Battered by Storms

A Dystopian Shifter Romance

Jemma Weir

Jemma Weir

Contents

Also By

Chapter One

Oliver squinted at the horizon, trying to scan the grey and dusty terrain past the low sun. The ground was flat and still for miles to his left. On his right, it was similar for half a mile until it turned into rolling hills that concealed what lay beyond from sight. In front of him stood an old farmhouse ruin consisting of little more than foundation stones and fragments of walls.

The open terrain and lack of trees or plants meant there wasn't much chance a Rift creature could sneak up on them without being seen, and he saw nothing he wasn't expecting. Which was good, but he didn't let his guard down. Rift scorpions often liked to set up nests in ruins like this one, and he wouldn't know for sure it was empty until he got close.

Better if something to hunt. Am bored, Thor, Oliver's wolf, said. He'd been complaining the whole patrol.

Patience, Oliver said, wiping his forehead as sweat dripped into his eyes. It had been oppressively hot all day, but he was hoping the evening would bring cooler temperatures. *If we don't find anything here, we can go hunt in Sam's woods.*

The suggestion cheered up his wolf, and they both appreciated that it was now an option they had. A few months ago, they'd only been able to shift and run outside of the full moon—if they'd wanted to do it—in the Rift Scar or if they went home. But when Hale changed the contract with Sam, wolves were able to shift whenever they wanted.

Hale good alpha. Made good changes, Thor said.

He had definitely made changes; not everyone was convinced they were good. If they had, more would have stayed.

Though, to be fair, he couldn't really blame them. Being sent to the Highland Rift Pack had originally been a punishment for Shifters. Somewhere that the alphas could send their troublesome wolves to teach them to behave. After a year of only being able to shift once a month, few would want to risk going back. But Hale had changed everything. Then he'd told them they didn't have to stay if they didn't want to.

Five Shifters had already accepted Hale's offer to go home in the past few weeks, and more were still undecided.

Want to stay, Thor said quietly.

Oliver didn't immediately answer. They both knew it wouldn't be that easy for them for multiple reasons. None of which he wanted to think about here.

We need to focus on the patrol, Oliver said, rolling his shoulders. Thor didn't like it, but he did listen.

He glanced to the right of the ruin, searching for the rest of his team. The two of them had circled to the other side so they could approach from two directions. They raise their hands flat, letting him know they were ready.

Normally, at least four or five rangers would be on each patrol, but they were spread thin with so many Shifters having left. Rather than skipping the shift, he'd taken the smaller group to patrol the border ruins instead. It would mean at least one of tomorrow's patrols would only need to cover deeper ground, but at least they got something done today.

Oliver checked the landscape one last time, but there was still nothing out there. He signalled to his team to advance and headed towards his side of the ruin with his rifle at his shoulder.

Thor pressed close, letting Oliver lean on his instincts as they pulled in a breath. Nothing but the Rift Scar stench of old meat left to rot in the sun. The ground was un-marked, showing no signs of anything but him having passed through. There was no sound but the crumble of the dry dirt under his feet.

Fresh sweat beaded on his neck as the ruin blocked his view of his team. It would have been easier if Amelia had been there. He could have felt her through their new pack bonds, and if that group had been in danger, he'd have known immediately. But she'd gone south of London with Mitchel so he could train to use his Frost Magic.

Want pack to come home, Thor said mournfully.

They won't be away long, Oliver said. They had only been gone a week, with another week to go, but it was hard. Oliver felt alone and isolated, which was stupid. He'd managed just fine before they'd become his pack.

Something that Oliver still could hardly believe. Mitchel wasn't a Shifter. Yet, with him being Amelia's mate, he'd been pulled into Oliver's pack somehow. Just like Hale had done to Sam.

It had saved Amelia's life, but if Oliver had understood how to use his alpha power better, he could have saved them without taking them from Hale's pack in the first place. Hale had been helping train Oliver to use the Alpha Magic for the last few weeks to make sure it didn't happen again. It had been an unexpectedly steep learning curve and something Oliver's father should have taught him.

Oliver shook his head and focused on what he was supposed to be doing. He would have to rely on his normal senses to protect his team, just like he'd done for the rest of the eight months he'd been living at the Highland Rift Scar. But he didn't have to like it.

He pulled in another breath, checking for any new signs of danger. He could smell his patrol now, the heat making them almost as pungent as the Rift Scar. But there was nothing else, no signs of Rift creatures.

He moved around the edge a little further until he reached the gap in the wall. Inside the house, undisturbed grey dust covered old stone floors, with no sign of anything having passed over it or having tried to bury under it.

'Clear,' Rafe called from the other side of the ruin.

'Clear,' Oliver said, lowering his gun.

Boring, Thor said. *Not good hunt.*

We aren't hunting. We're patrolling, remember? It's not the same, Oliver said, though he knew he was wasting his time. His wolf seemed to be particularly frustrated today. Thor sneezed at him mentally and ignored him.

His team moved into the building, still alert in case they'd missed anything. Rafe was a few inches shorter than Oliver, mixed race, with amber skin, tilted dark brown eyes, and black hair shaved in intricate patterns on his scalp. Cindy was shorter, just coming up to Rafe's chin, with wide shoulders and narrow hips. Her creamy skin had recently seen a bit too much sun and was scarlet in places. Her brown hair was cut short and spiked up with gel.

Both were Elementals. Cindy had control over air and Rafe over water. Though neither ability provided much use in the Rift Scar.

'This is the last ruin, right?' Cindy said, giving the space another once-over.

'Yes,' Rafe said, lowering his rifle to point at the ground, but he didn't let his guard down either. Both of them had been stationed up here for over a year and knew how quickly things could change. Even on a boring shift like today.

'What's next, boss?' Cindy asked, looking at Oliver, even though they both had more experience than he did.

It had been like that since he'd stood next to Hale as he'd dealt with the traitors last month. Everyone looked at Oliver differently since then. He wasn't entirely sure he'd done anything to deserve the extra respect or responsibility.

'Home,' Oliver said. 'You both have shifts tomorrow, and there isn't time to do anything else today.'

'It's only rapid response duty,' Cindy said, rubbing at a red patch on her neck. 'It's going to be a chance to catch up on some reading and listen to Rafe snore.'

'Great,' Rafe said, shaking his head. 'Now you've cursed it. Something is bound to happen.'

'Nothing ever happens. Not since the phones have been down around the Rift Scar. Maybe once they fix the tower, but until then. Nope,' Cindy said.

'How about the car accident and scorpions six weeks ago? Or the imps?' Rafe glanced at Oliver. Both events had nearly killed him, though he appreciated Rafe hadn't mentioned the wyvern. That attack still woke Oliver up in a cold sweat.

'Neither of those resulted in rapid response being called,' Cindy said, though she'd lost some of her humour. If the rapid response unit had been available and the cell towers had been up, maybe everything that had happened might have turned out very differently. 'But it doesn't matter. It's going to be quiet. Just you wait.'

Rafe grunted, shaking his head. 'I'll get my sleep at home, just in case.'

'Let's head back. I'll take point,' Oliver said, cutting Cindy off before she could argue.

Unlike the others, he finally had two days off. Though he wasn't sure it was a good thing without Mitchel and Amelia being about. But he'd hit the limit on how much work he could do in a week, and Hale had banned him from picking up more.

Go hunting in woods, Thor said, sending images of clean air filled with the scent of dirt, deer, and trees. That was Thor's solution to everything.

Okay, we can go hunting, Oliver said with a sigh. It was better than staring at the four walls of his studio apartment for the next two days.

Oliver rolled his shoulders and led them back the way they'd come, letting the other two watch his back.

STACI OPENED THE KITCHEN cupboard, supporting the broken door automatically as she put the clean coffee cup away. The door had been broken and fixed so many times that the chipboard would no longer hold a new hinge.

It wasn't the only old and broken thing in her mum's kitchen. Yellow striped wallpaper from the eighties covered the walls and was coming away at the corners. The cabinets that weren't broken had peeling laminate that had been glued back on more times than she could remember. The lino floor wasn't in much better shape. No amount of cleaning would turn the yellowed parts of the tile pattern white again.

But it was home. Staci had offered to upgrade the kitchen when she'd moved back in, but that had been before her mum had deteriorated. Now, it was better to keep things the same. Familiar.

A tingle of Storm Magic rippled in the distance, making her skin crawl. She tried to ignore it, but it had been persistently growing for the last few hours.

It wasn't fully formed yet, but it would be a fierce beast by tomorrow. Wild winds, treacherous lightning, and bloated rain clouds. It wasn't how the scientists saw a storm, but her magic wasn't science. Being a Storm Elemental gave her a view that they'd never have.

She reached out towards it out of instinct. But it was too far away. She might feel the growing pieces, but she'd have to go within five miles to affect them. If she got in her car and drove closer, she could break it apart ...

No. It was her day off, dammit, she was supposed to be spending it with her mum. It was Elliot's job to fix the storm. He was on call today and tomorrow, and this wasn't her problem to fix. Hell, she wasn't even supposed to be paying attention. But it was impossible to ignore when her whole body vibrated with the distant magic of the storm.

Why hadn't he replied to her? She'd texted him twice now and got no answer, not even a simple acknowledgement that he was working on it. The storm was in the Rift Scar's direction, making it even more dangerous than other storms.

'Sweetie, is everything all right?' Staci's mum asked. She was slim to the point of frail, her skin papery and thin. Her hair had turned wispy and white almost overnight. Staci missed the dark reddish brown, so much like her own—at least when she hadn't dyed it an off-colour pink.

'I'm fine, Mum,' Staci said, moving to sit down. She patted her mum's hand where it rested on the scarred kitchen table. Staci could feel every bone. Something that wasn't going to get better.

Her mum frowned, grey eyes hazing over as she looked around her. Confusion shone through as she looked over everything. They'd tried to keep the kitchen familiar, but it wasn't the same. Not when it was impossible to know where her mum was in her memories.

Staci forced her smile to stay on her lips as she bit back tears. She wouldn't cry. Not today. She'd done enough of that already. She was going to be here for her mum, even if she didn't remember Staci half the time. The doctor had said one more bout of pneumonia might be her mum's last.

Her mum settled again, gaze going to the window, a smile on her lips. 'It's such a beautiful evening,' she said. The sunset was turning the sky varying shades of pink, making the faint scattering of clouds look like they were on fire.

'There's a storm coming,' Staci said, shivering. She re-minded herself again that it wasn't her problem. Elliot would deal with it, stop it before it fully formed and hit the town. She had to believe that. Because the alternative was that Elliot was putting Huntly at risk.

The feel of the Storm Magic rose in volume. Every one of Staci's nerves burned. She hated these kinds of storms. Like they had a power of their own. After a heartbeat, the building storm faded back to a buzz in her mind.

'Oh, that's a shame. Are you like Frederick? He al-ways knows when there's a storm.' Her mum giggled, the sound carefree as if she was a teenager as she talked about Staci's father. He was a Storm Elemental like Staci, but her mum was human. 'You mustn't tell anyone that. My father would be furious if he knew I was talking to the Rift boy. He threatened to disown me, you know?'

Staci swallowed back her anger, looking away. This memory was old, from when Staci's parents had been young and just beginning to date. Staci's grandfather had been a man of his word, and when he'd found out her mum was pregnant, he'd thrown her out. Her mother had been too stubborn to care. Stubborn and in love.

'Yeah, just like Frederick,' Staci said. Except she was here, and her father wasn't. He'd walked out on them when Staci was a toddler. She didn't even remember him.

Her mother pulled her hands back into her lap, back straightening, the change quick and sudden as she stared at Staci with suspicion. 'Where's my daughter?'

Staci's chest tightened. 'I'm right here, Mum.' She didn't reach out, trying her best not to startle her mum. But Staci was already forgotten as her mum turned back to the sky, a smile playing on her lips.

Staci stood, needing to do something, anything, as tears threatened. Everything about dementia was hard, but not being recognised was the thing that Staci struggled with the most.

Trying to focus on something else, she wiped her eyes and grabbed her phone from where it was charging. There were no messages, nothing from Elliot at all.

'My goodness, Staci, look at the time; you should be in bed,' her mum said, struggling to her feet before Staci could message him again. Being remembered now hurt almost as much as being forgotten had. 'You want to be fresh and ready for your first day on the job now Jake's gone.'

Staci forced another smile. Jake had been her mentor after she'd finished magic college and come home, but he'd been gone for years now.

'You're right, we should both get some sleep,' Staci said, taking advantage of the memory. Her mum had been resisting going to bed for the past hour, but maybe this would finally get her there.

Then Staci could call Elliot.

Her mum stayed in that timeframe long enough to get her through the evening routine and into bed. She was too thin, her bones showing, and her skin loose. Tucking her into bed and turning on the baby monitor felt wrong even after more than a year of doing it. It took seconds for her mum to drift off, and Staci crept back downstairs, grabbing her phone.

Still nothing from Elliot. She called him this time rather than sending a text. Frustration ate at her as she listened to it ring. She could ask Florence to come round and watch her mum, but it was her day off, too. A night of peace. Staci didn't want to take that away from her without being sure something was wrong.

'What!' Elliot's voice was sharp. There was a background buzz over the line, something just beyond hearing.

'Why are you ignoring my text messages?' Staci said. If Elliot was going to be rude, then she saw no reason why she should be polite. So far, their entire working relationship had been Staci getting fed up with his self-important attitude and losing her temper.

'I'm not ignoring them,' Elliot said, voice muffled.

Where was he? 'Then why haven't you replied?' Staci asked, pushing away from the worktop to sit in her kitchen chair. It was that or pace, and she was too tired to pace.

She was beginning to feel like the mother of a teenage child. She'd never treated Jake like this. A few disagreements over how something should be handled, but not this attitude.

'It's not even a storm yet,' Elliot said. Interference cut him off briefly before he came back. 'You worry too much, Staci. Relax, I'm monitoring it, and if it gets worse, I'll head out and deal with it.'

The condescension in his tone made her grind her teeth. 'If you dealt with it now, you'd know it's not a problem.'

'Look, Staci, I know you're used to being in charge, but I've been using Storm Magic longer than you. It's fine.'

Considering he was only a year or so older than her, that argument didn't really inspire confidence. But it wasn't worth arguing with him over his experience.

'It's not fine,' Staci said. 'It's near the Rift Scar. It won't take much for it to get a lot worse very quickly.'

'Look, fine, I'll go and have a closer look,' Elliot said, then he must have covered the mouthpiece, his next few words muffled. 'Go back to your nice calm evening and leave it with me.'

'Let me know if you need any help arranging the rangers to go out there with you,' Staci said. He'd need an escort if the storm formed inside the Rift Scar. No one went in there without at least a few guns. So far, Elliot hadn't had to go in.

'I'm perfectly capable of doing my job,' Elliot said, making the phone hiss as he huffed out a breath. 'I told you. I know what I'm doing.'

Staci bit down on another rant. It wouldn't do any good. Maybe going into the Rift Scar would give him a bloody wake-up call.

'I'll call you if I find anything,' Elliot said, clearly taking her moment of frustrated silence as acceptance. Then he hung up.

Staci muttered a curse. Part of her wanted to go down to the border and take a closer look at the storm anyway, but she really didn't want to wake Florence and have her come over to watch her mum. She had to trust that Elliot knew what he was doing, which was easier said than done.

With one last look in the direction of the storm, she locked up and headed to bed. She wasn't hopeful that she'd be able to sleep, but she had to at least try.

THE TREK BACK THROUGH the Rift Scar to the car took Oliver and his team nearly an hour. There was no sign of any Rift creatures or anything of concern.

After stripping off their armour and guns, he drove them back to Huntly. They'd taken one of the old Land Rovers that Hale had bought for the rangers. For whatever reason, the older cars seemed to last better against the Rift Scar dust. It got everywhere and degraded metal over time.

Cindy and Rafe stayed silent for most of the drive. The patrol might have been quiet, but the heat was draining, and their gear wasn't light. That, plus the amount of overtime everyone had been pulling, was making everyone tired.

Ranger headquarters sat at the back of an industrial estate in Huntly. The old three-story building had once been a gym, but Hale had converted it long before Oliver had come to town. An armoury filled most of the ground floor. The second floor held space to work out. The top floor had a single studio apartment and a room with bunks for the rapid response unit to sleep during the night shift.

Hale had expanded into the ground floor next door in the last few months so Sam could work from there instead of her house. As rift surveyor, she had a lot of equipment. Her bosses at the Institute of Rift Studies and Defence, IRS&D, hadn't been happy about the change because they now had to pay rent. But it was in her job contract that they should have always provided her the space to work rather than making her use her garage.

Oliver pulled around the back of the building into a car park lit by a couple of motion sensor lights. They clicked on, though it wasn't fully dark yet, as he rolled into a space near the door. They all piled out and moved to grab their gear.

This part of town smelled of hot metal from the welder on the opposite side of the estate, gun oil from their building, and grease from the Chinese around the corner. Then there were the three of them. The rot of the Rift Scar and their sweat didn't make a good combo.

Go hunting? Thor asked.

The idea of being in the forest with clean air filled only with the scents of pine trees and wildflowers was more than a little appealing.

Soon, Oliver said. He needed to clean his gear and shower first. Shifting wouldn't remove the stench of the Rift Scar from his skin.

Before he could get his gear, his phone rang. He grabbed it, stomach dropping as a name that he didn't want to see flashed across his screen. His father.

His wolf growled in his head, unhappy as he withdrew back, even though their father wasn't physically present.

'You good?' Rafe asked, pausing by the driver's door. He watched Oliver oddly, making Oliver wonder if the growl had only been inside his head.

'Yeah, I've got to get this,' Oliver said. 'I'll see you inside.'

Rafe gave him another odd look, then turned and followed Cindy, who was already halfway to the headquarters' back door.

Not answer phone, Thor said, prodding Oliver to put the phone away. *Not want to speak to him.*

Oliver considered doing what his wolf wanted, ignoring the call, and going inside to get cleaned up. Pretend he'd never seen it. But you didn't ignore the prime alpha of Scotland, especially not when he was your father, and he was already angry with you.

We can hunt after I speak to my father, Oliver said, looking down at his phone again. At least, he hoped they could. None of the calls with him had gone well over the last few weeks. His wolf whined and backed away.

Oliver answered the call. 'Father.' He kept his tone neutral and even as he got out of the car.

'I'm tired of waiting for an answer,' his father said, sounding almost bored as he continued their last conversation with no pleasantries. 'Tell me how Hale made the pack lands feel alive?'

'I don't know. No one knows, not even Hale,' Oliver said, glad his father wasn't here in person—he wasn't a good liar. He knew exactly how the pack lands had been created. But that knowledge would put Hale's mate, Sam, at risk, something Oliver wouldn't willingly do.

'Liar. You're second in charge of the pack—despite your continued control issues,' his father said, voice a low rumble. A warning. Oliver shuddered. That rumble usually meant pain; his body remembered those past hits like his father was there, a fist in Oliver's gut. 'Hale clearly trusts you for him to be foolish enough to put you in that position. So, stop wasting both our time and tell me how he created the pack lands. How do they feel alive?'

Thor snarled in his head at the accusation about control. Oliver was careful to keep that anger to himself. There was no need to prove his father right.

Sorry, Thor said, huffing a breath, but then added, *Am not weak. Am alpha. Have own pack now.*

We can't let him know that, Oliver said. Being an alpha was something else his father would be furious about if he found out.

My pack, not let anyone take, Thor said, growling low, crouching in his mind like he was about to be attacked.

Oliver didn't answer his wolf. He couldn't. They both knew they'd have to give up their pack when he went home. There was no way Oliver was letting either of them anywhere near his father.

His wolf whined, knowing it was true. Knowing their pack was safer here. He couldn't protect them back home.

'The pack lands appeared after Shane and Lacey tried to kill Hale,' Oliver said, carefully picking his words; it wasn't something everyone knew outside the pack. He checked the back door to make sure no one had come back out. 'No one knows how or what happened.'

The growl that came over the phone made Oliver shudder. He reminded himself again that his father wasn't here. There was no pain coming. His body didn't believe him. He paced the length of the car, wishing he could walk away from this call as easily.

'Shane and Lacey died in a tragic accident in the Rift Scar. You would do well to remember that as you lie to me,' Oliver's father said, no longer holding any pretence of politeness as he snarled. Oliver flinched. 'Clearly, being away from home has made you forget yourself. Tell me the truth.'

'I don't know how the pack lands were created,' Oliver said again. His heart skipped a beat even as he lied. He only had a few more months before he had to go home. How was he going to lie to his father in person?

'You will tell me what Hale did to change the land, or I'll come down there and have him release you home. Maybe you'll remember how to tell the truth once you're standing in front of me.'

Oliver stopped pacing, turning back to the old redbrick ranger headquarters. He imagined his father doing just that. Then, what would happen if his father realised the truth about the pack lands and tried to take them from Hale?

If Oliver's father won a challenge against Hale, he'd gain the Highland Rift Scar's pack lands. His father would learn about Sam. He'd break everything. Kill Hale. Hurt everyone. No. Oliver couldn't let that happen.

He swallowed all the things that he wanted to say. All the anger and the pain. He had to find a way to make his father believe the lie.

'I don't know how they were created,' Oliver said again, careful to keep his tone neutral. 'But I can ask.'

Not tell father, Thor said, growling.

No, Oliver said. *But it gives us time to find a lie that he will believe.*

His father growled, making the phone vibrate in his hand. 'You have until tomorrow morning. Don't make me come there in person and challenge Hale over you.' His father paused, his voice now back to his previous cool tone.

'Though I imagine he'd be as happy as I was to get rid of you.'

'I understand,' Oliver said, stomach twisting.

'Don't make me regret giving you a choice,' his father said, voice sharp, nearly a snarl. The phone went dead, not giving him a chance to speak or argue.

Oliver leaned against the car, shoving his phone in his pocket. He needed to find a way to protect the secret.

Ask Hale, Thor said, whining, pressing close. *He help.*

Hale would challenge David. They would fight, and even if Hale won, the rest of the prime alphas wouldn't accept it, Oliver said. Only someone who was part of the prime alpha's pack could challenge them, and though Highland Rift Pack was in Scotland, Hale wasn't bound to any alpha. *They'd set an example. We need another way.*

He'd need to go home and keep the secret no matter what his father did to him. If he waited for his father to come to town and challenge Hale, there would be nothing Oliver could do.

They'd have to give up their pack, and he didn't have time to tell either Amelia or Mitchel what he was doing. Then he'd have to tell Hale he was leaving, but not why. Hale would never let Oliver go if he knew there was a threat.

Bile crawled up Oliver's throat. He didn't want to go home. Didn't want to do any of it. But if he didn't, Hale would be hurt. The pack would be hurt.

'You okay, mate?' Elliot asked, making Oliver jump and spin. He'd not heard anyone approach.

Elliot was shorter than Oliver, with short, dirty-blond hair, olive-green eyes, and sandy-white skin that tanned well when he spent time outside. Which clearly hadn't been recently. He'd only been in town for a few weeks, but they'd known each other in Glasgow for years.

'Peachy,' Oliver said, letting out a shaky breath.

'You don't sound okay. Really, what's up?' Elliot said, moving to lean against the Land Rover beside Oliver.

Oliver couldn't tell him the truth. But he also didn't want his friend to worry.

'My father has told me I have to come home,' Oliver said, missing out the reason why.

'That's great,' Elliot said, then he frowned when Oliver didn't agree. 'That's awful?' When Oliver still didn't reply, he shook his head. 'What happened?'

'My father is being his usual charming self,' Oliver said. 'He wants me to give him something that's not mine to give or come home.'

'Sounds simple to me. If you want to stay, then give it to him,' Elliot said, shrugging. 'What could be worth more than your freedom?'

'It could cost someone their life,' Oliver said. Though, that wasn't entirely true. Sam wouldn't die if the truth came out. She'd just lose everything. Her land, her home, her ability to stay in one place longer than a year. The government didn't like Earth Elementals. Or his father could use the risk of that truth coming out to control her. Either way, Sam's life wouldn't be the same.

'Who cares?' Elliot said, shaking his head. 'Why's their life more important than yours? Tell your father what he wants to know and stay here if that's what you want.'

Growing up in foster care had always given Elliot a more ruthless attitude than most. Or maybe that was just who Elliot was. But Oliver wasn't wired that way.

'I can't do that,' Oliver said, rubbing his face. He still stank of the Rift Scar.

Elliot gave a snort and shook his head. 'If you want to get anywhere in this world, you need to think of yourself first. Give your father what he wants. No one has to know it came from you.'

There clearly wasn't anything Oliver could say that would make Elliot understand why he couldn't do that. So, Oliver tried to change the subject.

'What are you doing here?'

Elliot seemed to hesitate a moment, looking at the rangers' building, then back to Oliver. 'I called earlier to see when you'd be finishing your shift. I thought I'd have better luck convincing you to go for some drinks in person,' Elliot said. He wore a light pink T-shirt, grey skin-tight jeans, and an over-the-shoulder leather man-bag. His clubbing clothes. Because, for some reason, he was convinced women loved the pink. 'Seems like my timing is excellent. If you don't look like someone who needs a drink, I don't know who does.'

Elliot had been asking Oliver to go out to Huntly's only club, Indigo, ever since he'd arrived in town two weeks ago. He wanted to say no. The urge was so deep that it almost slipped out on its own. But the idea of being at home, or even in the woods with his own thoughts, made the bile rise in his stomach again.

Fix problem first, Thor said.

There is only one option, to go home and lie, Oliver said. *To convince my father it's the truth.* No matter how much it hurt. Maybe the alcohol would make that decision a bit easier to accept.

Drinking bad. Not make feel better, Thor said, making a vomiting noise. *Woods better. We feel better if hunt.*

I don't want to feel better; I want to forget, Oliver said, though he might have to buy something a little stronger than what the bar served to help him with that.

'I could go for a drink,' Oliver said.

Elliot blinked like that wasn't the answer he'd expected, but he recovered quickly. 'First round is on me to celebrate my new job.' Elliot had been hired to be the town's second part-time weather warden, a job that wasn't easy to get. 'I might also have a surprise.' He looked around to check no one had come out and pulled out an unlabelled bottle from his man-bag. 'Wolfbite.'

Oliver smiled, taking the bottle. The wolfbite would help make him forget, even if just for a bit. The alcohol was so strong that it was toxic to humans, so not everyone would sell it. But there were plenty of people who made it under the table if you knew where to look. If he drank most of the bottle, he'd be able to get drunk for a little while.

'Indigo isn't going to know what hit it,' Elliot said.

'Give me half an hour to put everything away and shower,' Oliver said. Tomorrow, he would deal with his father, but tonight, he was going to forget about all of it.

Chapter Two

Staci repositioned the phone against her ear as she pulled down the kitchen blinds, blocking the early morning sunlight. The growing storm had kept her up most of the night as she'd tossed and turned. Now, she was left with a headache and a knot in her gut as she could still feel the storm at the edge of her senses.

She cursed and hung up the phone as it went to voicemail again. Why the hell wasn't Elliot answering her? He'd promised he'd deal with the storm. Had he lied? Or had something happened? Or maybe he was dealing with it right now? It had been late last night; perhaps the rangers hadn't wanted to go in until morning.

Dammit, why hadn't he given her an update? At least then, she'd know whether she should wait or just say screw it and go out there herself.

The storm gave a little surge as if to taunt her. Her skin crawled, and her head pounded a little harder.

'Do you think it will be a nice day today?' Staci's mum asked, forcing Staci to pay attention to something other than the magic.

Her mum was sitting at the kitchen table again, a cup of tepid tea in her hands as she stared out the window. So far this morning, she'd been stuck somewhere during the years Staci had been away learning how to use her magic. Her mum seemed to both remember Staci and seemed content with the condition of the kitchen.

'I think I'll have to work soon,' Staci said, rubbing her arms, trying to make the crawling sensation dissipate.

'You're doing such a good job with Jake,' her mum said, smiling. 'He told me yesterday how good your instincts are about what will become a storm and what will dissipate on its own.'

Staci smiled even though it hurt. Her mum had always been so proud of Staci's job. She'd talk to people for hours if she let them, no matter how much Staci squirmed. Now she wished for those moments to come again.

'Did I hear you say you had to work? Isn't it your day off?' Florence said, coming into the kitchen with a large shopping bag. She was a stout woman with rich brown skin and black hair piled into a bun. She was slightly older than Staci's mother at fifty-five, though you'd never have guessed it looking at the pair. Dementia had aged her mum early.

When Staci's mum was first diagnosed, Florence took the self-awarded position of nurse and carer. She looked after her mum just like she'd cared for Staci when she'd been a kid, and her mum had needed a childminder while she'd been at work. Without Florence, Staci wouldn't have made it this far.

'Maybe,' Staci said as Florence put the bag on the worktop and started unpacking it. 'I thought you were supposed to be off today too?'

'Pfft, a day off? You don't take a day off from family. Besides, what would you eat if I wasn't here to make you dinner?' Florence said. She seemed to believe that Staci was incapable of cooking. It was hard to argue with Florence when the food always tasted better when she made it. 'Now, tell me. Work? What is Elliot doing?'

Staci smiled and shook her head. 'He's not answering his phone.'

'That boy is as useful as a chocolate teapot,' Florence said, waving a vegetable about before she went back to unpacking the shopping. 'Go, deal with the storm; your mum and I will have another cup of tea and start the stew. You keep us safe like you always have.' Her unwavering confidence made Staci's chest ache.

Florence was one of those few rare people who never seemed to care that Staci was an Elemental. Humans had never really wanted to trust the magic that had come with the Rifts, even if they had no choice but to rely on it to stop the things that had come out. It had created tension and division that had never really gone away.

'Thank you, Florence,' Staci said, wishing she'd more than words to thank the woman.

'Once you're done with that, you bring back bread for dinner,' Florence said. 'The only bread at the local shop was the stupid healthy kind. Your mamma needs white bread, good bread.'

Staci smiled and nodded. Her mum was a bread addict. Between her and Florence, they could keep a baker in business. Staci's smile dipped. At least they could before. Getting her mum to eat now wasn't easy.

'I won't be long, but I'll call if anything happens,' Staci said before turning to her mum. She was staring out the window like neither of them existed. Staci wanted to kiss her mum goodbye, but she hesitated. She couldn't bear to be rejected if her mum had forgotten her again.

She shook her head and left without saying goodbye, grabbing her waterproof jacket from its peg behind the front door on her way out. It was sunny outside, but it wouldn't last much longer, especially not if Elliot didn't get his finger out of his arse and do his job.

She hopped in her old VW Bug and headed to Elliot's rental near the town centre. It was mid-morning, and the roads were quiet, so she made good time crossing town. Not that Huntly had a rush hour exactly, not like a city. But she still appreciated not being stuck at a junction waiting for all the parents to drop off their kids.

It also allowed her to think about what she wanted to say to Elliot. She didn't want to chase him off. He was supposed to be here to help so she could spend more time with her mum. The closest she got to a solution was that yelling at him would probably not help.

Maybe he'd prove her wrong? Maybe he'd already be out dealing with the storm when she got to his house.

Considering he'd promised to go out and update her on it last night, she wasn't optimistic, especially when it was still at the edge of her mind taunting her, calling to her. If they didn't do something about it soon, stopping the storm it produced would be impossible.

Elliot's two-seater Mazda was sitting in the car park when she arrived at his apartment building. Her last lingering hope that he might be out dealing with the storm faltered.

She walked up to his apartment on the fifth floor, trying to remind herself that she needed him. His door was peeling white wood, and he had no doorbell. She knocked hard. Maybe slightly harder than necessary.

Silence.

Maybe he was out dealing with the storm. But if he was, why was his car still outside? She hammered the door harder, muttering a string of curses that would have made her mum gasp.

'Sod off,' a man shouted through the closed door. It wasn't Elliot, but it was familiar.

Staci hesitated. What was Oliver doing here? He was a ranger, and Elliot hadn't yet needed to go into the Rift Scar. Unless that's why Oliver was here?

She knocked again, this time not stopping until the door was ripped open, revealing Oliver in the flesh. A lot of flesh. He towered over her at six and a half feet, his light brown hair dishevelled and slate-grey eyes red-rimmed like he was hungover. Since he was a Shifter and they weren't affected by alcohol, that was an impressive feat.

He was also completely naked. A narrow strip of hair peppered his chest before disappearing over his abs, drawing her eyes lower. Staci forced her eyes back to his face. If he'd noticed the wandering look, he didn't say anything.

'Oliver, where's Elliot?' Staci said, chin up, trying to ignore the heat in her cheeks. If Oliver was naked, then it wasn't likely he was here to help Elliot deal with the storm.

He just stared at her, eyes flicking to amber as his wolf peeked out. She suppressed a shiver that had nothing to do with fear. The wildness coming from Oliver was almost an energy in its own right. Something about him had always drawn her in, but the last thing she needed in her life was a party boy who was only here for a few months, so she'd done everything she could to avoid him.

'Oliver?' Staci said, voice sharp as she tried to get Oliver to focus on her. 'Are you listening to me?'

'Yes,' Oliver said as he rubbed his face. She got a whiff of vodka and something sweeter. Whatever he'd drunk to make him look hungover now must have been damned strong.

This was why she'd avoided him. She didn't need this chaos in her life. Yet part of her still wanted to reach out and touch him, ask him if everything was alright. Though why, she couldn't say; nothing seemed wrong except for the hangover.

'Is Elliot here?' Staci looked past him into the flat. It was small, with a combined kitchen living area and a short hallway presumably leading to the bedrooms and bathroom.

Elliot had not done much to decorate the all-white room, except for covering it with empty beer bottles.

Oliver followed her look, squinting at the sunlight. 'Why do you need Elliot?'

Staci sighed; this was getting her nowhere. She brushed past him into the apartment, not giving him an answer. Little tendrils of fire ran through her at the accidental touch. She ignored it.

'I called Elliot last night. He told me he was dealing with the storm,' Staci said, being careful where she stood. The mess was worse than she thought. 'But it's still growing.'

An empty unmarked bottle sat on the floor, next to beer, vodka bottles, and a stack of clothes. Going by the size, it had to be Oliver's.

'Did you and Elliot spend all night drinking instead of dealing with the storm?' Staci asked, turning back towards him.

He looked at her, frowning, then down at the clothes and bottles. Then down at himself. He cursed and grabbed a blanket that had been thrown over the back of the couch.

Part of her was glad to no longer have the distraction. The rest of her wanted the blanket to slip back off, which wasn't helpful. She couldn't let herself be drawn in. Oliver wasn't the kind of person to stay in your life. She couldn't afford to lose anyone else when her mum slipped a little further away every day.

Pushing back everything but the anger, Staci lifted her chin. She just needed to get Elliot and deal with the storm. Oliver would be a distant memory soon enough.

'Where is Elliot?' Staci asked again.

OLIVER GRIPPED THE BLANKET close to his body. Staci must think he was an idiot. No, correction, she must think he was even more of an idiot than she'd thought before. How the hell had he forgotten he was naked?

Better if had fur, Thor said, but he wasn't really paying attention, entirely focused on Staci.

If we were in our wolf form, we'd probably scare her, Oliver said, grabbing his jeans from the floor and dragging them on before she accused him of being a pervert. Though, she was the one who'd barged in.

Not scare Staci. She strong. Like alpha, Thor said, and Oliver couldn't disagree with that. *She'd like me.*

In Oliver's experience, most people didn't like Shifter's wolf forms. Even Elementals. But he didn't argue with his wolf about it either. It didn't matter. Staci didn't like any of him as far as he could tell.

Staci was tall and willowy, with faded pink hair thrown into a hasty bun, leaving a few wispy strands framing her face. She watched him with serious lavender eyes, a slight blush on her pale skin.

She was the main weather warden in town and had been for several years. She smelled like an incoming storm—ozone and electricity. But there was something more about her scent, the smell of sunlight-warmed skin.

He pulled in another breath, finding more layers underneath the base. Her embarrassment and anger mixed in with a flicker of desire. Mostly, she was angry.

Though the desire gave him a moment's pause, it was barely there even though she'd seen him naked. He fought disappointment. She wasn't interested in him. She'd made that clear the first time they'd met. He'd known that, but he kept hoping.

Hurt? Thor asked, pulling in one more breath. Thor was right. Under the anger, there was something that spoke of pain. *Help her.*

Oliver only just managed to stop his wolf from moving them forward. He was pretty sure that Staci didn't need anyone's help. Certainly not his. Nor would he be able to help after he went to tell Hale he was leaving.

Pain bloomed in his chest at the reminder. The wolfbite had done little to let him forget for long last night, but it had helped him pass out on the sofa so he didn't have to think at all.

Oliver tried to shake off the ache, realising Staci was still waiting for an answer. The storm?

'Elliot didn't say there was a storm,' he said. The hangover was easing now that he was on his feet, the pounding in his head dropping to a faint beat rather than a heavy metal competition.

'Where's Elliot?' Staci said, looking at the small hallway in front of her. She didn't wait for an answer as she headed down it. She got the bathroom first. The small white-tiled room made it really obvious that cleaning wasn't high on Elliot's to-do list.

The second door led into Elliot's room. He lay sprawled half under a blanket on the rumpled bed. A bottle of vodka sat half empty on the bedside table.

'Elliot, wake up,' Staci said, her tone harsh in the silence. He didn't react. The scent of Staci's embarrassment grew in his nose even through the odour of stale sweat.

After a few heartbeats, she moved to the window and threw open the curtains to let the sunlight in. 'Get up.'

'Gnarl, gar,' Elliot said, turning away from the sunlight. Oliver sympathised but didn't try to stop Staci.

'You told me you'd deal with the storm last night. Now it's getting worse,' Staci said, keeping her distance, but she didn't look away this time.

'There wasn't any storm; it's just some rain, and it's under control,' Elliot said, blinking blearily at her, seemingly unworried they were in his room as he reached for the vodka beside his bed.

Staci grabbed it first, pulling it out of reach. 'If that was the case, why's the Storm Magic dancing wildly in the back of my head right now? I feel it trying to form.'

'You're being dramatic,' he said, pulling a slow breath.

'Dramatic? I'll remember you said that when the storm destroys this tiny little flat of yours,' Staci said.

'I don't feel anything like what you're describing,' Elliot said, rubbing his face. The alcohol didn't stop an Elemental's powers, but it could hinder them and make a haze that needed to be waded through. It depended on the individual's power, the Elemental type, as well as the person themselves.

'Maybe if you'd not drunk yourself into a coma, you'd feel it,' Staci said, gaze going to the window. 'It's coming. There isn't much time left to stop it.'

Was Staci right? Had Elliot ignored the storm to go drinking? Oliver had known Elliot for years, and he'd seen him work hard to be qualified for this job. It was hard to imagine that he'd mess it up to go for drinks. Staci had to be wrong. Something must have changed since Elliot had spoken to her.

'Okay, the weather is a little worse,' Elliot said as he shoved himself up against the headboard, squinting towards the wall. 'What do you want me to do about it? It will go away on its own. A bit of rain never hurt anyone.'

Oliver stiffened at the casual lack of concern in Elliot's voice. Staci was livid, and Oliver wasn't much impressed by it either. But again, he stayed silent. Staci was already unhappy with him. Jumping in to fight a battle for her that he didn't even understand wouldn't help anyone. His wolf was strangely silent, watching the two of them.

'How about you do what you should have done at the start?' Staci said, putting the bottle out of reach on the chest of drawers. 'Your job. What the council hired you to do. Stop it before it becomes dangerous.'

'It isn't even a storm yet,' Elliot said, shaking his head.

'*Yet* being the operative word. Did you even go down to have a look?'

'It was after dark; no one is stupid enough to go near the Rift Scar then.' Elliot shrugged, looking towards the wall again, waving in that direction vaguely. 'It's not even a storm yet. It's just a little wind and rain; it will clear up on its own.'

Staci's face went from pale to red as her scent shifted to fury. 'Does this feel like it's clearing up on its own?'

'What happens if the storm is in the Rift Scar?' Oliver asked. He knew Staci had gone into the Rift Scar with patrols before to deal with storms but she'd always been able to shut them down, so he'd never seen what would happen if she didn't.

'Rift Scar storms pick up energy fast. Whatever magic is there feeds it and strengthens it. A small spring rain cloud can become a full-blown tornado under the right conditions. Or a snowstorm like you saw a few weeks back.'

'How long do we have until the storm turns into something like that?' Oliver asked, glancing at Elliot, who was stubbornly refusing to react.

'It's been growing all night, picking up power. We probably only have a couple of hours max,' Staci said carefully after a moment's pause. 'Maybe less, depending on how deep the storm is.'

'Get dressed, Elliot,' Oliver said, picking up a pair of jeans and a T-shirt from the floor that didn't look as rumpled as the rest and tossed them at Elliot. 'We're taking a trip.'

Elliot cursed but pulled his clothes towards him. Staci turned and stalked out of the room, presumably to give him privacy to dress.

'What's wrong with you?' Oliver asked. Elliot had everything he wanted, but he was carelessly throwing it away. Maybe if Oliver hadn't been faced with losing everything, seeing it might not have hurt so much.

'I don't know what you're talking about,' Elliot said, throwing back the covers. The scent of stale sweat got stronger as he moved. Oliver wanted to ask him to shower but giving him the chance to delay further seemed like a bad idea, going by Staci's fear.

'This town has given you a chance to do what you always wanted, and then you ignore a brewing storm?'

'Please,' Elliot said, sniffing the jeans that Oliver had tossed him, clearly deciding they were clean enough as he put them on. 'There isn't anything brewing. Staci just wants to be the centre of attention. She can't handle I'm better than her.'

Staci not want attention, Thor said, snarling. He wanted Oliver to step forward and wipe the condescending look off Elliot's face.

Oliver pushed his wolf back. Short of someone threatening the pack, he'd never seen Thor react that strongly against anything. *Calm down, let me deal with this.*

Thor didn't exactly back off, but he stopped pressing so hard.

'Staci has been this town's weather warden for years. The least you can do is respect her experience, even if you clearly don't respect her,' Oliver said, careful to keep his voice low despite his anger.

Elliot gave Oliver a surprised look like he'd missed the underlying anger until now. 'Look, Oliver, I know she's been here longer, but that doesn't mean she's right. Nor does it mean she's good at her job. I've heard more than one person raise concerns over her ability.' Elliot paused to pull on his T-shirt. 'You've known me for years, trust me. I know what I'm doing.'

Only trust Staci, Thor said, crouching low like he could burst free and attack Elliot.

Staci will not appreciate us beating up Elliot when he should be dealing with the storm, Oliver said, keeping a tight grip on Thor, though Oliver wasn't any happier. Elliot had always had a pretty inflated ego. But this was a whole new level. No wonder Staci was pissed at him if this was how he talked to her.

'Then you won't mind going into the Rift Scar to prove Staci wrong?' Oliver said.

Elliot paled. 'If Staci wants to drag you all into the Rift Scar, great. But I'm telling you, it isn't enough to become more than a light rain shower. I'm not going anywhere near that shithole.'

Oliver's stomach dropped at the declaration. Elliot was afraid; the scent of it soured the air. That's why he was denying the storm; he didn't want to go into the Rift Scar. But why the hell had he fought to come here? He had to have known that this could happen.

'This is your job; you will be going in even if I have to drag you,' Oliver said, making Elliot turn to him in horror. There wasn't a chance in hell he was going to let Elliot get away with leaving Staci to deal with this on her own.

Elliot glowered. 'Staci is overreacting, so now we all get to suffer for it.'

Thor growled, the sound slipping out of Oliver's mouth. Elliot flinched.

'If you didn't want to go into the Rift Scar, you should have picked an area without one,' Oliver said, stepping back towards the hall before he did something he would regret. 'We leave in five minutes.'

He left before Elliot could reply. He'd need to deal with this reaction later, but first, they needed to organise people to go into the Rift Scar. Cindy and Rafe were going to love this, especially after yesterday's conversation.

Staci was standing near the couch, not turning to look at him as he hunted through the rest of his clothes to find his phone. He dialled the rangers' headquarters number.

CHAPTER THREE

The pieces of the storm rippled on the horizon, right on the edge of merging. It sent a shuddering wave of energy across Staci's body like a thousand tiny needles. More painful than anything else. How the hell could Elliot think this was nothing?

'You okay?' Oliver asked. He was beside her, the spicy scent of wolf rising above the stale smell of the apartment, giving her a moment of almost clean air in the chaos. It did little to help clear her head.

She'd fallen against the couch, leaning against it heavily, heart pounding. No wonder he looked so concerned. Part of her wanted him to close the gap, to reach out and touch her. The rest of her remembered why it was a bad idea. Fortunately, the latter part won.

He'd put his phone away, finishing whatever call he'd been making. How much time had she lost? She'd not even heard him speak.

With effort, she forced herself to straighten and step away from the couch. Oliver gave her space, though he was watching her closely, body tense like he was braced to catch her if she fell again.

'I'm fine,' Staci said, taking a breath, trying to slow her heart rate as she pushed the magic away from her. 'The storm is strong.'

Maybe too strong. She'd never tried to stop anything this powerful before it was fully formed, and they still had to get to it. Not that she told Oliver either of those things. He didn't look like he believed she was fine as it was.

'The rapid response team are free and will escort us into the Rift Scar,' Oliver said, glancing towards Elliot's room. 'Would you mind giving us a lift to headquarters? Elliot isn't really fit to drive, and mine's not here. We can use one of the pool Land Rovers from there.'

She nodded slowly. 'No problem. All my gear is in my car, so I don't need to pick anything up.'

You didn't go anywhere near the Rift Scar in normal clothes. The place was dangerous, and it stank. So, she always kept her gear close, just in case. Grey thick Kevlar trousers, a long-sleeved T-shirt, an armoured vest, an old jacket, and heavy boots. She'd never be allowed a weapon without doing an extensive course. Considering the infrequency she went into the Rift Scar, it had never seemed worth it.

'You said it was your day off. Let Elliot deal with this,' Oliver said, eyes flashing to amber and back so fast she almost missed it. Another reason not to get involved with Oliver. Shifters were bossy and always thought they knew best.

'Like he dealt with it already?' Staci said, shaking her head. Going into the Rift Scar was never something she enjoyed. But she'd never hesitated to do it when it was needed. 'No, I'll come too. That way, there are two of us to deal with the storm.' She really hoped it didn't need two of them. She'd never worked with Elliot to break down a storm before, and this wasn't the place to experiment. But they might have to.

Oliver looked like he'd bitten into a lemon as he turned away, but he didn't argue, which was the main thing. He grabbed a T-shirt off the floor by the couch, sending several playing cards flying as he shook it and then put it on.

Somehow, Oliver managed to look just as good with the clothes on as he did with them off. The jeans clung to his butt, framing it, and the T-shirt stretched around his biceps, showing off the muscle she'd seen underneath.

She turned away again and pushed down all her twisty feelings about Oliver. She'd already decided she didn't want anything to do with him; her body just needed to get the message.

Elliot looked awful when he came into the room. He wore no armour or Rift gear, just his jeans and a white T-shirt. Staci shook her head and headed towards the front door. He was in for a shock if he thought that would help him. The rangers would have spare equipment.

Her little Bug wasn't designed for people as tall as Oliver, and he nearly had to fold himself into the front passenger seat. Elliot squeezed into the back, grumbling the whole time about how much better his car was.

They drove the short distance to the rangers' headquarters in silence, except for Elliot's moans about his hangover. The three storeys of ugly brown brick sat slightly apart from the rest of the industrial estate.

It was nice that they had the space. Staci's job didn't require her to have an office. She worked on call as the weather required, with people sometimes coming to the house to ask her for favours like extra water in certain fields. She saw the appeal of a fixed workplace, though. A separation between work and personal. Especially now she had Elliot as well. Three people had already tried to get her to do stuff on days she should have been off.

She pulled her Bug around the back of the building, slipping into a spot beside a battered-looking Land Rover.

Oliver and Elliot got out somewhat awkwardly. She followed behind them after grabbing her gear from the boot. She could get changed inside in the locker room and leave her good clothes here so they wouldn't get stinky.

The back door led into a large entrance room. To the right was a new section for the rift surveyor, Sam. To the left was the armoury. Ahead, just past the armoury, was a door that led to the kitchen and opposite that were the stairs up. This was the first time Staci had been here since the building work had been completed, and she noticed they'd also taken the time to paint and re-floor this section. It looked good.

Oliver swiped the card reader to let them into the armoury. The square white room was chilly, with extractor fans buzzing above her. Four metal tables were spread out throughout the room. Along the back wall was a door and an open hatch where she could see metal cages and a squat man pulling out a rifle.

A general hum of voices mingled with the rhythmic click of metal against metal, the sounds of guns being checked, and the swish of clothes as the group moved. Three men and two women stood around two of the tables, strapping on armour and other gear. She only recognised one of them.

Lance scared her just a bit. He was around the same height as Oliver but even broader in the shoulders, with warm bronze skin, dark hair, and a glove on only one hand. He never smiled, never seemed to be happy about anything. Today, that look was even darker than usual as he stared at Elliot.

'How far into the Rift is the storm?' Lance said, shifting his gaze to Oliver, then to Staci.

'I don't know,' Staci said quietly, wishing she could give them something more. But all she knew was that it was in the direction of the Rift Scar. 'When we get closer, I can try to be more specific.'

Oliver moved past Lance to the hatch at the back, asking the man there for something.

'You're not on rotation,' Lance said sharply, gaze following Oliver.

'You going to turn down an extra set of hands?' Oliver said, raising his eyebrow. 'Besides, you're not on call either and you're still coming.'

'I haven't worked a full seven days on,' Lance said, his eyes narrowing.

Staci watched them exchange the look that all dominant Shifters seemed to excel at. It said I'm the boss, and I'll not rip your head off if you don't piss on my land. She fought her smile at the image. It wasn't appropriate, considering the tension.

'I'll be fine. I've another day off after today,' Oliver said. His eyes didn't change colour, which she was sure was a good sign.

Lance grunted and turned back to Staci and Elliot. 'Go get changed,' Lance said, eyes not giving an inch. 'We leave in ten.'

'I don't have any gear,' Elliot said, straightening his back like he was trying to project confidence in his words. 'Besides, you don't really need two of us.'

No one looked impressed by his statement. If going into the Rift Scar was why Elliot had hesitated to deal with the weather, then Staci would be having words with the mayor about Elliot's future employment. She just hoped the mayor believed her.

One of the people she didn't know picked up a small pile of gear from the table she'd not noticed and handed it to Elliot. She had short brown hair spiked up. 'Don't worry, Oliver phoned ahead and organised this for you,' the woman said, giving Elliot a wink. 'Wouldn't want you to miss out.'

Elliot stiffly took the bundle. It was all grey—clothes and body armour—and a pair of boots on top. He gave Oliver a sideways glare but said nothing.

'Any other problems?' Elliot continued his silence, and Lance nodded towards the door. 'Then go get ready.'

Staci didn't have to be told twice, but she was surprised when Elliot meekly followed her out. The storm surged against her senses again as they reached the stairs, almost making her miss a step. She saw Elliot tense, clearly feeling what she did. Yet he'd have done nothing to stop it. She was going to have to do something about him after this. There was no use in having another weather warden if she couldn't trust him.

She showed him where the men's changing rooms were, then headed into the ladies. Once this storm was dealt with, she'd deal with Elliot and why he was lying. But for now, she needed to focus on what was ahead—going into the Rift Scar.

LANCE WATCHED OLIVER GEAR up. He stank of wolf-bite and stale sweat. Going by the strength of it, Lance should have sent Oliver home, regardless of his assurance that he was fine.

Not pup, Shade, his wolf, said. Oliver was five years Lance's junior. Five years felt like a big difference. Shade huffed a breath and added, *Oliver has hunted many times with us. Is good hunter.*

If he's unwell, he'll be slower, Lance said, looking at Oliver again, judging him. He moved smoothly, without any sign of pain.

Is alpha now, Shade said, not for the first time in the past six weeks. His wolf had sensed the change, though others had either not noticed or weren't talking about it, and Hale hadn't said anything. *Stronger than before.*

He's a long way to go before he can be a true alpha, Lance said. So far as he knew, all of Oliver's life had revolved around drinking, women, and fun. Power itself didn't make a leader, and Oliver, despite his protective instincts, hadn't shown Lance that he was anything but a party boy. Though the last few weeks, he'd been quieter.

Cannot learn from safety of den, Shade said, huffing a breath softly like he thought Lance was funny. *We good teacher. We help.*

It's Hale's job to teach Oliver, Lance said, turning away to check his rifle. He didn't want to risk his wolf getting too attached to the idea. Lance had no desire to be alpha or to teach one. Being an alpha meant letting others in and risking losing them. He couldn't do that.

It was bad enough that Hale had put him in charge of Shifters on patrol. The Elementals he could have dealt with, but the Shifters wanted to be connected and feel the pack. Lance couldn't risk opening himself up, not after losing his family.

Shade pressed close, fur brushing against the inside of their mind as Lance's chest started to feel tight. *We not alpha. We beta only. Is okay. Hale keep pack safe. Keep us safe. Hale will teach Oliver. Make him good alpha.*

Lance released the breath he'd been holding and almost laughed, though it would have held no humour. He'd thought Oliver was a risk, and here Lance was on the verge of a panic attack because someone had put him in charge. Stupid. He glanced at the others in the room, but no one seemed to have noticed his wobble. He'd gotten good at hiding it.

When Hale had asked Lance to be a senior rift ranger, he should have said no. But with so many leaving, there weren't many left with the experience needed to do the job. Against his better judgment, he'd said yes, at least until others were skilled up.

Or the attacks on the pack stopped.

Though Hale hadn't mentioned it—and being a senior ranger didn't necessarily mean that he was higher in the pack—it was obvious that some of the drive to promote Lance had come from the recent events. First, Shane and Lacey had tried to kill Hale, then the three rangers slacking had killed two people six weeks ago. Lance couldn't stand back while someone was targeting the pack.

So, he'd agreed to the extra responsibility, even though he knew he shouldn't have. This was why he'd not wanted to get attached to anyone. It made you vulnerable. Made you make stupid decisions.

He carefully stretched his gloved hand, feeling the painful tightness still lingering there. His scars. The permanent reminder of what he'd lost. The reason he didn't want to be truly integrated into another pack.

He'd lost his entire family because he'd made a bad choice. He might as well have lit the house on fire himself and watched them burn. It was all his fault.

We did not hurt family. We killed woman who did. She cannot hurt anyone now, Shade said, pressing closer, breathing with him. In and out. One at a time. Pushing the panic away. *Safe here. We know this.*

Sorry, Shade, Lance said, and Shade withdrew slightly, still hovering closer. *I know we're safe.*

But the safety didn't help with the pain. Every time he opened the pack bonds to Hale, it was like his family was being burned alive all over again, their pain his. Right now, the only thing that was letting Lance keep that trauma at bay was that Hale allowed him to keep the pack bonds between them locked down. Lance could barely feel his alpha at all.

Hale clearly thought that Lance just needed space and time to recover. It had been years, and none of it had got better so far. Maybe that was the price he had to pay for causing his family's death.

Lance rolled his shoulders and refocused on his team, trying to push away all his old pain. This wasn't the time to deal with it. He had a job to do and no one to blame but himself for joining the patrol and taking charge when he could have left Mac to lead the group.

There were four of them on rapid response duty today. Mac was a brown-haired man with sun-darkened skin, a weightlifter's build, and almost as much body hair as a wolf. Cindy, who'd spiked her brown hair again and Rafe, who'd shaved an intricate pattern on his head. The three of them were Elementals.

Zoe was the last member of his team and the newest. She was slim, with creamy white skin, brown eyes, and barely tall enough to reach his collarbone. She'd pulled her long dark brown hair into a French pleat to work. It was easy to overlook her, but with her police background, she'd more training than most of the people here combined. She was a Shifter, but she'd not been born that way.

Nearly a year ago, Zoe and her partner had gone to investigate a noise complaint. They found a scientist experimenting with Rift venom on wolves to create new Shifters. Any animal infected with Rift venom went feral, and whoever they bit or bled on could become a Shifter of that animal type. A wolf escaped and had taken chunks out of her and her partner before she'd killed it. She was the only one to survive the encounter.

The police had given her early retirement, not wanting a brand-new Shifter in their unit. She'd moved between several packs over the past year until she'd ended up here last month.

Hale had asked Lance to help train her. Teach her what it was to be a wolf, which was easier said than done. Coming into your wolf as a teenager was hard enough, but becoming one in your twenties, with human prejudice and fear of Shifters? It changed everything.

She didn't trust herself, and he didn't know how to help her with that. She needed someone who could teach her how important it was to lean on the pack and the connections there. But that was the last thing he wanted for himself, so he had no idea how to teach it to someone else. So far, Hale hadn't listened to Lance.

'Did you let Hale know about the storm?' Oliver asked, drawing Lance's attention back to him.

Oliver had already strapped on his Kevlar vest, swapped his jeans for the Kevlar-lined combat trousers, and was currently pulling on his heavy boots. The armourer had given him his weapons, too, and they were laid on the metal table in front of him. The rest of the team was ready and waiting.

Lance nodded. 'I called Hale after I spoke to you. He wasn't all that impressed by the lack of warning.' Or Elliot, but no one had been much impressed by him overall so far. 'He's going to come down and man the phone in case any other calls come in, but he's at least an hour away, so he said not to wait. Staci can take us to the closest edge, and we'll enter there. Patrol is working the far side of the Scar today, so there's no chance of having a clear path.'

Oliver nodded, face tight. There wasn't much else they could do. Taking civilians into the Scar was never fun, but clearing the way before them was usually preferred. Rift creatures moved regularly, so they could be walking into a brand-new nest and not know it until they hit it.

All his team except Zoe was experienced enough to know what to do if things went badly. So was Oliver. They'd be fine.

The three Elementals chatted quietly while they waited. Zoe kept apart, but that had been her normal attitude so far. Distant and quiet, only engaging when someone spoke to her directly. Lance had no idea what he was supposed to do with that. It wasn't like he was chatty. Hale should have assigned her to Oliver. Though he was as broody as Zoe today, watching the exit, dancing from one foot to another while he waited.

Staci appeared just after the five-minute mark. She'd re-tied her hair back into a bun and dressed in a long-sleeved grey T-shirt under a Kevlar vest and the same grey combats the rest were wearing. No weapons—or holsters for them—made her look incomplete. But she'd not had the training for combat in the Rift. She was a civilian. She smelled nervous, but you wouldn't know it by looking at her with her shoulders back and chin up.

Elliot took longer, and Oliver ended up re-strapping most of the protective gear onto him, delaying them even more.

'This is a waste of all our time,' Elliot said, just loud enough for everyone to hear. 'The storm isn't anything more than a few rain clouds.'

Something about his attitude raised Lance's hackles. He couldn't tell if two sets of traitors in three months were making him paranoid or if Elliot was the next problem they'd have to deal with. But how would him lying about the storm affect the pack or the rangers? Lance couldn't find any logic that fit. But it didn't make him feel any better.

'Then we'll have a quick stroll through the sunshine and be back for lunch,' Zoe said. Her tone had been mild, but she watched Elliot like a wolf watched a deer. Clearly, she'd seen the same things as Lance.

Elliot didn't say anything to that, especially when no one jumped on his bandwagon of not needing to go into the Rift Scar.

'Let's go,' Lance said, grabbing his rifle from the table and checking the safety.

By the time they finally piled into three old Land Rovers, it had been nearly thirty minutes. Everyone was as prepared as they could be.

CHAPTER FOUR

Oliver watched Huntly disappear behind him through the side mirror. The tall walls were an achingly familiar sight that he was going to miss. He'd not considered how much he'd feel that way about anything when he first came here.

Everything he'd done and seen at the rangers' base had given him the same sensation. The last time he'd gear up. The last patrol he'd go on. The last time he'd be in the Rift Scar. Not things he'd thought he'd ever miss.

Not want to go home, Thor said.

Me either. But they both knew there wasn't any other option.

Once the storm was dealt with, he'd go to Hale and tell him he was leaving. Not so long ago, he'd have been overjoyed at the prospect. Even as bad as his father had been, it had been home.

Had been his home. Not was his home.

He tried to shove his loss deep down. This wasn't the time to be mournful. He needed to get his head on straight to deal with the dangers that awaited them in the Rift Scar.

Lance drove silently, shoulders tense and knuckles white on the steering wheel. He'd had the same look in the armoury. Hell, he'd had the same look ever since Hale had made him a senior rift ranger. But his scent remained even, nothing of his emotions showing in the ginger and cinnamon mix. Oliver had never met anyone as good as Lance at hiding what they felt from their scent.

'What's wrong, Lance?' Oliver said, looking at the road ahead as they drove. Lance was dominant enough that their wolves could easily clash. Though he'd never seen Lance challenge anyone, even those who were being stupid.

Lance loosened his grip on the steering wheel a little. Not exactly like he'd relaxed, but more like he'd pulled all the tension inside.

'How well do you know Elliot?' he asked.

That wasn't the answer Oliver had expected. But he probably should have.

'We grew up in the same circle, but it wasn't until the last few years we became friends,' Oliver said. He didn't say that Elliot had got into trouble and Oliver had bailed him out. That wouldn't help endear him to Lance, though

Oliver wasn't sure he could endear Elliot to anyone at this point. 'He has been desperate to get a job working as a weather warden for the last year, but there are more people than jobs.'

'If he's so keen, what happened last night?' Lance asked, voice a low rumble as they followed the other two cars down the mostly empty road. 'Why didn't he come to us and tell us what was needed? We could have been prepared this morning.'

'I don't know,' Oliver said, then he stopped. Elliot had come to the rangers' headquarters last night. He'd claimed he'd been looking for Oliver to ask if he wanted to go out. Had that been a lie? Had he chickened out of going into the Rift Scar when he'd seen Oliver?

'But you believe Staci over Elliot?' Lance asked.

Oliver nodded. 'Staci has the experience.' Though it was more than that, deeper. He felt it in his gut that Staci was telling the truth. Her fear was just too real.

'So why did Elliot lie?'

Oliver winced. There weren't a lot of other ways to cut it. Either Elliot was lying, or Staci was. Or one was incompetent, and if that was the case, they'd never have got a job after school.

Elliot could be selfish, but Oliver couldn't imagine Elliot lying about the storm deliberately or out of laziness.

Fear, on the other hand, that would explain a lot. But if it was fear, his friend would never work as a weather warden again.

Lied about Staci, Thor said, letting out a small snarl. *Not friend now.*

Oliver didn't say anything to that. He didn't even know where to start.

Lance clearly took silence as permission to keep going. 'After everything that's happened over the last few months, the IRS&D are still watching us, waiting for someone else to screw up.' Lance's voice darkened at the words, the scent of his anger and wolf flooding the car. Oliver's reaction was little better. He opened the window.

The Institute of Rift Studies and Defence were in charge of anything to do with the Rift Scar, including the rangers. They were hands-off for the most part, dictating a general policy and best practice, then leaving the wardens to do their jobs unless something went wrong.

'IRS&D dealt with the three rangers,' Oliver said, turning to watch the trees that whizzed past them. They'd jailed the three men who'd failed to do their jobs. Apparently, all had pleaded guilty. By some miracle, the press hadn't yet caught wind of two deaths and three arrests.

'It doesn't matter if it was dealt with. People died because rangers weren't doing their jobs. We cannot afford mistakes,' Lance said, taking a breath. He'd opened his window as well, Oliver noticed.

'I don't know why Elliot would lie,' Oliver said slowly. His wolf growled in his head. Thor wasn't likely to forgive Elliot any time soon. 'He's wanted to be a weather warden his whole life. This is his chance.'

'Maybe he's not ready to be in the Rift Scar,' Lance said, not unkindly.

Oliver knew he should tell Lance about Elliot coming to HQ last night but couldn't find the words. Elliot had been his friend for years. He deserved the chance to explain.

'Let me talk to him again,' Oliver said, looking at Lance, watching his face for agreement. 'See if I can find out what happened.' He could do that. Another last thing he could do before he had to go home.

'Elliot has already lied once. Be careful the next one doesn't land us in trouble along with him,' Lance said. Something like pain laced his voice, though his scent only held anger, not a hint of anything else. 'Sometimes people aren't who we thought they were.'

So much more was under those words that Oliver almost asked what was wrong again. But Lance had never been good at sharing his past. Even if Oliver wasn't leaving, he doubted he'd be able to get Lance to open up.

They travelled the rest of the way in silence while Oliver tried his best to memorise everything around him.

STACI SHARED A CAR with Cindy, who'd introduced herself as an Air Elemental with no affinity for storms, and Zoe, who barely said two words the whole ride. Elliot sat in the back with Staci like a sulking child as he complained about being made to go into the Rift Scar.

They pulled off a single-track dirt road into a small patch of broken concrete where they would leave the cars. It was another half a mile before the Rift Scar started, but they'd walk from here.

Tendrils of the storm raced across her skin, calling to her magic. She looked up at the sky; it was still clear blue, not a cloud to be seen, but that wouldn't last much longer. By the time they got within a mile of the storm's core, there'd be no doubt to anyone what was out there.

Cindy opened her car door, bringing in the stench of the Rift Scar. Sour milk, putrid, rotten meat, and something underneath that was worse, defying description. She always forgot how bad it was. Elliot gagged, opening his door to vomit on the ground. The stench got worse, but at least it was outside the car.

'Great, just what we need, more stink,' Cindy said, nose crinkling as she got out of the car, ignoring Elliot as he heaved.

Zoe curled her lip and joined Cindy, the two of them going to the boot to open the locked storage; they pulled out weapons and strapped them on. The other two rangers did the same thing as they parked beside them. Oliver and Lance must have fallen behind because she couldn't see them.

Staci got out of the car, too, pulling her body armour back into place from where it had ridden up. She wanted to check her phone to see if Florence had gotten her update on what was happening, but she'd left it at HQ. The Rift Scar had no signal, and the dust ruined electronics. She'd have to wait until she got back.

Elliot groaned, but Staci ignored him. This was time she should've been spending with her mother. She wasn't going to give him any sympathy.

'Staci,' Elliot said, voice holding a whining pitch that hurt her ears. 'Look, I know you think there's a storm—'

Staci huffed a breath and moved around the car so she could give him the full strength of her glare; so much for ignoring him. 'Even hung over, I don't for one second believe you can't feel the strength of this storm. It feels like

I'm standing with one finger in a socket, every nerve in my body is pointing at the damned thing.'

'All I can feel is some rain,' Elliot said. But he was lying. She'd seen him react more than once on the way over. So why lie? Did he think it would help him explain his actions?

As if sensing the attention, the storm surged, trickling through her body like a slow burst of static. Every nerve was on fire. It was growing wilder with every breath she took. She opened eyes she hadn't realised she'd closed and watched Elliot. He was hanging out of the car, staring at the vomit on the floor.

'You aren't a good liar,' Staci said carefully. She was tired of this game.

'Look, think what you want. But I don't feel anything but a small rain cloud. I didn't feel anything more than that last night when you called and sent a hundred text messages either,' Elliot said, straightening to get out of the car. 'You're wasting everyone's time. But maybe this is for the best. The council will see this for the overreaction it is.'

The sound of the boot lid slamming shut was loud in the wake of his words. She was so angry she couldn't even speak. She spun, turning away from him before she did something she'd regret. Or maybe something he'd regret.

Did he really think the council would believe him? She felt the storm, felt it building on itself. The rangers would see the power of it by the time they got close enough to the core. The pieces were still slightly apart, right on the edge of forming. She'd never seen a storm take this long to gather before. They needed to stop it before it left the Rift Scar.

'Are you okay?'

Staci jumped and spun around. Oliver was attaching a strap to his rifle, frowning at her. She'd not even heard him arrive. It was starting to become a habit.

'I'm fine,' Staci said, trying to sound like she meant it. She didn't need Oliver's help. He didn't look like he believed her but didn't press.

'How far into the Rift Scar is the storm? And which direction?' Lance asked. He'd also strapped on his rifle and a smaller handgun in a thigh holster. All the rangers moved like they knew what they were doing, but Lance seemed to have an extra edge about him.

'I can't be sure. A few miles, at least, but not more than four,' Staci said, glancing at Elliot, but he didn't argue with her despite his earlier words. She pointed towards the storm. It was a straight line right into the Rift Scar. That's why she'd suggested this edge as they'd left. 'That direction.'

'Elliot and Staci, stay in the centre. I'll take the lead; Oliver rear; Cindy take the left; Zoe and Mac take the right; Rafe scout ahead,' Lance said. 'Staci will let us know if we head in the wrong direction, so don't go far, Rafe.'

The man with an intricate pattern shaved on his head nodded and started off in the direction she'd pointed at a slow jog.

'Oliver, you, Rafe, and Cindy swept this area yesterday, and there was no activity then, right?' Lance said.

Oliver nodded. 'No sign of anything passing through at all.'

'Why isn't a patrol in front of us?' Elliot said, finding a burst of energy despite how pale he still looked. 'That's the protocol. What if there are scorpions out there?'

'If we'd had a call yesterday, then we'd have been able to arrange it,' Cindy said, half under her breath.

Elliot turned red and opened his mouth, but Lance spoke first.

'We'll keep you safe,' Lance said, narrowing his eyes at Elliot, who shrunk back. 'If it looks like it's going to become dangerous, we'll go back.'

Staci moved to argue that they needed to go ahead anyway, but Lance turned his eyes to her, and the argument dried up. Elliot also didn't argue, which was good. The last thing she needed was Elliot telling the rangers she was overreacting. If they believed him, then they might not have gone into the Scar.

'Let's move. Safety is more important than speed, but let's remember we're on a deadline,' Lance said, moving to the front. 'Staci, let us know when we are getting closer.'

Staci nodded, though he couldn't see it, and then she fell into the middle with Elliot. Oliver was at her back. She could sense his presence almost as keenly as the storm. It made her feel safer somehow, which was foolish. All the rangers were there to keep them safe. She had no desire to analyse why he made her feel better and not the rest of them.

It didn't take long to reach the grey wasteland, dry and broken with the recent heat. The ground was uneven, with random dips and rises, the dirt crumbling under their feet, sending puffs of dust into the air.

It was quiet but for the sound of their breath and movement. No buzz of insects, no chirps from birds, no rustle of leaves. The Rift Scar destroyed everything from earth, and all animals and insects had learned to avoid it.

It was a shame Staci couldn't follow in their footsteps. But she had a job to do, and unlike Elliot, a little fear wouldn't stop her from doing it.

CHAPTER FIVE

OLIVER HAD BEEN WALKING for maybe thirty minutes when the breeze picked up. It didn't do much to cool the air, but the steady gust blew dust in their eyes and the rank, rotting stench deeper into their noses.

This section of the Rift Scar was all rolling hills, gullies, and more places that he could count where something could hide, waiting to attack. There was no sign of anything having passed through. But even so, his brain kept tormenting him with all the ways Staci could get hurt.

It was stupid and an attachment he couldn't afford when he was going to be leaving. Thor wasn't happy, either. He pressed close to the surface, not quite wanting them to shift, but there if they needed to move fast.

Staci walked with her shoulders hunched like she was being forced to bear extra weight. Elliot was the same, despite his words about Staci overreacting. Though Oliver was sure that Elliot would blame his hangover.

Rafe appeared ahead of them, running full tilt and motioning with his arm: *Creatures ahead*. The group stopped, closing a little tighter around Staci and Elliot.

Oliver searched the hills, searching for what Rafe had seen as the man slipped between them into the middle so he could catch his breath.

'Imps,' he said, gulping in air. 'Coming from the west and circling around behind us.'

'Stay close,' Lance said, though no one had needed the reminder. All the rangers were already as close as they could get, facing outwards, rifles raised to shoulders. 'How many?'

'Large group, three dozen at least,' Rafe said. 'They didn't see me, but it won't be long before they catch our scent if they haven't already.'

Oliver's stomach dropped. A couple of imps would have steered clear, but three dozen against eight? They might like those odds.

'There were no imps here yesterday,' Oliver said. He was getting flashbacks of six weeks ago. But the chances of a second wyvern in the Rift Scar were impossible.

'Maybe the storm is riling them up?' Rafe said. 'Forcing them to move away from their normal space?'

'It's possible, but I haven't seen it before,' Lance said as angry wolf energy spilt out of him, a warning that the imps wouldn't be able to sense. 'But the why doesn't help us right now. We need to find somewhere defendable.'

'I told you this would happen. I'm going to die because Staci wanted to fix a bit of rain,' Elliot said, words tumbling over each other.

Oliver glanced at him; he looked like he was about to faint. Staci was dealing with the news far better. She was pale but moving on the balls of her feet, waiting for them to tell her what to do.

'Shut up,' Lance said, not even looking at Elliot as he turned to Oliver. 'How close is the nearest ruin?'

'There's an old farmhouse with partial walls and a solid floor, a mile that way,' Oliver said, making the best guess at the distance as he nodded to the east. 'Open ground on one side, and these hills on the other. It was clear yesterday.'

'That's too far. We should make a stand here,' Mac said. 'Once we shoot a few, the rest will run.'

'No,' Oliver said, glancing again at Staci and Elliot. They had nothing to defend themselves. 'We are too exposed out here; if they don't back off and rush us instead, we won't be able to kill them fast enough.'

'This isn't another wyvern driving the imps out the Rift Scar,' Mac said, but he'd softened his voice. Everyone had seen how much damage that beast had done. 'We can scare them off.'

'Oliver's right, it's too risky. Even if fear isn't driving them, that big a group will take more risks. They might decide that the eight of us are worth the pain, and we'll have no protection,' Lance said. 'We go for the shelter and defend. Then we retreat.'

Oliver let out a huff of breath, a tiny fragment of fear easing. It wasn't much, but it was something. At least until Staci's fear hit Oliver's nose, sharp and biting.

'That storm is strong enough to become a hurricane if we leave it,' Staci said, making Oliver want to laugh. Of course, that's what she was afraid of. Not the clan of imps that wanted to rip them apart. The coming storm. 'We have to keep going.'

'Houses can be rebuilt, people cannot,' Lance said. 'Once we deal with the imps, we will head back. Warn people they need to find shelter.'

'I told you we shouldn't have come here,' Elliot said, his breath coming in sharp gasps.

'Enough. We need to get to shelter now,' Lance said, giving both of them a chilling look. Lance was good at that. They both shut up. But going by the set of Staci's jaw, Oliver didn't think Lance had heard the end of Staci's argument.

Mac nodded, accepting Lance's order as they repositioned themselves in the new direction. Rafe slipped into line with Cindy, evening out their protection box around Elliot and Staci. It was too dangerous to risk splitting up now against three dozen imps.

Staci had to give Elliot a light nudge to get him to move. She whispered quiet encouragement, but it didn't seem to make any difference as the stench of his fear grew stronger than the rot of the Rift Scar.

'If the imps didn't already know we're here, the fear is going to draw them right to us,' Lance said, voice too low for Staci or Elliot to hear.

He wasn't wrong. Imps liked to play with their prey, and fear only made that game more exciting. It was another reason they avoided bringing in civilians. Unfortunately, telling someone their fear was attracting the imps wouldn't help. Nor did they have the time to calm him down.

Oliver was starting to wish he'd let Elliot stay behind. He could have dealt with Elliot's problem another way. But that would have left Staci in danger. He didn't want that either.

Protect Staci, Thor said. He was so close that Oliver could practically feel fur under his skin. But they'd worked in the Rift Scar long enough that Thor knew not to try to shift when there was danger. It took too long and made them vulnerable.

They made it to the top of the hill and within sight of the small ruin before he heard the first high-pitched laugh. It loosely resembled a hyena cackle.

'Hold,' Lance said, voice steady. Everyone stopped except Elliot. Staci grabbed him before he walked into Lance's back.

Oliver moved his gun to point towards a slight dip in the ground as he caught sight of movement. An imp crouched in the dirt, grey skin partially blending in. The creature was child size, but with all the wrong proportions. Its arms were too long, knuckles dragging on the ground as it swayed from side to side. The breeze changed direction, bringing the smell of it to them. Elliot gagged, doubling over. Last night's vodka smelled almost as bad as the imp.

'I see one,' Oliver said, voice quiet. Another cackle came from further away.

'What are you waiting for? Shoot it,' Elliot shouted, wiping his mouth.

'Two here,' Zoe said.

'We need to get to the ruin,' Lance said. 'Anyone got a clear shot?'

'They're using the hill's edge as cover,' Zoe said, glancing at Oliver.

'Same here,' Oliver said, wanting to curse.

'Two more on this side,' Cindy said.

They needed to get behind cover before the imps surrounded them. The imp in front of Oliver started to sway, making a humming noise.

Elliot was muttering low under his breath about how he was going to die, his fear heavy in the air.

'Get your friend under control, Oliver,' Lance said.

'Me under control? You have a shot; it's standing right there. Why aren't you shooting it?' Elliot shouted, gulping in air.

'Elliot, take a slow breath,' Staci whispered. 'It's going to be okay. Oliver's got this. He's going to keep us safe.'

Oliver's whole body lit up at the way she said his name. She'd used it over all the others in the group. But Elliot knew Oliver. It made sense. It was logical. But none of that logic registered above the feeling of Staci's trust to keep them safe.

'There only looks to be seven or eight out there right now,' Mac said, looking at Elliot. 'Even with the stink of fear and panic, they should be backing off with our group being so big.'

'They know the rest of their clan is close,' Rafe said, breath steady and voice calm.

'We're going to be eaten alive,' Elliot whispered.

The imp in front of Oliver decided it was bored of waiting for them to make the first move, and it stood, making a loud cackle like he was trying to rally the others.

Oliver fired a small burst, hitting the imp in the centre of its chest. Black blood sprayed over the ground. Its cackle cut off with a scream as it fell.

He heard other shots behind him as the others took out more imps.

'Start moving towards the ruin,' Lance said. 'Rafe, take the lead.'

They swapped positions, and Lance ended up at Oliver's side as they retreated. Another imp stepped up on top of the hill, but this one was too far back. It was nearly black, with grey streaks running over its skin. The alpha.

It was a whole bloody clan. No wonder they were so damned confident. Lance's growl said he'd seen the creature too.

Oliver walked backwards, relying on the others to keep moving as he watched for anything approaching. He looked for another target. More shots came from his left. The stench of blood, so far all imp, filled his nose. They screamed and cackled.

Something caught the corner of Oliver's eye. Another imp rushing at them from the right. Someone shot at it, but it dodged, moving too fast for them to correct before it reached Oliver. The imp's claws hit his Kevlar as it rammed into him, throwing him backwards. He hit the ground hard.

STACI YELPED AS OLIVER hit the ground beside her, an imp on top of him. They rolled, imp going underneath as Cindy dropped inside the circle, slashing at it with her knife. The imp tried to get away, clawing at Oliver's Kevlar as the pair struggled wildly until they rolled again, and the imp was on top.

There was nothing Staci could do. She had no weapons and no way to use her magic to help. She wanted to scream, but there was so much noise it would have been lost in the chaos.

Black saliva dripped onto Oliver's face. Cindy moved in fast, slicing the blade into the imp's neck, catching the spine. The beast went limp against Oliver. Kicking the creature off him, he rolled to his feet, searching. When his eyes caught hers, some of the tension flowed out of him.

Her heart remembered how to beat again, one painful pound after another. He'd been worried about her? While the damned imp was trying to kill him? Idiot.

'Keep moving,' Lance shouted, more gunfire blasting Staci's ears.

Oliver and Cindy moved back to the circle edge like nothing had happened. No words, no celebration. They started moving towards the ruin again, faster this time. The imps pulled back, watching and cackling.

Staci shoved Elliot to get him moving. Tiny flecks of electricity danced between them, singeing her fingers. She cursed and pulled her hand back. He didn't even seem to notice. His eyes were too wide, the whites flashing as he tried to look everywhere at once. She wanted to do the same, but she focused instead on the old, broken shell of a house in front of her. She could make out the individual stones on the walls now. It was so close. Ten metres. Five. Then they were there.

The rangers spread out after a few words, each picking a broken wall for protection. The wind gusted over them, sending dust into her eyes, making them water.

'How many are dead?' Oliver shouted, looking over at Lance.

'Four, maybe five,' Lance said. His rifle was at his shoulder, and he was crouched behind a low wall. Staci searched for the bodies. They almost blended in; if not for the black blood, she might not have seen them at all.

'Dammit, that should be enough to make them back off,' Oliver said, looking back at her. Her heart missed another beat as she saw his fear. All of their fear. This wasn't normal, and they were worried.

'They seem angry rather than afraid,' Lance said.

Staci didn't know how he could tell, but she didn't care at this point.

Elliot whimpered beside her, tiny sparks of light flickering over his skin. He was losing control, and this close to a storm, that was dangerous.

'You need to calm down, Elliot,' Staci said, barely hearing her words as her ears rang.

'This is your fault,' he said, turning to her as he backed up against the tallest wall. It reached just above his head. His anger was better than fear. She could deal with an insult or two to keep him there. 'You couldn't just leave it alone.'

'If you'd come out here last night, none of this would have happened,' Staci said, glancing at the others. Everyone was still pressed against the walls for cover, guns barking intermittently. She just had to keep Elliot angry until they killed the imps.

Elliot's magic spread wider, prickling against her skin like a thousand tiny needles. It felt like lightning, but it couldn't be that. Carrying lightning was dangerous. It would drain your magic as you tried to contain it. Or it would connect you to the storm, which would drain you instead. There was no benefit.

She'd been lucky that the one time it had happened to her before she'd learned how to use her magic, the weather warden had been there to help her. But she'd been taught better since then. Elliot would have had that same training. Surely he wouldn't be that …

Sparks crawled over his skin again. White and blue arcs of light. It wasn't just a little bit of static. It was lightning. She could feel it now that his magic was growing more erratic.

She muttered a curse, glancing in the direction of the storm. They were still too far out for Elliot to interact with it, but it was only getting closer; she needed to calm him down before he got dragged in. The last thing this storm needed was more power. She'd never be able to rip it apart then.

When she'd been struck by lightning, the old weather warden had helped her ground it, but this wasn't exactly a safe place to do that. Nor was she sure exactly how he'd done it safely since they don't teach it.

'Whatever you're doing, stop,' Staci said, reaching out to touch him, anything to soothe him. But he slapped her hand away. As his skin hit hers, she felt his magic connect with her.

Lightning flared between them, grounding inside her in a blinding flash of light. Her skin was two sizes too small as it writhed, trying to get free and connect back to the storm.

She couldn't let that happen. But she couldn't keep hold of it forever, either. She was going to kill Elliot if they survived today.

'What the hell is wrong with you?' Staci whispered to Elliot as her vision cleared. The magic tugged at her again, sensing somewhere other than the storm it could go. She fought it, sweat beading down her spine. How the hell had Elliot been keeping it contained all this time?

'You can't do that.' Elliot was paler than before. He shook his head, stepping back from her. 'No one can do that.'

The storm surged, feeling closer than before, almost like it was within range now, though it hadn't moved. It was so tempting to reach out, connect with it. But it wouldn't help her control the storm. That wasn't how Storm Magic worked.

'Me? I didn't do anything. You brought the lightning here,' Staci said, stepping towards him and then stopped as an imp screamed a challenge. She flinched away from the sound; she'd nearly forgotten the fight despite the noise.

The magic was so loud in her head that it was hard to think about anything else.

'This is all your fault. The storm. The attack. All of it.' Elliot was moving along the wall, so close to the edge that one more step would take him beyond the protection of the rangers.

'Elliot, stop,' Staci said, reaching out, but as she did, the lightning tried to travel down her arm towards Elliot. She dropped her hand. 'You need to stay in the ruin.'

Elliot wasn't listening anymore. He took another step, nearly touching Rafe. 'No, you're going to kill us all,' Elliot said.

Staci didn't get a chance to reply as Rafe fell backwards into Elliot, spinning him to the side. An imp landed on top of Rafe as they fell into the circle. He tried to throw off the imp, but it scored a long strip across his shoulder.

The man never even screamed as blood sprayed over the grey dirt. One of the other rangers turned and rammed a knife into the shoulder of the imp. Staci moved as they rolled, ending up half outside the ruin as well.

Elliot took advantage of the distraction and bolted.

'Elliot!' Staci shouted. She hesitated to follow, not wanting to leave the limited protection of the ruin. But she wouldn't be able to forgive herself if she let him run off either. She started after him, her heart beating so hard she could hear it.

A black imp appeared in front of Elliot, and he nearly crashed into it, feet sliding on the dry ground as he scrambled to stop. The imp slashed at him.

She grabbed him by the back of his Kevlar and shoved him out of range. Those claws skimmed his skin rather than taking off his arm. She didn't risk looking away from the imp to check if he was okay as he landed with a grunt.

It snarled at her, face twisting as it showed razor-sharp teeth. She wouldn't have time to run. The others were too far away to help. She was on her own. The lightning flickered down her arm, the white light drawing the imp's eye. It growled and lunged forward.

There wasn't time to think, only react. She grabbed the imp's black arm rather than trying to dodge. Lightning surged down her arm, trying to ground itself in the imp just like it had with Elliot. Except this time, she didn't hold it back.

She let all of it go.

OLIVER TURNED TO FIND Staci, her hand on the arm of the black imp.

She was too close to risk shooting. Too far to reach her in time. He saw her death, felt it in his soul.

Light flashed between them, blue and white, and then the creature convulsed, screaming in agony so loud that it made all the other imps stop.

The alpha imp fell away from her, still screaming as it hit the ground. Fear filled its scent, and then a bullet took it in the head, spraying blood around it.

The rest of the imps screamed again, picking up the fear and the loss of their alpha. They bolted as one, heading deeper into the Rift Scar, careless of the bullets or their kin that had been left behind.

Oliver didn't wait to see if there were stragglers as he ran towards Staci. He needed to know she was okay.

Cindy caught his arm as he passed her. He snarled, showing teeth, then snapped his mouth shut and forced himself to remain still. Cindy wasn't his enemy. He knew better than to react like this.

Stopping us from helping Staci, Thor said, pressing him to move. Cindy wasn't pack, wasn't in danger.

'Careful touching her. That looked like lightning,' Cindy said slowly, letting go of him, showing no urgency. No fear. Not many people could have kept their reaction so neutral.

Oliver nodded, wishing he could afford the time to apologise, but he'd do that later. But first, he needed to check on Staci.

She didn't look like she'd been hurt physically, but she was staring at the imp she'd touched.

Is afraid. Tell her will be okay, Thor said, urging him to move closer, to wrap their arms around her. Something Oliver doubted she'd appreciate. Nor was this really the place.

Thor didn't like it, but he knew that just because the imps had left didn't mean they wouldn't return. He needed to get her back in the ruin.

'Staci?' Oliver said, trying to get her to look at him. She didn't look like she'd heard him.

Despite Cindy's words, he couldn't stop himself from reaching out and touching her arm. His skin tingled, but he didn't feel any pain. She let out a sharp breath and pulled back, her scent changing to fear as she watched him.

'You're safe,' Oliver said, wanting to touch her again, but he held back. 'They've gone.'

'I didn't mean to,' Staci said, eyes returning to the dead imp. 'But I couldn't stop it.'

'You didn't do anything wrong. You stopped the attack and made all the imps run,' Oliver said, stepping closer. He wished they were somewhere a little more private, without half a dozen ears listening to every word he said.

Staci shook her head but didn't answer him. He wished he knew more about Storm Magic, but whatever was wrong, she was clearly upset. She shuddered, turning deeper into the Rift Scar. The wind stirred again, sending a sudden cold blast over them.

'Mac, Oliver, get Staci and Elliot back into the centre,' Lance shouted, bringing everyone's focus to him. 'Zoe, check Rafe's arm. Then the rest form a perimeter in case they come back.'

Oliver wanted to snarl at Lance and tell him he wasn't leaving Staci, but she turned almost like she was in a dream and started walking back towards the centre.

Touch her, make her feel better, Thor said again, whining. But Oliver ignored him and moved back to the edge of the ruin.

Mac dragged Elliot to his feet and shoved him back to the centre without a word. He had a bright slash of red over his arm, and he clutched it to his stomach. Rafe had a gash on his shoulder that was much deeper, and the blood had soaked down his sleeve and was dripping onto the ground as Zoe helped him put pressure on it.

Oliver took a breath and trusted that Zoe would care for them as he turned back towards the Rift Scar. There was no sign of any movement. All the remaining imps were dead. A dozen of them now, black blood seeping into the grey soil. A third of the clan.

'How are they doing, Zoe?' Lance asked, not looking away from the field.

'Rafe's got a deep laceration on his shoulder. He's going to need stitches and checking out at the hospital,' Zoe said from behind him. 'Elliot's aren't as deep, but he's probably going to need stitches too.'

Elliot made a noise, halfway to a moan, but at least he was staying put this time. Staci and Rafe said nothing.

'Once you've finished patching them up, we will head back,' Lance said.

'We can't; the storm is getting worse,' Staci said. 'We need to keep going. Stop it.'

'No, we're going back,' Oliver said. The idea of putting Staci in any more danger made his chest tight. No way was he letting her put herself at risk after this.

'We can't go back now,' Staci said, turning to him, voice sharp. 'The imps are gone. You killed them. We need to stop the storm now, or it's going to be so powerful I won't be able to stop it.'

Her fear was so potent that he wanted to pull her into his arms. But even Thor could see that she wouldn't welcome that touch now.

'No. Oliver is right. That group might be dead, but what happens if others attack? We have two injured and have already used a significant amount of ammo. We're going back,' Lance said, voice low as his wolf rose. Not that a wolf would help against Staci. She wasn't pack or a Shifter to be swayed.

Not control Staci, Thor said, pressing hard until Oliver stepped between Lance and Staci. Their power rose like a wave around them, wild and angry. *Mine.*

What? Oliver said, breath catching. *Thor?*

Thor ignored the question. Instead, he pressed close to the surface, like he wanted to challenge Lance.

Not the time or the place, Thor, Oliver said, shoving against his wolf until he fell back a step, letting them both take a breath.

He'd deal with what Thor had meant later. Right now, Lance was still watching him. He'd not moved, hadn't reacted at all. Typically, Lance didn't get involved in pack dominance, but Oliver had challenged him. And worse, he'd done it as an alpha. Something he was trying his best not to let the pack know.

He could feel Staci behind him. Feel her heat and the tiny tendrils of power that came from her. The need to protect her went soul-deep, even if it meant fighting Lance.

Which was stupid. Lance didn't want to hurt her, he'd just been reiterating what Oliver had said.

Oliver turned away first, though Thor fought him over it. He didn't want to fight Lance. He didn't think he'd win for a start. But also, Hale had been teaching him better than this.

Lance's angry energy whipped about him before it calmed, too. However, Oliver doubted that Lance was just going to let it go. The other rangers were staring at Oliver, though none except Zoe were Shifters to have sensed exactly what had happened. But they'd been around the pack long enough to know it was something.

'We'll follow the same formation as before, except Mac. I want you to scout ahead, but not too far, and Rafe will take your position,' Lance said as if nothing had happened. 'When we get back, we can get warnings out to the locals about the storm.'

Both men nodded. Ideally, Rafe would have been in the centre since he was wounded. But, after that attack, they needed every weapon they could use just in case. He'd already drawn his handgun, holding it by his non-injured side.

'It's already too late,' Elliot said, breath catching as Zoe tightened the bandage.

'I thought you said there was no storm?' Oliver said, voice tight.

'There wasn't,' Elliot said, looking at Staci. 'Staci did something to make it worse.'

Staci turned towards Elliot, and Oliver grabbed her arm before she could step forward, feeling the power under her skin again.

Elliot lie, Thor said, snarling. *Not Staci's fault. She saved us. Help her hurt him for lie.*

Calm, Oliver said. *He's clearly hurt and upset; he doesn't mean it.*

His words did little to soothe Thor. At this point, nothing would. Not when he'd declared Staci was his. Which should have been obvious far sooner after the way Thor had been all day. Oliver wanted to ask Thor about it but now wasn't the time.

'We're going back,' Lance said again before anyone could speak. 'We'll warn the town, and they'll fall back on their storm protections.'

'What about the other patrols?' Rafe said. 'Won't they be hit by the storm?'

'They're on the other side of the Rift Scar, near the coast,' Lance said, glancing at Staci. 'Will that put them out of its path?'

Staci nodded slowly. 'It's coming this way.'

'As long as they don't deviate, they should be fine,' Lance said. 'Now, let's go home before we've any more surprises.'

The wind picked up, throwing the dust loosened from their fight into the air and stirring the scent of death. Oliver expected Staci to argue again, but she said nothing, wrapping her arms around herself as he dropped back to the rear, leaving her alone with Elliot.

He forced himself to pay attention to his surroundings as they started walking again. He wanted nothing more than to wrap his arms around Staci and carry her home. But he didn't.

Resisting was the hardest thing he'd done all day.

CHAPTER SIX

STACI FOLLOWED THE OTHERS, barely seeing where she was putting her feet. The storm called to her, right at the edge of her mind, like a siren. It had coalesced after the imps had retreated and wanted to grow, be more, be bigger. It knew she could give it that if she connected with it.

Letting it in would be easy, especially when her fingers still tingled from the last of the lightning. But she couldn't afford to give it any more power; it was already dangerous enough. There wasn't anything she could do to stop it now.

Grinding her teeth, she glanced at Elliot. She wished she knew how he'd been able to gather the lightning or why he'd been holding it in the first place. They were too far from the storm for it to have come from there. But after his accusation, she doubted she'd get a straight answer from him.

Had the others believed him? Did they think the storm was her fault? How the hell was she going to prove it either way? It was her word against his.

Unfortunately, she wouldn't be able to do anything about it until the storm was over. They would have other priorities they'd need to deal with first: storm protections to be put in place. People to be warned.

She needed to get back and make sure her mum and Florence got to safety. This was the last thing her mother needed. She was never going to understand what was going on.

The temperature dropped quickly as the rain started. It was light, but it wouldn't stay that way for long. She could feel the weight of the water in the clouds, ready to be released.

Staci shuddered as she felt the storm prod at her again. She focused on the muddy ground at her feet, refusing to look towards it. Bloody Elliot. Why the hell hadn't he dealt with this last night? None of this would have happened.

'Staci?' Oliver said softly. The question in his tone made her wonder if she'd missed something.

Swiping the rain from her eyes, she looked at Oliver, then past him, seeing the cars. She'd not even noticed the ground had changed from grey to brown. It was just as well the rangers had been with her. She could have been attacked by a pack of imps again, and she wasn't sure she'd have noticed.

Elliot was ahead of her now, and the rain had turned his bandage pink where the blood had soaked through.

'Are you okay?' Oliver asked, moving closer. His long-sleeved T-shirt was soaking wet and clinging to his arms, showing every muscle.

'I'm fine,' Staci said, but Oliver didn't look like he believed her. Hell, she wouldn't have believed her either.

Oliver started to say something, but instead, he shook his head and walked beside her silently as they covered the last few dozen metres to the car.

The stench of the Rift Scar was fading under the smell of fresh rain. Or maybe she'd just got used to it.

No one spoke as they removed their soggy armour and weapons, putting them into the boot. Staci followed suit, handing it to Oliver when he put his hand out. She felt lighter, but the armour had been blocking the wind. Her thin grey T-shirt didn't stand a chance against the rapidly increasing gusts.

Someone helped Rafe and Elliot out of their gear, but there was little to be done about the damp bandages without cover from the rain.

'How bad will the storm be?' Oliver asked, so close behind her she could feel his warmth despite the chill of the rain. 'How far will it spread?'

Staci let her attention be pulled to the storm, feeling more than just its draw this time. It was so strong it was hard to focus on what it was becoming rather than just the pull. It was filled with fast-moving winds and tingling lightning. Dangerous. Powerful.

'Category 2 hurricane at least, maybe worse. Heading towards Huntly,' Staci said as the wind gusted, trying to rip her hair out of her bun.

Staci glanced at Elliot, but he hadn't reacted to her comments. He was just staring at his arm, ignoring everyone, jaw muscle twitching.

Lance nodded at Cindy. 'Take Mac, warn all the farms in the area, then get to a shelter. Send a text when you're done to let me know you made it to safety.'

Mac and Cindy got into the closer car and sped off. Staci's stomach dropped as she realised she'd not even considered those closer than Huntly. By the time they made it to the town to warn them, it would already be on top of the people here.

'I'll warn the mayor and get him to send messengers to the other towns,' Staci said, crossing her arms to hide the tremor in her hand as the storm prodded her again. She could warn the town first, then get her mother. She'd have time. Just.

'Take Oliver with you,' Lance said.

'I'm fine,' Staci said, but she didn't look at Lance when she said it. It was a myth that wolves could smell when someone was lying. At least, she thought it was.

'I'm not asking, Staci,' Lance said, voice soft as he glanced at Oliver. She'd never heard Lance sound so careful before. 'Oliver said your name three times before you looked at him. He'll drive you to see the mayor, then to a storm shelter.'

Lance wasn't wrong, but dammit, she didn't want Oliver following her around. Resisting the storm was hard enough; the last thing she needed was something else to tempt her.

'What about me?' Elliot asked, sounding like a child. 'I need a hospital.'

'How about you take responsibility for your mistakes and talk to the mayor,' Staci said, wishing she sounded less petulant.

'My—'

'Enough.' Lance exhaled slowly as he turned to Elliot. 'I'll take you, Zoe, and Rafe to the hospital.'

Staci wanted to argue but didn't think it would make any difference, and they didn't have a lot of time. Elliot got in Lance's Land Rover without a word, and after a quick shake of their heads, Rafe and Zoe followed. Lance lingered a moment, eyes on Oliver.

'We'll talk after the storm,' Lance said, then he turned away before Oliver could reply and got into the driver's seat. There seemed to be new tension between the pair, but whatever had happened, she'd missed the source.

That left Staci with nowhere to go but Oliver's car. He was quiet, not saying anything for or against being made her personal chauffeur as they both got in. She shivered as the car started. Blowers that had been set to cold on the way here blasted her. Oliver cursed and turned them off, then switched it over to heat.

They were both dripping wet, and the seats were trying their best to soak up all the water. She shivered, picking at her T-shirt, wishing she had brought her change of clothes with her. Not that she had anything to get dry with.

'Everything is going to be okay,' Oliver said as he reversed the Land Rover; it easily handled the muddy ground as they sped off towards Huntly.

He couldn't know that. No one could. Not with a storm like this. But she didn't say that. They'd find out soon enough how bad it was going to be.

BY THE TIME OLIVER caught sight of Huntly's walls through the heavy rain, the wind was battering at the car, trying to drive him off the slick road. The storm clouds had been following them steadily. Occasionally, he'd get a dry patch of road before it caught up again.

The sound of the storm siren blared out as they drove into Huntly, the warning a long, sharp wail telling the residents to seek shelter. A small measure of tightness eased in his chest. The more notice people had, the more chance they'd be able to find safety.

He glanced at Staci. She was turned away from him, showing one cheek smeared with grey dust. Her damp clothes clung to her, and her hair was more out of her bun than in it.

'Where do you want to go?' Oliver asked. She'd not said anything the whole drive. But her scent spoke for her, shifting between fear and anger. He couldn't blame her after Elliot's words.

Elliot wrong, Thor said, still furious that they hadn't done anything to Elliot after he'd insulted Staci.

'The mayor will be at the council building this time of day. There's a shelter there,' Staci said, glancing at him before she turned to look back out the window.

'The storm siren is going off. Are you sure you still need to see him?' Oliver asked. Part of him wanted to take her to the nearest shelter and make sure she was safely away from everything. But the rest of him knew he didn't have the right to tell her what to do.

Staci shook her head, tucking a rogue strand of hair behind her ear. 'I need to speak to him. He'll think that I'm going to fix it, even with the warning.' The anger came back so sharp that it bit into Oliver's nose. 'We should have taken Elliot with us.'

'He needed a doctor,' Oliver said, slowing to give the car in front plenty of space as they approached a junction.

'He had a scratch. A basic first-aid kit could have treated it,' Staci said, giving him a sideways look. 'He didn't want to face up to his mistakes. Take responsibility for letting this storm happen.'

He could feel the question in her voice, and his stomach dropped as he realised why. No one had spoken for or against Staci. They'd all been silent.

Thor growled.

'Elliot isn't as strong as you are,' Oliver said. Thor growled again, not liking how he was still trying to defend Elliot. But Oliver still couldn't give up on his friend. There had to be something more going on. 'Or as experienced.'

'I told him there was a storm. He didn't believe me, or he just ignored me. Then he lied.'

Oliver didn't know how to answer that as he wove through the traffic as other people headed for cover. Most were going the opposite way from him.

'I don't know why Elliot said that,' Oliver said at last, loosening his vice grip on the steering wheel as he pulled into the council car park.

He parked the old Land Rover as close to the front door as he could get, which was easy as the place was nearly empty. The council office was a two-storey brown brick building. The front entrance had glass doors and a small overhang that was doing nothing to stop the driving rain.

Staci's lips thinned, and he thought she'd get out of the car without saying anything else, but she stopped, turning full to him. 'Do you think I'm lying?' Staci stared at him, watching his reaction.

'I—' Oliver's phone chose that moment to ring. He'd left it in the centre console, and it vibrated loudly against the plastic.

'Answer it, it might be important,' Staci said when he hesitated. 'I don't need you to babysit me while I tell the mayor how we fucked up.'

She got out before he could react and jogged towards the front door. Oliver cursed, wanting to go after her. But he didn't. With the storm, he couldn't risk ignoring any calls.

He grabbed the phone, heart skipping a beat when he saw the name on the screen. His father again.

He'd not had a chance to phone him this morning or speak to Hale because of the storm. He'd thought he'd have more time.

Oliver almost didn't answer it, wishing he'd followed Staci.

Help Staci. Need us, Thor said. But it wasn't true. Staci didn't need anyone. She was fierce all on her own, and anyone who got in her way beware. *Not mean can't help.*

After this call, Oliver said, taking a breath as he answered the phone, putting it against his ear. Staci disappeared through the glass doors. Alone.

'I have been calling for an hour,' his father said, not offering a greeting.

'I was in the Rift Scar,' Oliver said, fighting the instinct to apologise. He'd done nothing wrong, and his father would only see it as a weakness.

His father grunted. 'So that's your decision, then? You want me to come to Huntly to collect you?'

Oliver let out a slow breath. It did little to ease the tightness in his chest at his father's words. Oliver didn't want to do this. He wanted to be inside beside Staci as she faced the mayor about the storm.

'The weather warden needed to go into the Rift Scar. I haven't been able to see Hale,' Oliver said, leaning in the old seat, damp clothes uncomfortable as they stuck to him.

'I don't care about a storm,' his father said, voice half growling. 'You had one simple task. Call me with your answer. Have you forgotten your lessons already?'

'No,' Oliver said. His wrist ached from the memories that came too fast to follow. All pain. All the times he'd forgotten his lessons in the past.

When his father tried to teach him those lessons again, would he be able to hide that Sam was an Earth Elemental? Or how the pack lands had been created?

Not tell. Protect pack. Protect alpha, Thor said, snarling, pressing closer.

But Oliver could feel his wolf's fear. Their father would be their alpha again. It had been eight months since he'd been near his father.

'If you make me come out there, boy, you and Hale will both regret it,' his father said. His wolf was in those words, a harsh snarl vibrating through his voice.

'No, I'll speak to Hale today,' Oliver said, leaning forward, wanting to move, to do something. But the rain was hammering down outside, and the wind was hitting the car in sharp bursts.

'You'd better. Replacing Hale wouldn't be difficult, but it would cause a stir,' his father said. This time, his wolf wasn't in his voice, and somehow, the casual threat was so much worse for it. 'I expect to hear that you're on your way home by lunchtime.'

'As soon as the storm is clear, I'll talk to Hale.'

'By lunch.' The connection died before Oliver could answer. He checked his phone. The signal was gone, so that timing had just been poor, rather than his father being dramatic.

Not want to go back, Thor said, curling into a tight ball. *Want to stay here with Staci and our pack.*

Staci doesn't need us, Oliver said, loosening his grip on his phone before he crushed it. He rubbed his wrist, feeling the echo of old pain. *And Hale will take care of Amelia and Mitchel.*

Oliver pushed open the door and got out of the car, ignoring his wolf's growl. Staci might not need him, but he could be here for her today, anyway. Then he'd take her to safety, and as soon as the storm passed, he'd find Hale.

STACI SHIVERED AS SHE entered the council building. The air-con was still running on cold, slicing through her wet clothes. She paused on the mat, anyway, letting the water drip down as she scanned the hallway. The building was split into a couple of sections with a sign in front of her. An arrow pointed to the left, with Mayor printed in bright black letters under it. She turned that way.

At the end of the corridor, there were a few soft seats against the wall in the corner and a white table in front of them. Against the right wall was a waist-high reception desk. Behind it stood a stout, dark-haired woman frantically gathering her things into a box with seemingly arbitrary grabs. Valerie, the mayor's assistant. Or the council building's receptionist. Staci had never been sure. The woman seemed to do everything all at once.

'Where's the mayor?' Staci asked, shoving back some loose strands from her bun.

Valerie looked at Staci like she was crazy before recognition slowly came. 'Staci? You look awful.'

Staci nodded, walking carefully across the tiled floor so she didn't slip on the water she was generating. There was no one else in the waiting room. That was a first in all the years she'd been weather warden.

'He's screaming for an update in his office,' Valerie said. 'I'm going to the storm shelter before any idiot asks me to do anything else. Tell him he should be in a shelter, too. You're more than welcome to stay.'

'Thanks, but I need to go find my mum,' Staci said. There was a shelter near her house, and Florence would have taken her mum there. Storms might be common, but hurricanes weren't frequent enough to justify all buildings having shelters—especially old council buildings like Staci's.

'Be careful,' Valerie said, nodding at the door behind her. 'Go. You know the way.'

Staci hesitated, thinking about Oliver. She didn't know if he'd follow her, not after what she'd said. He was Elliot's friend. Part of her wanted him with her, but the rest didn't want to rely on anyone.

'There might be someone else joining me,' Staci said at last, glancing over her shoulder, but no windows faced the car park.

'If he comes in before I lock the doors, I'll send him through. Otherwise, he'll need to wait outside,' Valerie said. 'Use the same door you came in when you leave. It will let you out even if it's blocked from letting people in.'

'Thanks, Valerie,' Staci said, steadying herself as she went through the door that Valerie buzzed open. The floor changed to carpet that soaked up some of the water still dripping from her.

A half a dozen doorways lined the small space, but only one was open. She could hear the mayor's voice. She steeled herself as she started towards it.

The mayor sat behind his desk at the far end of the room. He was a well-built, balding man in his fifties who prided himself on his fitness. His suit jacket was thrown over the chair behind him, and his shirt was pristine as he leaned forward on his elbows.

'Don't tell me to calm down, Charles. This is ridiculous. There's a storm coming straight towards us,' Joyce King said. She was a heavy woman with a turkey neck made worse by her high-collared shirt and overly tight suit jacket. Her hair was up in a perfectly neat, if severe, bun. 'Once again, the weather is a mess. This has to stop.'

She stood with one hand on the desk, leaning forward like she was trying to loom over the mayor as she complained. Other people would have been intimidated, but the mayor just watched her with half-lidded eyes.

'Mayor Charles,' Staci said when neither seemed to notice her.

Joyce straightened, then recoiled from Staci, face growing pale. 'You. This is your fault,' Joyce said, practically spitting.

Joyce had hated Staci for years. Saving someone's life should have made them grateful, but when Staci had pushed Joyce out of the way of lightning, she'd accused Staci of trying to kill her. No one had believed Joyce, thankfully.

Staci turned back to the mayor. She didn't have time for this.

The mayor sighed. He didn't seem worried, which, considering his window was rattling in its frame, was a surprise. 'Do you know how bad the storm is going to be?'

'There's a Category 2 hurricane coming,' Staci said, forcing her shoulders down. There had never been weather this bad in all the years she'd been weather warden.

'Then why haven't you done something about it?' Joyce asked.

'I tried—'

'Tried? It's a storm, girl; that's your job. To stop them,' Joyce said.

'We went into the Rift Scar to stop it, ma'am, but imps attacked us,' Oliver said, making Staci jump. 'We were lucky to get away with only two injured.'

Joyce flinched, and the mayor leaned back in his chair as he focused on Oliver. The reaction was nothing like how the mayor had treated Staci.

She turned to Oliver. He stood with his feet slightly apart, hands at his side, eyes a solid amber as his wolf shone through. Well, okay, she'd give the mayor his fear. Oliver looked pretty pissed. Then there was how his wet T-shirt clung to him, highlighting every muscle. He looked good, too. Real good.

'What are you going to do about it, Staci?' the mayor asked.

'There's nothing to do but prepare,' Staci said, dragging her gaze away from Oliver. 'The siren is already doing its job to warn people.'

'We haven't had a true storm in over a decade.' The mayor's eyes never left hers, blame obvious.

He wasn't wrong. Staci should have dealt with the storm as soon as she'd felt it. Instead, she had trusted Elliot would do his job because she'd wanted to spend more time with her mother. All of this was her fault.

'It won't happen again,' Staci said.

'Bloody right, it won't happen again,' Joyce said, turning her back to Oliver like he was nothing. 'Staci has been doing a sub-par job for the past year, using her mother as an excuse. We bring in help, and it has only made things worse. I think it's time you reconsider my request to have her removed as weather warden.'

Staci's stomach dropped. Joyce had tried to have her removed? Staci shouldn't have been surprised, but the words hurt, slicing through old wounds.

'Joyce,' the mayor said, voice harsh as he stood. Joyce backed away in surprise. 'You forget yourself. You're not the mayor. The town didn't vote you in, and this isn't your decision to make.'

'When the town finds out that you hired an inept weather warden and allowed her mistakes to cost this town, maybe they'll finally see the truth. How many people were hurt during the cold snap or other freak weather events over the last few months?' Joyce said, lifting her chin, though there was too much extra neck for it to have the effect she was going for. 'Staci is incompetent and should be removed and sent somewhere she won't be a danger to the people around her. Just like her father—'

'Stop. You've been warned already. Don't make me warn you again,' the mayor said; this time, his voice was quiet. Joyce didn't continue, but for once, Staci wished she had.

Staci struggled to get a full breath. Her father had left when she'd been a child, abandoning her mum and leaving her to raise Staci alone. That's what she'd been told. But Joyce smirked like she'd won some kind of victory. Like she'd been waiting to say those words for a long time.

'Staci wasn't the weather warden who missed the storm,' Oliver said, stepping closer. She could feel him at her back. Feel his heat despite the chill of her wet clothes. She wanted to lean back into him, press herself against him. But she couldn't afford to let herself rely on him when she knew his presence was only temporary.

Then his words registered. He'd given up Elliot. Defended her.

'Elliot?' the mayor said, narrowing his eyes and turning to Joyce. 'He ignored the storm?'

'Don't be ridiculous. Elliot has been trained by the best weather wardens out there,' Joyce said.

'Your son isn't infallible, Joyce,' the mayor said. This time, he'd softened his voice. A courtesy Joyce would never have extended.

Elliot was Joyce's son? Staci struggled with the idea of the bigoted woman being related to a Rift Bloodline. She'd not even known that Joyce had a son. But maybe that explained Elliot's attitude towards Staci.

The wind slammed into the window, making a loud crunching noise. They all paused, expecting the glass to break, but it held. The storm surged with it, slipping past Staci's defences as her emotions roiled. All that energy coiled in her gut, looking to connect to her. She pushed it away, fighting the desire to pull it in.

'We'll deal with this later. For now, we should take shelter,' the mayor said, picking up his jacket and turning to Staci again. 'You're all welcome to weather the storm here.'

Oliver touched Staci's arm, sending a wave of warmth through her, making her feel safe and pushing the storm further from her mind. 'Where do you want to go?' he asked like he knew she wouldn't want to stay here.

She wanted to tell him she could do it alone, but she had no car to get across town or phone to call anyone. Florence would be worried. 'I'll give you directions as we go,' Staci said, stepping away from his touch. The storm surged like it hadn't liked the moment of inattention to it.

Joyce shoved past them before they could leave, stalking down the corridor out of sight. 'Don't take any heed of Joyce, Staci,' the mayor said as he followed them into the hall and locked his office. 'She's afraid of storms, has been for years.'

'So, she was lying about my father being sent away?' Staci asked before she could think better of it.

The mayor's eye twitched. 'We'll talk about it after the storm.'

She wasn't sure he meant it, but they were out of time with the storm growing closer. She nodded and led Oliver back out into the reception area. He didn't ask her about her father or the rest of what had been discussed. He just stood at her back like he was her private guard.

For the first time in a very long time, she felt safer for it, even with the storm raging in the back of her mind, trying to get past her defences. But she couldn't afford to get used to it. Oliver wasn't going to be around for that much longer.

She needed to be able to stand on her own. Because soon she would be. Fighting back useless tears, Staci led the way out of the front door. The wind slammed into her, stealing her breath, and making her eyes sting harder.

Her mum wasn't gone yet, she reminded herself. She wasn't alone.

But it was only a matter of time.

Chapter Seven

Lance parked next to the hospital's accident and emergency entrance. It was an old, two-storey building with a flat roof and shutters on all the windows. A small group of nurses were running between them, trying to force them shut as the wind slammed the white-painted wood against the concrete wall.

Did good, Shade said, sounding like he believed it. *All safe now.*

Zoe had called ahead to the hospital to warn them about the storm. Going by the sound of the sirens a few minutes ago, they'd passed the warning on.

At least something had gone right today. He could still feel the soul-deep chill of how close the fight had been; going by the silence from the others, they could feel it, too. He should never have gone in without a team to check ahead.

Beat imps. Made them afraid, Shade said. *Won fight.*

It wasn't us that made them afraid, Lance said. Staci had been the one to frighten them. If it had just been Lance and the rangers, they'd all have been dead. Overwhelmed.

Did not happen, Shade said, giving Lance a small growl. *Stop chasing tail. We not pup to play stupid games.*

Lance wished it was that easy to let the thought go, but it wasn't. He'd almost killed his team. There had been too many imps coming at them from all sides. If Hale had been there, he'd have thought of a way to save everyone.

Not dead! Shade said, slashing at him this time. The pain was brief, but it helped push the negative thoughts back. *None died.*

His wolf was right. No one had died, but they knew how close it had been. Maybe after this, Hale would realise Lance wasn't fit for this job.

He got out, ignoring his wolf's answering growl. An arctic blast of wind hit him hard, cutting straight through his wet clothes, but at least the long awning protected them from most of the rain. Three nurses came out pushing two wheelchairs as they hunched against the cold.

'No venom, just imp claw wounds,' Lance said as he opened the back door. One nurse helped Elliot into the first wheelchair. He was acting like his legs had been wounded, not his arm.

Zoe had opened the other back door for the second nurse to help Rafe. The bandage on his shoulder was soaked red. He refused help getting out of the car but reluctantly sat in the other wheelchair.

'What do you want to do?' Zoe said as she watched the two men disappear inside.

'I need to move the car,' Lance said.

Zoe's lips thinned, and she gave him a sideways look, not giving up. 'I meant about Elliot?'

Lance hesitated, not wanting to get involved. 'The weather isn't ranger business.'

But as he looked at her, he could tell that wouldn't be enough of an answer. She'd been here long enough to know about the recent troubles and smart enough to know this felt wrong.

'It's coming from the Rift; you and I both know who will be blamed for it,' Zoe said, looking back towards where Elliot had disappeared. 'Don't you want to know why Elliot lied?'

She was right. The reason for that lie could answer a lot of questions. But getting answers would mean investigating. Lance's chest tightened at the idea of getting involved in that. Of what had happened the last time he'd been part of an investigation.

Not like before. Not tracking, Shade said. He pressed against Lance until he could nearly feel his wolf's fur. *We just learning. Asking questions.*

Until those questions lead to unwanted attention, and someone gets hurt because of me, Lance said.

He hated he was hesitating. This was why he'd told Hale he didn't want to be a leader. People relied on them. Wanted them to make decisions, but Lance's decisions had cost his family their lives.

Questions not hurt us. Crazy woman hurt us, Shade said, lying down to lick his furless paw. *Crazy woman dead.*

She might have been, but she was never far from his mind. He stretched his hand, feeling the scars against the leather. It was damp and uncomfortable, but removing it meant people would see the scars and stare.

He would see the scars and remember what they meant.

If do nothing, might bring worse things, Shade said quietly. *Might hurt more people.*

Hale can speak to Elliot after the storm. He can figure out what Elliot is up to, Lance said.

If wait, might be too late, Shade said. *Here now. Get answers now.*

Lance cursed silently. Shade was right; if Elliot was here to stir up trouble, they needed to know now. He didn't have time to wait for Hale.

'Go inside, watch him,' Lance said at last, looking back at Zoe as he heard the siren of another ambulance approaching. 'I want to know what he has to say.'

Zoe smiled and turned to follow the nurses inside. It was the most excited he'd seen her about anything since she'd arrived. At least someone was happy with his choice.

He parked in the first space he could find, then jogged back the short distance to A & E's entrance, getting even more soaked. In the few years he'd been in town, he'd not needed to spend much time here, so he had to ask at the desk where the others had been taken. They gave him a once-over, nose wrinkling as they took in his damp, stinking gear and gave him directions.

The hospital was the busiest he'd ever seen as staff ran around, presumably preparing for the storm. He caught sight of Rafe standing in the hallway, ignoring the wheelchair beside him as he talked to a doctor. Pascal was around six feet tall, with dark skin, pale hazel eyes, and short black hair. He was often the one neck-deep helping rangers with Rift Scar wounds.

'I'll take any help I can get,' Pascal said, hands on his hips. 'After you've been treated. You won't be any use if you pass out from pushing yourself too hard.'

Rafe ran his hand over his scalp and turned to see Lance. 'Do as he says,' Lance said, pre-empting the question he knew was coming. 'You can help after.'

'I don't need my arm to use magic.' Rafe didn't look at Lance as he said it.

'And if you pass out from blood loss halfway through, I'll have to help fix you rather than keep the water out,' Pascal said. 'If you get fixed up now, we will both be able to use our magic together.'

Rafe sighed and went to run his hand over his scalp again, this time using his injured side. He cursed and nodded slowly.

'Maybe if the weather warden could stop feeling sorry for himself long enough, he could help too?' Pascal said, the scathing tone unusual for the ordinarily even-tempered man.

'If that boy wants to still be the town's weather warden after this, I'll do overtime for the next month,' Rafe said, shaking his head. Not that was much of a bet. They'd all been doing extra. 'He should have listened to Staci.'

It was interesting that Rafe had also believed Staci over Elliot, the same as Zoe had. Neither of them would have known for sure he'd been lying.

'I have a treatment room ready for you,' a young nurse said, motioning to the wheelchair.

Rafe sighed and sat down. 'Let me know if you need me.' The nurse was already rolling away before he could finish.

'Where's Elliot?' Lance asked Pascal before he could turn away.

Pascal scowled again but gave him a room number. 'Watch out for that one. I studied with him for a bit in Glasgow. Weather wardens have both Air and Water Magic crossover, so they bring them into some of our classes. He's an arrogant twat, thinks he's better than everyone, and wants them to know it.'

'I'll bear that in mind,' Lance said. It was interesting that Oliver had a different impression of Elliot. But Oliver wasn't an Elemental, so maybe Elliot treated Shifters differently? Either way, it didn't matter right now. Arrogance would work in Lance's favour.

Lance followed Pascal's directions to Elliot's room. Zoe was standing outside, leaning against the doorway. Lance nodded at her but didn't say anything as he stepped into the room.

Two nurses were working on Elliot's arm, slowly removing the last of the sodden bandage. The wound was surprisingly small, considering how close he'd been to the imp. The younger one was offering quiet, comforting words as Elliot moaned. The older nurse was pulling out antiseptic and other tools she'd be using to clean the wound.

'This is your fault,' Elliot said as he caught sight of Lance, breath coming in quick gasps. 'I told you we shouldn't go into the Rift Scar.'

The room stank of the chemicals they were using, hiding most of Elliot's scent. Not that he needed it to know that Elliot was full of shit.

'So, you wanted us to let the storm run its course?' Lance said, keeping his voice soft and reasonable.

'No. Staci was overreacting. There was no storm until her fear changed it,' Elliot said, shaking his head, not meeting Lance's eyes. 'She lost control of her magic. She's just too worried about losing her job to admit it.'

All lies. Lance knew enough about how magic worked to know that Staci couldn't affect the storm from a distance, which was why they'd gone into the Rift Scar in the first place.

'So why didn't you stop her? Surely you could have broken it apart if she was close enough to the storm to make it worse?' Lance asked, keeping his voice light, drawing Elliot out. The nurse cleaning his wound paused, holding the wash she was about to pour over his arm, giving Elliot a chance to answer.

The arrogance came into play here as Elliot thought that through. Lance saw him consider his options. Did he risk admitting Staci was better than he was?

'I would have, but the imps attacked. I was hurt before I could do anything,' Elliot said, this time looking at Lance. Elliot barely kept the look for a heartbeat before he had to look away. He was playing the victim. In his book, that was clearly better than being weaker in magic than Staci.

The nurse poured the antiseptic wash over his arm, and Elliot screamed, cursing about not being given a warning. Lance expected the nurse to tell him to leave then, but she didn't as she wiped Elliot's arm, checking the wound from different angles.

'How did she affect the storm?' Lance asked, drawing Elliot's focus back to him.

Elliot hesitated, not expecting the question, or maybe it was deliberate to make him look like he didn't want to get Staci in trouble. 'She called the lightning. You saw her use it on the imp. She could only do that if she had been calling the storm.'

Lies and half-truths. He was right about the imp, but they'd been too far away from the storm for her to have pulled the lightning from there. But it had to have come from somewhere.

Lance didn't know enough about Weather Magic to know what the options were. He'd have to find a weather warden who did.

'Right, that's you all cleaned up. Now it's time for the stitches,' the younger nurse said. She nodded at the older nurse, who got up and made a motion that it was time for Lance to leave.

Lance followed her out. His nose stung from the abuse of the chemicals, and it was a relief to put some distance between him and them. Zoe followed him.

'Do you believe that Staci did something wrong?' the older nurse asked, pushing herself in front of him once they were out of hearing range of the room. He was taller than her by over a foot and a half, but she stood there, eyes narrowed, unconcerned by his size. Zoe moved to his left, positioning herself to react if needed, but didn't interfere.

'No,' Lance said. The nurse's stance relaxed a fraction.

'That girl is going through enough without the likes of him trying to ruin her life,' the nurse said, shaking her head. 'Ain't none of us believe Staci would ignore a storm. What you gonna do about these lies?'

Lance opened his mouth and closed it. Staci wasn't pack. She wasn't family or even a friend.

Protect, Shade said. Not a question. A statement. *Is Oliver's pack. Needs us.*

Lance almost sighed as he remembered how Oliver had stepped in front of Staci to challenge Lance. If his wolf thought Staci was pack, that would make her Oliver's mate. Shade ignored that thought, which meant he'd already known. Stupid wolf and his secrets. Which made three mates in less than six months.

'I won't let Elliot lie about what happened,' Lance said.

'Good,' the nurse said, shivering as the wind battered the building with a sharp blast of air.

'Do you know how to get in contact with the previous weather warden?' That was Lance's best chance at confirming what had happened.

'My friend would have his number. I'll get it for you.'

'Thank you,' Lance said. He couldn't call until the signal was back up, but it would be a good start.

'Are the two of you staying for the storm?' the nurse asked, glancing at Zoe.

Lance nodded slowly. He could hear the strength of the wind outside. There was little point in trying to get to another shelter now. He may as well help the hospital weather the worst of the storm. 'Yes. If you need help, just ask.'

The nurse smiled. 'Good, because there's a lot to do and not much time.'

Somehow, that just about described how he'd felt ever since he'd found out about the storm.

Chapter Eight

Oliver gasped as he stepped outside into the rain. It was icy against his already wet clothes, seeping straight to his skin. Staci missed a step, clearly feeling it, too. They dashed towards the car.

He wanted to reach out and touch her, offer support or comfort. Anything that would have eased her tears. He could scent them even over the residual cloying perfume stink that had clung to Joyce and the heavy rain.

That arrogant, pathetic little woman deserved to be forced to be outside in the storm. The way she'd been excited by Staci's reaction to talking about her father had made his stomach roll.

Broken, toxic, Thor said. It had become his wolf's new favourite word, though in this case, it was accurate. Joyce was clearly bitter, twisted, and afraid. None of which was Staci's fault, but she'd clearly become Joyce's outlet. *Protect Staci?*

There isn't anything we can do, Oliver said, as Staci got in the car without a word, wiping her eyes.

Touch. Feel better then, Thor said.

It's not that easy, Oliver said. Staci had made it very clear, more than once, that she wanted nothing to do with Oliver. After Elliot, those feelings were probably even stronger. His wolf disagreed, but he settled down in the back of his mind, watching.

Oliver got into the car, feeling the seat squish under him. He wished he'd kept something in the car that could help dry them, but there was nothing, just damp seats trying to soak up more moisture.

'Which way?' Oliver asked as he started the engine. Water dripped down his face, and he swiped it away. Thankfully, they hadn't been inside so long that the car had lost all its heat.

She gave him the direction and address, and he pushed the car into gear and headed out of the car park. The streets were already overflowing with rain, becoming shallow rivers that would only get worse before it got better.

'Did you know Elliot was from here?' Staci asked, not looking at him.

Oliver glanced at her, surprised by her question, as he pulled out to go around a long row of illegally parked cars.

There must have been a shelter nearby because the roads weren't so bad they were impassible.

'No,' he said, focusing on what he could see of the road. 'I thought Elliot was an orphan. He was raised in a group home.'

'Clearly, the mayor thinks Joyce is his family,' Staci said.

'Most of the kids in that particular group home all had at least one Elemental parent,' Oliver said, rolling his shoulders. He'd been there once to see Elliot when he hit eighteen. It hadn't been a bad place, but there were a lot of kids who'd been abandoned. 'Not all human parents want to keep a kid that might get magic.'

Staci turned away. 'Joyce abandoned her son.' She shook her head. 'When she found out he might have magic, she sent him away? But she must have known the father was an Elemental?'

Oliver hesitated to add anything. Nothing about Elliot's past made excuses for his present, but it might help her understand. 'Elliot wasn't born an Elemental. He was ten when his family broke down near the Rift Scar. He doesn't remember much except wandering off and being stung. He survived, but it meant he came into his magic much earlier than most.'

'Ten?' Staci whispered. 'At least that explains why he keeps saying he's been doing magic so much longer than me.'

'I'm not making excuses for him. He lied, and he will need to answer for the damage today. But I wanted you to understand why things might be difficult for him. Different.'

Staci was silent, watching the rain pounding down on the passenger window as he took another turn, avoiding a car that had skidded into a lamppost. He slowed to check if anyone needed help, but it didn't look like anyone was inside.

'You said Elemental kids. Why no Shifters?' Staci asked, looking at him intently.

'No pack would leave a Shifter in a group home if they knew about them. Someone would always take them in,' Oliver said, giving her a light smile and didn't add that sometimes the parents weren't given the choice.

All kids who become Shifters had to join a pack. It was safer for everyone, especially in the beginning. Normally, it wasn't an issue, but a few one-night stands ended with a father who didn't know they had a kid until they became a teenager and changed for the first time.

'That must be nice, having the protection and support of an alpha and pack,' Staci said, but she looked away.

Which was probably just as well. Oliver wasn't sure his expression would have agreed with her statement.

Hale good alpha. He keeps us safe, Thor said. *Not all like Father.*

But some can be, Oliver said, but he didn't correct Staci. He couldn't do that without going into his past, and that was something he wasn't going to burden anyone with.

They were almost halfway to Staci's shelter when the first lightning strike lit the sky. Staci shuddered like she'd been struck. Her scent grew stronger in the car, merging with the smell of the storm.

'Staci?' Oliver said, looking her over, searching to check if she was okay.

She shook her head, staring out through the front window. Then her eyes widened. 'Oliver! Stop!'

Oliver had already pressed the brakes before she could finish the words, or he'd seen the man in the middle of the road. The car skidded to a stop, aquaplaning for a terrifying heartbeat before Oliver got it under control. The man leapt out of the way. But he didn't go far because as soon as the car stopped, he came back hammering on the window.

'Help, please. You have to help me,' the middle-aged man shouted through the window. 'The kids are stuck. Please.'

Oliver looked past the man to see a single-storey old wooden house. Huntly Primary School was displayed on a sign out front. An old tree had fallen onto the roof, tearing a hole right through it.

A school bus sat nearby. Someone had tried to attach a rope to the back of it, but the tree was thicker than two men's arm spans. The bus would never have the power to move something that big.

Had the kids been on that side of the building when it fell?

He shoved the thought away, feeling sick. No point in dwelling on what he couldn't do. The man was asking for his help.

'What do you need?' Oliver asked, screaming to be heard past the wind, even as he opened his window. He'd have opened his door, but the man was in the way.

'When the tree came down, it blocked the door and trapped the kids inside a classroom,' the man said. 'We can't get them out. The building isn't designed to handle a hurricane. It's already crumbling against these winds.'

Oliver cursed, looked at the dark sky; more lightning flashed in the distance. The wind and rain were bad enough now, but the building would be ripped apart if it got much worse.

'Stay here, Staci,' Oliver said, rolling the window up and pushing out into the storm. His door was almost ripped from his fingers, and he had to force it shut.

'Like hell I will,' Staci shouted, following him out. She had to use her entire body weight to shove the door closed. 'Mr Patterson, right?'

The man nodded, squinting. 'Staci?'

'Yes. Show us where the kids are?' Staci shouted.

'Do you have a shelter for after we get them free?' Oliver asked. They were cutting it tight to get somewhere safe before the storm became too dangerous to travel.

'The shelter at the school isn't big enough for all the kids. It was originally a house, and we've been using the space for storage,' Mr Patterson said, fighting to be heard over the wind. 'But the bus will get us to the high school shelter. It's not far.'

As they stepped into the school, the wind's pressure stopped so suddenly that he stumbled. He only just caught Staci as she fell into him. She was scalding hot like the cold wasn't affecting her.

She stepped back from him, not making eye contact, face flushed. Oliver wanted to ask her if she was okay, but there would be time for that later. He forced himself to turn away and follow Mr Patterson in a slow jog. They needed to help the kids.

He could figure out what was wrong with Staci later.

STACI PULLED IN A breath and followed behind Oliver. She wanted to reach out and touch him so badly it hurt. Which was stupid, considering they were rushing to save children. But she couldn't help how her body felt.

The look on his face when he'd told her about Elliot had broken her heart just a little. But that pure protective growl at the idea that any Shifter had been abandoned had shattered it. It was hard to understand why she'd thought Oliver had been a flake in the face of that. Even more so as they jogged through the school behind Mr Patterson.

The school's corridor was narrow, with light blue linoleum floors and walls painted with large flowers and cartoon animals. She remembered them from her childhood, and they'd not aged well. The storm battered the building, making it creak and rattle. Rain poured down the hallway around the corner, and they moved wide to avoid slipping.

The tree was impossible to miss. Its massive trunk blocked the corridor, crushing an entire wall and blocking most of the door. It lay at a slight angle, leaving a metre-high gap to crawl under at the far side. The roof had collapsed around it, stopping the worst of the wind seeping in and some of the rain. Some of the thinner branches had been torn away, but it wouldn't be enough. Short of a chainsaw, they weren't moving the tree.

Her old teacher, Mr Patterson, led them under the trunk. An older woman was crouched at the other side, one hand pressed against the wall like she could touch the children through it. She was talking slowly and calmly to someone on the other side.

'That was the only door,' Mr Patterson said, stopping by the older woman. Staci could hear a child crying. The quiet noise made her heart ache. 'There aren't any windows in this room. I thought it would be safer for them to be here with the wind.'

The guilt in his voice was ragged. Staci wanted to tell him it wasn't his fault, that his choice had been a good one. But his face told her it would be a wasted effort.

'Even all of us together won't be able to move that tree,' Staci said, voice low enough that it wouldn't be heard by anyone else. Oliver looked back at her, face as bleak as she felt. With the roof already half destroyed by the tree, it wouldn't take much for the wind to take the rest of the building and the children with it.

'Is the shelter in there?' Oliver asked, but Staci wasn't surprised when Mr Patterson shook his head. If it had been, then they wouldn't be as worried.

'Please, we have to help them,' the woman said, tears staining her face. She was a teacher that Staci knew by sight but not by name. 'They're frightened.'

'You can hear them?' Oliver asked. The woman nodded slowly. 'Then the wall must be thin?' Oliver looked at Mr Patterson. 'Is there an axe?'

'I tried cutting the branches. We don't have time,' Mr Patterson said, putting his hand on the woman's shoulder as she swallowed back a sob.

'Not the branches. The walls,' Oliver said, putting his hand against the painted flower that was there. The entire building was shuddering.

Hope stirred. The building wasn't dealing with the wind outside it. The construction would have been weaker inside, especially if it was just a dividing wall.

Mr Patterson's eyes widened, and he nodded at a fire axe he'd left on the floor beside the tree. Oliver took it before Mr Patterson could. Even if you took just human strength into account, Oliver massively outweighed her teacher. But as a Shifter, he was even stronger.

'Get the kids to move back,' Oliver said, changing the grip on the axe.

The older woman talked in the same tone as before. Calm and patient. Somehow, her voice held no sense of panic despite the fear on her face. Staci couldn't replicate that, so she pulled back out of the way. Mr Patterson showed Oliver a point in the wall that he thought would be far enough away from the kids but still in the room.

'Everyone is together, all touching the wall?' the woman said, head tilted as she listened to faint little voices behind. 'Tommy? Good. Now, I want you all to keep real still with me. Okay?'

After a moment, she turned to Oliver and nodded. The wall splintered against the axe. Staci hoped the children had listened to their teacher. It didn't take long to make the whole wide enough for them to throw a coat over the broken wood and free the small children. All five were barely six years old, with tear-stained faces as they clung to their teachers. Mr Patterson was as patient as she remembered.

'Is that everyone?' Oliver asked.

'The parents picked up the rest of the kids,' Mr Patterson said, tears unshed in his own eyes as they helped the children under the tree. 'Thank you.'

They moved through the school as fast as they could with the kids. When they hit the front door, the wind rattled it so hard she thought it would come off its hinges. The rain was coming in nearly horizontal. There was no way the kids would make it through that without help. The way they flinched, they knew it too.

'I want you to hold on to me and Miss Stoat,' Mr Patterson said, picking up a child in each arm. Oliver copied him and picked up two more. Miss Stoat took the last one.

There were no more children for Staci to hold, so she moved ahead to grab the front doors. The freezing wind was so close to breaking them that they shuddered in her grip. She wished there was something she could do, some way to lessen the surrounding weather. But the storm had control now. Even if she was strong enough, splitting the storm apart would take too long to send the pieces away.

With a slow breath, she opened the door, holding it in place as the others carried the kids out. The sky had grown darker as the storm's edge reached them. The feel of it rippled through her, the promise of its power all around. But she refused to give in to the pull. She needed to get the kids to safety and then find her mum. If she let the storm in, she wouldn't be able to do either.

Forcing the door closed, she moved to follow the others. Mr Patterson made it to the bus, with Miss Stoat following. Oliver handed her the children he was carrying.

The lightning flickered in the sky, so close that the hairs on her arms stood on end. It was too close. She traced it, feeling it searching for somewhere to connect. For a moment, she was sure it would try and strike her like Elliot's lightning had, but there was something bigger and more attractive out there. The bus.

Oliver stood with one hand on the side, blocking the wind as he handed over the last child. Panic burned in her chest. No! She couldn't let it go there.

It started to flow towards the bus, so much power that it would have killed Oliver instantly. She held out her hand, pulling the strands of the storm towards her. Calling it. The storm responded, changing its path with a thrill of power and energy. Then it hit her.

Lightning flared through her. Into her, around her. Fire sparked down every nerve in her body, lighting her up until she thought she'd burn up from the power of it.

It felt good in a way she didn't have words for. The storm was part of her.

OLIVER SPUN AS HE heard Staci shout. She stood a few metres away, hand outstretched. A flash of light burned his eyes, and a clap of thunder rattled his teeth in his skull.

'Staci!'

Oliver fought to clear his vision, to see what had happened. His wolf tore at his control, trying to push him aside. But teeth and claws wouldn't help Staci if she was badly hurt. His wolf snarled, backing off.

Help. Needs us, Thor said, panting, pacing. *Go now.*

I'm trying, Oliver said, blinking, trying to see past the afterglare of the flash. He wanted to step towards her, but if he hurt himself, he wouldn't be of any use to anyone.

The wind lashed at him like it wanted to press him against the bus, and the rain ran into his eyes. But he fought against all of it. He needed to find Staci. Help her.

Slowly, his vision cleared, the afterimages fading to shadows before he finally saw Staci. She was hunched over where he'd last seen her, hand clutched to her chest. He moved to step towards her.

'Careful,' Mr Patterson said, grabbing Oliver's arm to stop him from going forward. He let go when Oliver growled at him. 'She grounded the lightning. It's inside her now. Touching her could hurt you even with your wolf healing.'

Oliver remembered the imp earlier that day, how it had screamed in pain.

'He's right. Stay away from me,' Staci said, opening her eyes. They were lit with a light of their own. Her skin crackled as she moved, tiny flecks of light sparking in the darkness. 'Please.'

'What happened?' Oliver said, but he didn't reach out again.

The wind suddenly dropped to nothing, and the rain stopped. Oliver pulled in a breath, scenting Staci all around him. No burned flesh. Which shouldn't have been possible, even for a Storm Elemental. The silence was deafening.

'Go, take them to safety. I'll be fine here,' she said. But she sounded wrong, disconnected almost. She rubbed at her arms, sending more sparks around her.

'You don't look fine,' Oliver said, stepping closer. He wasn't going to leave her alone.

Staci's anger flared, and with it came a gust of wind. Mr Patterson let out a sharp breath behind him. Oliver couldn't blame him; the show of power was pretty incredible.

'There is nothing wrong with me,' Staci said, then she took a slow breath as she looked up at the sky. 'It's just so beautiful out here.'

Oliver looked up at the black clouds, not seeing whatever she did. He nearly said as much, but Mr Patterson stepped closer.

'She's connected to the storm,' he said, lowering his voice so she'd not hear him. Not that she seemed to be paying attention anymore as she stared at the sky. 'We need to get her to let it go, then get her in a storm shelter.'

Like it was that simple. Going by how Staci was staring at the dark sky, Oliver wasn't even sure she remembered they were there. She looked drunk, happy for the first time since he'd known her. Which was sad because her smile lit up her whole face.

Fight storm. Kill it, Thor said, snarling, searching for something he could attack, except this wasn't a physical enemy.

'The storm has stopped.' But that wasn't quite right. The wind and rain had stopped, but the clouds were so dark it looked like night.

Mr Patterson hesitated for a moment. 'It's paused, doing as she asked. But it's not gone.'

'How do you know that?' Oliver asked. It was obvious that the man was human, and it wouldn't be the first time someone who didn't understand magic made a wrong suggestion.

Mr Patterson shivered as the wind picked up for a moment, piercing their soaked clothes. Even inside the bus, the kids would be feeling it, too. They needed to get out of here before the storm came back.

'I was there when she caught lightning for the first time,' Mr Patterson said, glancing at Staci. 'I've never seen the old weather warden so shaken. He said that the way she'd broken up the storm was something that most people took decades to learn. If they learned to do it that way at all.'

'I thought controlling storms was the whole point,' Oliver said.

'I don't understand it now any better than I did then, but he insisted that if it ever happened again, she needed to let go of the storm and find shelter. He was the town's weather warden for twenty years, and I've never had cause to doubt him before,' Mr Patterson said.

Oliver bit back a curse, turning back to Staci. Light sparked over Staci's skin again, tiny flickers of light arcing. Touching her wasn't the only issue. It wouldn't be safe to drive her anywhere or put her on the bus with the kids when she had that power inside her. Regardless of whether Mr Patterson was right or not, his only option was to find a local shelter.

'You said there was a small shelter here?' Oliver asked, looking at the school.

'It's at the back,' Mr Patterson said, giving directions. 'It's big enough for the two of you. Just be careful; while the lightning is inside her, she might accidentally hurt you.'

Cindy had said the same after Staci had shocked the imps, and Oliver hadn't been hurt then. He had to hope the same was true here.

Staci not hurt us, Thor said, sounding confident, like he had no doubts. *We protect her. She protects us.*

Only if she remembers who we are, Oliver said as the sky rippled, lightning flashing, but it didn't ground this time.

'You should go. I'll take care of Staci,' Oliver said.

'Be careful. I'll send someone to check on you both when the storm is over,' Mr Patterson said, returning to the bus. Then he stopped and turned back to Staci. 'Tell her thank you. Thank you both.'

Oliver nodded as Staci turned away from the sky to follow the bus. He gave a silent prayer for it to get safely to the high school. The storm stayed calm here and now, but he could feel the breeze stirring again. It wouldn't be safe out here for long.

'You should go, take the car,' Staci said. She looked distant still, but she must have been paying some attention because she'd said car, not bus.

'I'm not leaving you alone,' Oliver said, moving closer until he could feel the hairs on his arms rise. 'We should get inside. Before the rain starts again.'

The comment seemed to surprise Staci, and she blinked up at the sky, holding out a hand like she'd not realised it had stopped. That probably wasn't a good sign.

Staci not hurt us, Thor said again.

You can't know that, Oliver said, watching another spark crawl over her skin. Thor growled and snapped as Oliver hesitated to reach out. *Thor?*

Our mate always knows us, Thor said.

Oliver exhaled sharply, feeling like the world had tilted. *Staci can't be our mate.*

But even as he said it, in his head he re-ran every time he'd seen Staci. The first sight of her wild pink hair getting thrown about in the wind. The instant attraction and pull to get closer to her. Just like how Amelia had described her connection to Mitchel. A mate bond. But that link felt weaker now.

Was not safe to take mate back to Father, Thor said quietly, not looking at him. *Would not stay here forever. Needed to protect mate. Built wall. Like Hale showed us.*

Oliver's chest ached as he felt his wolf's pain, how much it had hurt to cut Staci off from them. How hard it had been for him to hide it from Oliver. *You should have told me.*

Protect you, Thor said.

Oliver shook his head, focusing on Staci. The rest he would deal with later. Knowing she was his mate didn't guarantee he would be protected from the magic, no matter how certain his wolf was. But he needed to know now if it would be a problem, not after they were stuck inside the shelter.

He reached out carefully, placing a single finger on her wrist. He felt the power inside her; it danced like a live wire, but it was like there was something between them. A barrier. He wasn't sure if that was the block Thor had put on the mate bond or if it was normal. He might never know now.

Am sorry, Thor said.

It's okay; as long as we can touch her, it's fine, Oliver said.

'You shouldn't be near me. It's not safe,' Staci said. But she sounded more focused as she stared at his finger on her wrist and didn't try to back away.

'Looks like it's not hurting me,' Oliver said, wrapping his hand around hers, holding her gently. The feel of the magic didn't change. 'Let's go inside.'

'I don't know if I can,' she whispered. She shivered, looking up from their connected hands. The smell of the storm was so strong he could no longer separate it from Staci. He missed the scent of sunlight-warmed skin that normally came from her.

'Then I'll help you,' Oliver said, tightening his grip and moving them to face the school.

She let him lead her. Each step was slow and hesitant. The rain started again before they reached the front doors. She shuddered, and he tightened his grip, pulling her forward with him.

The school had no warmth as he dragged the door open and stepped inside. The wind slammed the glass closed behind him, the weather changing rapidly.

'It's so strong,' Staci said, brow furrowed, hand tightening against his.

'Let it go,' he said, now they were undercover. He followed the directions Mr Patterson had given him to the shelter. Staci gripped his hand tightly.

'If I let go, it will rip the school apart and us with it,' Staci said, voice matter of fact. There was no fear there.

'We're almost at the shelter,' Oliver said, picking up the pace.

She leaned into him as he reached a door with a small staff-only sign. He tried the handle, but it was locked. The door didn't look particularly sturdy, nor did the walls around it, so he suspected that it wasn't part of the storm protection. But if he was wrong and he broke the handle, he'd have no way to seal them away from the storm.

Staci stiffened in his arms, breath catching as another gust hit the school. He was out of time to second-guess himself. He twisted the handle; the crack of the cheap metal was lost in the clap of thunder that echoed through the school.

He'd been right. A storm door was set in the floor, flush with the concrete. He pulled the old metal hatch up, relieved it wasn't locked. A steep concrete staircase led downwards into darkness. He grabbed his phone and turned on the light app without letting go of Staci.

'Let go of the storm,' Oliver said again, turning back to Staci, giving her a light tug so she looked at him as he started down the stairs.

She hesitated for a heartbeat, then nodded and closed her eyes. She gasped, body jerking before she sagged. He shifted his grip to wrap his arm around her waist, stopping her from falling.

The wind hit the school in a brutal blast, shaking the building. Then, there was a painfully loud screeching noise, and he saw a piece of the roof fly off. Lightning flashed in the black sky above them, showcasing the damage.

He tightened his grip around Staci, heart beating fast as he pulled the hatch shut and slammed the thick bolts into place. The volume dropped but didn't stop as the building above them screeched and whined, metal screaming as the wind tore at it. Oliver ignored it, helping Staci down the last of the stairs to the basement level.

The room was two metres deep and easily as wide and long. It had old stone walls, a rough, wooden floor, no windows, and only one hatch above him as an exit. Going by the amount of dust, it had obviously not been used in some time.

Storage lined one wall, holding blankets, water bottles, ration packs in foil wrappers, and other miscellaneous storage. Along the other wall was a sofa covered in a white sheet. It looked like it was designed for two or three people to take refuge.

The shelter would protect them, or it wouldn't, so he didn't waste energy worrying about anything except Staci.

'Are you okay?' he asked.

Staci choked out what might have been a sob or a laugh. He couldn't tell. 'It's so damned powerful,' she said, looking up at him. Her eyes were still glowing, but it was duller now.

'You're safe with me,' Oliver said, wishing he could do more to protect her. But his wolf couldn't fight the storm.

'You didn't have to stay,' Staci said, closing her eyes and resting her forehead on his chest with a shudder. Having her lean into him felt good, and he wanted her to stay there forever.

'There's nowhere else I'd rather be,' Oliver said, and despite the storm raging above, he meant it. Not just here in this space but in this town and pack. With his mate, it felt like home.

But with his father threatening him, how did he find a way to stay here with her?

Hale help us, Thor said, pressing close like he could also help transfer some of his warmth to Staci.

Oliver hoped his wolf was right as he tightened his grip, letting her recover. They just needed to get past the storm, and then they'd go to Hale and see if there was another way. One that wouldn't end in his father ruining everything.

CHAPTER NINE

THE STORM SURGED ABOVE Staci, tearing at the school like it was trying to reach her again. She tried to ignore it, reminding herself that it was dangerous no matter how good it had felt to be connected. Or how much control it had felt like she'd had. It was all a lie. With the lightning inside her, connecting to the storm would have been draining her of her magic. It would have taken all of it if she'd stayed connected.

But it hadn't felt like that at all. It had felt like she was part of the storm.

Of course, it had also stolen part of her awareness like she was drunk. Like there was only the storm and its power, which was dangerous in its own way. Only Oliver's touch had brought her back to her senses. So maybe it didn't matter if the storm was draining her; it was still a bad idea to connect.

Staci shuddered, half from the fear, half from the feel of Oliver against her. He was still here. She wasn't sure whether she wanted to hit him for not listening or if she should bury in closer. Unfortunately, neither option would get them warm or dry, and now they were no longer in the storm, she was feeling the cold.

She pulled away from Oliver slowly, shoving her hair back from her face. He let her, dropping his hand from her back until she stood alone. The storm grew so loud she couldn't hear anything else. It tried to bridge the gap between them, tugging at her, reminding her how good it had felt.

Oliver took her arm. The storm grew dimmer and quieter at the touch, sending a different kind of pleasure through her. She could almost feel him and his worry for her.

'You okay?' he said, shouting slightly to be heard above the noise. The wind was so powerful it sounded like trains were roaring past, rattling and shaking. Despite the noise, there was no movement in the shelter itself. Whoever had built this place had done it well.

'Yeah,' Staci said, taking a breath slowly as the energy settled. Her magic wasn't supposed to do that. It was either in her control or it wasn't. Another person shouldn't help her balance it.

'You don't look okay,' Oliver said. His eyes were glowing their beautiful amber colour.

'I just felt dizzy for a minute, but I'm fine now,' Staci said, this time pulling away slowly; she needed to see how bad the effect of the storm was without him.

As soon as she lost contact with Oliver, it hit her like a thousand tiny insects were crawling over her skin, trying to bury inside her. She fought against letting it in; it wasn't easy, but she managed. Now, she just had to keep this up for the next few hours.

Oliver waited for a minute like he wanted to be sure she wouldn't fall over, and then he turned his phone around the room, lighting everything up.

'It looks like it should have everything we need,' Oliver said.

Seeing it made her regret leaving her phone at the rangers' headquarters. If she'd had it, she could have called Florence and checked on her mum, unless the cell towers were down, which was likely.

The storm flared savagely, telling her to let it in. To come outside. She struggled to shove it away.

'Staci?' Oliver said from behind her. She realised he'd been talking, and she'd missed it. She couldn't even blame the volume of the wind. While it was wild, it wasn't deafening. He must think she was stupid.

'I'm fine. I was just wishing I had my phone,' she said, then stopped, shivering. Great. Now he was definitely going to think she was stupid. 'I mean, I know it won't have a signal, but it would be good to have it.'

She risked a look at Oliver as she finished rambling. He was holding a blanket in his hand, the plastic wrapping rustling. She'd missed that sound, too, though she could probably blame that on the noise of the wind and rain above.

'I asked if you wanted a towel?' Oliver said, voice gentle.

'Please.' Her hand shook as she reached for it. Static sparked between them even though she'd not touched him directly. She pulled the towel back, fingers tingling.

'Sorry,' Staci said quietly, rubbing her fingers together. She'd nearly forgotten about the lightning inside her. She should have grounded it outside somewhere it couldn't have hurt anyone. But there hadn't been space or time. At least the lightning didn't seem to be hurting Oliver.

'It's okay,' Oliver said, not commenting on her lack of control as he grabbed another towel from the rack. 'The fastest way to get warm and dry will be to get rid of the wet clothes. I'll turn my back so you have privacy.'

Staci couldn't help the flush that warmed her face at the idea of them both naked. If he noticed her blush, he didn't say anything about it as he placed his phone on the ground, angling the light away from them. Then he turned away to give her privacy as promised. But he hadn't asked her to do the same.

Staci froze as he pulled his T-shirt over his head. Water rolled down his broad back like a caress, becoming lost in the waistband of his combat trousers.

She tried to remember why she'd walked away from him all these months. He was a ranger. He was only here for a year; then he'd be gone, and she'd be alone. When she was already losing her mum, it had been too much to bear. Except that hadn't been the only reason.

He'd had a different woman every week, practically living in their local pub, The Dead Imp, showing off to the rest of the rangers. He'd been loud and shallow. Or at least that's what she'd let herself see but she'd missed all the good things about him. How careful he'd been to help her to the shelter when she'd been out of it. Staying with her when she knew Mr Patterson had told him it wasn't safe. How he'd rushed to save the kids without even knowing who any of them were. The way he'd defended her even after everything he and Elliot had been through. Then, finally, he'd accepted her no that first time she'd given it. He'd not pressured her, or tried to convince her that he was all she needed, unlike some of the other rangers.

Everything she'd thought about him had been wrong. She'd not given him a chance to show her who he was before. She felt like she'd wasted the last few months hiding from him. The idea of losing him had paralysed her.

'Do you want to talk about what happened?' Oliver asked as he took the towel and rubbed at his head and back.

Staci flushed and spun, her heart beating too fast as she tried to remember what she was supposed to be doing. Getting naked. With Oliver.

The thought did little to help calm her, so she focused on his question instead as she pierced the plastic wrap, sneezing as the dust puffed into her face. The material was soft, if a little smelly.

'Nothing happened. I caught the lightning,' Staci said. The last thing she wanted to do was talk about it, but maybe it would help keep her on task. She put the towel at her feet and tugged at her sodden long-sleeved T-shirt. The parts that hadn't been touching her skin were so cold she nearly gasped as she pulled it off.

'Did it hurt?' Oliver asked, though there had been a hesitation like he'd been going to ask something else and had stopped.

'No,' she said, shivering, this time mainly from the cold. 'It felt different. Not good or bad, exactly. Like I was powerful. Whole.' Staci stopped. She must have sounded stupid. 'The lightning is like a bridge, letting me feel and be part of the storm.'

At the reminder, the storm prodded her, asking her to let it in. Even knowing what would happen, it was still tempting. She didn't tell Oliver that part. There wasn't anything he could do to help her, so there wasn't any point.

'That sounds pretty intense,' Oliver said. She heard his zipper come down, the sound loud despite the wind above them. She didn't turn around, but it was a close thing.

'The feeling is a lie. The storm just wants to grow. It takes but never gives back,' Staci said, pulling at her sports bra. The elastic clung to her, feeling like it had shrunk a size. There were no clasps to loosen on this design, either. Sexy, she was not, and that made her doubly glad that he had turned away from her. If he still wasn't looking. That thought made her struggle out of the material just a little faster, somehow managing not to choke herself.

'Does that mean you're still holding it?' he asked. He didn't sound afraid, but she still hesitated with her answer. Most people were afraid of lightning.

'Yes,' Staci said, shivering as a tiny spark arced across her arm, but it was just that, a spark. Unlike earlier with Elliot's lightning, this didn't seem to be fighting to escape her. 'I have it under control, though.'

'What would have happened if you hadn't caught it?' Oliver asked over the sound of his heavy wet clothes falling to the floor.

'It would have hit the bus,' Staci said as she wrapped the towel around herself and tucked it under both arms. She was so cold her fingers felt clumsy, but the towel felt a million times better than the wet top had. 'You were all still getting the kids on the bus. If anyone had been touching the ground ...' Her stomach still churned as she thought about where it had been going to strike.

'Thank you,' Oliver said, letting out a long exhale.

She wanted to turn and see him, see if he really meant it. The one and only time she'd saved someone from lightning had resulted in a very different reaction.

Shaking her head, she refocused on getting undressed. Oliver had said he'd give her privacy to change, but he hadn't said he'd give it to her forever. Going by the sound of his clothes hitting the ground, he was probably already done.

She undid her trousers, sliding them and her knickers down as fast as she could. The material caught against her feet, heavier than she was expecting. She lost her balance, tipping as she tried to hold the towel and pull her leg out.

Hands caught her, holding her tightly. The link to the storm cut off, and she could only feel Oliver. Like he was part of her again. She hadn't realised how loud the storm had been in her mind until it was gone, and she could relax.

'You said you wouldn't look,' Staci said, voice shaking as she took a slow breath. She felt trapped with her legs tangled and him the only thing keeping her upright, but she couldn't quite make herself care.

'I smelled your fear,' Oliver said, helping her back upright. He'd wrapped the towel around his waist, and most of the water was already dry on his chest.

She flushed. If his sense of smell was that good, that wasn't all he'd have been able to pick up. But he never mentioned it. Yet another example of how he'd given her space and not pushed her when he could have.

He put one of her hands on his shoulder, then bent slowly once he was sure she was stable and untied her boots. She'd forgotten to take them off in her hurry. Very stupid.

But if she'd done that, Oliver wouldn't be kneeling at her feet, ever so carefully helping her remove their excess weight. She lifted her foot once the laces were loose, and he easily slid the first one off. Then, the second one.

She nearly groaned when his fingers brushed against her leg as he gripped her trousers, holding them so she could tug herself free. He could have run his hand higher, but he didn't.

Now she was free of the clothes, Oliver stood up, once again checking her balance. 'Do you still feel dizzy?'

It took her a minute to remember why he was asking her that. That had been what she'd told him. That was why he was being so careful, like she was a doll that might break.

'I'm okay now,' she said, blushing. But at least that meant some of the heat had returned to her face if no other part of her body. She pulled back slowly, missing his heat the moment she let go.

'I'm here if you need me,' Oliver said.

'But not for much longer,' Staci said, trying to sound casual about it like it was a joke, but it didn't come out that way. No matter how she saw him now, he was leaving in a few months. She'd missed her chance.

Oliver stared at her for a long moment, eyes flashing to amber. 'I've been thinking about asking Hale to stay,' he said. 'Maybe permanently.'

Staci's heart skipped a beat as she considered his words. 'I thought your contract was only for a year?' All the Shifters she'd met had stayed a year maximum except Hale and Lance. 'Are you allowed to extend it?' Would he want to? Working in the Rift Scar wasn't exactly a safe job.

'Hale is letting us stay as long as we want.'

The idea of him staying permanently sent a thrill through her. She tried to imagine what that would be like, but before the thought could fully form, the storm flared, sending something crashing into the ground above with a loud thud. She barely heard it over the spike in energy, but it must have been bad because Oliver grabbed her, pulling her close as he stared at the ceiling.

The connection to the storm broke with his touch, and she shuddered, feeling dizzy for real this time. She listed against him, and only Oliver's grip kept her upright.

'Maybe you should sit down?' Oliver said as he helped her over to the sofa in the corner, pulling at the large dusty sheet covering. More dust rose, making them both sneeze.

As the air cleared, she saw that the sofa was actually a metal-framed double bed with large cushions placed against the wall. Her brain stuttered as it gave her other options on how they could use it to warm up. All of them were familiar fantasies, even if the setting wasn't something she'd have picked.

For the first time ever, she seriously considered what would happen if she took that leap to make her fantasies a reality. But just because Oliver was staying, that didn't mean he still wanted her. Or that she could bridge the past times she'd rejected him.

Except she'd seen the way he looked at her. That was more than just the kindness of a friend.

When Staci shivered again, he grabbed and unwrapped another towel from the unit, carefully placing it around her shoulders. She wanted to reach out and touch him, tell him he didn't have to keep his distance, but the storm was surging loudly in her mind, making it hard to think.

'How long will the storm last?' Oliver asked.

'We're nearly in the centre of it now,' Staci said, tilting her head just as the noise dropped with a suddenness that left its own kind of deafness. The power shifted, the calmness trying to pull her back in.

Staci fought it, trying to push it away. She didn't want the storm. She wanted Oliver. But the words wouldn't come as the storm pressed against her.

'I'm going to wring out our clothes,' Oliver said, tugging the two ends of the blanket a little closer before he stood and stepped back to give her space.

The storm surged again the moment he moved back, overwhelming her senses. But instead of the previous chaos, she felt calm, like she was floating in a still lake. The moment of surprise was enough to let it drag her under.

OLIVER THREW THE DUSTY bed cover in the corner, avoiding looking back at Staci. The towel had swamped her, making her look tiny and vulnerable, and it had been nearly impossible for him to back off and give her space. Especially when her desire was thick in his nose.

No matter how much she might smell like she wanted him, she'd done nothing to suggest she'd changed her mind from when she'd said no six months ago. As a Shifter, you learned early that what someone said and did was more important than their scent. It saved any miscommunications.

Ask again, Thor said, sending images of them curled up together.

I'm not going to put pressure on her while we're naked and freezing in a basement, Oliver said. Though he wanted desperately to put his hand back on her skin. Whenever he let go of her, she seemed to grow more distant.

Touch her, Thor said, shaking out his fur like he was wet too. *Ground her here with us.*

She's not a wolf to welcome casual touching, Oliver said. *If we do that, we will scare her off.*

Thor growled, sending images of Oliver as a pup and an older wolf nipping him to teach a lesson. *Was happy when we said we stay.*

That wasn't something he should have promised until he'd figured out a plan with Hale. Things might not go the way he wanted.

Once we sort out things with my father, we can talk to her. Court her, Oliver said, stumbling over his word choice as he tried to explain it to his wolf.

Not need court. Is mate, Thor said.

Shaking his head at the unhelpful attitude, Oliver took their clothes to wring them out in the corner before hanging them on the edges of the shelves. The whole time, Staci didn't move or speak. While she'd never been exactly chatty with him before, she wasn't someone he'd known to be silent like this. Even the desire was slipping away until, once again, all he could smell was the storm.

'Staci?' Oliver said. She didn't react to her name. Her eyes were shut, head tilted slightly back.

He moved closer slowly, not wanting to startle her. Mr Patterson had said to bring her inside and help her break the connection to the storm. She'd done both so that should have meant she was safe.

Except she looked worse than she had when she'd stood in the middle of all that chaos.

Oliver reached out and touched Staci's limp wrist on her knee. It was freezing, so cold that he almost pulled away from the shock of it. He moved his other hand to her cheek and neck. All of her was icy.

'Staci,' Oliver said again, urgently this time. Staci still didn't react, and he tightened his grip, saying her name again.

That she wasn't shivering was a bad sign. It meant she was slipping towards hypothermia. The towels should have been enough to keep her core body warm, even staying still.

He searched the room, looking for anything that would heat it, but there was nothing but more towels and blankets. Cursing, he left Staci only long enough to take one of the blankets, ripping it out of its plastic. It was massive and clearly intended to be used on the double bed.

But the blanket would only keep the heat in, and she seemed to have no heat at all.

We can warm her, Thor said. Oliver expected him to press for them to shift, to grow fur. *Not time. We warm without fur.*

He hesitated, debating his options to get them warm, then decided that, in this case, asking forgiveness was the better option. He shoved the cushions off the bed, then stripped their towels away, barely registering her perfect porcelain skin as he stepped over her to lie on the bed and pulled her back against his chest. She was so cold he couldn't help his gasp.

He wrapped the blanket around as much of them as he could, but Staci still wasn't reacting. No sound or movement.

'Come on, Staci,' Oliver said. He should have done what Thor had said, touched her. If he'd done that, he'd have

seen she was freezing and been able to do something sooner.

How long did it take for someone to warm up? He
didn't know. Worse, this was probably related to her magic, which might mean he was doing the wrong thing.

Every time he'd touched her, it had brought her back to
the surface, but she wasn't reacting this time.

'Staci, you need to wake up,' Oliver said, rubbing her
arms, but it didn't seem to be helping to warm her up.

Call her, Thor said.

I am, Oliver said, leaning his chin on top of her head,
pulling in her scent. It was faint under the storm, but it
was there.

No. Call with magic, Thor said, showing them how it
had felt when Staci had touched them. How muted it was
now in comparison to the first time he'd seen her. *Break
wall.*

Oliver hesitated as he struggled to understand, but his
wolf's knowledge of their magic was often better. It was
almost like his wolf had a rule book about how their magic
worked that Oliver couldn't access.

Not read. Not have book. Just know. Trust Thor.

Oliver smiled despite his fear and nodded, letting his
wolf rise so high that he was a hairsbreadth from shifting.

Thor wrinkled their nose. Even in their human body, the room smelled terrible. Damp. Stale. Dusty. And the storm. So much of it that everything else was nearly buried. He wanted to be in the woods to show Staci their home and land.

Focus, Thor, Staci needs us, *Oliver whispered impatiently in Thor's mind. But he had not forgotten why he was here.*

He put a hand on Staci's chest as it rose slowly. Not enough movement, even for sleep. He had been too slow to convince Oliver to help, but he would fix it now.

He focused on the walls he had built. There were three, all weak after David had hurt them. Alpha. Pack. Mate. The last one had been hard to build, but he had not wanted to be like Hale and hurt for so long.

The magic was not something Oliver understood, but Thor did. He had learned much. Remembered more. They did not need the wall now. If they needed it again later, he could rebuild once David's damage had healed.

Thor let the wall to his mate crumble the rest of the way, and warmth flowed in. Magic. Magic that wasn't ours but belonged with us. It flowed in wildly, searching for a safe place. It was weak, exhausted, hurting. Thor reached through it, searching until he found Staci, then wrapped himself around her, offering her his strength.

Staci gasped, gulping in air like she had not been getting enough until now. She would be safe. He would be able to help her.

'You're okay, Staci,' Oliver said as Thor fell away. He said the same thing over and over. That link between him and Staci fluttered brightly in his mind, making him wonder how he'd missed it the first time he'd met her.

Thank you, Thor, Oliver said, rubbing his hands over Staci's arms as she shivered so hard that her whole body practically vibrated. Shivers were good; shivers meant her body was trying to get warm.

We protect our mate, Thor said. *Stay. Keep her safe.*

Yes, Oliver said. *We are going to stay.* He'd find a way to figure it out.

'What happened?' Staci asked, teeth rattling as she tilted her head to look at Oliver.

He couldn't tell her why he was able to help, though he probably should have. But announcing that she was his mate wasn't something he could just casually drop into conversation. Especially not when he was pressed naked against her.

'You were freezing,' Oliver said, thinking he should probably move back, but she was still shivering. 'I didn't know how else to warm you up.'

Staci didn't move, but he felt her fully realise what position they were in. She didn't stiffen, but the tension in her body changed even under the shivers.

'Thank you,' Staci said slowly, swallowing. 'I was in the storm. I hadn't meant to reach out. But it was right there.'

'I think connecting to it might be a bad idea,' Oliver said carefully, remembering what Mr Patterson had said.

Staci let out a small laugh, turning away from him. 'You touching me helps,' Staci said, voice so quiet it was like she was afraid to say it out loud.

'Then I'll hold on as long as you need me,' Oliver said.

Now the walls were down, he could feel her through the link between them. She was pleased at his words, but there was also an edge of fear, though he couldn't find the latter's source.

After a minute, the shivers started to slow, and Staci placed her hand over his where he'd wrapped it around her waist.

'I thought I had it under control, but the core arrived, and it was like it just sucked me up inside,' Staci said, voice tight. 'I couldn't get out. Then I felt you.'

She turned her head to him again, her emotions rolling like a rainbow. Too many to count. Even in the pack, the connections to Amelia and Mitchel were never this clear.

Her teeth were no longer chattering, he realised. Her body was no longer cold. That seemed too fast of a change, but since the cause had been magic, he had no way of knowing if it was normal.

'I can feel you more than before,' she said quietly, eyes dropping down to his lips. Her arousal grew sharp in his nose. 'Like a piece of you is connected to me, keeping me grounded.'

Again, he considered telling her about being mates, but this really wasn't the place or time. He didn't want to make her feel like she was trapped. Unfortunately, his body wasn't on the same page, and now she was safe; it was having all sorts of inappropriate reactions to her being so close.

He started to move back a little, not letting go all the way, but not pressed so close that she'd feel his attraction to her.

She grabbed his arm, stopping him. 'Don't let me go.'

'I'm not; I just thought you might appreciate a bit more space.'

'You don't have to,' Staci said, and it was hard to remind himself that it was just because she was afraid of the storm coming back, not because she wanted him.

'I don't want to make you uncomfortable,' he said, settling on that as a safe answer.

'Do I look uncomfortable?' Staci said, turning her head around to watch him. With her back still pressed against his front, it meant his erection was solidly pressed against her thigh. There was no way she'd have been able to miss it, but she didn't pull away.

'No, but I remember what you said last time I asked you out,' Oliver said, biting back a groan as she shifted position a little, her soft skin rubbing against him, adding friction.

'That was six months ago. What if I've changed my mind?' Staci said, eyes dipping to his lips again. 'What if I was wrong?'

Told you, Thor said smugly, then he backed off, pulling back to curl up into a ball to sleep. Sex was a human thing, not a wolf thing, and he had no interest in that except it meant that he was close to his mate.

Oliver wanted to argue with his wolf, but that would mean taking his attention off Staci, and he couldn't bring himself to do that.

'Have you changed your mind?' he asked, still not as sure as his wolf. Staci had been pretty damned clear in the past.

Her eyes moved up to his again, and she smiled. 'Very much, yes. When I met you, I made a judgment about who I thought you were, and I was wrong.' A faint blush coloured her cheeks, and he could smell the edge of embarrassment at her words.

'What makes you think you're seeing me right now?' Oliver asked, and Thor growled at him.

'Because the man I thought you were wouldn't have run into a school to save children he didn't know. He wouldn't have protected me from the storm when he could have left. And he would have kissed me already and not asked any questions,' Staci said, pulling in a breath. 'I'm just sorry it took me so long to see it.'

'So, what do we do now?' Oliver asked. His skin tingled where it rested against her stomach. He kept still, letting her take the next step. Her words plus the arousal didn't mean she wanted to have sex with him; it just meant she was willing to give him a chance. He wasn't going to risk pushing her away now.

'I have an idea,' Staci said, pushing up on her elbow until her lips touched his, gently at first, tasting of sweat and the rain. Then she freed an arm, wrapping it around his neck, pulling him closer, tongue seeking entrance into his mouth.

He groaned, sliding his hand over her stomach, then up and across her breast. She arched, pressing against his very painful, very hard erection.

As much as he wanted to continue, he forced himself to stillness. He had to be sure. That morning, Staci hadn't wanted this from him.

'Are you sure this is what you want?' Oliver asked, his whole body rigid as he fought to stay still. To give her the space to say no if that's what she wanted. It might kill him, but he'd do it.

She rolled over, breasts touching his chest, making his body tighten. He could feel the hardness of her nipples. He doubted the cold had anything to do with it, not with the heat that seemed to roll off her.

'I've wanted you since the first time I saw you,' Staci said, lips almost touching his as she spoke. 'Wanting you was never the problem. Keeping you was.'

Oliver shuddered at her words, wanting more. She'd wanted him too. 'I'm not going anywhere.'

Again, he knew he shouldn't have made that promise yet. Not with Hale's life at stake. Staci's, too, if Oliver's father found out about her. But he couldn't make himself take it back. He would find a way for it to work. Because even if this was the closest he ever got to her, he never wanted to leave her alone again.

Stay, protect pack. Protect mate. Protect Hale, Thor said. *Stronger together.*

Staci leaned in and kissed him again, taking full advantage of the better angle. He tasted every inch of her mouth until they were both gasping for breath and his father was far from his mind.

STACI DIDN'T LET OLIVER back off from the kiss. She was tired of saying no, of holding herself back. Of not seeing Oliver for who he really was. She'd wasted so much damned time. Now, she was finally sure what she wanted and could feel the same impatience within him.

She could feel him like he was part of her. Like he was the storm that she'd so recently been lost in. Except this time, she didn't care if she got lost. She didn't tell him that, of course—either part. She didn't want to scare him off.

Oliver moved to her neck, kissing down her skin an inch at a time, lingering when he hit a spot that had her whole body arching against him. His hand cupped her breast, thumb moving over the nipple in a lingering stroke that made her groan.

It felt good to have him against her, like every part of her he touched was linked to her core by a live wire. She leaned forward, returning the favour, kissing the muscle on his neck. She could feel the echo of his pleasure through the new link between them.

With them both being naked, there was nothing to block the sensation of his erection pressing against her thigh. She'd felt it almost as soon as she'd woken up. But her thigh was the last place she wanted it.

Lowering her hand, she traced the lines of muscles along his stomach until she reached his erection. He hissed as she ran her fingers over his length, and he jerked against her. She moved her hand again, sliding it slowly against him, deliberately keeping the touch light.

Oliver growled, sending a vibration through her deep enough that it tightened every muscle she had. He pulled her in for another kiss. She forgot what she'd been doing as she tasted him.

His hand brushed her hip, more tendrils of fire sparking through her as it travelled over her thigh. She pulled back from the kiss, gasping in a breath as his fingers slipped further between her legs, just brushing her core and no more. She arched against him, wanting more.

Oliver groaned, burying his head against her neck, teeth grazing skin so lightly that she felt like the two points of her body he was touching were connected. Then his fingers slipped inside her.

Every part of her tightened against him, and she stood on the edge, but she wasn't ready to fall over it alone. She wanted him inside her first.

'No more games,' Staci said, gasping as Oliver grazed her neck with his teeth again. 'I want you now.'

Oliver chuckled as she rolled onto her back, pulling him with her. She widened her legs to give him space to settle against her. He still didn't quite go where she wanted, balancing most of his weight on his arms. The length of him was still too low, and she groaned, arching her back. Trying to pull him closer.

He gave her a low half laugh, half growl, eyes glowing as his wolf stared out at her. She reached out, running her finger over his cheek. 'I love it when your eyes are amber.'

She saw something akin to shame flash across his face and felt him retreat. He started to turn away, but she caught him, holding him in place. 'Don't hide,' she said, but he refused to look back at her.

'It's because I'm weak. Dangerous,' Oliver said, not raising his eyes. 'A Shifter should always have control over their beast.'

'You're not weak,' Staci said, cupping his chin, forcing him to look at her. He was more than strong enough to stop her if he wanted to. 'I've seen weakness. I've seen what it does. You're not that. You're not dangerous.'

She could feel that he didn't believe her, not really. This was a wound that went deep and had festered a long time. The clarity of how she knew that should've scared her, but she felt no fear right now. She wished she could show him that because she was sure of one thing: he wasn't dangerous.

Staci wrapped her arms around his neck and lifted herself to capture his lips in another kiss. His tongue darted out, hesitantly at first. But after a heartbeat, the kiss grew deeper, and he slowly lowered them back to the bed, crushing his entire weight against her.

His heat burned her as his erection pressed close to her core, the tip of his sex right at the edge, almost inside her, like he was giving her one last chance to back out. 'I want this,' Staci said, shifting her weight just enough that he slipped inside.

He moved slowly, almost painfully so, as he sheathed himself inside her. Staci let out a small cry as she wrapped her legs around his waist, shifting so he could go even deeper. He groaned, one hand moving to her hip as he started moving.

With each stroke, it was like she could feel every sensation he did along with her own. She'd had sex before, good and bad, but never like this. Never like she was two people.

Her core tightened to almost painful levels, and she clawed at Oliver's back, so close to the edge that she couldn't catch her breath. Then she fell.

She cried out as lightning danced over both of them, bright sparks of light that she couldn't tell were real or in her head as Oliver joined her with his release.

He shuddered against her, moving once, then twice more, and she fell over another ledge she hadn't seen coming.

When she could breathe again, she blinked at Oliver, loving the way his amber eyes caught the light from the phone. Both their chests heaved as they tried to get enough air.

'You're beautiful,' Oliver said, hand moving down the side of her face. She could have argued with him, but right now, she felt the truth of those words more than any of her own insecurities.

'You're better than any storm,' Staci said, feeling the words spill from her without thinking. She might have blushed if her entire brain had been working, but Oliver kissed her, stealing all her thoughts.

He was hardening inside her, swelling against muscles still twitching from the last orgasm. She moaned, rolling her hips, wanting him to move again.

She had a brief, fleeting worry about protection, but she was on the pill and, to her knowledge, Shifters didn't carry any kind of disease that she could catch. Besides, it was already a bit late; he'd already filled her up.

Oliver smiled against her mouth, lifting his hips until he was almost entirely out of her. Then, with a quick thrust, he was moving again, faster this time, not giving her a chance to catch her breath.

Neither of them got the chance to breathe for a very long time.

Chapter Ten

Oliver woke on his back outside in the sunshine. He blinked up at the blue sky, trying to figure out where he was. Old ruins spread out on either side, unfamiliar.

He remembered falling asleep, Staci on top of him. He could feel her like he was inside her still, except she wasn't here with him. The conflicting sensations made the ruins waver and his body jerk. Staci moaned against his neck. Again, not really here in this place.

Wherever he was, he wanted to go back to her.

His vision blurred, and he blinked, finding everything had changed. He lay in the storm shelter with Staci, inside her still as she clung to him, the scent of their sex so strong it was all he could smell.

She squinted at him, her eyes filled with a light of their own, even more so than when she'd been in the storm. She looked fierce. 'I was dreaming about Huntly Castle,' she said sleepily. 'About being hit by lightning.'

The room spun, and he was back on the grass in the sun again. This time, Staci was on top of him, naked where she was pressed against his chest, him still inside her.

She blinked at him, then at the ruins as she pulled back so she was straddling him. He wanted to reach up and caress the curve of her breast, but unfortunately, she was only half paying him attention.

'How are we here?' Staci said, reaching down to touch the grass beside them. He groaned as the movement made her tighten around his sex.

'I don't care, but I suggest we make the most of it,' Oliver said, moving his hips until it was her who gasped.

She finally looked at him properly, and he reached up to cup one of her breasts, brushing his thumb over her nipples, making her arch against him. He wanted to spin them so she was against the grass, but the sight of her above him was too good to move them, even if it meant extended torture.

'I've never had a dream this vivid,' Staci said. Something about the word dream tugged at him. But whatever it was could wait. 'It's just like I remember. But you weren't here.'

'I hope that doesn't mean you entertained other men outside in the sunlight?' Oliver said, jealousy surging at the idea. Not that he had any room to talk about past lovers, though few of them had liked the outdoors as a location.

Staci flushed, looking around again. They were hidden between two ruined walls, out of sight of anyone who might be about. He could feel her small surge of excitement at the idea of being here. Of the risk of being caught.

Despite the feeling running through her, she shook her head. 'That's not what I meant. I never had sex with anyone here. There was just a storm. My first storm.'

'Would you like to have sex with someone here?' Oliver asked, trying to sound nonchalant and failing. Staci shivered again, hands moving to his stomach for balance instead of the grass. He loved the weight of her pressing against him.

'I've never considered it before,' she said, moving her body, sliding up his length. He almost came just from the look on her face as she bit her lip.

He lowered his hand from her breast to her hip, not seeking to control but to feel her move against him. She lowered herself back down his length, hesitantly at first, watching him. He let her see and feel what he felt. The pleasure and excitement of watching her move against him.

Her confidence grew, body moving faster, breasts bouncing, stomach taut. She was tight and hot against him as she lost her rhythm, nails digging into his stomach as she fought to find it again.

She came with a cry, static sparking around them both. Her body arched back, and he grabbed her hip, holding her steady as he jerked once, twice. He came hard, whole body going wire tight as he emptied himself into her.

It felt like he was marking her, claiming her. Part of him distantly felt an echo of the sensation, like he was doing this twice over. Not an echo of Staci this time, but an echo of himself.

The sun wavered, and again, he saw the ceiling in the bunker for a moment before he was with Staci again in the grassy ruins. She sighed, collapsing on his chest, breath coming fast, body twitching along with his as the release still captured them.

He felt good in a way he had never felt after sex before. Like he was where he was supposed to be. His mate was safe here, smelling of him. Everyone would know not to touch her.

That was the alpha in him, and he doubted Staci would appreciate the sentiment. Not many women, even Shifters were happy with being marked.

'That was ...' Staci didn't finish, lifting her chin to look at him. She was sweaty, with cheeks flushed red, and her breath came in little puffs still. 'Satisfying.'

He pulled her tighter to him, thinking of all the extra words he wanted to add to that, but instead, he nodded. 'Satisfying.'

'Now maybe we can figure out where we are?' Staci said after a few more breaths, though she made no move to get up.

A drop of rain hit Oliver's face, cold despite the warm sun above. He blinked up at the blue sky. Dark clouds were closing in fast, much like earlier.

'A storm is coming,' he said, almost feeling it gather above. But as a Shifter, he didn't have that kind of magic. Or he shouldn't.

Staci closed her eyes, pulling in a breath. 'I remember this storm,' she said. It didn't sound like it was a happy memory.

'What happened?' Oliver said, shivering as the world around them swayed and shifted.

He stumbled, trying to catch Staci as he found himself on his feet, standing in another part of the ruins, dressed now. He could still feel himself inside her, the real world intruding, making it hard to think of anything else.

But Staci's fear trickled into his nose. Thor growled, low and deep, as it vibrated around him. Not a sound that was inside his head. He looked down to see his mostly brown wolf pressing against Staci's legs, offering additional support.

Staci followed his look, breath catching as she met Thor's eyes. Her fear eased, dropping away as something else rose in its place, part curiosity, part awe. 'He's beautiful.'

'Don't tell him that. He thinks enough of himself as it is,' Oliver said, ignoring the long white teeth his wolf showed him.

A small group of children appeared, herded by a younger Joyce and Mr Patterson and two blond teenagers; one looked a lot like Staci, and the second looked like Sam, Hale's mate.

'That's me,' Staci said, reaching out as the group passed, but she didn't touch anyone. Not that it seemed to matter. No one seemed to react to their presence as they filed inside a small opening in the ruin. The metal door was rusted and heavy. There would be no closing it to block off the coming storm.

Thunder rolled above them, and the clouds grew darker. Young Staci stopped, looking up at the sky. Mr Patterson said something to her that was lost in a gust of wind. She turned and walked inside with the others.

'How are we seeing this? I didn't even think I remembered it this clearly?' Staci said, turning back to Oliver.

'I don't know,' he said, but he suspected he did. Mates could share dreams and memories. Sam had used Pack Magic and the dream to save Mitchel. But it wasn't like Oliver could just tell Staci that. At least not without making it look like he was trying to force something on her.

He could damn near feel Staci not believing him, but she didn't argue as the rain came down all at once, freezing, soaking him to the skin in moments. He could feel its call here with Staci, like a whisper in his mind.

Staci pulled him towards the entrance to the small shelter, and as they stepped inside, the water disappeared off them like it had never happened.

'Shame that it's not that easy to get dry in real life,' Staci said, giving him a smile.

'I dunno. I think I liked our way of getting dry just fine. I highly recommend a repeat without the storm interfering, of course,' Oliver said.

Staci blushed but didn't look away.

'If we're going to let the freak children stay in this town, they should bloody well contribute,' Joyce said, jerking him out of the moment to the small crowd that couldn't see them.

His Staci stiffened against him, and Thor growled. He wanted to do something, anything. He hadn't been a fan of Joyce before. Seeing this side of her, he liked her even less.

'Joyce,' Mr Patterson said, voice firm enough that several kids looked at him in surprise. 'She's only fourteen. Even if she had the power, I'd never ask her to use it without training, and neither should you.'

Oliver could have kissed the older man for his words.

'I'd forgotten that he'd said that,' Staci said, voice strained. 'Every time I think about this day, I remember her words, but I can't believe I'd forgotten his.'

'This was the first time you sensed the storm?' Oliver asked. He could feel it through her. The strength and excitement of what he could do if he just reached out. No matter how many times Elementals had described their power to him, this had never been how he'd imagined it would feel.

'Not the first time I sensed it. But it was the first time I used my magic,' Staci said quietly, leaning into Oliver. 'I didn't want to leave my mum, and if I admitted I had the magic, they would've sent me to magic school, and all of them were far away. I'd been so sure that ignoring it would be enough. In hindsight, it was naïve of me.'

Oliver wished he felt that about his family. But even ignoring his father's punishments, his mum had been cool at best. He'd never felt the need to be close to his parents.

Being sent away was about the best thing his father had done for him, and even that was a risk now.

'It's not naïve to want to stay with those you love,' Oliver said, wrapping his arms around Staci. He watched as the teacher got the kids to do star jumps to combat the growing cold.

STACI FELT MAGIC STIR inside the storm. Jake, the weather warden at the time, was starting to break it apart. Oliver looked up like he sensed something, though Shifters couldn't feel magic.

'The weather warden,' she said, closing her eyes so she could focus on the feel of him separating the storm. She'd been amazed back then by the skill and delicate touch he'd used against the raging energy. 'I saw what he was doing, how he took it apart piece by piece.'

The thundering rain stopped slowly, along with the gusting wind. After a moment, the sun broke through, shining in through the open doorway, sparking off the puddles.

'Finally. I don't know what took him so long,' Joyce said.

Staci jumped and turned to see Joyce heading for the exit, heels clicking on the old stone floor. This part she remembered just fine.

'Joyce, you know you're supposed to wait,' Mr Patterson said. 'Just because the rain has stopped doesn't mean the storm is under control.'

Joyce ignored him as she stepped outside into the sunlight, careful where she put her stilettos. 'If you think I am going to hang around here after weather like that, you are mistaken. A little bit of rain isn't going to stop me.'

The lightning hummed in the air, the last to break apart. But unlike the rain and wind, it wasn't listening to direction. It slipped and slithered in the sky, refusing to be dismissed. Staci stiffened, remembering what was coming; she wanted to warn them, but this wasn't real; it was just a memory.

'The storm isn't done,' her younger self said, making all eyes turn to her. Staci remembered how insecure those mistrustful and doubtful looks had made her feel. It rose every time she talked about her magic.

'Really? Now you want me to believe you have power after it's all over. Please, girl, I've seen toddlers make better liars,' Joyce said, scowling at the room.

'I knew the lightning was coming. I could feel it,' Staci said, glancing at Oliver; he shivered, looking in the direction it was forming.

'I can feel it too,' he said, though he shouldn't have been able to.

The power of the lightning rippled over her skin as it slipped free from Jake. Then, the storm above changed. No longer calm, it reignited, all the elements springing back together in a bright spark of power.

The rain and wind hadn't returned yet, but it would only be a matter of time before the whole thing slipped out of control again. The lightning grew in strength, searching for a target. Something it could ground itself in. Joyce.

Her younger self stood frozen for a moment, staring at the sky. Then she bolted forward into the sunshine and shoved Joyce so hard she stumbled into the muddy grass, hissing in pain as she landed on her hands and knees. But it was better than what would have happened if she'd stayed where she'd been. Lightning struck her younger self, the blue light blinding.

Staci tightened her grip on Oliver's hand as he stepped forward like he could protect the girl in the memory. But he couldn't. This had already happened. She'd survived.

It took a minute before the light settled. When she could see again, her younger self stood alone with an occasional spark dancing across her skin. Staci looked for signs of the struggle she'd felt today, but all she saw was fear as her younger self stared at the sparks.

'You tried to kill me,' Joyce said as she crawled backwards, mud dripping off her in wet slops.

Staci flinched at the accusation, wishing she could step forward and tell her teenage self that no one would believe Joyce. Not then, and not later.

Thor snarled beside her and lunged at Joyce but passed straight through her, nearly planting his nose in the wall.

'Thor,' Oliver said disapprovingly. His wolf growled, shaking out his coat.

'As in the god of thunder?' Staci asked, lips twitching as she looked between him and his wolf. She knew she should care that his wolf had attacked Joyce, but she couldn't make herself worry about it.

'I was really into the show when my wolf surfaced. He attached himself to the name early on,' Oliver said, sounding a little defensive.

'I love it. Thunder to match my lightning,' she said, turning to Thor again. He really was beautiful, and he was pleased with her words. She could feel it wash through her like an echo.

Oliver smiled and shook his head as Thor trotted back to them, moving to sit so he was pressed against her leg.

They watched her past self struggle against the left-over lightning inside her. It wanted to ground itself.

The humour drained out of her slowly as she remembered that struggle. 'I'd forgotten how afraid I'd been. Of getting the magic. Of being sent away. Hell, even Joyce's words had frightened me. It was my first look at what others would think of me when I really did have magic.' Staci thought back to earlier and Elliot's accusations against her. 'That I was dangerous.'

'You're not dangerous,' Oliver said, turning to her. 'I see someone who risked herself to save a young woman who clearly didn't deserve it. You protected them—all of them—from the storm, stopping it. And you did it without any training. I see someone who has the strength to move mountains.'

'All I did was react. The weather warden had already broken apart the rest of the storm,' Staci said, shaking her head.

'You stopped the storm. I felt it break free from the weather warden, but you stopped it, split it apart. It's completely gone now,' Oliver said, looking up. 'You did that.'

'That's not possible ...' she trailed off, feeling the storm. She realised he was right. Jake wasn't controlling the storm; it was just gone. 'But that's not how the magic works.' It was the opposite of what she'd been taught. She felt Oliver hesitate. Not saw, but felt it. Like she knew he was holding something back. 'What is it?'

Oliver pulled her closer to drop a kiss on her forehead. 'Mr Patterson told me that the old weather warden had been shaken up at what you'd managed to do here. He'd said it was something that took years to learn, if they could learn it at all,' Oliver said, looking at her younger self.

Had she done something? She thought back to how she'd felt that day, but all she remembered was the fear. Nothing about what she'd done. She thought about today instead. How she'd stood in front of the school, the lightning inside her, and the storm above. The rain and the wind had stopped like she'd been in the eye of the storm.

But that wasn't how her magic was supposed to work; it was time-consuming and tedious to push away the parts of the storm. They didn't just stop on command. At least it shouldn't. She'd never been able to do that before.

No, that wasn't right. She'd never *tried* to do that before. Because she'd been taught to do it another way, taught to never catch lightning. Today, her fear had made her react the same as she'd done as a teenager.

'That's two storms you've stopped,' Oliver said, rubbing his thumb over the back of her hand. 'Though I'd appreciate it if you didn't scare me so much next time.'

'I'm not really sure stopping the second storm counts as a success,' Staci said, shivering as she remembered the power that had filled her. 'I only stopped it for a little while, and then it dragged me under into darkness. Only feeling you helped me find my way back.'

'If you ever get lost again, search for me, and I'll be your light in the dark,' Oliver said. There was another moment of hesitation inside him, like he was holding something back.

She wanted to ask what it was, but this time, she was afraid of the answer, so she leaned into him instead, enjoying the feel of him against her.

The dream flickered, and they were watching Mr Patterson and Joyce run for shelter with the kids again. Staci shivered; she didn't want to relive it twice.

'I think I preferred the other dream,' Staci said quietly, looking up at Oliver. His eyes flickered to amber. 'Where the sun warmed our skin ...'

Oliver groaned and pulled Staci into a kiss. The world shifted, and they were alone once more in the grass. 'I think I did too.'

She pressed herself against him, wanting to go back to their moment of peace before she relived her past.

CHAPTER ELEVEN

LANCE STOOD IN AN empty patient room, looking out at the hospital's car park. The soaking-wet tarmac sparkled in the sunlight, and all he could hear was the plink of water dripping from the building.

The winds had died down about an hour ago, going from wild to nothing, almost between one heartbeat and the next. But his ears still rang after the never-ending screaming wind, rattling metal, and lashing rain. It had felt like it was going to tear the building apart.

They'd managed to escape flooding as Rafe and Pascal had done their best to stop the rain from getting in. It had been touch and go as part of the roof lining had been ripped free. But now the winds had died down, they'd been able to get up and put in a temporary patch.

The power had stayed on by some miracle, and the hospital was quickly returning to normal. It wouldn't be long before people injured in the storm would start flooding in. Pascal was worried about being overwhelmed and had asked if Lance and Zoe would continue to help, this time as crowd control. Lance had said yes. Right now, there was no way they'd get a call to ranger headquarters about the Rift Scar, so their time was better used here.

We good at guarding, Shade said, pleased with the designation. *We good at fighting.*

Guarding isn't the same as fighting, Lance said as he shook his head. In a fight, it was easy to just switch off everything else and focus on the movements. Guarding meant you were watching, waiting.

Guarding better than mule, Shade said, curling his lip.

Carrying things was helping, Lance said without conviction. They'd both been getting itchy with all the lifting and shifting between floors to avoid the chance of damage if there was flooding. It gave him too much time alone in his own head to dwell on everything that Elliot had said.

Not alone in head. Am here, too, Shade said, pressing close. *We together.*

I know. I appreciate it, Lance said. Zoe was already down in A & E, but he'd needed a moment alone before he joined her. It had been a long time since he'd had to be around this many people he didn't know.

Lance turned as he scented damp earth tones that meant Rafe was close. He was the palest Lance had ever seen him. Between the injury and working with Pascal to stop the rain from coming in, he had clearly strained himself to his limit. He also seemed to have abandoned his sling. Elementals didn't get the fast healing that Shifters did, so he had to be hurting. But he didn't let it show.

'Pascal is looking for you. Something about Elliot,' Rafe said.

Lance grunted, shaking his head. They'd moved Elliot to the second floor with the rest of the patients during the storm. He was more than healthy enough to have been helping, but he'd made so much fuss that they'd had no choice but to assign the man a bed. It was a good thing the hospital wasn't at max capacity.

'What'd he do?' Lance asked, pushing away from where he was leaning against the window frame.

'Didn't ask,' Rafe said, smiling. 'I'd rather dance with another imp than deal with that spoiled prick.'

'Thanks.' Lance shook his head, wishing he had the same luxury. 'Go rest. You look like shit.'

'Yeah, yeah,' Rafe said, but he flexed his fingers, giving a faint wince. 'Pascal found me a spare bed to use. I'm going there next.'

'Go, I'll deal with Elliot,' Lance said. Rafe offered a weak smile and left.

Lance headed up to the second floor, searching for Pascal. The hospital had a strange calm about it now that the storm had stopped. Or maybe the chaos had just been so intense before that now it felt like peace. Nurses still moved about the hallways, checking on the patients. He found Pascal at a nurses' station.

'Finally,' Pascal said, handing the nurse the file he'd been reading. 'I need you to see this.'

Lance didn't get a chance to respond as Pascal headed to a small four-man room. The walls were white, and the floor was grey linoleum. It smelled of Elliot's sweat, fear, and anger. It was strong enough that it overpowered the antiseptic they used to clean the place.

Elliot was up on his feet, messing with the window at the back of the room. The shutters were open, but even from here, Lance could see the window was locked. Not that Elliot trying to go out a one-storey window would have been a huge concern. It wouldn't likely kill him, though it would hurt a lot.

'It's wrong,' Elliot said, muttering under his breath. He was flashing the world his arse but didn't seem to notice or care. 'It wasn't supposed to happen like this. Not possible. They said it wasn't possible. It was supposed to be my storm.'

Lance hesitated, not liking the words. They could mean a lot of things. Elliot clearly wasn't all here right now.

'I tried talking to him, but he just bashed the window. He's been like this since the storm stopped,' Pascal whispered. 'I can't tell if he can hear me or not.'

'What wasn't supposed to happen, Elliot?' Lance asked quietly, moving slowly closer, picking one of his statements.

'It wasn't supposed to be like this. They said the storm couldn't be stopped.'

Threat to pack, Shade said, snarling low. *Not let him hurt anyone.*

Calm, Lance said, though his own panic had spiked. Elliot had known the storm would be this bad, and he'd done nothing? He'd been sure the man was lying, but not that he'd done this deliberately.

'Who said that?' Lance asked. Pascal had gone quiet, but Lance could smell his anger and uncertainty. Elliot wasn't entirely himself, and Pascal had a duty of care as his doctor. But Elliot had clearly tried to set the storm against the town.

'They said she wouldn't be able to stop it,' Elliot said.

A voice came from further down the hall. 'Mrs King, please, if you'd just wait—'

'No, I will not wait; take me to see Elliot, now!' Joyce said, voice high and clipped as she interrupted the speaker.

What the hell did she want with Elliot? From what little he knew about her, she was concerned with politics and money, neither of which seemed relevant to this. Unless she was upset about the storm and wanted to blame Elliot, she was a proud hater of anything that came from the Rift Bloodlines.

If that was the case, he needed to get his answers now before she caused him to shut down and stop answering questions.

'Who told you Staci wouldn't be able to stop the storm?' Lance asked, stepping a little closer. It wasn't hard to guess that Staci was who he'd been referring to.

'They were wrong. She tore it down,' Elliot said, voice falling to a whimper. 'She stole my storm.'

'Who told you,' Lance said again as Pascal looked towards the door, clearly hearing the sound of stilettos too.

This time, Elliot didn't answer, and they were out of time. Lance stepped back a moment before Joyce entered the room. She stopped and glared at Pascal, then stiffened as she saw Lance. They'd not interacted much, but she'd no doubt recognise his ranger uniform.

'Why is this ranger in Elliot's room? He's not a doctor or nurse,' Joyce said, brushing her hands down her perfect clothes. Clearly, she'd avoided all the weather.

A man in a suit followed her in, wringing his hands. He was one of the hospital administrators. 'Mrs King, please, if you would just give me a moment to—'

'He should not be anywhere near my son, especially since it's the ranger's fault he was injured in the first place,' Joyce said, interrupting.

Elliot turned around at the word son, staring at Joyce with surprise. He wasn't the only one. The silence in the room spoke volumes.

Lance shook off his own surprise and focused on the rest of what she'd said. The accusation was very deliberate, implying a bias against her son. It would make it easier for her to make people discount anything Lance said. Shade snarled, liking Joyce even less.

'If your son had told us about the storm last night, we could've had a patrol go ahead, and then he'd have been able to follow behind safely,' Lance said. He had to talk over her when she tried the same interrupt tactic on him. 'Instead, Elliot lied about how bad the storm was.'

Elliot flinched at the accusation. He looked sickly, especially with the bandage on his arm. If he wanted to play the part of a victim, he'd have an easy time with it.

'How dare you!' Joyce said, stepping forward. 'My son tried to save this town while Staci let disaster strike again, and the thanks he gets are unfounded accusations.'

'Staci tried to save this town,' Lance said, catching sight of Zoe as she slipped into the room and moved to lean against the wall. Out of the way, but again, close by if needed.

'If not for that dangerous woman, there wouldn't even be a storm,' Joyce said.

The words made Lance's stomach drop. Elliot was the only one claiming that, and he'd not had a chance to speak to his mother yet. Not with the phones down. There was only one way she'd be able to re-iterate that information.

First, Elliot says the storm is deliberate, and now Joyce knows too much. But neither was enough on their own to prove the pair had done something wrong.

The suit who'd followed Joyce stepped forward. 'Mrs King, I assure you—'

'I don't need assurances. The storm is over. Why's my son still here when you said he only needed stitches?' Joyce's voice grew louder as she lifted her chin.

'Your son is free to leave anytime,' the man in the suit said. 'It was simply not safe—'

'Get your things, Elliot. We're leaving,' Joyce said, interrupting again as she glared at everyone. 'Clearly, this place cannot see how the pack is trying to bully my son or how they blame him for their mistakes.'

Lance shut down the growl that rose, not wanting to rise to Joyce's games, but he hadn't missed she'd said pack, not rangers. Neither had Zoe, as her anger rose in the air as strong as his. He glanced at her; she was rigid but hadn't moved. He tried to calm himself so he didn't feed into that anger more.

Elliot jumped at his mother's command and grabbed the shoddily folded pile of clothes on the chair.

'Mrs King, your son isn't in any danger here,' the suit said, finally getting in a complete sentence as he glared at Lance.

'Don't worry; when I gather the council to tell them all about how Staci caused this storm, I'll make sure to include this hospital's negligence.' Joyce turned to Elliot again, scowling harder. 'Cover yourself up, for goodness' sake, boy, you're not a savage.'

Lance dug his fingers into his palm to stop himself from speaking. Or worse. Shade was livid.

Not let them hurt pack, Shade said, snarling.

Enough, or you're going to set a bad example for Zoe, Lance said. *Nothing we can say or do to Joyce now will help Staci; we need another way.*

Shade didn't like it. *Promise will help.*

I promise, Lance said, even though he knew what it would mean. This was turning out to be so much more than just a storm warning gone wrong.

Shade backed off, and the prickling of his wolf's energy against his skin eased. Zoe didn't relax, but without his anger adding to the mix, it would be easier for her to convince her wolf to stand down, too.

Elliot flushed like he'd not realised he was flashing everyone. He clumsily pulled on his trousers under his gown and then chased after Joyce as she left without a word. The suit followed Joyce, still trying to placate her.

'I don't like this,' Pascal said quietly, anger tightly controlled. He took two slow breaths. 'If what he said was true ... He can't get away with doing that to us. Not to our town.'

Lance moved to stand beside Zoe before he answered, putting his hand on her shoulder, letting her feel more than just the anger of his wolf. It wasn't much since he wasn't her alpha, but it would help. Zoe relaxed a little, leaning her head back against the wall and closing her eyes.

'He's not going to get away with it,' Lance said, tightening his grip on Zoe's shoulder before he let go.

'What are you going to do?' Pascal asked.

'Talk to someone who understands the magic,' Lance said, fishing out the piece of paper the nurse had given him.

It had the town's old weather warden's number on it. 'Are the landlines up?'

'Yes, they came up about half an hour after the storm finished,' Pascal said.

'Good. Tell Rafe to go home when he feels better,' Lance said. 'Unfortunately, me and Zoe won't be able to help like we promised.'

She opened her eyes; there was no sign of her wolf in them, and from experience, he knew how hard that had to be. She nodded slowly.

'I'll tell him,' Pascal said as a nurse appeared at the door asking for him. 'Let me know if you need any help.'

'We will,' Lance said, though right now, there wasn't much he'd be able to help with. Pascal followed the nurse out.

'What do you want me to do?' Zoe asked. She'd relaxed now, though she wasn't any less angry.

'Find out what Joyce would get if the storm had done major damage to the town,' Lance said. 'She knew to say the exact same thing Elliot did, and unless he was able to sneak to the reception desk to make a call in the last hour, I doubt they've had a chance to talk to each other. This has to be more than just a grudge against Staci. Joyce is too politically and financially motivated to take a risk for that.'

'And the council?' Zoe asked. 'If Joyce is going there now, I doubt we will have answers in time as to her motivations.'

'Leave that to me,' Lance said, looking at the number again. 'Another weather warden, one with experience, will counter whatever lies Elliot is spouting.'

Lance also needed to warn Staci if he could, though with the cell tower down, that wouldn't be easy. She could be anywhere. But he would worry about the parts he could do now.

And ignore the tightness in his chest that he was putting people in more danger by helping. Doing nothing would be worse. He just had to keep telling himself that until he believed it.

Chapter Twelve

Staci woke slowly. She was warm and comfortable, with a solid weight pressed against her back. A shadow of her dreams replayed, showing her visions of having sex with Oliver in the sunshine. Him under her. Then, on top of her, moving so slowly, she wanted to scream.

She wanted to stay in that dream, but a warm breath fluttered across her shoulder. She opened her eyes to see an arm wrapped around her waist. Oliver's arm. He was pressed against her back, their legs twisted together, the only light coming from the torch on his phone.

It hadn't been a dream. She'd really had sex with Oliver.

The realisation made her heart skip a beat. After so long of saying no, she could barely believe the memories were real. Or at least some of it was. They'd clearly never been outside in the sunshine, not with the storm raging. Though why she'd dreamed they'd both been out at Huntly Castle, she didn't know.

She ran her finger down Oliver's arm, enjoying the warmth coming from him. This hadn't been where she'd expected to end up today, especially after all her fears. He'd stayed and protected her from the storm in a way she'd never imagined was possible.

The storm was …

Staci stiffened, hearing only silence. There was no energy dancing over her skin. Nothing around her. The storm was gone. Just like in her dream.

She searched for it, reaching out to the furthest edges of what she could feel. A calm breeze danced over Huntly. The rain was gone, purged out of the sky like an over-squeezed sponge. The lightning was little more than a few sparks flickering between the clouds. Even what had been inside her was gone now.

It hadn't just passed over them, progressing into the next town. It was just gone. Which wasn't possible. A storm like that didn't just stop, nor did it move so fast she'd no longer be able to feel it, despite what had been in her dream.

'You okay?' Oliver asked, running his thumb over her stomach where his hand rested. His voice was deeper, rough with sleep.

'Yes.' Staci nodded, wrapping her hand around his arm so he knew her fear wasn't connected to him. 'The storm is gone.'

'Isn't that a good thing?' Oliver said, dropping a light kiss on her shoulder. She sighed, wanting more.

Their dream conversation played through her head, along with his promise to pull her back if she got lost. He was right. The storm being gone was good, even if she didn't understand it.

'It's just strange,' Staci said, settling on that as her answer. It wasn't like Oliver had really been in her dream. She snuggled in a little closer, letting his scent fill her nose. It was a musky spice and something a little like wet dog, though she would never tell him that.

'What do you want to do?' Oliver asked. Amazingly, there was no innuendo in that question. She was tempted to add it in herself, but she felt the pull of reality. Of the things she should be doing.

'I need to go home and check on my mum,' Staci said. Not being home would upset her, and Florence would get her back there as soon as she could. 'It's safe to leave now.'

Oliver kissed her temple and pulled back the blanket off himself, letting it fall between them. 'Then that's what we'll do.'

She didn't miss the 'we' as the cold air hit her bare skin briefly before his side of the blanket settled around her. 'You don't have to come with me,' she said, turning to watch him sit up. His body was all muscle, with barely an inch of fat anywhere to be seen. She could trace the lines for hours.

'If you keep looking at me like that, we might never leave,' Oliver said, smile growing as she flushed. 'I hung our clothes over the shelves to help them dry, but I expect they're going to be damp still.'

She hesitated to stand. Sex was one thing, but walking around without clothes was something else. He must have sensed her reluctance to move because he placed another light kiss on her shoulder and climbed over her to get out of bed.

More cold seeped in like he'd been her personal heater, but the storm didn't intrude. A thread of tension she hadn't realised had been there eased.

He crossed the room with a confidence and grace she envied as he gathered up their clothes; he gave her a towel along with her pile. If they'd been anywhere else, at any other moment, she'd have settled with watching Oliver, but they needed to go.

She sighed as she unwrapped herself from the blanket so she could get cleaned up with the towel and drag on her clothes. He'd been right. They were still damp, and she couldn't bear to pull on her sports bra. It had been bad enough to get off, so she tucked it in her pocket.

She turned around to find Oliver already dressed and watching her with his beautiful amber eyes. She wanted to go over to him and wrap her arms around him. Kiss him and tell him how beautiful his eyes were. To get a chance to see him strip out of those clothes a piece at a time. But she didn't move, either towards him or the door.

The longer Staci dawdled, the more she realised it wasn't just the draw to Oliver that made her hesitate to leave. She was afraid to see how bad it was outside. How much damage the storm had done. To see if her mum was okay. Or find out how many people the storm had hurt.

'Your mum will be fine,' Oliver said as if he'd read her mind.

Staci nodded, trying to let herself believe the words. Oliver picked up his phone, sending the light spinning around the room. 'How late is it?' she asked.

'Early afternoon. We've been here a couple of hours,' Oliver said, tapping the screen. 'No signal still.'

She wanted to ask how long the storm had been over, but that wasn't a question either of them could answer. But the phones still being down meant it couldn't have been that long. They were usually quick to repair that and the power. Of course, it wasn't often that the storms were hurricane-strength.

Staci took a deep breath as Oliver went to the heavy hatch in the ceiling. He shoved hard, making metal scrape loudly against concrete, the screech reminding her of the storm ripping at the school. Something that did nothing to ease the knot in her stomach as he revealed blue skies.

Blue skies and no roof.

'Shit,' Oliver said, exhaling slowly as they climbed out into what had been a corridor to take in the damage. No one was going to be coming back to school here anytime soon. 'I felt it, but I never imagined.'

There was no furniture, just broken fragments of walls, some half crumbled to nothing. The cartoon designs had survived in places, though they were much more torn. The roof was completely gone. It looked like a dystopian TV set.

The fallen tree was still slumped against the school, visible from here because of the missing roof. It was a stark reminder that she'd been safe and warm with Oliver while others might not have been.

'Come on, let's see if the car survived,' Oliver said, bringing her focus back to him. He offered her his hand, and she let him lead her through the ruin and help her climb over the debris.

As they finally made it out of the school, she could see the surrounding houses had fared better. However, they were far from undamaged. Tiles were missing off roofs; light posts had been knocked to the ground; a tree had fallen into a semi-detached house, splitting it down the middle; someone's trampoline was wedged in a front window, glass shattered and ragged. It wasn't the only window broken in the chaos. But the houses themselves were still standing. The road was flooded, too much water too fast for the drainage to cope with, and going by the smell, it was heavily mixed with sewage now. It looked like power was out in the surrounding area because all the houses appeared dark.

Guilt crawled into her gut and took up residence. Elliot might have been the one to ignore the storm last night, but she could have done something sooner, and she hadn't. This was all her fault. People had suffered because Staci had wanted more time with her mum. Because she'd been selfish.

But her mum was slipping away, and time was precious. That selfish part of her would happily watch the town burn to stay with her mum. More guilt moved in on that thought.

She hated conflict at the best of times, but this was inside her, twisting and churning. The guilt for not working warred with the guilt for not spending more time with her mum before Staci lost her altogether. It hurt so much it was an almost physical pain.

Oliver's hand tightened around hers like he'd sensed her pain, or maybe he just scented it. Either way, it helped ease some of the pressure and calmed the cycle in her mind.

It was too easy to let him take that weight, but despite the connection between them, part of her was still afraid to rely on him. He might have said he wasn't leaving, but doubt gnawed at her now they were back in reality. Would he really want to stay in a place where he had to go into the Rift Scar all the time?

She stomped down on the fresh pain that the thought had brought. She would deal with it later. Right now, finding her mum had to be her first priority.

They found the old Land Rover sitting a few feet from where they'd left it; the driver's door was dented like something had slammed into it. Oliver let go of her hand to brush a stray branch off the windscreen and walked to the driver's side.

'It looks okay. Let's see if this thing will start,' Oliver said, pulling keys from his pocket. The car was unlocked, but they'd both remembered to shut their doors as they'd rushed to help her old teacher. Not that it made much difference. They'd already soaked the seats from their previous excursions into the rain.

'And if it doesn't?' Staci said, shuddering as the seat squelched when she sat down.

'Then I get to walk you home,' Oliver said, opening his dented door. It creaked but complied. 'Though I may still have to if the roads are blocked.'

Nothing was blocking this street, but it was luck mostly. The fallen trees and lampposts were leaning towards the houses, and most of the other cars had been parked in driveways, not on the road.

Oliver started the car on the first try, turning off the fans before they could blast them with cold air this time. 'Sometimes the old beasts are the best,' Oliver said, running his hand over the steering wheel.

The engine felt loud in the silence as he pulled away, and she let it fill the space between them as she took in the damage to the neighbourhood. More broken windows, fallen trees, and random twigs and leaves scattered everywhere. Someone's front lawn was strewn with part of a shed.

They'd barely driven five minutes when the destruction seemed to reduce tenfold. There were still leaves and crap everywhere, but no more missing roof tiles or fallen trees. She'd seen storm damage before. There was a path to it, a range of effect, but this town wasn't that big. A storm like the one that had hit them should have affected all of it. More than just the school.

A few people were out sweeping or checking cars or properties. No one looked hurt, but there were a lot of nervous glances at the sky as if they didn't trust the change in weather.

'Most of them had decent warning to get to safety because of you,' Oliver said, making her turn to him.

'If I had done my job, then none of this would've been needed.'

'This is on Elliot, not you,' Oliver said, moving to wrap his hand around hers. He couldn't keep it there long because the car was manual, but she enjoyed the moment of warmth and peace it gave her.

'I feel like we've had this argument before,' Staci said. 'Except we were on the opposite sides.'

'I never thought you were responsible for the storm,' Oliver said, glancing at her. But after a moment, he smiled. 'But since you think we're on opposite sides, you must already know I'm right?'

Staci couldn't help but laugh. Shaking her head, she leaned back into the squishy chair a little, missing the warmth of Oliver's hand as he took it back to change gear. He gave it right back to her.

Worry over how long Oliver would stay intruded again. She shoved it away. One problem at a time. First, she needed to check on her mother. Then she'd worry about her future.

OLIVER FOLLOWED STACI'S DIRECTIONS until he pulled up in front of an older two-storey detached house with a large garden out front and a stone wall around it. Leaves were scattered over the grass, and a tiny river of water flowed onto the street, but the house itself looked undamaged.

Staci stared but made no move to get out, hand gripping her seat belt so tight her knuckles were white.

'She's going to be okay,' Oliver said, though he had no way of knowing that for sure. But he wanted to offer Staci something. Anything that might make the pain he'd felt in her the whole drive ease off.

Protect mate, Thor said, whining. He could feel her pain too, deep and cutting, but not physical. *Make her not afraid.*

Just as soon as I find out what's hurting her, I will, Oliver said, wishing he could read more than just emotion from her.

An older woman opened the front door, relief evident in how she clutched her hand to her chest. She was round in the middle, with spindly thin legs, dark skin, and black hair that flowed down her back in thick curls.

'Florence,' Staci said, breath escaping in a rush as she fought with the seat belt to get out of the car. He helped her, pressing the button to release the lock. She shoved the door open and met the woman in the middle of the stone path, hugging her.

Oliver got out of the car slowly, reluctant to intrude but not yet ready to leave.

'I was so worried, girl. Don't you dare do that to me again, y'hear?' Florence said, leaning back to stare at Staci, then pulling her back into a hug.

'I'm sorry, I tried to get to the shelter,' Staci said, voice breaking a fraction. 'But I found somewhere else safe. I promise.'

Florence made a shushing noise that reminded Oliver of his grandmother, who'd passed when he'd been a child. That same warmth and comfort flowed from her. Longing rose in his chest, and he shoved it down. He couldn't afford to want this kind of comfort. His father would use it against him.

The reminder of his father sent a stab of pain through him. He'd missed the deadline, but with no signal and the fallout from the storm still gripping the town, there wasn't much he could do about it. Hopefully, his father would wait long enough for Oliver to figure something out with Hale.

Staci pulled back from the hug. 'Is she okay?'

'Your mum is fine. She's having a good day,' Florence said, kissing Staci's forehead before stepping back. Then Florence focused on him. 'And who's this rather bedraggled-looking young man?'

Oliver self-consciously brushed his hands through his hair, though he doubted it would improve his appearance. Staci looked back at him, a blush colouring her cheeks, and just like that, he no longer cared how he looked.

'This is Oliver. He's been helping me,' Staci said.

Florence smiled widely, sending a knowing look his way, then turned and bustled back inside, calling over her shoulder as she moved. 'Then come, come. I've water boiling for tea.'

Staci's blush faded slowly as she watched him. 'You don't have to if there's someone you want to check on.'

'I don't really know anyone else in town,' Oliver said. He could check on the pack, but they were spread widely and could be anywhere. They would all check in with Hale once the lines were back up.

Staci hesitated still, glancing back at the house. Seeing that look hurt, which was stupid because he'd known her for all of five minutes.

'But, if you don't—'

'No. It's not that. It's just …' Staci looked down at her hands. 'My mother has dementia. She can be … difficult. But don't worry, she's human. I inherited my powers from my father's side.'

The last part was tagged on quickly in a way that told him she'd been asked that question more than once. He could understand why. Someone with the ability to control the weather, suffering from something like dementia, was a terrifying thought.

'I'd love to come in and meet your mother,' Oliver said, moving down the small stone path until he was almost touching Staci. He wanted to reach out more than anything but didn't want to scare her off.

'The house is a bit outdated. I mean, it's clean, though you might not think that looking at it,' Staci said, glancing over her shoulder like she was judging her house and finding it lacking.

'I'm sure it's perfect,' Oliver said, still giving her space.

Not need space. Need comfort, Thor said, giving him a mental shove.

Thor reached out for Oliver, touching Staci's arm. Even through the T-shirt, he could feel the connection. Feel her unease. They offered what comfort they could. Staci relaxed a fraction, turning back to him.

'I've not had anyone over since ... In a long time,' Staci said.

'I can go if that's easier? I can pick you up later to get your car and things from headquarters,' Oliver said, stumbling slightly over the last part. He was assuming none of them had been damaged. Something he should have thought about sooner, but Hale would be all over that.

Staci shook her head slowly, placing her hand over his. The connection between them grew deeper. He could feel her pain still, an internal conflict she was fighting. 'No, I want you to come in.'

'Then I'll go where you want me and leave anytime you need. Just ask,' Oliver said, leaning closer.

Staci lifted her chin, eyes on his. He moved a hand to the back of her neck, so close he could almost taste her already.

'Do you like milk and sugar with your tea?' Florence called from inside.

Staci closed her eyes and leaned into him with a groan.

'Just milk, please,' Oliver shouted back as Staci pulled away from the brief hug and slid her hand into his.

He let her lead him into the house. The entrance was a straight corridor that ended in a door, with a small split off to his right. A narrow staircase was tucked against the wall, the bannister done in aged pine, carpets looking slightly threadbare.

Laughter came from the room ahead of them. Then, another woman's voice rose as she said something in reply to Florence.

Staci led them in that direction, past walls decorated with floral wallpaper and wood panelling. Staci had not been exaggerating when she'd said old-fashioned. But he could feel the history of the place everywhere he looked. Small lines marked the doorway ahead of him, with dates next to each one. Tiny children's drawings marked the bottom of the walls; they were faded like someone had tried to wash them away, but the pens had stained the wood.

This home was lived in. Nothing like his parents' house, which was pristine, and any mark removed to protect the perfection shown to outsiders. A shell that hid the rotting underneath. He'd have chosen to live here over his parents' home a thousand times over.

The kitchen was outdated, with old black and white linoleum and peeling cabinets, but like the rest, it felt lived in and well-used.

'Staci, you're home. We've been worried sick,' a frail woman said, struggling to stand. The resemblance to Staci was unmissable. She had the same narrow nose and long face. Age had worn away at her, digging in heavily around her forehead with frown lines. But the laughter lines were visible now as she smiled at her daughter.

Staci went to her mum, pulling her into a careful hug. 'I'm fine, Mum,' she said, pulling in a deep breath like she was drawing in her mum's scent.

Thor pressed him to do the same. Staci's scent was the static of the storm and sunlight-warmed skin, laced with her pain and joy. Florence smelled like fresh bread and ginger. But Staci's mum was the strongest, chemicals hiding almost all of her natural scent. But just there, under it all, he caught a hint of lavender. The combination had buried deep into the furniture. It would be years before the scents faded.

Again, he couldn't help but compare it to the sterility of his home. Scents were erased, scrubbed away, and removed. Good and bad until it could have been a show home.

'And who do we have here with you?' Staci's mum said, pulling back to give Staci a knowing look. 'A boy?'

'Oliver, at your service,' Oliver said, nodding towards her.

'You can call me Melanie,' her mum said, offering her hand to Oliver to shake. He took it gently, feeling all her bones. 'My daughter never brings her boyfriends home.'

'Mum!' Staci said, face flushing. Her mum just laughed, giving her a wink.

The flush faded too quickly, and Staci's expression changed, longing rising above all that conflict. He wanted to reach out and touch her again, but she was closing down, pulling away.

'What's wrong, Staci?' her mum said, reaching out to her daughter as she sensed the change.

'Melanie, honey, why don't you sit? It's been such a long day. You must be exhausted,' Florence said, struggling to hold onto her equally strained smile.

'What a wonderful idea! Staci will be home from school anytime. I want to be rested for her,' her mum said, re-taking her seat. Then she looked up at Staci and Oliver, frowning. 'Florence, you didn't tell me we had guests?'

Staci's scent changed to a pain so sharp it stung his nose. When she'd said her mum could be difficult, he'd assumed that meant her mum would be grumpy or obstinate. He'd not imagined that this had been what Staci meant. Changing from being a daughter to being unrecognised. Even though he didn't like his family, he couldn't imagine how having his mother not even know him would feel.

'I need a minute,' Staci said, walking away from the kitchen without looking at anyone.

Florence's face held an echo of the same pain. She gave Oliver a small shooing motion. 'Go, be there for her. All this on top of the weather, it's been hard. She could use a friend right now.'

Staci's mum frowned harder, not really following but watching Florence like she held all the answers. Oliver nodded and backed up a step, moving to follow Staci. How did he help her with this pain? He had no experience of this kind of loss.

Hurt like when lost pack, Thor said quietly, bringing the feel of his temporary pack being torn away from him. Creating it had been an accident, but the loss hadn't hurt any less for it. Then, his wolf showed him the feeling of being whole again when Amelia and Mitchel joined his pack. *New pack made pain less.*

Staci's mum is sick, and she won't get better. Nor can she be replaced like that. She will only ever have one mum, one family, Oliver said, following the most recent scent through the house into a flowery living room. Staci stood in the middle of the room, back to him.

Make her our pack. We be her new home, Thor said.

Which was easier said than done. Even if Staci wanted to be in Oliver's pack, Sam still had no idea how she'd done it, and he'd still not found a way to tell Staci she was his mate.

But either way, now wasn't the time to add complications. He needed to be there for her with what he had to offer and hope that was enough.

STACI'S CHEST ACHED IN a way she didn't have words for. She'd missed her mum so much, and then to see her so clearly, just to lose her again. It hurt to take a solid breath. Her throat burned. But she refused to cry. She was done crying. Her mum had always been there when Staci needed her. It was Staci's turn to be there for her mum.

But it was easier said than done as she stared around her living room. Like most of the other rooms, this one was all floral design right down to the patterned carpet. Everywhere she looked, she saw her mother, saw their life together. Saw what she was losing. She wished she was a child again and could curl up on the sofa with her mum's arms around her, telling her it would be okay.

Oliver's large arms wrapped around her, pulling her against his warm body. It was so close to the echo of her thought that a sob escaped her. She should have told him to go. He didn't need any more of her drama than he'd had to deal with already. But she hadn't wanted to say goodbye, not yet.

'I can't do this,' Staci said, voice breaking. 'I can't keep losing her.'

'It's okay,' Oliver said, sliding his hand over hers. She felt his calm with that touch. His confidence in her that she was strong. He was wrong. She wasn't strong. She was falling apart.

The desire to lose herself in his arms was so powerful that she almost gave in to it. But it wasn't that simple. He might be here now, but she still wasn't sure how long that would last.

'For how long?' Staci said, anger rising in the wake of the tears. She shrugged out of his arms, wrapping her own around herself instead, but she didn't turn to him. 'Do you really want to spend the rest of your life working in the Rift Scar?'

'I'm not going anywhere. I'm right here,' he said. 'If you'll have me?'

She turned to him. He looked at her with such calm patience and tenderness that she almost broke. It had just been her and Florence for so long that she didn't know how to let herself rely on him being there every time it got too much. If she was wrong, she wasn't sure she'd survive losing him, too.

A knock came from the front door, saving her from answering. Swiping away her tears, she turned away from

Oliver and his extended hand. It was harder than it should have been. Then she called to Florence to say that she'd get it.

She opened the door to find Mr Patterson standing there, still in his wet, dirty clothes from earlier. Staci stared at him, unable to find words. What was he doing here?

'Are the kids alright?' Staci asked, though her throat tightened at the idea that they'd been caught in this mess any more than they had already.

'Yes, they're all fine,' Mr Patterson said, nodding quickly. 'They're being reunited with their parents as we speak. Even better, so far, there have been no reports of serious injuries or casualties.'

'That's great news,' Oliver said, coming up behind her. She could feel his heat. It would be so simple to lean back against him, but she kept herself straight, refusing to give in.

'Yes. But now we've another problem,' Mr Patterson said, eyes tightening. 'The council is meeting. Someone has accused you of deliberately creating the storm. You need to be there. Give your side of events.'

Staci felt the air leave her in a rush as his words hit her. They were blaming her?

'That's ridiculous,' Oliver said, half-stepping in front of her. 'I was there. Staci didn't do anything wrong.'

Mr Patterson stepped back two paces, raising his hands. 'I agree. But if they declare she was responsible, they'll remove her as weather warden.'

That wouldn't be all they did. They'd put her in prison and pump her full of Rift venom so she couldn't use her power to hurt anyone else. She'd not be able to support her mum.

'They can't do that. They'd need witnesses,' Oliver said, looking back at Staci.

'The rest of the council is gathering now. It's taking longer than normal because the phones are still down. Once everyone is together, they won't wait for witnesses after a disaster like this,' Mr Patterson said. 'They'll react quickly to show the mayor is in control.'

'Who's gathering them?' Staci asked.

'Joyce King,' Mr Patterson said, running his hand through his hair. He knew precisely what Joyce thought of Staci. He'd been there when that hate had been born.

'Elliot is Joyce's son,' Staci said, feeling sick. Joyce had been out to get her since she saved the woman from being hit by lightning. Now, Joyce might finally have her chance to do it.

'Then she's even more reason to want to blame you for this,' Mr Patterson said.

Oliver growled. The sound made Mr Patterson pale, but he didn't take another step back, making him either brave or stupid. But she didn't back away either, so maybe they were both just stupid.

Staci touched Oliver's arm, feeling his anger on her behalf. 'Don't. It's okay. It's not his fault Joyce is a bitch.'

'Elliot might not be perfect, but I can't believe he would let them blame you like this,' Oliver said.

'I hope you're right because it's Elliot's word against mine,' Staci said. She wasn't convinced Oliver was seeing his friend all that clearly. Oliver was a natural protector. Elliot's story and history made him someone that needed that.

'Who'll be there at this meeting?' Oliver said.

'The council is made up of the heads of the families who came back to rebuild this town a hundred years ago. It's a carryover from the Fae War that never got disbanded,' Staci said. 'They have a voice, but the mayor makes the decisions.'

'The mayor was supportive of you earlier?' Oliver said, sounding hopeful.

'The families have a lot of influence in the community. When it comes time to vote the mayor in, he needs their support,' Mr Patterson said, shaking his head. 'If Joyce convinces them you're at fault, he won't have a lot of choice but to concede to the majority voice.'

'How long do we have?' Staci asked, glancing back towards the kitchen. Florence hadn't come out, but she'd shut the door, protecting her mum from the sound of more visitors.

'Not much. Most of the council was close by already in shelters,' Mr Patterson said. 'My car is working. I can drive you there now if you want?'

'I'll drive her,' Oliver said, voice low in a growl.

Part of her felt the safety in his words. His need to protect her. But at the same time, that safety scared her. She couldn't afford to rely on it. 'I'll be fine. This doesn't involve you. You've already done enough today.'

Oliver turned to her. His eyes were amber again, the colour bright and strangely comforting. 'I'll tell them what happened, that Elliot ignored the storm. I won't let them blame you for this.'

She couldn't argue with that and didn't want to, so she nodded slowly. Some of the tension in Oliver eased. Staci left them only for a minute to tell Florence a short version of what was happening. Then she followed Oliver back to the Land Rover and the squishy seats. Mr Patterson got back in his car, planning to meet them at the courthouse.

'It's going to be okay,' Oliver said. 'I promise.'

'Don't,' Staci said quietly. 'Don't make promises you can't keep.'

She kept herself faced away from him as he started the car. She could feel he wanted to say more, do more. But there wasn't anything else they could do. Except talk to the council. Which probably wasn't going to go well despite Oliver's reassurances.

Wrapping her arms around herself, she stared out at her street, watching it disappear behind her. She'd fight Elliot's accusation with everything she had. She couldn't lose any more time with her mum. Not even if it hurt to be with her.

Chapter Thirteen

Oliver forced himself to loosen his grip on the steering wheel. Everything still seemed to be working fine with the car, but if he broke the wheel, they wouldn't get very far.

Staci huddled in on herself as they drove through town, moving into the more damaged section the storm had passed through again. She didn't look at him, but he could smell her fear.

Protect, Thor said, sending Oliver images of them hunting everyone who was hurting Staci. Joyce was at the top of that list.

I know you mean well, but we cannot hurt them, Oliver said, reminding his wolf what would happen if they did. Their own cage, and never being allowed to shift until they were little more than a hollowed-out shell. That was what happened to Shifters in prisons. Or at least that's what the prime alphas told them.

Take mate home. Keep safe, Thor said, sending images of them living on Sam's land, alone and safe from anyone who wanted to hurt Staci. Melanie had even been included. Of course, his wolf's idea of hiding out didn't involve a house.

If only it was that simple. But Sam's land wouldn't protect Staci if the courts decided she was in the wrong. Nothing would protect her. Thor snarled angrily at the idea that they couldn't help Staci.

We protect her by telling the truth, Oliver said, slowing to go around a fallen tree that someone had cut to allow traffic to pass. Even though he'd reassured Staci that Elliot would do the right thing, Oliver was more than prepared to throw him under the bus if he didn't.

Thor hesitated at that thought. Not believing Oliver. But Staci was their mate. Elliot, on the other hand, was lying to protect himself.

Staci straightened in her seat as the council building came into view. This was the Staci he had met before. Closed off. He hated seeing it, feeling the walls going up, though he understood it. This was her life on the line. But more than that, this could cost her time with her mum.

Strong, Thor said. The confidence of his wolf's words made Oliver smile. His wolf would think that. But Staci didn't have to be strong alone.

Not alone. We here. We protect our mate, Thor said.

Oliver didn't argue. His wolf was right. They were going to do everything they could to protect Staci.

The council building had weathered the storm well, bar a few stray branches on the ground out front. There were more cars here now as he searched for a parking space. He wished he knew more about the council to know if this was everyone or not.

Before he'd finished pulling on the handbrake, Staci opened the door, stepping out into the sunshine. The seat squelched as she moved, but she didn't seem to notice as she focused on the building.

He wanted to say something hopeful or meaningful, but words escaped him as he got out of the car.

'You don't need to do this,' Staci said, not looking at him. 'I know Elliot is your friend.'

You our mate, Thor said, almost pushing Oliver to say the words out loud, but he caught himself just in time. Thor wasn't happy.

'Oliver.' The voice that called out over the car park made Oliver shiver. It was familiar and powerful. Oppressive. His father.

Thor shied back from their shared mental space, crouching low, huddling around their pack bonds to

Amelia and Mitchel. Not that their father should be able to see them when Oliver was in Hale's pack.

Oliver turned to watch his father approach. He looked out of place in his fitted suit with a silk shirt underneath. When he hit the halfway mark, he stopped, waiting for them to come to him. It was a power play that had no place here.

Staci gave Oliver a questioning look, but he couldn't find the words to give her an answer. He could barely find the air to breathe.

'Someone you know?' Mr Patterson said, moving closer to stand beside them.

'My father,' Oliver said, finally managing to get the words out. His father shouldn't be here. He should be back in Glasgow waiting for Oliver to tell Hale he was leaving. It was only mid-afternoon. For him to be here now, he must have started driving long before the midday deadline.

Not go with him, Thor whispered.

It might not be that easy. Telling his father he wasn't going home over the phone was one thing. Telling him in person, with all that weight and power behind him, was something else entirely. Oliver should have spoken to Hale sooner, warned him.

Not wanting his father to focus on either Staci or Mr Patterson, Oliver headed towards him.

'I can't talk to you right now. I have to do something first,' Oliver said, fighting the feeling of his father's power. Oliver might be an alpha in his own right, but his father had been his alpha for a long time, longer than Hale. Even broken, the old pack bond between them shivered.

'No. Now,' his father said, eyes never leaving Oliver's, using every inch of that power against the old link. Thor shrunk back deeper.

'We have an appointment with the council,' Mr Patterson said, clearly not liking Oliver's father's attitude. 'Whatever your business is with Oliver, it can wait until after that's concluded.'

His father smiled without humour. 'Go on without Oliver. I'm sure you won't miss him,' his father said, barely glancing at Staci and Mr Patterson.

If Mr Patterson had been a wolf, Oliver would have said he bristled at the dismissive tone. Oliver stepped a little further in front of the older man. If Mr Patterson got hurt because his father took offence, it wouldn't help anyone.

'It's okay, I won't be long,' Oliver said, nodding at the two of them. Staci stared at him for a minute, then nodded.

'Family first,' she said, almost too quiet to hear as she turned away and headed towards the building. He wanted to tell her that his father wasn't like her family, but he kept silent.

Mr Patterson looked like he wanted to argue again, but he turned away and followed Staci.

THE FRONT DOOR OF the council building was open when Staci tried it, and she stepped through. She wanted nothing more than to turn around and run back to Oliver, stupid though the instinct was. She'd hated how he'd looked as she'd left him. Closed off in a way she'd never seen him. His father wasn't part of the pack, or at least not one she'd seen before. Why was he here?

Seeing his father only reinforced her fear. No one in the pack stayed. Oliver would want to go home to his family.

'I'm sorry, Staci,' Mr Patterson said, their footsteps the only other sound in the building. 'This isn't fair. You've done a brilliant job as our weather warden.'

'I should've done more,' Staci said as Mr Patterson brought her back to the problem at hand. They were alone in the corridor as they turned towards the mayor's office. Valerie probably wasn't back in reception, so they might have issues getting into the back rooms if the door was locked.

'You did everything you could,' Mr Patterson said with that same soothing tone she remembered from her childhood. It wasn't helping much today, unfortunately. 'You did more than anyone else could have expected.'

'More?' Staci put her hand on his arm to bring him to a stop. Something underneath his words, but she couldn't place it. 'You say that like I did something special?'

Mr Patterson didn't immediately speak as he stared at her.

'Tell me what you mean.'

'I saw the school,' Mr Patterson said, taking a slow breath. 'The storm stopped there.'

'Storms break apart,' Staci said, but she remembered her fear when she woke and found the storm gone. Storms might break apart, but they didn't do it that quickly. 'I didn't do anything; the storm was too powerful.'

'I was there when you caught lightning before, remember?' Mr Patterson said, raising a hand to stop her from interrupting. 'Jake, the old weather warden, was shaken up. He let slip that he thought you'd been the reason the storm had been stopped. Not him.'

'I didn't do anything. I didn't know anything about my magic back then,' she said, shivering. His words echoed what Oliver had said in her dream. It was hazy now, some of the detail missing, but she remembered feeling it had been vivid at the time. 'I don't remember doing anything except be too late,'

'And yet, I don't doubt Jake,' Mr Patterson said. 'You did everything you could to help this town. You need to believe that.'

'If I had gone after the storm last night, none of this would have happened,' Staci said, wrapping her arms around herself. She winced at the feel of her damp T-shirt. She should've changed before coming here. There were a lot of things she should have done today.

'Enough self-pity,' Mr Patterson said, voice sharp enough to make her stop and stare at him. He never raised his voice. 'If you go in there believing you deserve to be blamed for what happened, then all you're doing is going to make them believe it too. You've done nothing wrong.'

Staci stared at him, hearing what he was saying. He was right about belief. She was doing herself no favours by doubting her actions. She straightened. Elliot was the one who'd ignored the storm. She'd warned him. She'd done everything she was supposed to.

'That's better,' Mr Patterson said, nodding. 'Now let's show them how wrong they are to doubt you.'

She offered him a tight smile and searched one last time for Oliver, but he wasn't there. She shoved the hurt that brought deep down for later. Right now, she needed to rely on herself.

Mr Patterson led them down the hall and pressed a button under the desk that unlocked the door on the back wall. How he had a way inside would be a question she'd ask later. If there was a later.

No. No more doubts. She pulled her hair out of her bun as she walked, regathered all the loose strands, and put it back up. All the doors were closed this time. She was about to ask which room they were in when the far door opened, and Lance stepped out.

He was still wearing the clothes from the Rift Scar, rumpled and dirty. But somehow, he looked dangerous, whereas she must have looked like a drowned rat. He nodded at her as he closed the door. The last time she'd seen him, he'd been going to the hospital. What was he doing here?

'Is everyone okay?' Staci asked, trying to remember the name of the man who'd been hurt and failing. 'Your scout?'

Lance blinked at her, frowning. 'Rafe? He's fine. Needed some stitches, but nothing was damaged badly. He's resting at the hospital now.' Lance looked at Mr Patterson behind her, then back to Staci. 'Elliot also needed a few stitches, but you'll see him soon enough.'

Staci scowled. Of course Elliot was here. He'd all but promised to tell the world this was her fault.

'Why are you here?' Staci asked, trying not to squirm under his gaze.

'Making sure that Elliot's version of what happened today isn't the only one they hear,' Lance said, eyes flickering to gold. 'You did good work; they should know it.'

Staci stared at him, unable to find her voice. 'Thank you,' she said at last.

Lance gave her a minuscule nod. 'We protect our own,' he said. Then he was moving past her before she could ask what that meant. She wasn't a ranger.

But she couldn't help the warmth that grew at the idea of having that support. Or the gratitude that he'd come here to offer help.

'Seems like you've made some good friends here,' Mr Patterson said.

Staci took a breath. Friends she hadn't even known she had. She closed the gap to the meeting room door but hesitated before opening it. Doubts lingered despite everything.

'You've got this,' Mr Patterson said, offering her a smile and opening the door for her.

With no choice but to go forward, Staci stepped into the meeting room.

OLIVER ONLY TURNED BACK to his father when Staci disappeared inside. 'You're here early,' he said, struggling to keep his back straight and shoulders back as his father's power battered against him.

'So that's why you've been too busy to answer your phone?' Oliver's father said, glancing briefly at the council building where Staci had disappeared. 'I've seen you with better.'

Oliver's anger sharpened, and it was an effort to keep his voice even. Shouting at his father never ended well. 'Does Hale know you're here?'

His father laughed. It echoed through the silent and empty car park. 'That fool doesn't deserve the breath it would take to tell him. This is my territory. I can go where I please.'

Oliver shivered at the spike of power that followed the words. Almost as if his father's wolf was trying to reach out and claim the area.

Not his, Thor said, but the words were almost a whisper.

'If you'd done as I'd asked, I wouldn't need to be here at all.' His father stepped closer to Oliver. 'Yet instead of finding you already on your way home, you're here. Why?'

'Everyone had to take shelter from the storm,' Oliver said, trying not to take a step back. Retreat was a weakness to his father. 'It's only just cleared.'

'Seems like you had time to entertain your new whore,' his father said, looking him up and down.

Oliver bit back a growl, shoving it down deep. But it didn't help. The backhand that hit him was quick. Or maybe he was just too slow as he fell to his knees from the force of the blow. He landed in one of the many puddles, fresh water soaking into his combat trousers.

Face stinging, he turned back to his father. He realised that he should have seen that coming as he licked his split lip. He'd been away too long. Forgotten the rules.

'It's bad enough that you drag me down to this middle of nowhere shitshow, but I'll not have you shame me as well,' his father said. 'Control yourself; I'll not have a child of mine flashing their wolf's eyes.'

Keeping his eyes down, Oliver tried to calm Thor. His wolf whined in his head. Afraid and sorry. They'd both been careless.

'Well?' his father said. 'What do you say?'

'Sorry, sir.' Oliver flinched as his father stepped closer. Old fear. Old pain. But this time, there was no strike.

His father grabbed Oliver's chin, forcing his head up until his eyes were visible. Oliver braced for another blow, but it didn't come.

'Better,' his father said, letting go of his chin with a rough shove. 'I should never have sent you here. I see it's done nothing but make you weak. More so than you were already.'

Oliver clenched his jaw until his teeth ached. His anger was a hard edge that was nearly smothered by his fear. But he couldn't fight his father. He wasn't powerful enough; he didn't have enough control. It had been beaten into him every day since he'd been a child. It didn't matter that he had Amelia and Mitchel. Or that he had a mate to protect. Oliver was never going to be strong enough to beat his father. He should have spoken to Hale when he'd had the chance.

'Since I've had to come all the way out to this shithole, I want answers, and I will get them,' his father said, beginning a slow circle around Oliver. They were alone in the car park, the storm keeping everyone who might have normally been out and about inside.

His father stopped behind him, making his skin crawl. He wanted to turn around, back away, run. But none of those were an option. He'd done all of them, and only stillness had ever helped. Sometimes, not even that.

'Tell me how Hale made the pack lands?' his father said, voice heavy with power. It was a weight against his chest, the need to give an answer. Submit.

Oliver struggled against the pressure. All those hours he'd spent with Hale, learning to be an alpha, felt like he'd been a child playing with Lego. Now, with his father challenging him, it was like he'd been asked to build a brick-and-mortar building with the same skills.

But there was too much at stake to give in. He needed to protect Hale and his secret, Amelia, Mitchel, and Staci.

'Answer me, boy,' his father said. The power of alpha increased tenfold. It felt like he was being suffocated, while at the same time, something inside him was tearing at him, trying to split him from his pack ties to Hale.

Oliver didn't dare open his connection to either Hale or his pack to pull in more strength. He was alone in this fight. Worse, it was a fight he didn't think he could win, even if he did have that strength.

He was failing Staci. Failing his pack.

A different pain bloomed as another blow struck his face. He couldn't catch himself this time as he fell to the ground, face scraping against the rough surface, the sting barely felt among the rest. He could smell his blood and the bitter scent of the tarmac, still wet from the rain.

'Answer me!' his father said, feet close to his face now, the pressure of the power smothering him.

Oliver choked back a scream.

LANCE LEFT THE COUNCIL building through the side exit, pulling in fresh air with relief. Joyce's perfume was so strong it had almost made his eyes water. It had done little to hide her toxic joy as she tried to blame Staci for everything that had happened.

Sharing what the old weather warden had told him about the local storms with the council had felt good. Watching Joyce's fury grow had felt even better. She'd clearly not expected that.

Deserve worse, Shade said, growling low. *Try to hurt pack. Should hunt. We good hunters.*

Patience, Lance said. *She will get what she deserves just as soon as we know what's really going on. Zoe is getting the information now. Then we can hunt.*

Though Lance's hunt, in this case, was calling the police to deal with them. But he didn't tell his wolf that.

Not like Joyce hurting pack, Shade said, still growling. *Not like Staci's fear.*

Lance didn't either. It set an edge of panic in his chest about what could happen. He couldn't lose another pack, not even someone who wasn't technically even pack yet.

Shade pressed close, helping ease some of the tension. He'd done everything he could to help the council find the truth. All they needed now was time.

Staci strong alpha's mate, Shade said.

She was. But all going well, she'd have an easier time defending herself now. It was still up to the council whether they believed Staci or Joyce. Lance was counting on the former.

'Answer me!' A man's voice echoed through the quiet area, followed by a wave of unfamiliar wolf power.

Intruder, Shade said, snarling, pulling in a deep, searching breath. They couldn't scent anything except the wet tarmac and the fading storm.

Lance searched the area, trying to pinpoint the direction the voice had come from. He pulled out his phone; he had service but no messages. Nor had Hale mentioned any new wolves were due in town. Lance followed the sound around the front of the building, stopping for a heartbeat when he saw what was happening.

Oliver lay on the ground, eyes down, blood dripping from a split on his cheek. A man in his late fifties stood over him, foot pulled back like he was about to kick Oliver.

'Stop!' Lance shouted.

The man froze and turned slowly, as if he didn't want to make it look like he was following a command. David, Scotland's prime alpha and Oliver's father. He was shorter than Oliver, with silvering hair and amber eyes that shone bright before fading back to a muddy brown.

'Step away from Oliver,' Lance said. Shade put all their power into the words, pulling on their link to Hale before Lance could stop him. There was a burst of surprise from Hale, but he didn't block the pull.

Lance shuddered at the connection, fighting old memories of the last time his father had reached out through their pack bonds. Of feeling the pain of the fire, then nothing as his father severed the connection, saving Lance from the backlash of his death.

David's eyes widened, and he stepped away before he checked himself. Those brown eyes flashed amber again as he growled.

'You don't have the power to tell me what to do,' David said, shoving his power around them in a wave. But it was too little too late; Lance had already seen the weakness. 'This is my land.'

Lance shook his head. David might be a prime alpha, but Hale didn't belong to him. Which meant there were no pack ties between Lance and David. He was also a long way from home. Lance, on the other hand, was close to Hale's power base and their own pack land.

'You're not my alpha,' Lance said, continuing forward.

David took another step away, so Lance wasn't close enough to strike when he finally drew level with Oliver.

Coward. Weak, Shade said, snarling quietly. *Should challenge.*

No. Lance fought a moment of panic at the idea of being a prime alpha. Of having all those connections bound to him.

Did not mean it, Shade said, wanting to turn their back on the old man. But he was too dangerous for that. *We should just kill. Someone else could be the prime alpha.*

No killing David, Lance said as he crouched next to Oliver. Lance hesitated, then added, *Unless he attacks us.*

Shade wasn't happy, but he accepted the decision.

'Oliver?' Lance asked, putting his hand on Oliver's shoulder. The pack bonds grew brighter between them, but without one of them being the alpha over the other, that was all he could do.

The scent of Oliver's fear was thick in Lance's nose now he was close. Staci was there too, the scent of their shared sex heavy on Oliver's skin. Damp, mildew, and dust were also faint undertones. There was only a hint of blood, which meant he wasn't bleeding badly.

Is he okay? Lance asked. His wolf always seemed to know more about the pack bonds than he shared.

Still pack, Shade said. *But hurting. Old alpha try to steal Oliver. But old alpha not stronger than Hale.*

Lance bit down on his growl, wishing there was something more that he could do. Shade filled the pack bonds between him and Oliver with what little comfort he could offer, but only Hale could help Oliver heal.

'You okay?' Lance asked, tightening his grip, trying to draw Oliver's attention.

Oliver blinked rapidly, not focusing on anything at all. That wasn't a great sign after David's psychic attack.

'Oliver is mine,' David said, moving again to take another step forward. 'I have come to take him home.'

Lance pulled on the pack power from Hale again, letting it roll out over the car park. Every second he was connected hurt like he could feel his father burning again, but this was worth the pain. David flinched from the wash of power. A taste of the power Hale could call if David was to challenge him.

'Oliver's not your pack anymore,' Lance said. 'He's Hale's.'

As if Hale had sensed the thought, the feel of him grew sharper and was joined by a faint tug, Hale searching for them. Headquarters was a good ten-minute drive from here at the best of times, but with the storm debris, it could be longer.

The feel of Oliver's wolf rose under Lance's borrowed power. It spread out cautiously like he was afraid he would be attacked. The scents in the car park grew sharper as more of the pack's power gathered. The bitterness of tarmac and old car exhausts peppered through angry Shifters.

His wolf is trying to keep them safe, Shade said, pulling back so Oliver's power could grow. *But is still hurt from attack.*

'He's my son,' David said. 'He'll always be mine.'

Oliver flinched at the words, but his wolf grew stronger, power spreading over Oliver almost like a bubble. Lance could see it through Shade's eyes. It was something only alphas could do and was used to protect their pack from other alphas trying to steal their people. Clearly, Hale had been teaching Oliver.

David stiffened. 'No!' he said. 'You're not an alpha. You're nothing but a weak, pathetic little mutt.'

Can Oliver protect himself now? Lance asked.

Might not be enough, Shade said. *Old link still strong. Old alpha could break other bonds.*

Then we keep his father away from him, Lance said. Right now, the best way to do that would be to get Oliver to leave if he could.

Lance moved his arm from Oliver's shoulder to offer his forearm instead. Oliver hesitated for a moment, then gripped it, letting himself be pulled to his feet. Their magic overlapped, making Lance's skin tingle before it balanced. The two of them held so much of Hale's power that Lance could nearly smell the man.

Oliver didn't look at his father as he let go of Lance's arm and wiped the blood from his face. The scratch was already healing, and his eyes were a bright, nearly glowing amber. Blood smeared a bright red line down his dirty, damp T-shirt. It looked like Lance wasn't the only one who'd not found the time to change.

'Go inside. I'll join you in a minute,' Lance said. Oliver looked Lance in the eye, but there was no challenge there despite the amber glow of his wolf. He nodded once and turned towards the building.

'Don't walk away from me, boy. I didn't come out to this shithole to be ignored,' David shouted. Oliver didn't answer, didn't even look back. 'Oliver!'

Lance moved to block David as he tried to follow. Oliver's shoulders were hunched like he was expecting a blow.

That wasn't something that came from one strike; that was something that came from many.

Should kill evil alpha, Shade said. *Hurt own pack. Own pup. Should remove. Let Hale take all packs.*

No. It's too dangerous, Lance said.

Would not lose.

But the other primes wouldn't be happy about the challenge, Lance said. They wouldn't tolerate someone coming in that they didn't approve, though they'd deny any interference.

Shade hesitated on that one, trying to understand. He wasn't sure why the other prime alphas would care, but he trusted Lance's judgement enough to believe him.

'Oliver is nothing more than a broken, weak little mutt,' David said. He'd not tried to go around Lance. 'Hale was supposed to show him how to be a real Shifter. Clearly, he's failed.'

'Oliver has never been weak,' Lance said, turning fully towards David, who was practically foaming at the mouth with his anger. 'And there's no way in hell he will be going back to you.'

That wasn't something Lance could guarantee. But knowing how vulnerable Oliver was to his father's attacks, there was little doubt that Hale would do everything he could to keep Oliver safe.

'You think Hale is strong enough to protect him?' David said, finally finding the courage to step towards Lance. 'He can't. He isn't strong enough to stop me from taking my son back. Nor is he strong enough to stop the rest of the prime alphas from doing the same.'

'Then why are so many wolves still here?' Lance said, letting his lips curl into a smile he didn't feel.

David growled. 'Not for much longer.'

'Ahh, so you intend to force them?' Lance asked, shaking his head. But he didn't believe David. That knowledge would spread if the prime alphas forced their Shifters home against their will. Questions would be asked. Questions the prime alphas didn't want people talking about, like how the Highland Rift Pack was no longer a place of punishment.

'You know nothing about how a pack should be run. Your father was so weak he couldn't save his family from something as mundane as a fire,' David said, showing he knew exactly who Lance was.

Lance stepped forward, Shade's claws razor sharp as he pressed to force a challenge. Hale filled Lance's mind, bringing not calm exactly but something more reasonable. Lance shuddered as he fought the need to tear David to shreds.

Win or lose, there would be consequences. He had to remember that.

Either David sensed he'd lost, or maybe he could feel Hale's power approaching because David sneered and half turned away. 'Tell Hale that I want my son returned to me by the end of tomorrow, or I'll take him by force.' He gave Lance one last up-down look, turned, and walked away to a Mercedes parked near the car park exit.

Lance didn't release his breath until the car disappeared out of sight. Carefully, he closed the link to Hale down to a trickle. Enough that he could be found, but not enough that he could feel Hale.

We did good? Shade asked, leaning against Lance. His wolf hadn't understood everything that had happened. Why they couldn't attack or why David would hurt his son.

Yes, we did good. Oliver is safe. That was our win, Lance said, turning to follow the same path inside that Oliver had taken.

The heat was growing so fast that steam was rising from the building. If only everything was as easy to purge. Like the rage. Hale had cooled it, but it wasn't gone.

But at least rage was better than pain. If only by a small measure.

Chapter Fourteen

Staci entered the meeting room with a confidence that didn't last. Nearly a dozen people were seated around a glass-topped table. Some were familiar, but not all. They were dressed in a mix of casual jeans, dresses, and suits that wouldn't have looked out of place in a boardroom. They turned to Staci as one, making her feel like she'd been weighed and judged unworthy.

Nervous laughter bubbled under the surface, but she stamped down on it fast. They already didn't look impressed; random bursts of giggles wouldn't help them take her seriously.

'What's this?' Joyce said, face turning a faint shade of red. She was standing behind her seat like she'd been addressing the room before Staci had entered.

Elliot sat next to her. He'd found time to change and was now dressed in a clean pair of pale jeans and a T-shirt. He looked up at Staci, lips thinning.

'Ah, good, you made it,' the mayor said, motioning to a spare seat.

'Made it? Why's she here?' Joyce said, her eyes narrowing as she took in Staci's clothes and hair. Staci forced herself to keep her hands at her sides. She might not be perfect like Joyce, but she hadn't been outside fighting to rescue kids from a school in the middle of a storm. Or being attacked by imps in the Rift Scar.

'When you make accusations against someone, they have the right to be present to defend themselves, Joyce. Surely you haven't forgotten that basic rule?' the mayor said, raising an eyebrow.

'She almost destroyed the town. She shouldn't have any rights.' Joyce tightened her grip on the back of the chair when no one else in the room agreed with her.

Staci slipped into the white leather seat before they changed their minds. Mr Patterson hadn't entered with her, and the door clicked closed now she was clear of it. She folded her sweaty hands on her knee, keeping her back straight. She didn't think her fake confidence fooled anyone, but it was the best she had.

She glanced at the door again. Where was Oliver?

'Back to what you were saying, Joyce? You believe there have been problems?' the mayor said, waving a hand at her to get on with it.

'Ever since Staci came into her power, there have been problems,' Joyce said, levelling another glare at Staci. 'First, she almost killed me playing with lightning.'

'With respect, Joyce,' a petite woman said, leaning forward. She could have been anywhere between thirty and late forties, with brown hair, hazel eyes, and bronze skin. 'My husband was there that day, and his version of events vastly differs from yours.'

'Mrs Patterson,' Joyce said, the condemnation in the tone nearly dripping it was thick. 'I was there when she leapt outside while your husband was still inside babysitting a class of scared children. He couldn't possibly have seen what happened.'

'Your version of events that day aside, Joyce, I'm unaware of any other problems,' the mayor said, leaning forward on his elbows. 'More to the point, since Staci has been weather warden, we've never had a storm that has done more than minor damage.'

'Speak for yourself. How many times has there been flooding that has wiped out an entire crop? How often has the rail line been blocked because a tree has fallen? We all know how chaotic the weather can be here, how erratic,' Joyce said, waving her arms. 'Heatwaves and freezing weather in turn. Other towns in the area don't have these kinds of problems because they have properly trained people doing their job.'

'They do happen in other towns, I can assure you,' the mayor said, 'and frankly, all the bad weather we've had recently has been when Staci was out of town. Not because of her.'

'Charles, please, she's unskilled at best, criminal at worst,' Joyce said, shaking her head slowly like the mayor was a child who needed to be lectured. Maybe that was how she saw him; she certainly didn't seem to be showing any respect. 'Just admit that we need someone who knows what they're doing. There are far better-qualified people that can do her job.'

'You mean someone that would ignore a storm because they'd rather go drinking?' Staci said, not bothering to look at Elliot.

The rest of the table shifted nervously, but no one else spoke. They clearly didn't like Joyce, either—that much was obvious—but they were all unwilling to stand up to her. Outside of Mr Patterson's wife's unexpected support. Which at least answered the earlier question about how he'd known what was happening.

'Of course you would say that,' Joyce said, scoffing, waving her hand towards Elliot. 'My son has already told us how the storm wasn't bad enough to cause this damage.

Until she went out there.' Joyce pointed towards Staci like she thought the group might not know who she was referring to.

'Yes, Joyce, you and Elliot have gone through your version of what happened. If you've finished with your examples of previously perceived misdeeds? I believe it's time for Staci to give us her version of the events,' the mayor said, glancing around the table.

Joyce's mouth opened, then snapped shut as those around the table nodded. She pulled out her chair, sat in it aggressively, and then settled herself to glare at Staci.

The room turned with her. Staci managed not to squirm in her chair by sheer force of will. Detailing everything that had happened from last night until they left the Rift Scar took far less time than she thought it would. There was no expression on the council members' faces, nothing to give away their thoughts, even though the mayor quickly stopped Joyce's attempt at interruptions.

'After that, I headed into town to speak to the mayor and let him know about the storm,' Staci said, wrapping up what happened.

'She clearly worked with the pack to get her story the same,' Joyce said, curling her lip at Staci. 'My son told them there wasn't a storm, and now they're covering for her.'

The accusation against the pack made Staci stiffen, especially after the way Lance had tried to help her. It also reminded her that Oliver still wasn't here. Something she couldn't afford to be distracted by right now.

'What has the pack got to do with this?' Mrs Patterson asked. 'I thought it was the rangers who went with her? Elementals and Shifters.'

Joyce flushed and lifted her chin. 'Hale has already proven to be ineffective after events last month. After two deaths, he's clearly covering. The rangers might as well be pack for all that it matters while he is in charge.'

The room went deathly silent at those words. Staci had heard rumours about rangers failing to do their job and being jailed, but she'd assumed they were just that.

'Those who broke the law have been punished,' the mayor said, standing, face going red. 'Unless you have evidence of something more, I'd be very careful of the accusations you so casually throw around.'

'You're all missing the point,' Elliot shouted, standing now as well. 'Staci made a mistake, and to cover for it, she created the storm. Why can't you see that?'

Staci dug her nails into the palm of her hand to keep her mouth shut. So that's what he'd told them? She was glad she'd not been here to listen to that.

'Look, we are here to talk about the storm, nothing else, so let's stay focused,' one of the older women sitting to the mayor's left said, leaning forward. She didn't even acknowledge Elliot.

'You are right as always, Bethany. My apologies,' the mayor said as he sat down, smoothing his jacket. 'Please continue.'

The old woman nodded, then turned to Joyce. 'We understand you want to protect your son, Joyce, but Staci has lived here almost her whole life. We know her. Your son, however, has not. Why should we believe his version over hers?'

Elliot flinched at the harsh words and sat abruptly. It was like he was just realising that the room wasn't as impressed with him as he was with himself. Maybe if he'd had that wake-up call a bit sooner, they wouldn't be here now.

'Surviving being stung by a Rift scorpion as a child isn't a small thing,' Joyce said, but it was obvious that she was trying for sympathy. This group wasn't giving it to her, though. 'I sent him away so he could be trained properly. But he's part of this town. He's finally got a chance to come home. Why would he risk that for—if Staci is to be believed—a few drinks?'

'Sending him away was a choice you made,' an older man said, glancing at the rest of the group. 'You could have brought him home anytime once he'd learned control. He didn't need to be a weather warden.'

Staci watched the agreement pass through the group. Joyce could see it, too, because she leaned forward to slam her hands on the table.

'This is ridiculous,' Joyce said. 'My son almost died going into the Rift Scar to stop that storm. He will be forever scarred after this. And this is the thanks he gets?'

'I wasn't aware that shallow scratches caused scars?' Staci said, looking at Elliot. It was childish, but she couldn't stop herself, not after how he'd spoken about her.

'Enough, we're going in circles,' the mayor said, giving Staci a warning look. 'I've given everyone a chance to explain their side, and I've been given two very different versions of what happened.'

Staci's gut tightened.

'My son has no reason to lie,' Joyce said, straightening her back. 'There was no storm before she made it.'

'If that's the case, you'll need to find another weather warden to provide evidence that she can create a storm out of nothing so quickly. From the information Lance provided us from our previous weather warden, what you're claiming isn't possible,' the mayor said. 'Until—'

'Only because he believed the pack was telling the truth. The old weather warden wasn't here; my son was,' Joyce said, pushing to her feet, face turning red.

'Enough, Joyce,' the mayor said. 'Until you bring us more evidence, I've no choice but to remove Elliot from his position as temporary weather warden while we investigate the accusation that he ignored the storm.'

'You can't do this,' Joyce said. 'You need him.'

'It's done. Besides, this was always a temporary assignment. The position was given an extended budget to utilise two part-time weather wardens so Staci could take time to care for her mother. Replacing Staci was never part of the scope.'

Staci looked away at the word 'temporary'. It was a reminder she didn't need that her mother was short on time.

Joyce stepped away from the chair. 'You'll regret this. Staci has no control. You all heard how the primary school was destroyed?' Joyce said, pointing at Staci. 'That was her fault. Is that what you want? Her own father nearly destroyed this town because he couldn't control himself. Now she's going to finish what he started.'

Staci felt like she had been punched in the gut. Her father had almost lost control? No one answered Joyce. But more than one eye was cast her way. Why had no one told her this?

'That matter isn't up for discussion here,' the mayor said, his voice very quiet. He knew what had happened, and he'd not told her. Who else knew?

'Why? Because you're protecting the Elementals and their savage children,' Joyce said. More than one person glanced at Elliot. He flinched ever so slightly, jaw muscle twitching.

'That's enough, Joyce. This meeting is over, and my decision stands. Staci remains as the town's weather warden,' the mayor said, standing. The rest of the table copied him.

'This isn't over,' Joyce said, then with one last glare at Staci, she motioned to Elliot, and they stalked out of the room. Elliot didn't look at anyone as he followed his mother's direction.

Mrs Patterson let out a breath as the door slammed shut. 'I, for one, would like to personally thank Staci for helping the kids today,' she said, giving Staci a smile. 'And my husband. If she hadn't been there, I dread to think what would have happened.'

There was a general wave of agreement through the room, and Staci flushed, not liking the attention even though it was positive. They'd believed her over Elliot. The relief might have been longer lived if not for the comments about her father.

'Yes. Thank you for today and every other day that you've protected this town,' the mayor said, nodding at the group. 'I think it's time we're done for today. I'm sure we all have places we'd rather be after the storm. If anyone needs anything, please let me know, and I'll do my best to offer assistance where I can.'

'Thank you,' Staci said, voice almost lost as they said their goodbyes. She stayed in her chair, head still spinning. Her job was safe. Her mum was still dying. Something had happened with her father that no one was talking about. All of it was too much, and Oliver still wasn't here.

'He wasn't a bad man,' the mayor said, making Staci jump. The room had cleared out. 'Your father was just untrained.'

Staci wrapped her arms around her waist. 'What happened?'

'That's not my place to say,' the mayor said, holding up his hand as she moved to argue. 'Talk to Florence. She was there.'

'And if she won't tell me?' Staci asked. She'd always avoided asking about her father because it had made her mum sad. But she'd never asked Florence.

'She will tell you if you ask, especially with where things are with your mum,' the mayor said. 'You did good today, Staci. You saved lives, and you protected this town. Go home and rest. All of this stuff with Elliot will sort itself out.'

Staci wanted to press about her father, but the set of the mayor's jaw said that she'd be wasting her time. She thanked him again, then stood and left. The corridor outside was empty. She stopped, taking a breath. She was okay. No one was sending her to prison. She still had her job. There was clearly something more going on, but she didn't care right now.

She wanted to tell Oliver. Celebrate with him, but there was still no sign of him. Her stomach twisted as she remembered the tightness in his body as he'd stood in front of his father. Had something happened?

Shaking herself, she headed towards the door.

OLIVER STUMBLED THROUGH THE doorway of the council building, staring at the sign in front of him. It pointed to the left, directing him towards the mayor's office. He was supposed to be there for Staci. But how was he supposed to help her when he could barely stand on his own?

Will rest first, then help, Thor said. He was panting heavily, pacing in a circle, never stopping as he fought to keep the fragile new wall up. Even with the borrowed power Hale had sent him, it felt like it would crumble any moment.

They needed more than rest. His father had ripped through every defence he had. His whole body vibrated from the backlash of the pain. He could feel Hale without any barriers between them. If not for the distance, Oliver wouldn't have been able to keep up the walls that gave Amelia and Mitchel their privacy, either.

He felt raw. Burned on the inside. Even Shane's theft of the pack bonds from Hale months ago didn't compare, and that had been brutal.

An arm wrapped around Oliver's waist a moment before he scented Lance. Oliver let himself sag against the support. Lance had locked down his connection to the pack, so the tingle of power was gone. But the memory of it was still vivid. Oliver had always known that Lance was powerful, but he'd never really understood. Lance had to be damned close to Hale's level, if not stronger.

His father didn't follow behind Lance. That didn't mean he'd left, but at least Oliver would have a moment of peace before facing the man again. The thought made his gut churn.

'Let's sit,' Lance said, turning them in the opposite direction to the mayor's office.

'Staci—'

'Staci will be fine. I already spoke to the mayor and council and told them what happened.'

Oliver's legs threatened to give out as the relief hit him. Lance had no issue supporting the extra weight as they rounded the corner to a small reception with soft seats. There was no one else there but the two of them.

Lance lowered Oliver gently into a beige seat. Every movement hurt like there were blades in his joints.

'How do you feel?' Lance said, moving back to crouch in front of Oliver.

'She's really going to be okay?' Oliver asked, ignoring Lance's question.

'I spoke to the old weather warden, and he told the council what was and wasn't possible with the magic. Then I told the council about everything Elliot had done since last night when Staci told him about the storm, which was mostly nothing. They seemed inclined to believe me,' Lance said, glancing over his shoulder. 'It helps that no one likes Joyce or outsiders. The boy might be her son, but he hasn't been part of this town since he was a child.'

Oliver winced. Elliot had always been stuck as an outsider. Coming into his power so young had put Elliot ahead in learning magic, but even more on the outside for it. But that didn't excuse what he'd done today.

'Now, tell me how you feel?' Lance said, the scent of his wolf growing sharper. His eyes went to Oliver's cheek.

Oliver touched the area. It stung, and his fingers came away with fresh blood. He'd forgotten with the rest of the pain. Now he'd remembered the whole side of his face throbbing like it wanted to make up for lost time.

'I'll heal,' Oliver said, though he knew Lance was asking about more than the physical injuries. After the rescue, he also deserved a better answer. 'I feel like I've been broken into pieces and glued back together badly.'

Lance nodded. 'Psychic attacks always feel worse than physical ones. They also take longer to heal.'

'Funny that no one ever mentioned that was something I should worry about,' Oliver said. He'd been beaten enough times over the years that he'd thought that was the worst his father could do. But this was different. Somehow, it felt like even more of a violation.

'There are a lot of things the prime alphas don't want people to know,' Lance said, standing. He went to the water cooler in the corner and filled a cup. 'Normally, when you're in a pack, you're protected by your alpha.'

'It felt like he was able to go around Hale,' Oliver said, shuddering. It was like there had been no protection at all.

Lance was quiet for a moment, then he took a slow breath and handed Oliver the cup. 'Maybe the way Shane severed everyone's family pack links has left you all vulnerable?'

Oliver took a sip of the water as he considered that. Shane had shredded their bonds after stealing the pack from Hale, but that was only one side of the link, and Shane clearly had no clue what he was doing. If they were right, then other members of the pack could be hurt the same way his father had hurt him.

'Why don't you fight David?' Lance said, watching him. 'He attacked you. No one would have blamed you.'

'He'd have knocked me down before I got the first blow,' Oliver said. Not that he'd ever tried, but he imagined how much worse it would have been if he had.

'You're over a foot taller than he is and more than that wider,' Lance said, taking the seat beside him, tugging down the sleeve of his T-shirt. It had ridden up to show a flash of twisting burn scars.

'Physical difference doesn't do me much good when he can floor me with a look,' Oliver said. Even to himself, his voice sounded bitter. It didn't matter if Lance was right. Even if Oliver was bigger, it didn't make him any less weak.

Thor was strangely silent on the matter, listening to Lance.

'You're not weak,' Lance said, making him wonder if he had spoken the last part out loud.

'You're one of a few who believe that, then. Poor control. Weak. Useless.' The words spilt out of Oliver before he could stop them. He looked away, automatically hiding his eyes.

'Control issues?' Lance asked, and then when Oliver continued to say nothing, he thumped him on the shoulder.

'Hey!' Oliver said, rubbing the spot. Lance hadn't been gentle, and his eyes were hard as he stared at Oliver.

'Are you turning into a wolf because I made you angry?' Lance said. 'Are you attacking people without thought? No? Because I've seen what happens when someone like us loses control. I've seen the cost of it. Your control is just fine. Trust me.'

'I can't control the colour of my eyes,' Oliver said, turning away as he admitted the truth. The shame that came with that pressed on him like a weight.

'And?' Lance said, clearly wanting more.

'And that makes me weak,' Oliver said, turning back to Lance, who just stared at him.

'Since when?' Lance said. 'Your eyes changing doesn't tell me you've lost control. If anything, it tells me your wolf is paying more attention than you. Which is not something I find hard to believe.'

The backwards insult gave Oliver something to hold on to in the chaos in his head.

'Who told you—' Lance cut off before he finished. This time, it was Lance's eyes that changed, his wolf shining through. 'Your father? I think I like him even less than before, which is saying a lot. Trust me when I tell you this because I know. I've helped the police track Shifters who've lost themselves to the point they're little more than feral beasts. Your control is fine.'

Oliver let the silence hold between them, thinking. Everything he'd been told ran through his head. He was weak. He lacked control. How many times had his father told him that?

'Is Hale weak when his eyes change colour?' Lance asked, leaning forward in the seat. It creaked under the change in weight.

'No,' Oliver said, then froze. Stupid. He was so damned stupid. Why had he never questioned that?

'Your father's eyes changed more times than I could count while I argued with him,' Lance said. 'Humans fear the change. But those who are Shifters know that colour alone isn't a loss of control.'

'My father's eyes changed colour?' Oliver asked, rubbing his forehead when Lance nodded.

How many times had that happened and Oliver hadn't noticed? Was Lance right?

'All of this is moot. He's here to take me home. With the pack bonds half there still, I have to listen to him,' Oliver said, but he didn't look at Lance. Only an hour ago, Oliver had been so sure he was going to stay. But that was before his father had come to town. He'd been naïve earlier to think there would be any other choice but to go home. 'I'm not seeing I have many options other than to leave.'

Not leave mate, Thor said.

I was wrong to think I could keep her safe against my father, Oliver said. *I can't protect myself, let alone anyone else.*

Thor snarled, pacing. But he knew Oliver was right. They'd been naïve to think they could stay here with Staci.

'You always have options, Oliver,' Lance said, looking down at his hand, fingering the leather. 'What does he want from you?'

'He wants to know how the pack lands were created,' Oliver said. 'He thinks I know.' There wasn't any point in adding that he did.

'You should've told Hale.' Lance's voice didn't hold reproach, which was a surprise. 'He could have dealt with this.'

'I thought I could convince my father no one knew, but he grew impatient,' Oliver said. 'He called last night and said if I didn't give him an answer, I needed to come home. That if I didn't, he'd come and challenge Hale. I can't let him do that.'

'Hale doesn't need our protection,' Lance said. This time, there was amusement in his tone and scent. 'Especially not from your father.'

'You saw my father. His power? Even if Hale wins that fight, he'll end up at odds with the other prime alphas.' Oliver paused and looked away. 'I can't let that happen.'

'And your new pack? Staci?' Lance asked. 'What happens to them as you sacrifice yourself?'

Oliver started to deny that he had his own pack or Staci, but looking at Lance, it was obvious it wasn't him guessing; he was sure.

Lance alpha, too, Thor said, still pacing. *He help us fight?*

No one else could fight our father without starting a war, Oliver said. *And we would die if we tried alone.*

Oliver didn't want to die, but he had a fleeting moment of realisation that it would also protect everyone. His pack, Staci, Hale's secret.

Not leave mate alone, Thor said, swiping at him, making the pain sharper.

I didn't mean it, Oliver said, reaching out to his wolf, offering comfort. *We'll find a way to keep Hale's secret from him without it coming to that.*

But now he'd felt his father's psychic attack, he was less sure about how he'd be able to do that.

'Going home will protect everyone,' Oliver said. He had to believe that it would.

'Except you,' Lance said, leaning back. 'I think that's something Hale should have a say in. He shouldn't be much longer.'

Oliver stood, feeling the fatigue weigh him down immediately, but he needed to move. Hale would challenge David if it meant keeping even one person safe. It's what Oliver would do. If that happened, all the prime alphas would go after Hale.

'No. The best thing I could do for everyone is leave,' Oliver said.

Staci's sharp inhalation was Oliver's only warning that she was there. Her scent came a moment later, bringing the sharp sting of anger and pain. He spun to her, taking in her pale face and narrowed eyes.

'You're leaving?' she asked. She stood there frozen, waiting for him to answer. But he said nothing. He couldn't form the words.

He didn't want to leave her, but he didn't know how to tell her that without dragging her into his father's games. Thor raged at him, trying to force him to go to her. But he stayed where he was.

She shook her head, then turned and walked away, the scent of her pain and anger tearing at his nose.

'Staci, wait,' Oliver said, cursing as he followed her.

STACI'S HEART POUNDED IN her ears as she doubled back to the entrance. Stupid. She'd been so damned stupid. He was leaving. She'd known he would. None of the Shifters stayed longer than a year.

But he'd said he would stay. He'd lied to her.

She pushed open the front door and stepped out into the sunshine; it was humid and hot. There was no wind. No air at all. Or maybe that was just her.

After a few more steps, she stopped, realising Oliver was her way home. She couldn't catch her breath.

'Staci, please,' Oliver said, touching her arm. Bone-deep weariness filled her, along with a wave of fresh pain that went deeper than before. 'Tell me what happened with the council?'

She pulled her arm out of his grip, turning to face him, and that weariness faded under her anger. At least until she saw a graze down his cheek and blood on his shirt. Oliver was hurt.

'What happened?' she said, feeling cold. She almost reached out to him, wanting to help ease his pain, but she held herself still.

Mr Patterson came over from where he'd been standing beside his car, but he paused when he saw Oliver, like he wasn't sure if he should interfere or not.

'It's not important,' Oliver said, wiping his cheek with his muddy sleeve. 'I'm fine. What happened with the council?'

Clearly, he wasn't fine, and she wasn't important enough for him to tell her what happened—because he was leaving.

'I didn't get fired. Turns out the town likes me better than Elliot and his mother. Who knew?' Staci said. Something he'd have known if he had been there. The angry thought helped her keep her distance, even though he seemed to waver on his feet.

What had happened?

'That's good. I'm glad,' Oliver said, moving as if he wanted to reach out to her, then pulled back. If he wanted to do that, then why was he leaving?

'When were you going to tell me you're leaving?' Staci said, digging her fingernails into her palm. She wouldn't cry here. Not for him.

'It's not that simple,' Oliver said.

'Make it simple,' Staci demanded, but she got silence. She turned away, glad the council seemed to be gone already. The last thing she needed was Joyce and Elliot to still be here and see this. Seeing Staci in pain would have made Joyce's day.

'Let me take you home,' Oliver said.

Staci didn't want to be alone in the car with him. Hell, even out in this open car park, half of her wanted to close the gap between them and clean his cheek. How could she be so mad at him and still be worried that he was hurt?

'Is everything okay?' Mr Patterson said, stepping closer. Maybe Oliver wasn't her only way home.

'Mr Patterson, would you be so kind as to give me a lift home?'

She couldn't tell what her old teacher thought, but he nodded.

'I'm sorry, Staci,' Oliver said, his amber eyes intense on hers. But it wasn't enough. He'd clearly made his choice.

'Sorry doesn't fix the lie, though, does it?' Staci said, turning away from him and following Mr Patterson to his car.

'Staci, wait,' Oliver shouted after her, still not contradicting her statement. She ignored him.

She had to ignore him, even if her foolish heart wanted to stop and give him another chance to explain. But she'd given it to him, and he'd said nothing. He was leaving. Maybe not today, but soon. She wasn't going to wait for him to break her heart. No. She was going to do it all by herself. Because that's what walking away felt like. Being broken into a thousand tiny pieces.

Oliver didn't follow her this time. Mr Patterson opened the car and let her slide in. She didn't even have the spare energy to apologise for being damp and dirty.

The victory of the council was well and truly lost in the wake of everything with Oliver.

CHAPTER FIFTEEN

Mr Patterson let Staci travel in silence, for which she was grateful. She wasn't sure she would have been able to make conversation.

'Thank you, Mr Patterson,' Staci said as he pulled up outside her house.

'Call me Barry,' Mr Patterson said, giving her a smile. 'I'm not your teacher anymore.'

Staci nodded, moving to open the door, but Barry touched her arm, stopping her.

'You know that Shifters don't have the same freedom we have,' Barry said, frowning. 'They're bound to their pack and families in ways that are hard to understand. If Oliver is leaving, it might be he doesn't have a choice.'

'Then why not say that?' Staci said, turning to her house. 'He could have explained, and he chose not to tell me. Or even why his face was scratched.'

'Not everyone is as fortunate as you to have a family that cares about them,' Barry said, letting go of her arm. 'Give him some time to explain if he can.'

Staci nodded, though she was far from convinced. She was so tired she just wanted to be inside, sleep for a week, and forget she'd ever met Oliver.

Her street was no longer empty as she got out of the car. People were sweeping dead leaves from their gardens and asking their neighbours how their houses and families had weathered the storm. Staci hurried inside, not wanting to get caught in the conversation.

Florence appeared in the corridor like magic the moment she closed the front door. She took one look at Staci and opened her arms. The tears that Staci had been holding back started to flow as she stepped into Florence's embrace.

'What happened?' Florence said, tightening her grip around Staci.

'He's going to leave,' Staci said. Other words came, but even to her, they made no sense. It was like the pain wanted out. If she'd been alone, she might have screamed her rage.

It felt like it took a long time for the tears to stop. Eyes burning and throat aching, she pulled back from Florence. The woman who had been a second mother to her growing up looked down at Staci with so much warmth and patience that the tears almost started again.

'I know it hurts right now, but it will get easier,' Florence said, wiping away Staci's tears with her thumb.

'He's not even been in my life a day,' Staci said, voice harsh from crying. 'It shouldn't hurt this much.'

'Love is fickle like that,' Florence said, smiling, eyes growing distant. 'My husband and me were love at first sight. I could have lost him the next day and felt the pain as deeply as I did when I lost him five years ago.'

Staci wanted to argue that she didn't love Oliver. But she couldn't find the words and didn't want to hurt Florence by saying something careless. Just because Staci was in pain didn't mean she should drag Florence down with her. They had enough pain in their lives already.

'What happened with the council?' Florence asked.

'They fired Elliot,' Staci said, wishing she could feel that relief again, but everything just hurt too much as she gave Florence a shortened version of the meeting.

Part of Staci wanted to ask about her father, but she wasn't sure she could take any more blows today. Instead, she glanced towards the kitchen, searching for her mum.

'Your mum is napping,' Florence said, looking down at Staci's clothes, picking at the now grungy-looking T-shirt.

'Go shower. There's enough water in the tank for a quick one.'

A shower sounded good. Normal.

'I'll make some stew for when you're done. You must be starving after all that magic,' Florence said, giving Staci a little nudge towards the stairs when she didn't move on her own.

'I don't say this enough, Florence. But I don't know I could do this without you.' Staci's eyes stung with tears.

Florence's eyes shimmered with her own. 'Nor I without you. Now go before you make me weepy, too.'

Staci did as she was told, dragging herself upstairs a step at a time. Having something to do helped with the pain a little. It gave her something else to think about, at least for a little while.

OLIVER ESCAPED LANCE'S WATCHFUL eye with the excuse of cleaning up. The first place he'd found was the council building visitors' toilet. The room was cramped, with peach tiles and a tiny sink so close to the toilet that you almost needed to sit down to use it.

He splashed water on his face, making his cut sting. It did nothing to make him feel better.

The image on Staci's face as she left made his gut churn. He wanted to get in his car and race after her. Tell her he was stupid, that he wasn't going anywhere. But he'd made his choice.

Wrong choice, Thor snarled.

It's the best chance I have of protecting her, Oliver said, heart breaking all over again at the idea of life without her. But he had no choice if he wanted to protect her.

A mate was a weakness he couldn't afford going home. His father had leveraged his connection to family and friends more than once over the years. Staci would just give him more power.

Oliver needed to let go of all the links he had. He'd have to see Hale to do that, but not until it was time to go. Going by the fact his father was already here, that wasn't likely to be long.

But for now, Oliver needed to be on his own. Carefully, he built the wall that Hale had taught him. It was about as strong as a sandcastle; one strong wave would wash it away. But it helped to mute Hale from his mind. Hale let him.

Oliver pulled a handful of paper towels from the dispenser and carefully wiped his face. The blood and dirt were better, but he could do little about his pale, washed-out skin. Sighing, he threw the towels in the bin and left the bathroom.

Lance was propping up the wall outside, head tilted like he was listening to something. He turned to Oliver as the door closed.

'I'm going home,' Oliver said, sending images to his wolf of his small studio apartment as Thor got excited.

Not home, Thor said, angrily digging his claws in.

We need to gather what little shit we have and leave, Oliver said.

He didn't wait to give Lance a chance to argue as he turned towards the exit.

'At least wait until Hale gets here,' Lance said, grabbing Oliver's arm as they stepped into the sunshine.

'There isn't anything else to say. I'm going.' Oliver pulled himself free. Though, he only managed because Lance didn't try to hold him.

'Hale isn't going to just let David win. You know that,' Lance said.

'Hale said we all had a choice,' Oliver said, closing the distance to his car. 'I'm making mine.'

'You're making a stupid one,' Lance said. 'One you're going to regret.'

'I regret a lot of things. Protecting my pack and mate isn't on that list,' Oliver said, opening the car door, using it to support his weight as the half-lie registered. He did regret how he'd left things with Staci. He was definitely going to regret losing Amelia and Mitchel. But Hale would take care of them.

Lance held the door as Oliver climbed inside the soggy seats. The car smelled like Staci, adding to the pain.

'Tell Hale I'll come see him later,' Oliver said, gut tightening again. 'He can release the bonds and do everything that needs to be done, then.'

Thor snarled at the idea, digging his claws deeper. Oliver tried to soothe him, but it was impossible.

'He'll tell you the same thing as me. You don't need to do this,' Lance said.

'And if Hale challenges my father, or vice versa? It won't matter who wins or loses, the fallout will be massive,' Oliver said. Lance didn't have an argument for that. They both knew it was true.

Oliver pulled the door closed, not managing to say goodbye as he started the car and headed towards the exit. He probably should have. This was the last time he'd see Lance, and he owed him more than that after the last eight months. Something else he'd be able to regret later.

Stupid, Thor said, turning his back on Oliver. *You hurt us for nothing.*

Not nothing, Oliver said, tightening his grip on the steering wheel. *To protect others.*

Thor didn't answer this time, but he was still furious in the back of Oliver's mind.

Oliver lived near the middle of town in a studio flat on the top floor of a three-storey building. He parked in the small private area reserved for residents and got out. He still felt shaky and weak, but he refused to let it show as he locked the car, checking it was secure before heading inside.

Not home, Thor said, again showing him images of Staci and her small old-fashioned house.

Not an option, Oliver said as he unlocked the door to his flat.

He'd rented the place when he'd first come to town. It had just enough room for a bed, TV, a small kitchenette, sofa, and his weights that he'd tucked into the corner. The walls were white, the floor a basic wood vinyl, and the bathroom was a pale grey.

It looked sterile. The only piece that showed that someone lived here was his clothes thrown in the corner. This flat wasn't permanent. Something that had never bothered him before. Hell, he still had his suitcase on the floor in the corner rather than buying a set of drawers. At least that would make it easy to pack and leave.

A floor-length mirror hung on the wall opposite him. His eyes were amber. Shame rose, an old familiar feeling.

He wouldn't ever be good enough to meet his father's standards. He'd always be weak. Useless.

Not weak, Thor said, pacing in his head.

Oliver blinked at his reflection in the mirror. The amber didn't change back. It wouldn't, not until Thor backed off.

Lance said amber not bad, Thor said, replaying the conversation like Oliver might have forgotten it already. *We not dangerous. Not out of control. Lance good alpha. He knows.*

After so many years of being told the opposite, Oliver couldn't make his brain realign. But at the same time, despite the amber colour telling him otherwise, he didn't feel out of control.

Oliver closed his eyes, letting his wolf fill his mind. Thor wanted to run, shed their skin, and lose themselves in the woods. Then, go to Staci and curl up at her feet. Be home. The instinct was strong, but it wasn't uncontrollable. Hell, they mirrored his own desires for the most part.

But the first meant returning to the pack lands and dealing with Hale, and Oliver wasn't ready for that. And he doubted Staci would appreciate the second.

What if Lance was right? Had his father lied to him all these years?

Staci like our eyes too, Thor said, voice so quiet he almost missed it.

Another stab of pain hit him, and he turned away from the mirror, throwing himself onto the sofa. He needed to let her go. She'd be safer here because even if he wasn't weak or out of control, he still wasn't strong enough to fight his father.

Nor was he willing to let Hale do it for him.

Going home was his best choice, no matter how much it would hurt.

LANCE PACED THE CAR park. The pack bonds thrummed in his mind, not open exactly, but enough that he could feel Hale tugging on them for his location. He wanted to shut them down, but Hale wouldn't know where he was then.

At least the car park was almost empty. All the council that had been here were gone now, back to their lives, assessing the damage from the storm. If only his life was that simple.

Being a rift ranger here was supposed to be easy. A job. But it was quickly turning into something complicated.

Losing one family had been hard enough. He didn't want to lose another one.

Oliver not lost, Shade said.

It's not just him. First, Shane and Lacey betrayed us. Then Amelia almost died because of more traitors in the pack. Now Oliver is in danger, Lance said, very aware he was spiralling, but he couldn't do anything about it.

Coming here was supposed to mean no connections, and instead, Hale had made it into a real pack. Shifters were choosing to stay. Not many, not yet. But Hale was a good alpha. How much longer before the pack grew?

Peace. Calm, Shade said, pressing close.

Zoe was relying on him to teach her. But who was he to teach anyone? He couldn't even keep his own shit together.

'Lance?' Hale's voice was soft, and his presence a gentle brush against his senses.

Lance opened eyes that he'd not realised he'd closed. How long had Hale been here?

'It's okay,' Hale said. His hand was on Lance's arm. The one without scars. Warmth spread out from the touch, helping push the panic back a little further.

Shade spread that warmth deeper, taking the feel of pack and wrapping it around them. For the first time in a very long time, Lance didn't feel the loss of his family in that connection.

But it would only be temporary. Their problems couldn't be solved so easily.

'It's not okay,' Lance said.

Hale offered Lance a smile and backed off. He was good at that. Knowing when to step back and when to help. It was part of what had made him such a good alpha. It was also why Lance was still alive when that had never been his intention as he'd come to the Highland Rift Scar.

'Tell me what happened?' Hale asked. Just like that, they were back on topic, like Lance's minor breakdown hadn't happened. Yes, this was definitely why he'd survived here. He owed Hale a great deal.

Lance suppressed a growl as he gave Hale the quick version of what David had done and said, along with the deadline he'd given.

'What did Oliver say before he left?' Hale asked.

'Oliver said he's going to come see you soon,' Lance said, shaking his head. Oliver was going to sacrifice himself for nothing. 'Get you to let go of the pack bonds and give you his pack, I presume.'

Hale didn't react to the last part. Not that Lance had doubted he'd already known.

'David has a lot to answer for on how he's treated that kid,' Hale said, like he'd forgotten he was only a few years older than Oliver. 'He knew his son was an alpha and gave him no training. Then he sends him here because he followed his instinct and created a pack.'

Lance opened his mouth, then closed it with a snap. That was why Oliver had been sent here? Lance couldn't even imagine what his life would have been like if his father hadn't trained him to control his alpha instincts and magic. Especially doing the job he'd been doing.

'He's made Oliver believe that he's weak and broken,' Lance said at last. 'That he can't control his wolf. Not training him would reinforce that belief.'

'When I arrived here, I didn't like David. I like him even less the more I learn about him,' Hale said.

'Is that why you didn't join his pack?' Lance asked.

Hale looked at Lance, then away. For the most part, the two of their wolves got along, but with tensions running high, there was no need to push their luck. 'He wasn't strong enough to bring me into his pack.'

There was no boast in the words, just a simple fact. But it confirmed something Lance had already suspected. Hale could beat David if he wanted to.

'Why's David here now? What's changed?' Hale asked, pulling in a breath. There was still a faint hint of the man, but most of it had dissipated.

'He wants Oliver to tell him how the pack lands were created,' Lance said. It was a secret that Hale had been guarding heavily since Sam became his mate. But something had changed with Oliver recently. 'Does he know?'

'Yes,' Hale said, not giving away more than that.

Fortunately, he didn't need to. Lance had only ever seen one thing that could change the land like that. Earth Magic. Since Sam owned the land, it wasn't hard to guess that she was the source. Because of the way the government persecuted Earth Elementals, there was no way that Hale would let that knowledge out. It would mean that Sam would lose her land and be made to move every year.

But if Oliver told David, then the prime alphas would know. They'd have leverage against Hale. A way to change the pack to how it was before. As much as Lance didn't like the changes for himself, he knew they were better for the pack.

'What do we do now?'

'We go see Oliver, see if we can talk him round,' Hale said.

'I don't think it's going to be that easy,' Lance said. 'He was convinced that leaving was the only option. He's trying to protect you from a confrontation with his father.'

'David isn't going to challenge me,' Hale said, eyes flashing gold. 'He knows he'd lose, especially here. Now we just need to convince Oliver of that.'

It might not be possible, but Lance didn't say that. Hale was much better at these things than Lance was. Maybe he'd get Oliver to see reason.

OLIVER'S DAMP CLOTHES RUBBED, and he stank. He knew he should go get a shower but even the idea felt like too much effort. It wouldn't help him forget everything that had happened. Forget the hours spent with Staci under the storm.

A knock at his front door drew him out of his spiral of self-pity. The knock itself wasn't a surprise, but as Oliver forced himself to his feet, the scent he caught was.

Elliot. Along with a hint of his blood and desperation.

Despite the blood, Oliver hesitated. He didn't want to deal with anyone, especially not Elliot. But the blood might mean he was hurt and needed help.

He opened the door to find Elliot leaning against the door frame. His bandage was spotted red, and his nose was swollen, blood smeared across it from a split at the bridge.

'I'm sorry,' Elliot said, voice nasal because of the damage to his nose. 'I didn't want any of this.'

Oliver bit down on his first reaction. It wasn't helpful.

Not friend. Try to hurt mate, Thor said.

No. Not our friend. Maybe he'd never been our friend, Oliver said, tightening his grip on the door, feeling the wood start to cave.

'Which part? The bit where you tried to frame Staci for causing the storm?' Oliver said. 'Or the part where you ignored the storm in the first place?'

'It wasn't supposed to be like that,' Elliot said, looking up at Oliver. 'I swear. My mother just wanted me to stay full time. She just wanted them to lose confidence in Staci so I could be the only weather warden.'

'So you agreed to let the storm hit the town? There were people in its path, real lives you could have destroyed. For what? Being able to come home to your mummy?' Oliver said, voice low. Thor wanted to snarl at Elliot. Oliver wanted to finish the job on his nose. He did neither. 'What would you have done if someone had died?'

'No one died,' Elliot said. It wasn't lost on Oliver that Elliot didn't bother to deny any of the rest. He touched his nose, fingering it carefully.

'Why are you here, Elliot?' Oliver said, wanting nothing more than to slam the door shut and forget he'd ever met Elliot.

'Your father wants an answer,' Elliot said, using the bandage to wipe his nose.

'Why would my father ...' Oliver broke off, forcing himself to stay still. He thought about how his father had been waiting for him at the council car park. There was no reason for him to know Oliver would be there. Unless he hadn't been there for Oliver, he'd been waiting for Elliot.

How many times had he asked about the pack lands over the last few weeks? Oliver hadn't even thought anything of it. He'd just changed the subject and moved on. It was pack business, and Elliot wasn't pack.

'He gave my mum the leverage she needed to get me hired,' Elliot said, not looking at Oliver. 'It was a perfect deal. Your father just wanted a small piece of information. I would reach out and reconnect with you and get it.'

Oliver's gut sank further. He should have seen something sooner. Known something was wrong when Elliot asked those questions.

'I thought it would be easy. Get you drunk, and let you rant about how rubbish things were here in this crap job,' Elliot said, shaking his head. 'But you didn't hate it here.'

If Elliot had come two months ago, before everything had changed, his visit might have gone exactly like that. Things had been rough back then. One shift a month had been hard.

But why even bother with this game at all? It wasn't like he was a Shifter to need permission to come and go. 'Why not just come home on your own?'

Elliot laughed, shaking his head. 'The only thing I know how to do is control a storm. I deserve that after everything I've been through. That job should have been mine, not Staci's.'

'So everyone else has to suffer because you wanted something?' Oliver said. He realised he could have forgiven the lies and the need to come home. But not how Elliot treated Staci. Even if she hadn't been Oliver's mate, how Elliot tried to take away another person's freedom was unforgivable.

'I needed a job. Your father gave me a guarantee,' Elliot said.

'So what now? You didn't trick me into giving you the info he wanted, so you're going to ask me? Threaten me?' Oliver said, narrowing his eyes. Staci had won the council over, meaning Elliot was out of a job. Oliver's father couldn't help Elliot now. 'Why are you here?'

Elliot was silent so long that Oliver nearly slammed the door in his face. 'Your father took Staci. He wants you to meet him. He'll release her if you agree to go home with him and tell him the truth.'

Oliver froze, barely risking taking a breath. His father had Staci? No, she'd gone home. Mr Patterson had taken her home. 'Not possible.'

Protect mate, Thor snarled. *Not let anyone hurt her.*

'Your father said to tell you that her house is an old-fashioned detached two-storey building and that the inside could use an update,' Elliot said. There was nothing in his tone to say how he felt about what he was saying.

That was Staci's house. His father had been inside. She'd have welcomed him in, not knowing how dangerous he was because Oliver had been trying to protect her.

Find Staci, Thor said, growling, pressing so close that Oliver felt the need to shift to four paws. He pushed his wolf back. Four paws wouldn't help Staci. *Track. Find.*

Staci isn't pack. I don't know how to track her, Oliver said, feeling helpless.

Mate, Thor said, pulling at the wall he'd built. It was keeping everything out, though, not just Staci. If they let it go, his father would be able to shred him without any effort at all.

Elliot knows, Thor said, urging them to motion. His wolf was right. They didn't need to track her. Elliot was going to take him there.

'Where is she?' Oliver said, stepping closer to Elliot.

'I've got to drive you out there,' Elliot said, curling in on himself like he was expecting a blow. 'They said no pack.'

He didn't need to say the threat that implied. Oliver closed his walls a little tighter to make sure no hints of fear or anger escaped. He hadn't missed the usage of 'they'. This wasn't just Oliver's father; it was Joyce, too.

'If either of them hurt Staci, I'll make you regret you ever met me,' Oliver said.

Elliot flinched, looking away. 'They just want you to answer the question,' Elliot said, but he was trembling.

'Your mother just tried to have Staci removed as weather warden and failed,' Oliver said, voice still more wolf than human. 'Tell me, what do you think she'd do next to get what she wants?'

'She wouldn't hurt Staci,' Elliot said.

Oliver let the silence hold in the wake of that statement. He sounded like he believed it. 'Just a whole town filled with people. Those she was happy to murder?'

Elliot didn't answer as he turned away towards the stairs. He knew the risk of the storm. He knew what could have happened, probably more than most.

Oliver followed, forcing himself to breathe slowly. He should have given himself to his father in the car park. Then Staci would be safe. But he'd just wanted a bit more time with her.

Fight, Thor said. *Kill David.*

We're not strong enough to challenge him, Oliver said. *Besides, fighting him would still hurt Hale.*

Lance said we strong enough, Thor said, but he didn't say it like he believed it. *Join pack. Then challenge. If kill David when in his pack, not affect Hale.*

Oliver exhaled slowly as he considered what his wolf was suggesting. He still wasn't sure they could win a fight, but as part of the pack, the challenge was his right. Right now, his father was away from his power. He'd be weaker.

If win, Staci would be safe, Thor said.

If we win, everyone would be safe, Oliver said, though prime alpha wasn't a position he'd ever sought. And there was no guarantee the rest of the prime alphas would accept it either.

But he'd do it to protect Staci. Which only left one question. Was he strong enough to challenge his father in the first place?

It was a risk he might not have a choice but to take.

Chapter Sixteen

Lance let Hale drive. He'd taken his own car, an older model Ford Focus. He didn't need to look up directions, seeming to know where Oliver's place was.

'When Oliver came to town, I was worried about how he'd get on with the rest of the pack. Especially when it had been implied he had control issues,' Hale said, glancing at Lance like he'd sensed the question. 'It didn't take long to realise—like many of the others who'd been sent here—that wasn't his problem.'

'But you made sure you knew where he lived, just in case,' Lance said, shaking his head. Before Hale had found his mate, Lance had always assumed that Hale's closed pack bonds had meant he'd left most of the pack to take care of themselves. He'd certainly not interfered with anyone's business. But knowing how he'd helped Lance when he'd first come to town should have told him that wasn't true. 'And me? What did you hear about me when I arrived?'

Lance shut his mouth with a click. He shouldn't have asked. He didn't want to know the answer.

'That you were hurt soul-deep, and you needed time to heal,' Hale said, slowing as they pulled into a small car park in front of a block of flats. Oliver's borrowed Land Rover was parked in a space at the back.

'I shouldn't have ...' Lance cut off, unable to finish. He hadn't meant to start this conversation. But he didn't know how to get out of it.

'I learned where you lived, and I checked on you daily. Sometimes more than once a day. I paired you with people who understood your pain and knew how to keep you safe,' Hale said, leaning back in the seat to watch him. 'I gave you space because you needed it.'

Lance struggled to take a breath. He knew he'd only made it because of Hale. But there was so much more than just being there in that sentence. 'And now?'

'Now we're changing. You're changing.'

'That's why you assigned Zoe to me?' Lance said, realising finally why he'd asked. 'You wanted someone who wouldn't pressure her to be connected to the pack.'

Hale nodded.

We best teacher, Shade said. He was ridiculously pleased at Hale's words.

Hale is manipulating both of us, and Zoe, Lance said, though he couldn't find any anger for it.

'She doesn't trust me because she knows how much control I have over her.' He paused and looked up at the house. 'But she still needs to learn. You can help her do that. Help her trust herself. Be the person she can ask for help.'

'What if I can't be that person?' Lance asked, that fear choking him again.

'Then I wouldn't have paired you together,' Hale said, pushing open the door, letting in the humid air.

Lance wasn't fast enough to find his words after that statement.

Trusts us, Shade said, pressing close. *Is good thing.*

What if we fail?

Alpha trust us. Not fail, Shade said, then he shook out his fur and lay down. Settling to watch, leaving Lance with nothing to do but get out of the car and focus on why they were here.

He pulled in a deep breath, testing the air. Oliver had been through here, along with several people Lance didn't know. The scents were so layered that they became a giant mass. But over it, there was Elliot, who stood out because it was new.

Lance couldn't help his growl. 'Elliot was here.'

'Do you know how long ago?'

'Not without shifting,' Lance said, which wasn't possible here unless they wanted to be arrested. The law stopping Shifters from changing anywhere but pre-registered places might be being challenged in the court system, but it wouldn't get a result for years yet. 'There are too many other scents.'

'Let's go see Oliver,' Hale said, heading towards the door to the block of flats in front of him. 'If Elliot is there, we'll deal with him. Maybe he will volunteer an explanation.'

The last part wasn't so much a question as a statement. One that was practically a growl.

'Zoe is digging into Joyce's and Elliot's backgrounds. Hopefully, she can find something useful in their history that explains why they'd want to cause the storm.'

'Deliberately?' Hale asked as he entered the building. The entranceway walls were a pastel green, and the floor a pale grey linoleum. The building was three storeys high, and going by the numbers, each floor had four flats.

'Looks that way,' Lance said, filling Hale in on the rest he'd learned so far. Elliot's admission at the hospital. That he was Joyce's son. How they'd tried to get Staci fired and blame her for the storm.

'You're sure Joyce said pack, not rangers?' Hale asked as they reached the top floor. 'She hasn't exactly liked the pack, but we've never been actively at odds with her.'

'I'm sure,' Lance said. 'She was furious that I was talking to Elliot.'

'She'll be even less happy knowing that the council sided with Staci over her son,' Hale said. 'If she wasn't angry with us before, she will be now.'

Lance didn't answer. They were close enough that Oliver would hear them now if they kept talking. By the time they reached the top landing, the scents had thinned out, and Lance could pick up a hint of Elliot's blood. But that didn't say much. It could've been from the scratch on Elliot's arm.

Oliver's door was the furthest from the stairs and done in an off-white. Hale moved to knock, though Oliver would already know they were there. The door swung open on its own at the pressure. It hadn't been shut properly.

Lance followed Hale inside, searching for Oliver. But there was no sign of him and nowhere for him to hide in the open studio apartment. Not even with the mess.

'Oliver wouldn't just leave his flat open,' Hale said as he pulled out his phone and dialled Oliver's number. A ringtone blared from the small sofa. Making Hale curse. 'His father wasn't here. We'd have scented him.'

'The only scent I recognise is Elliot,' Lance said.

'Are there any connections between David and Elliot?' Hale asked.

'Not that Zoe has found, but she wouldn't have been looking at that angle,' Lance said.

'Get her to,' Hale said. 'This all feels like we're missing something. Like we're only seeing half the picture.'

Lance did as Hale asked, sending a message to Zoe to search for the extra connections.

Hale doubled over, grunting in pain like he'd been struck. His wolf spread out from him in a violent, angry wave.

'Oliver,' Hale gasped, falling onto one knee.

Lance cursed, kneeling with Hale as his anger swarmed around them. Shade added to the power. They might not know what had happened, but someone was hurting their pack, and they'd do whatever they could to protect it.

Oliver pulled in the scents around him. Pine trees, wet earth, heather, wildflowers, and woodland animals. No scent of his father or Staci.

They'd driven about twenty minutes outside Huntly and parked in a lay-by used by the forestry to get in and cut the trees. From there, Elliot had led him through a cramped animal trail with no sight or scent of anything but the animals who used it and an older scent from Elliot. The storm had hit the old forest hard. The ground was littered with branches and uprooted trees.

Shift, Thor said, pressing for four legs and more speed.

It was tempting, even knowing the risk of what would happen if he was caught. It would be easier to run through the unfamiliar woods on four paws. But even if it wasn't illegal, it would take too long to shift, and if Staci was hurt, he'd need hands. His wolf backed off at the logic, letting Oliver keep control.

He started to ask how much longer they had to go, but the wind changed direction. He got a face full of Elliot's sweat, but there was a hint of Joyce's awful perfume under it. They were close.

We need to let Amelia and Mitchel go, Oliver said. The longer they left it, the harder it would be.

No, Thor said. *Will not give up pack. Will not abandon them.*

If we still have them when my father pulls us into the pack, we'll lose them anyway, Oliver said.

No, will hide them where he can't see.

And if we lose?

Not lose. Best hunter. Lance said so.

That's not what Lance had said, but Oliver didn't let his wolf catch that thought. If he was confident, then that was good.

I don't like putting them at risk, Oliver said at last.

Then we kill David fast, Thor said.

They passed under a small, overturned birch tree. The silvery trunk was at an angle over the path, roots half torn out. Just past it, the woods opened up into a clearing.

Oliver saw his father first. He'd removed his jacket since Oliver had last seen him, and he stood in the middle of the clearing with his arms crossed. Joyce was beside him, wearing a peach dress suit, hair pulled back in a severe bun.

'Where's Staci,' Oliver asked. Not giving either a chance to speak.

'You don't get to question me, boy,' his father said, stepping towards Oliver.

Instinct told him to back away, to run. His memories told him that running would hurt worse in the end. But both were buried under a new desire. One that went against his own preservation. To protect Staci.

'You let Staci go—unhurt—and I'll give you what you want,' Oliver said, lifting his chin.

His father curled his lip, stepping forward. 'You'll give me what I want either way.'

Oliver saw the blow coming this time, but he let it land. Pain lanced up his jaw and cheek as he landed in the damp pine needles. Blood filled his mouth, and he spat it out.

Pushing back to his knees, Oliver looked up at his father. His power spread around him, clawing at him, trying to find a way in. The attack earlier was a feather's touch in comparison to this.

'You're mine,' his father said, putting his hand in Oliver's hair and pulling his head back at an uncomfortable angle.

The pressure doubled until it was like the heat of a furnace that rose around him. There was no way to accept him or to step away from Hale. There was just pain and an attack.

'It's time for you to come home.'

The power ripped at the walls he'd built around himself. With Staci earlier, he'd chosen to drop them, but not here. It hurt. Burned like there was a fire in his blood, scalding him from the inside out.

That link to his father flared into life like it had always been there waiting. The anger, the disappointment. The toxic weight of the past. How could he have forgotten how this had felt? How bad?

His connection to Hale wavered against the pressure. Despite his decision to submit, Oliver tried to hold on to it out of desperation. It was the only sliver of light in the darkness. But it was slipping away, and Oliver couldn't do anything to stop it.

Hale flared in his mind, trying to hold on, offering him strength. But it only made the pain worse.

'Stop resisting me, boy,' his father said, tightening his grip. 'You're mine.'

Hale hesitated at the pain the fight was causing. That hesitation was enough. The link between them snapped. Oliver screamed, collapsing down on the ground.

There was only his father and his pleasure at winning in Oliver's head. No more Hale.

Oliver's stomach twisted, bile eating its way up his throat. But he couldn't afford to throw up. Not at this angle. He'd choke to death.

In his mind, Thor tried to shield them, but his father's wolf snarled, pinning Oliver's wolf, dragging him down, teeth ripping into his neck. Thor didn't try to fight, but his father's wolf didn't stop or let go.

Oliver searched for his links to Amelia and Mitchel but couldn't feel them. Hopefully, they were just buried in his mind, safe. Though for how long, he didn't know.

'Hale thinks he's so much better than the rest of us,' his father said, coming closer. Oliver couldn't make his eyes open to watch. 'But he couldn't even keep a hold of one of his own pack.'

Oliver struggled to take a full breath. Hale had let go because he hadn't wanted to hurt Oliver, but it was doubtful his father would care even if Oliver could pull in enough air to tell him.

'You have what you want,' Joyce said, voice distant. 'Now it's my turn.'

Oliver struggled to open his eyes and sit up. It took two attempts as he nearly threw up. This wasn't going to plan. How were they supposed to challenge his father if he couldn't even get to his feet?

'Yes, yes,' his father said, standing and turning away. 'Evidence that Elliot left town before the next storm hits will be sent once I return home.'

'That wasn't the deal,' Joyce said.

'I can't exactly give you what you want from the arse end of nowhere, can I?' his father said.

Oliver tried to tune them out, searching the clearing for Staci. But he couldn't smell or see her? Where the hell was she?

'Where's Staci?' Oliver asked, forcing the words out.

His father spun, turning that snarl on Oliver as his father's wolf pressed harder on Thor. It hurt; hell, just breathing hurt.

'You have what you want. Let her go,' Oliver said.

'Stupid boy. Does it look like she's here?' Joyce said, shaking her head. 'We don't need her here. We need her nice and comfortable while the storm grows so big that it will destroy her as she tries to stop it.'

Oliver shook his head. She wasn't here. But she wasn't safe either.

'Start the storm,' Joyce said, turning to Elliot. 'This time, don't hold it back. Feed it and send it straight towards Huntly. They'll beg us to come up and clean up the mess then.'

Elliot glanced at Oliver, a tiny flicker of uncertainty, but then Elliot straightened his shoulders and turned away, back to his mum. He'd made his choice. A storm like that would tear the town apart. People would die. Elliot was going to let it happen.

His father filled his vision, blocking out the other two as he grabbed Oliver's hair again, tugging his neck so far back that only the grip kept him upright.

'Tell me how the pack lands were created,' his father said.

The need to comply slithered through Oliver. With his father's wolf still at Thor's throat, it would have been easy to give his father what he wanted.

'I don't know,' Oliver said, struggling to catch a breath. Trying to make the lie believable.

His father cursed and threw him to the ground, then kicked him in the ribs hard enough that something cracked. Oliver screamed.

'You always did enjoy the pain, Oliver,' his father said, standing over him. 'You must have, or you'd have learned your lessons better than that. Never lie to me.'

Oliver couldn't take a full breath as his father kicked him again. Lower this time, so nothing broke. Or at least if it did, he couldn't hear it.

'Tell me the truth, how do the pack lands feel alive?' his father said.

Oliver screamed as his father pressed on him with all the power he'd used earlier. Only this time, there was no link to Hale to shield him.

LANCE CAUGHT HALE AS he sagged, pain lacing his scent and the power that spilt out around them.

'What happened?' Lance asked.

'David ripped Oliver from the pack. I couldn't hold on without hurting him,' Hale said, shuddering as he pulled back the energy until Lance could only just feel Hale again. 'It shouldn't have been possible for him to do it like this.'

'His father was using his old family link to control Oliver earlier.' Lance pushed Shade down as his anger grew at the memory.

'Something else we'll need to fix to protect the rest of the pack. Bloody Shane. His legacy just keeps on giving,' Hale said as he pulled back, breathing still uneven. 'We need to find Oliver. I don't have any way to track him now. He's no longer pack.'

'David wouldn't be stupid enough to attack Oliver in town again. He wouldn't have backed off when I arrived earlier if he was. He's afraid of you,' Lance said. Not that it really helped. There was a lot of land around Huntly where David could have gone. 'Was there anything before the link cut?'

'Oliver had locked the pack bond down until David attacked him. After that, he was in too much pain to do anything. There wasn't enough to tell me where he was,' Hale said, straightening a little more, breath coming more slowly.

There was someone who would still be able to track Oliver. If Lance could convince her that Oliver was an idiot and hadn't meant to walk away.

Will help, Shade said, *is mate.*

Sometimes anger can make people do stupid things, Lance said. But in the end, she might have been angry, but she hadn't known the whole story. Maybe if she did, she'd help Oliver.

'Staci will be able to find him,' Lance said.

Hale raised an eyebrow, quickly picking up on what Lance meant. 'Another one? You're sure?'

Lance nodded. 'My wolf is, and I trust him.'

'Three mates in nearly as many months,' Hale said, closing his eyes. 'I've not even heard of that many in one place ever.'

'Yeah. Though Staci might not be all that happy with Oliver right now,' Lance said.

'He told her he's leaving?' Hale guessed.

'He failed to answer her question when she asked. Then, he didn't explain. Easier to walk away from someone who's mad at you,' Lance said. 'Is there anyone who knows her well enough to ask her for help?'

'Most rangers know her by sight, but little more,' Hale said, then hesitated. 'Sam and her are similar ages. They grew up together, though they aren't close.'

'Where is she now?' They'd lose an hour if they had to go to Sam's house to get her.

'She went to ranger headquarters to check on the equipment. Make sure nothing was damaged in the storm,' Hale said, jaw muscle working. Obviously, he didn't want to involve her, but they might not have another choice. He pulled out his phone.

'Having another mate explain to Staci what the link between her and Oliver is might help. Sam could explain how to use it to track Oliver,' Lance said.

'If Oliver hasn't told Staci that she's his mate, then this could get very complicated,' Hale said as he dialled.

Lance grunted. Somehow, he suspected that no matter what they did, it would be complicated, but it would be worth it to rescue Oliver.

STACI SHOWERED FOR AS long as she had hot water. Clean and dry and still feeling fragile, it would have been easy to pull on her PJs and just slob on the couch, but she was too restless to be that still. Besides, she still needed to get her car and phone from the rangers' headquarters.

She dragged on a pair of light blue jeans and a grey T-shirt. Then, she braided her hair into a French pleat to keep it out of the way. She was done with it being in her face today.

But rather than going downstairs, she dithered. Tidying away shit that didn't matter. Cleaning the bathroom, though Florence had already ensured it stayed spotless. Anything to avoid going downstairs and explaining what had happened to Florence.

She wanted to forget Oliver and their day together. But ever since she'd finished getting dressed, it was like he was there in the back of her mind. She could turn in a circle, and there he'd be, far away, but in that direction. Which was stupid. She needed to get used to him not being around again. He was leaving. Going home to his family. He was going to forget about her soon enough.

Just like her mother was.

Staci turned towards her mum's room. How much longer did they have? Not long enough.

Then, without her mum to care for, Florence would go back to her life. They'd see each other less, too. Staci would be alone in this house.

Stop it, they aren't gone yet, Staci thought to herself. She wasn't alone. Straightening her shoulders, she finally braved leaving her room. She'd wasted enough time already.

The scent of stew filled the house when Staci opened her door. The hunger she'd not noticed before flared into life, making her stomach growl as she went downstairs.

The old house held so many memories. Childhood games, playing with her mother because none of the other kids' parents would let them play with an Elemental. Maybe Joyce had done the right thing by sending Elliot away. Maybe he had kids like him around as he grew up. She wasn't about to ask him either way.

Florence sat at the kitchen table, humming. She had a small embroidery ring in her hands, the stitches tight and brightly coloured. She looked up at Staci, gave her a bright smile, and immediately put the ring on the table.

'Sit,' Florence said. 'I'll bring you some stew.'

Staci did as she was told. When Florence used that tone, there was no arguing with her. Florence dished up a large bowl of the spicy-smelling stew and put it in front of Staci.

'Thank you,' Staci said, throat tight.

'I'm always here if you need me, Staci,' Florence said, wiping a tear that had escaped. 'Now. After. Always.'

Staci nodded, not trusting her voice as she picked up her spoon. The stew was as spicy as it smelled. Ginger and peppers flooded her taste buds, making her hunger jump further into focus.

She'd nearly inhaled half the bowl when someone knocked at the door.

'You eat, I'll answer that,' Florence said, standing. Staci opened her mouth to argue. 'If they're looking for you, it can wait until you've finished eating.'

Staci put another spoonful into her mouth, and Florence turned to the door. Another knock came, more urgent this time. Their neighbours were rarely that impolite.

It wasn't Oliver, though how she was so sure, Staci didn't know. But with the issues with the council resolved, who else would be calling on her?

Florence's voice was quiet, as were the replies. Staci couldn't make out words or even the gender of the visitors.

The silence was followed by the closing of the door and more than one set of footsteps coming towards the kitchen.

'Staci, they'd like a word,' Florence said, lips thin as she looked behind her. 'They say it's urgent.'

Three people stepped into the kitchen after Florence. Lance was still wearing the same gear from earlier. He leaned against the door frame, giving her a quick nod. Hale took up position on the opposite side. In casual jeans, he could have passed as a university student, except for his expression. But Staci had seen the other side of Hale before, the power that made him alpha.

Seeing the two men wasn't exactly a surprise after everything that had happened today with Elliot, but the third person was unexpected. Sam looked tiny, standing between the other two. But she didn't work for the rangers even if she was now dating Hale.

Staci put her spoon down, stomach twisting. She was starting to regret the speed at which she'd eaten the stew.

'Hey, Staci,' Sam said, moving to take the seat at the table next to her. 'How're you doing?'

'What's wrong?' Staci asked, ignoring the question. She was tired and hurt. She didn't want to play any more games. 'And before you start with more politeness, know that I've had a shit day. You've never visited my house before, let alone with rangers. Tell me what's wrong.'

Sam glanced at Hale. He nodded, and Sam turned back to Staci.

'Oliver is missing,' Sam said.

Staci's heart stopped. Her chest compressed so tight she couldn't get a full breath. Missing. Not left. Florence's hand settled on Staci's shoulder. The connection helped Staci take a breath at last.

'We think his father took him, and we want to get him back,' Sam said when the silence drew on.

'Why do you think he was taken?' Staci asked, looking from Sam to Lance. 'You were there. Oliver said he was leaving.'

'It's not that simple,' Lance said. 'Oliver doesn't want to go home. He doesn't want to leave you or the pack.'

Staci felt dizzy, replaying the conversation with Oliver in her head. He'd refused to answer her. Refused to explain why his face was grazed. What was it he'd said to Lance?

'The best thing I could do for everyone is leave.'

He'd not said he'd wanted to leave. Why hadn't he corrected her? Why let her think he was choosing to leave after everything they'd been through? Her stomach sank. So she wouldn't try to convince him there was another way. So she'd be mad at him.

'Bloody Oliver,' Staci said, looking away from Lance.

'Oliver was going to see Hale, have him release the pack bonds. But now Oliver is missing, and the bonds have been severed by force,' Lance said.

'I don't care if Shifters have their own rules they follow or not. That's kidnapping,' Florence said, tightening her grip on Staci's shoulder. 'You should be calling the police.'

'The police won't help,' Lance said. 'They never help with any personal matter involving Elementals or Shifters. Unless a human is involved too.'

Florence didn't argue; she couldn't. Lance was right. Staci put her hand on top of Florence's, in part for her own comfort. A lot about being Rift Bloodlines wasn't fair or equal. Some she understood. But this?

'Why are you here rather than looking for him?' Staci asked, turning back to Sam. She'd clearly been designated to explain because she was the only one sitting.

'Wolves—or maybe all Rift Bloodlines, who knows—can create a connection to a person. We call it a mate bond,' Sam said, looking at Hale for a moment. Something unspoken passed between them. Then Sam faced Staci again. 'We think that you have this connection to Oliver.'

'There's no magic between me and Oliver,' Staci said. But as she finished, she realised that wasn't exactly true. There had been something different between them after the shelter. But that had been Staci's magic, not a mate bond?

'Did you dream together?' Sam asked, leaning forward on the table.

Staci fought her blush at the memory. It was hazy now, but she remembered them in the grass, naked with the sunlight on their skin. It had felt so good, like they'd been connected, and the sex had been a combination of their physical bodies, dream bodies, and an echo of what Oliver had felt. Then, later, he'd stood beside her to watch the lightning fall. He'd told her something that Mr Patterson had later repeated. Something she couldn't have known.

Not wanting to reveal the details and not trusting her voice, Staci nodded.

'For me, when the connection to Hale was first created, I could feel where he was. Like he was my north on a compass.'

Staci turned away from Sam, searching. That link she'd felt earlier to Oliver. The one she'd been trying to ignore.

'You feel it?' Sam asked.

'Yes,' Staci whispered. She couldn't feel anything past a direction. Was he okay? 'What does his father want?'

'To punish me,' Hale said, speaking for the first time. His anger was so intense that she could nearly feel the weight of it. 'I changed the pack, allowed Shifters to stay if they want. Gave them land to change on and be their wolves for more than one day a month.'

'That all sounds like a good thing,' Staci said, though she knew very little about the Shifters.

'It's complicated,' Hale said. Which was clearly short for *I'm not going to talk about it.*

'It's a good thing,' Sam said, giving Hale an annoyed look. 'Shifters might want to stay rather than go home.

This would become a permanent pack rather than a transient one.'

'Oliver could stay?' Staci said, knowing there was more to the words than just that, something harsher. Otherwise, Hale wouldn't have avoided it. But she wanted to be selfish for once.

Sam nodded. 'If he wanted to.'

'He wants to,' Lance said, drawing Staci's focus again. 'He was trying to keep you safe.'

'You want me to track Oliver?'

'We think you're the only one who can,' Sam said. 'I can help show you what I know about my bond.'

Staci looked up at Florence. 'I'll take care of your mother, child. You go help your man.' Florence squeezed Staci's shoulder, then let go and added, 'Then give him a slap for worrying you.'

A smile rose despite the fear churning in Staci's gut. She stood. 'Thank you.'

As Staci followed the others out, she realised there was one thing no one had said, and she couldn't bring herself to ask. What was Oliver's father doing to him? She'd seen how Oliver had been hunched over like he was in pain and the scratches on his face, seen them and ignored them because he'd refused to tell her what had caused them.

She searched that tug towards Oliver. She wished it told her something about whether he was okay. But if she could feel him, he was alive. That meant she could help him.

Chapter Seventeen

The pain was never-ending. The question came over and over. *How had the pack lands been created? How did they feel alive?* Each time it was asked, power lashed at Oliver, adding a new wound to the rest.

Oliver said nothing.

The magic buried deeper, searching for a way to force him to answer. But all it could do was make him feel pain, and Oliver had lived with pain for a long time. He knew how to deal with that.

Ironically, he had his father to thank for that. Years of abuse had taught him well. How to continue even when everything ached. How to hide how bad the wounds were.

Stronger than him, Thor whispered. He was still on his side, their father's wolf's teeth in his neck.

But they couldn't keep accepting the pain forever. There'd come a point where even they would break.

Then we fight, Thor whispered.

How they'd have the strength after this, Oliver didn't know. But he let his wolf have his hope.

Another wave of pain burst through Oliver's wrist, bones crunching together. Old memories rose of his wrist breaking as his father had forced him to shift with it pinned. But there was no demand to shift because a wolf couldn't give his father the answer he needed.

'Answer me!' his father shouted, adding more weight to his wrist.

Oliver screamed, unable to help himself as the bone snapped. But he didn't answer the question.

Without warning, the pressure of the magic lifted and was gone. The pain didn't go with it. If anything, he felt more raw without the weight of the magic against him. Physical aches joined the psychic ones until he almost vomited.

He lay shuddering in the pine needles, skin slick with sweat. He felt like he was on fire, burning from the inside out. Part of him knew he needed to move, to get up. But he could barely draw a breath. This stink of his own sweat and pain overpowered even the pine needles under him.

'You've always been a spoiled brat,' his father said, voice moving away from him. 'I wasted years trying to teach you better, and this is the thanks I get? Lies? Silence?'

His father's wolf let Thor go, stalking back a few paces. Oliver could feel Thor's blood, hot and wet in his fur, coating his neck. Thor moved to lie on his belly, crouched, watching for another attack. Their father's wolf watched them just as closely.

Oliver forced his eyes open so he could see his father. It took two attempts to clear his crusty eyes before he could see the clearing again. His father had crossed the length of it and now sat on a fallen trunk, older than the fresh storm damage. Elliot was kneeling on the far side of the clearing, eyes closed. Tiny gusts of wind caught his clothes, but the rest of the clearing seemed calm.

'I should have done more when you were a child,' his father said, shaking his head like he was disappointed. 'Maybe then you'd have learned better.'

Laughter bubbled up in Oliver's gut, and he couldn't help as it escaped. It had no real amusement, and the pain that came with it didn't make it worth it.

'You think you didn't hurt me enough?' Oliver asked when he could breathe again.

His father moved to his feet, rage turning his face pink. Being questioned and laughed at were both triggers for the man.

'How much longer is this going to take?' Joyce asked. She didn't look at all concerned that Oliver was being hurt.

'It will take as long as it takes,' his father said, turning away from Oliver.

Oliver released a breath. He'd not meant to start another fight. He needed time to recover first.

'At some point, that stupid girl is going to sense this storm. I'd rather be gone before then,' Joyce said.

'If Staci does appear, I'll deal with her,' his father said.

Oliver growled, forgetting about recovery. Forgetting about everything but the threat to his mate.

'You don't get to touch her,' Oliver said, forcing himself to his knees. He had to hold his breath against the pain to stop himself from screaming. He clasped his broken wrist close to his body, using it to shield his ribs, and then stood.

'You don't tell me what to do, boy,' his father said, turning back to Oliver.

Oliver looked down, not up to look into his father's eyes. 'I won't let you hurt her.'

His father snarled, stepping forward, hand raised. But this time, Oliver didn't react. His father faltered, stopping three feet away.

The shock nearly made Oliver lose his balance. He finally saw what Lance had. Age had crept in, and grey now streaked his father's hair. Those muscular arms that had once been heavy and bursting out of shirts didn't fill the material. His forehead was furrowed with lines, and his eyes sunken.

He looked so different from Oliver's memories that he thought for a moment his father must have been sick. How long ago had that happened? Months? No, years. Filtering through his memories, he saw the changes now he looked for them. This wasn't the strength of Oliver's childhood.

Thor rose close to the surface, pressing against Oliver, giving him strength. *We fight.*

'Control yourself, boy,' his father said. 'You shame yourself by showing your wolf.'

'No,' Oliver said, too angry to care that his eyes were the wrong colour. Right now, he wanted Thor right where he was.

His father's eyes widened, and he rocked back a step like Oliver had struck him. The balance had changed, and now Oliver was stronger. His father knew it. His father's wolf backed off like he had sensed the change too.

'Do as I tell you, boy,' his father said, but there was hesitation there this time.

Oliver straightened, no longer afraid, at least not for himself. He could fight his father if he had to. He might even win. But he had to protect Staci first. That was why he'd come here.

'Make Elliot stop creating the storm,' Oliver said.

'Tell me how they made the pack lands feel alive, and it will all go away,' his father said.

'No,' Joyce said, stepping closer. 'That isn't the deal.'

'Shut up, Joyce,' his father said, snarling, eyes flashing to amber. Just like he'd always told Oliver was a sign of losing control.

How had Oliver missed it all these years? How many times had he seen his father's wolf like this? A flash here or there as the anger got the better of him. Yet Oliver had accepted it.

His father started to raise his power again. His wolf crouched lower, ready to lunge. Thor stood, no longer willing to submit.

We not weak, Thor said.

No, Oliver said, rolling his shoulders, testing his range of movement. *No, we're not weak. We were never weak. But I don't know we're strong enough to fight them like this.* Not physically or psychically, not after what his father had done.

Attacking us cost him, Thor said, shaking out his coat. *Scent weakness.*

Oliver pulled in a breath, searching for what Thor had seen. Pine trees, fresh dirt, rain, and wildflowers. Over it all was pain and blood, all Oliver's. He almost didn't look past it, but the wind changed, and a new scent registered.

Bitter and sweet at the same time. Pain and weariness. It was coming from his father. His exhaustion. That's why he'd stopped. Oliver had forced him to go to his limits.

'Answer the damned question, boy,' his father said, eyes changing to amber.

The change made Oliver flinch. 'Your wolf is showing.'

His father snarled at him, showing teeth like he was already half wolf. 'I'm not weak like you are.'

'Control your son, David,' Joyce said, finally starting to sound uncertain. Oliver took far more pleasure than he should have at the sight of it. 'He's already caused enough problems.'

David snarled, stepping forward. 'My son? Your son fucked up the entire plan because he couldn't keep one damned storm going.'

'If your son hadn't dragged Elliot into the Rift, none of this would have happened,' Joyce said. 'Staci would have gone out there with the rangers and failed to stop it. Then, I'd have been able to convince the town of the truth. That she's useless. Instead, they now believe she's indispensable.'

'I don't care about that stupid bitch,' David said. 'You said your son could level the damned town.'

'You wanted to hurt Huntly?' Oliver asked, turning to Elliot. He still sat quietly, eyes closed. This had always been Elliot's plan. To destroy the town. But why?

'The mayor was told to say no,' his father said, turning away from Joyce with a snarl. She stepped away while he wasn't watching. Putting space between them. 'But he had to give Hale what he wanted. There should never have been any lands for the pack to shift whenever they wanted.'

'So you attacked Huntly because they did what the prime alphas should have done years ago?' Oliver said.

Power lashed out, slashing at Oliver without warning. But this time, he didn't accept the pain. He fought it. His wolf did ... something. It happened so fast that Oliver couldn't follow it, and the power slid away from them.

His father grunted and flinched back from them, stumbling into the log.

'I'm done playing games,' Oliver said again, taking a step towards his father. It hurt, but he refused to show his pain.

His father growled, forcing himself back to standing. Oliver didn't want to fight. He still wasn't sure he was physically strong enough with his broken wrist and ribs. But he'd do it to find Staci.

'If I can't control you, then I have other ways to make you talk,' his father said as he pulled out something from his pocket. Light flashed off the surface as he drew it up higher. Gun. 'Tell me how Hale made the pack lands feel alive?'

Oliver snarled but didn't move. For his father to have brought a gun, he must have known Oliver was stronger. He'd known that this was how it would go.

'No,' Oliver said. The word came easily this time, with no pressure weighing him down to answer.

His father pulled the trigger too fast for Oliver to move. The bullet bit deep, dragging a scream from him.

STACI NEARLY TRIPPED OVER another root as she followed Lance and Hale down a narrow path through the woods. The sun was starting to set, and the shadow of the trees was making the footing harder, at least for her. Hale and Lance seemed to have no problems.

Sam followed behind—much to Hale's annoyance. He'd wanted her to stay in the car when they'd parked in a lay-by, or better yet, take the car and drive home. But Sam wasn't about to let anyone tell her what to do. It was one of the things Staci had always liked about her, though they never really spent a lot of time together.

'Is this still the right direction?' Hale asked as they moved into a slightly wider path, letting them walk two abreast.

Staci concentrated, feeling the link like it was a magnet drawing her forward. 'Yes.' She wished she could feel more than just a direction. Then maybe some of the twisting in her gut would ease. Though she doubted anything would help until she saw him for herself.

'We're going to find him,' Sam said, moving close enough to put her hand on Staci's shoulder.

Staci nodded, though the words did little to ease the twist in her gut that said they were too slow.

'And the storm?' Hale asked, glancing at Staci. He'd not asked her if she was sure about the storm. He'd just accepted that she was telling the truth when she'd told him about it.

Staci changed her focus to the storm. Its pieces were growing too fast to be natural. Yesterday, she would have said it wasn't possible. Today, she'd learned a lot. Every one of her instincts told her to stop and rip the storm apart, but if she did that, they'd take longer to find Oliver.

'Yes,' Staci said, frowning as Hale and Lance exchanged a look. 'Why?'

'Elliot was at Oliver's house just before he went missing,' Hale said after a moment of hesitation.

Staci missed a step; only Sam kept her from falling into the damp mud. 'Elliot is his friend. Why would he do something that would hurt Oliver?' Except even as she thought it, she realised Oliver had stood by her. That would have felt like a betrayal if Elliot had found out.

'Elliot clearly only cares about himself. If hurting Oliver got him what he wanted, I wouldn't put it past him to do it,' Lance said.

It was good to know she wasn't the only one who saw the real Elliot. 'But what does he get?' Staci said, holding onto the link to Oliver in her mind like it could help ease the fear.

'Elliot was upset that you'd stopped the storm,' Lance said, holding aside a branch so the rest of them could pass through, then he moved back to the front. 'And now another one is forming. Whatever he wanted, he didn't get it the first time, and it feels like he's trying again.'

She almost said she hadn't done anything to the storm, but she stopped herself. He was the third person to tell her that.

'Doesn't Joyce own a construction company?' Sam asked.

Hale and Lance stopped, turning to stare at Sam.

'What?' Hale asked. 'Since when?'

'Always,' Staci said, looking at Sam, who nodded in agreement. 'Her family has run it for generations, right back to the repairs after the Fae War; they built their brand on it and are still used by the council today. I think Joyce's uncle runs it, but she's part of the business.'

'Is the company struggling?' Hale asked.

Staci felt sick even thinking about the direction in which Hale was going. She glanced at Sam, who shrugged. 'I don't know.'

'I'll get Zoe to check,' Lance said, pulling out his phone.

'Joyce is pretty cold, but surely she wouldn't put the town at risk just to make a bit of money,' Sam said, but no one responded.

Sadly, Staci could see Joyce doing something just like that. With a son who could make a storm at will, she'd be able to target people. Worse, no one would have known better because that wasn't how Storm Magic worked. They'd have blamed it on wild storms and thanked Elliot for limiting the damage. Which was why they'd been so desperate to get rid of Staci.

They continued silently for a few minutes when a sharp crack echoed through the woods. Staci froze, searching for the source.

'Stay here,' Hale shouted as he and Lance bolted.

'Was that a gun?' Staci asked, her hand on a tree as she watched the two men disappear. She turned to Sam, who'd gone pale. She drew level with Staci, balancing on the balls of her feet.

'Yes,' Sam said.

Staci started running before Sam had finished. She wasn't anywhere near as fast as the men or as fit, and her breath came in harsh gasps within moments. Sam kept pace beside her, avoiding the roots and rocks with ease.

The small storm that was forming doubled in size, sending a wave of power over Staci. She stumbled and would have fallen if Sam hadn't caught her.

'Are you okay?' Sam asked, breath coming fast as she searched the woods. They'd stopped in a small cluster of pine trees, the bracken ahead of them bent and broken from the others' passage.

'It's just the storm,' Staci said, trying to push it away. She had to get to Oliver. But the storm wouldn't be ignored. It doubled again, making her gasp.

This wasn't possible. Elements took time to gather. How was Elliot feeding this thing? She searched out with her magic, looking for the source, and when she found it, she could have cursed.

Elliot had used the small storm to keep her attention. Then, while she was focused on that, she'd missed the other fragments he'd been building further away. Small clusters of rain clouds, high-speed winds, and lightning. Now, he was pulling them together. It was going to be so brutal that none of them would be able to walk away.

'How bad?' Sam asked. The wind flared up at her words, stirring the pine needles and other forest debris.

Staci hesitated to answer. He'd built a storm that would destroy this forest and everything for miles around. But she couldn't say that. 'Bad. Worse than this morning.'

'Destroy it,' Sam said as another gust hit them, this time forcing them back a step.

'Oliver—'

'Hale and Lance can help Oliver,' Sam said. 'Only you can help with the storm.'

Staci shuddered. She could feel Elliot manipulating the air currents and moving the water. The damned thing pulsed like a beacon. It was too big to destroy in the normal way.

'I don't know if I'm strong enough,' Staci said as another wave of elements merged with the main storm. She doubled over, and Sam helped her to the ground this time rather than holding her up. The mud was still wet from the rain, and it soaked into her jeans.

'You heard Lance; Elliot was pretty upset that you'd destroyed the earlier storm,' Sam said, crouching next to her. 'You're stronger than him.'

'But I don't know what I did,' Staci said, bracing as another gust of wind hit them. It felt like the magic was searching for her, prodding at her.

'I saw you catch lightning before anyone had trained you to use your magic,' Sam said. 'Magic is more about sensations and feelings than science. Use that instinct.'

Staci hesitated. Sam was human, but she wasn't wrong. Staci had followed her instinct that day and presumably today if she had stopped the storm earlier.

'I'll stay with you,' Sam said. She didn't glance in the direction the guys had gone, which was more than Staci had managed.

She wanted to find Oliver. Make sure he was okay. But if she let the storm grow, it wouldn't matter if she found him. The storm would tear them apart.

'Move back a little, just in case,' Staci said as she settled more solidly into the muddy ground. It squelched as she moved, water soaking into her knickers. The wind already felt like it was targeting her; the last thing she needed was for Sam to get hit by something worse.

Once Sam was a few feet away, Staci closed her eyes, trying to push away the distractions. Her fear. Everything.

Then she let herself feel the storm. All of it.

Elliot was twisting the parts so carefully that she could barely even see what he was doing. Any doubts about Elliot having made last night's storm dissipated. But how had he controlled it from so far away?

A problem for later. Staci needed to stop this one now, and she was more than close enough to manipulate it this time.

Elliot would feel her the moment she meddled, so she hovered, watching it.

She always saw the storm as three main parts. The rain, the wind, and the lightning. She knew a storm was a lot more than those pieces. There was air pressure, heat, and cold. But none of that helped her visualise the storm. Like Sam had said, it wasn't about science.

This one was the largest she'd seen. The sheer amount of rain in it would cause flooding beyond anything Huntly had seen before. The winds would be over a hundred miles an hour. Then there was the lightning. It slivered through the storm like a snake, dancing back and forth. She didn't open her eyes, but she suspected it was growing darker by the second as the clouds gathered.

Normally, she would push away the pieces, but just like the earlier storm, this one was too big. She shivered as the wind picked up. The rain started, a single drop on her cheek. Then another. It would get worse quickly.

How had she controlled the storm earlier? The lightning had created a connection. But starting with that didn't seem like the smartest idea, considering the risks and how lost she'd become without Oliver's touch. She needed to try something a little less extreme.

Taking a breath to help steady herself, she did the opposite of what she'd been taught. She reached out, touching the storm with her magic. It tried to suck her under.

The storm was everything. It was life. It was the air in her lungs. It wanted her to become part of it and share her power.

No! Staci struggled to remember that she didn't want the storm to get stronger. She wanted to do the opposite.

It was so hard to think. The storm felt amazing. It was a freedom she'd never looked for or wanted, but now she had it, she didn't want to let it go. Nothing mattered in the storm. Not Oliver. Not that he was missing.

Pain slid through her as she thought about Oliver, and she reached for the link to him, holding it close even if it didn't tell her he was okay. But it did help ease the compulsion of the storm, the desire to let it fill her and forget about the real world.

A piece of the dream flickered through her, hazy now. But she remembered Oliver's promise. If she ever felt lost in the storm, she should look for him and use him as her anchor. He'd meant the mate bond.

She pulled it closer to her, and the storm's compulsion slid away. She released a breath, nearly laughing with relief.

Had this been what had happened to her father? Had he become lost in how good the storm felt? Without knowing what had happened, she wouldn't know, but either way, it didn't help her now.

Lightning flickered against her senses, and she tilted her head up, focusing on the storm again. She'd been so lost in the power she'd not seen Elliot had been manipulating the magic. Now she could see clearly. It was so close that the hairs on her arm stood on end.

Elliot gave it a nudge. Telling it that she'd be a good target. It twisted faster, searching until it found her. It was too powerful; if it hit her, it might kill her.

Staci caught it with her magic before it fell, holding the power in her mind. It hurt. Elliot pushed against her control. She struggled against him, feeling the lightning shift and twist.

'Sam, I need you to move further back,' Staci said. If Sam answered, she never heard as she struggled with Elliot.

His grip on the magic slipped just a little. His power was running low. She pushed harder, sending the electricity away from her and Elliot. But it was a bright flare in the sky now; she opened her eyes to watch it. Elliot and she were the best targets, and the lightning wanted to hit them.

The bolt slid back towards Elliot as his power flickered again. She tried to catch it and bring it back. But it was too strong. Part of the bolt slipped free from her grip, falling and striking Elliot with so much force, she heard the blast from where she sat.

The other part sprung back, splitting from the rest of the bolt. It moved too fast for her to stop and slammed into her in a white flash.

Oliver's leg throbbed. Each beat of his heart sent more blood pooling to the surface. His father hadn't hit anything vital, but there was still time.

'Tell me what you know,' David said. 'Or I'll shoot your other leg.'

Coward, Thor snarled. *Not deserve to be alpha.*

Footsteps came with a rattle of branches, and then Hale and Lance were in the clearing with Oliver. The energy of their wolves lashed at him. Foreign but familiar at the same time. His father's energy was barely there against the wave of power from Hale. But his father didn't need magic when he had a gun.

Hale was beside Oliver before his father had a chance to react, eyes a gold so bright they nearly shone with their own light. Oliver realised he'd never seen Hale angry before, not like this.

He smelled faintly of Staci. It wasn't strong enough that she'd entered the clearing with the others. But enough that he knew she'd come with them. He wanted to search for her. But he didn't want to risk drawing attention to her if she was there.

Protect mate, Thor said, fear thick.

Hale won't let anything happen to her, Oliver said. Especially not when he caught a hint of Sam's scent, too. He wouldn't have let Sam anywhere near something dangerous.

Hale moved to crouch, but his father snarled. 'Don't touch my son. Oliver is mine. You can't take him back.' The gun wavered towards Hale before he pointed it back at Oliver.

Joyce backed up slowly, pale, glancing at Elliot. He was still kneeling, eyes closed, not reacting to anything that was happening.

'This is how you treat your own family?' Hale said, his voice calm despite the scent of his rage in Oliver's nose.

'He needed to learn a lesson. One I think you need to learn too,' David said, this time moving to point the gun at Hale.

Oliver stood, being as careful as he could of his leg. It ached even though he didn't put any weight on it. He needed to shift and seal the wound or get someone to clean and stitch it. But he couldn't do either here.

'Put down the gun, and we can discuss this,' Hale said. He sounded calm. Reasonable. Patient. But it wasn't making any difference, and while Hale was fast, he wasn't faster than a bullet. If his father took a shot, one of them would be hurt before they could get the gun away.

'Liar,' Oliver's father said. 'You've been after my position ever since you came to this town. You think I'm stupid, and I can't see that?'

'I don't want to be prime alpha,' Hale said, trying to take a step closer, but his father snarled. 'I want this to end peacefully, with no one hurt. You can't shoot all of us.'

Joyce made a noise in her throat as she reached the edge of the woods, then she turned and ran. Good riddance. It wasn't like she'd be hard to find when all this was over.

His father snarled, gun wavering to Lance, who'd taken another step closer. 'You think you're stronger than me?

I'm a damned prime alpha. You're nothing compared to that.'

'Please, David. Put the gun down. We can deal with this peacefully,' Hale said again. But it was obvious that Oliver's father wasn't interested in doing any such thing.

'You think you can talk your way out of this?' his father said. 'I should have killed you all those years ago when you came into my territory.'

'You needed me,' Hale said. 'I helped you bring the pack here back under control.'

'I don't need anyone,' his father shouted, his wolf so close to the surface that his eyes weren't changing back. 'I'm in control.'

But he wasn't, and now all of them could see that. Even if his father walked away from this, it wouldn't be the same. This was what losing control looked like. It was more than just the yellow eyes. There was a wildness there.

'You don't have to do this to prove you're in control,' Hale said, trying to take another step forward. This time, his father changed his aim back to Hale. He stopped.

A gust came out of nowhere, catching the leaves from the tree and shaking them like a rattle. It brought a biting cold with it that chased away the heat of the day.

Elliot made a noise, drawing his father's eye. Not long enough for them to move in. The rain started as a light drizzle that soaked into his clothes quickly. Dark had spread through the clearing faster than the coming evening called for. The storm was getting worse fast.

'Stop this,' Oliver said, limping slightly in front of Hale. If he could get his father to focus on him, maybe the others could have a chance. 'You've won. You have me, and I'm not going anywhere.'

'You were always mine,' his father said, curling his lip. 'The weak, pathetic child who grew into a weak man. I should have shot you before I let you leave.'

Lightning flared in the sky, casting shadows over them from the trees. But it didn't strike. Instead, it moved unnaturally, writhing back and forth.

Everyone glanced at Elliot, but he couldn't do this alone. Staci was fighting the storm he was making. If the lightning struck her ...

Stop Elliot, Thor said, bracing them to move. But they couldn't do anything with his father waving the gun about. *No more games. David not in charge.*

'Stupid Elemental, can't even do a simple task,' his father said.

Thor was right. It was time to stop letting his father lead them.

'I've had enough,' Oliver said, stepping past Hale and a little further from Lance. There was now a good four feet between them. 'You keep telling me how weak I am. But you're standing here with a gun, threatening us rather than proving your wolf is stronger.'

His father snarled, skin rippling along his throat. The start of a change.

'I challenge you,' Oliver said.

His father's eyes widened. Fear and panic flashed through his scent. This was what his father had been afraid of all this time. That Oliver would be strong enough to challenge him?

'No.' Something passed over his father's face. A decision. The gun started to move.

He wanted to lunge at his father, but his leg wouldn't hold him to cover that distance. He tried to move anyway, nearly falling as he put weight on his damaged leg.

The two fast bangs killed his hearing for a heartbeat. Then light flashed through the clearing so bright that it couldn't have just been from the gun. The pain came slower, maybe because there was already so much other pain for it to reach past.

He fell to the ground, legs no longer doing what he wanted. His vision swam.

There was shouting distantly, screaming. But no more gunshots.

Shift, Thor said, trying to force their body to change, no longer caring about rules or laws. But their father's wolf was there. He lunged at them, pinning Thor again, stopping him from shifting.

This time, Thor struggled, fighting against the other wolf with teeth and claws. But every second that passed, they lost more blood. Lost more strength.

He needed to shift. Needed to find out if the others were okay. But there was nothing but darkness and pain.

STACI STRUGGLED AS THE lightning writhed inside her. There was so much of it that it strained against her magic, burning through it so fast that she thought there would be nothing left. But it was more than that. It was temptation. Light. Life. Everything.

She clung to her link to Oliver as the chaos tore at her. It was all that stopped her from giving in to the power and letting it pull her under. That and the knowledge that he was still out there, somewhere, and he needed her. She didn't know how she knew, but she felt the certainty of it right to the core of who she was.

After several very long heartbeats that felt like hours, her magic contained the lightning, and she no longer felt like she was about to explode. She was shaking, and each breath hurt. But the pain was good. It meant she was more than just the storm.

Now she was in control, she searched for Elliot, but there was no sign of his magic. Had the lightning been more than he could handle? Or was he just waiting for her to lose concentration so he could attack her again? Either way, she couldn't afford to wait around and find out. The storm was rapidly getting worse.

As if to emphasise her point, lightning twisted in the sky, trying to form. She caught it, and this time, without Elliot fighting her, it did as she asked, halting. Without the connection to the storm, she'd never have been able to do it. She focused on the bolt splitting up, and it dispersed into small flickers of sparks like fireworks in the rain.

'Staci?' Sam said, voice nearly lost in the sound of the storm.

Staci nearly jumped. She'd forgotten about Sam.

'I'm okay,' Staci said, opening her eyes. Sam was pressed against a tree, barely visible through the driving rain. It was so cold that each drop felt like a needle stabbing her. The wind picked up again, making the trees creak and her braid whip about behind her.

They might be okay now, but if Staci didn't do something about the storm soon, neither of them would be for much longer. She'd seen what had happened to the school. None of them would survive that.

Staci reached into the storm and took hold of the rest of the elements. After the lightning, the wind and rain were easy to hold, but that didn't mean the storm was just willing to submit. It fought against her touch, trying to push past her link to Oliver and remind her how good it had felt to let it in. Her skin crawled as the instinctual awareness crept over her mind.

The wind stopped first, halting so quickly that Staci almost fell, not realising how much she'd been fighting to stay sitting. Then she did the rain, and slowly, it eased off until all she could hear was the dripping of trees around her.

'Staci?' Sam asked again, stepping away from the tree she'd been holding onto.

'I've got it,' Staci said, but now she did; what did she do with it? She couldn't just send the parts away; even if Elliot was out of commission, the elements were still too big. But she couldn't keep hold of it either. The drain might not have been as severe as the magic college had led her to believe, but holding it wasn't free either.

She still wasn't sure how she'd dispersed the storm in her dream, but she had an idea about how she could stop this one. She needed to break it up into smaller chunks. That way, she could limit how much rain or wind she sent to a certain area. It was also the reverse of what Elliot had done.

Focusing on the rain first, she sliced off a piece of the storm and nudged it towards the Rift Scar. The storm didn't like being split; it fought against her, offering her power instead. Without her link to Oliver, the storm wouldn't have let her focus long enough to do the work. Which made her wonder how Elliot had managed to keep the pieces separate as long as he had. Another problem for later.

The clouds shifted, moving miles in a few heartbeats before it slipped free from her magic on the edge of the Rift Scar. The clouds above her thinned, showing the hint of a moon through the haze. If she hadn't been connected to the storm, nudging the pieces apart would have taken more than an hour. This was how Elliot had made the storm last night, and it was scary how easy it was.

She did the same with a slice of the wind, sending it out in a different direction where there would only be fields. Then she repeated it over and over until all that was left of the storm was the lightning inside her, but without the rest of the elements to feed it, that was fading on its own.

Staci opened her eyes again, though she'd not remembered closing them, and shivered. The rain might have stopped, but it was still cold, and she was still wet.

'I did it. I stopped the storm,' Staci said, turning to Sam. She'd kept her distance like Staci had asked, but she was dancing on the balls of her feet, looking over her shoulder. Staci's stomach sank; Sam had been calm before. 'What happened?'

Sam turned back. 'I heard more gunshots.'

Staci pulled on her link to Oliver, even though she knew it wouldn't tell her anything, but she felt it waver, nearly slipping from her.

'We have to find them,' Staci said, stumbling to her feet, fighting against numb legs from sitting still so long. Sam caught her, helping her stay upright. 'Something's wrong with Oliver.' That link to him had never wavered until now.

'We're not far from Hale,' Sam said as she put her arm under Staci's, helping her walk. Every step helped the chill in her bones, letting her move a little faster.

It wasn't long before she heard the faint murmur of voices and a deep, savage growl. They ducked under a broken branch and entered a clearing dripping from the fresh rain.

Oliver's father was straining against Lance's grip, cursing. Lance showed no sign that he was struggling to keep the man pinned. A gun lay on the ground a few feet away.

Elliot was flat on his back, not moving, skin marked with faint pink lines. She couldn't tell if he was unconscious or something worse, but she couldn't seem to care right now as she searched for Oliver. She saw Hale first. He was crouched with his hands pressed against Oliver's chest. Blood seeped through his fingers.

'No!' Staci shouted, forgetting about everyone else as the link between her and Oliver wavered again, pulsing in and out of focus. She scrambled to him, sliding on the wet earth, putting her hand on his face. Pain flared so deep that she hissed, pulling back.

Sam knelt beside them, touching Oliver in the same spot as Staci, but she didn't pull back in pain. Staci knew logically it was because Sam couldn't feel Oliver the way she could, but it didn't help her anger that Sam could touch him, but she couldn't.

'What happened?' Sam asked.

'Oliver challenged his father. He shot Oliver rather than fighting,' Hale said. Even though he wasn't moving his hands, blood was pooling onto the grass. It was too much, too fast. Even a Shifter couldn't survive this kind of wound without medical help. Or shifting. It might have been against the law to do it in public, but someone would have to catch him first.

'Help him shift,' Staci said, turning to Hale. She didn't know much about Shifters, but she knew that the alpha had the power to force the change.

'I can't,' Hale said, eyes gold as they turned to Sam. 'I'm not his alpha.'

'Then make him do it,' Staci said, glaring at Oliver's father. He was twisting and spitting curses at Lance.

'There isn't enough time,' Hale said.

'We have to do something,' Staci said, tears burning her eyes. She wiped them away roughly. Crying wasn't going to help Oliver.

'Let me try to help,' Sam said, though Staci didn't know what she could do as a human. But at this point, she'd accept any help she could get.

'I can't capture his wolf,' Hale said, shaking his head. 'You won't have a connection.'

Sam hesitated, but she glanced at Staci. 'We could use the mate link like Amelia did?'

'Oliver pulled Amelia into his pack first. Neither Staci nor Oliver has a connection to us,' Hale said.

Staci didn't follow what they were talking about, but Sam was trying to help, so she kept silent, focusing instead on Oliver. He didn't react at all as they talked. His chest moved erratically, like he couldn't get a proper breath. His skin was so pale he looked like he was almost dead already.

'But Staci could use the dream. Tell Oliver to accept you in?' Sam said.

Hale hesitated, looking at Oliver's father again. 'It might not be enough.'

'Please. I'll try anything,' Staci said, putting her hand over Hale's. 'Help me save him.'

Hale turned back to her, his eyes pure gold. This wasn't the calm, easily forgettable man from earlier. This was an alpha, and he was pissed. Hale nodded once. 'Tell him he needs to accept me as alpha, and I can force him to change and heal.'

'How?' Staci asked, looking from Sam to Hale.

'You go into the dream,' Sam said. She put a hand on Staci's shoulder. 'He will hear you there.'

'The dream hadn't been intentional, and he's not exactly in a condition to repeat what we did,' Staci said. She probably should have been embarrassed, but she wasn't. There were too many other emotions getting in the way.

'You just need to touch him. Follow the pull. Let it draw you in,' Sam said.

The link between Staci and Oliver wavered again, fluttering like she was losing him. She put her hand back on his cheek, choking on the scream that tried to escape her. There was only pain. Nothing else existed.

Her mind fought her, trying to protect itself from that pain to stop her from following the link. But she'd only just got Oliver in her life. She wasn't ready to let him go.

She needed to calm down. Focus. She took a breath and closed her eyes, pulling on one of her oldest memories of her mother. The two of them sat side by side as her mother tried to teach a bored five-year-old how to meditate. There was rain running down the window. Even then, she'd been drawn to the sound. It had helped quiet her mind. Cookies were baking in the kitchen. She released her breath.

The link between her and Oliver became something more than just pain. She could feel him underneath. His fear for her. She followed it, trying to tell him she was okay. That she was right here.

The darkness changed shape. Shifting into a stream of colours, then back into darkness, and a different kind of pain.

CHAPTER EIGHTEEN

STACI FLINCHED AS SHE heard a young boy scream.

Opening her eyes, she found herself in a small study with floor-to-ceiling bookshelves filled with old books. Two tan leather armchairs sat in front of them, and a large antique desk stood in front of a massive window.

A boy of maybe ten lay on the wooden floor in the centre of the room, curled in a ball. Oliver's father, fifteen years younger, stood above him, wiping blood off his fist with a hanky.

'Next time, boy, do as you're told the first time I ask,' Oliver's father said.

The room wavered. An older boy, maybe twelve this time, knelt at his father's feet. One eye was black, and his nose was bloody.

Another shift. More pain. A broken wrist. A punch to the gut. There and gone, too fast for her to react.

Then, the boy was an adult, and it was Oliver. It always had been. Each image showing another vision of his abuse.

He lay on the ground, naked, body writhing. 'I can't,' Oliver said.

His father stood, coming over to Oliver with a quick stride, then kicked him over onto his back. He grunted, pain so obvious that Staci could nearly feel the ache of it.

'Can't. Hurts.' Oliver's eyes flashed to amber as he blinked at his father, pleading with him, but his father snarled.

'Control yourself, boy,' Oliver's father said. Oliver tried to pull away, but it was useless as his father stepped on his wrist. 'I'll not have a son of mine so carelessly show his wolf eyes. Either you're a wolf, or you're a man. You'll not be both together. Now shift.'

The change ripped through Oliver, making him scream. As his throat changed, the sound became a choked howl.

Staci stepped forward, but Oliver grabbed her arm. Not the man on the floor, but her Oliver. He was wearing the clothes from earlier, clean and dry here.

'Don't,' Oliver said. 'He's not really here. None of this is real.'

'Then the minute I get back to where he is real, I'm going to kick his head in,' Staci said. She couldn't remember ever being this angry.

Oliver smiled at her, twisting them so her back was to the scene on the floor. It did nothing to stop the sound as she heard bones breaking. Oliver shifting.

'That I'd love to see,' he said calmly as he leaned his forehead against hers.

He might have been calm on the outside, but she could feel the echo of her own rage from years of pain and abuse.

'Why are you here?' Staci asked. 'There are so many other choices.'

Something warm and soft pressed against the back of Staci's legs, and she looked down to see Thor. He watched her with those intelligent amber eyes.

He think is his fault, Thor said, answering before Oliver could.

'This isn't your fault,' Staci said, narrowing her eyes at Oliver. 'You didn't do anything to deserve this.'

Oliver looked away from her, and she grabbed his chin, bringing him back to look at her.

'Nothing you could have done would have made you deserve to be treated like this. Nothing,' Staci said.

She couldn't even imagine how hard it had been for him to grow up with this hatred. She'd always had her mother and Florence. Always had their love and comfort. She wished she could share some of that with him.

'It's easier to say than to do,' Oliver said at last, looking past her. 'Even knowing he was wrong. That he's broken. Years of memories tell me it's me that's the problem.'

Staci reached up to put her hand on the back of Oliver's neck; he focused on her again. She didn't know much about trauma, but she suspected it would be years of therapy before he came close to dealing with this kind of pain.

The room dimmed, colours leaching away, and then everything brightened again. She cursed. She'd forgotten why she'd come. Even now, she struggled to remember what Hale had told her.

'Hale said you had to let him in,' Staci said, glancing down at Thor. 'He'll help you shift and heal.'

Oliver touched his chest where Hale had been putting pressure. 'My father shot me,' he said like he'd also forgotten he'd been hurt.

'Oliver, you need to find Hale,' Staci said, but he didn't react. 'Please listen to me.'

'Why are you here?' he said, finally looking at her. 'I hurt you.'

'Lance told me why you said what you did,' Staci said, gut twisting. None of this was him reaching out to Hale. 'Oliver, are you listening? You need to accept Hale.'

'My father said he took you. Said he'd let you go if I rejoined his pack,' Oliver said, reaching up to cup her face. 'You're really okay?'

'He never touched me,' Staci said, putting her hand over his. 'Now, find Hale.'

Thor pressed harder against her as Oliver shook his head.

'Let me go. It's better this way,' Oliver said. 'If I'm not here, he won't have any reason to hurt you.'

'No,' Staci said, pulling Oliver's hand away from her face. 'I don't accept this.'

Tears stung her eyes as his expression didn't change. She needed them to be somewhere else. Somewhere that Oliver's father had never been. A place he'd never been hurt.

Oliver opened his mouth, but she tore at the dream, focusing on one memory, one place that mattered right now. The room wavered; the smell of old dust and faint mould rose. Above her, the wind raged, and the rain lashed down.

She saw the moment Oliver registered the new location because the room solidified. The small shelter was as cramped as she remembered. The bed held the blanket Oliver had thrown over them, and the only light was the faint glow of Oliver's phone camera. Their clothes were dripping wet, just like when they'd first come in here.

'If you want to let go and say goodbye, then we do it here. In this room,' Staci said. They'd appeared in the same places where they'd stripped off their wet clothes.

'Staci—'

'No,' Staci said, cutting him off. She had to swallow a lump in her throat before she could continue. 'You tell me you're going to leave in the same place you told me you'd stay.'

'This isn't my choice.'

'Like hell it's not your choice. Hale is out there reaching for you. Trying to help. Trying to save you. All you have to do is accept him.' Staci stepped closer to Oliver. 'Or you can tell me you're going to abandon me. Leave me alone in this world.'

Oliver growled in sync with Thor. The pair were together now, side by side.

'Tell me that's your choice, and I'll leave you to die,' Staci said, words choking at the end.

Oliver closed the gap, wrapping his arms around her tightly, sharing his warmth as she shuddered. She lay her head on his chest, squeezing her eyes shut as she waited for his answer. 'I'm not going to leave you alone.'

'Then fight, dammit!' Staci said, looking up from his chest. Ribbons of light fluttered around them, passing through his wolf into Oliver.

She pulled back to get a better look at them, not entirely sure what she was seeing.

Two blue-white streams were so closely entwined she could barely separate them as they shot off into the distance. Another one, dark and writhing, looked like it had jagged barbs, chaining Thor's leg to Oliver's, then spun out in the opposite direction.

A third and final ribbon flowed between her and Oliver. This light was pale lilac and hit the centre of each of their hearts. Oliver stared at it, then gently ran his fingers over the bond.

She shivered. It was like he was touching every part of her. He pulled back, smiling like he knew how good it had felt.

'Is it always so ... visual,' Staci said, turning again to the white-blue link, wondering who was at the other end of that.

'That's my pack,' Oliver said like he'd sensed the thought. 'But I've never seen it so clearly like this.'

'How do you find Hale?' Staci said, looking around.

A new ribbon she'd not seen before was hovering near the edge of the room. It was blue and so thick and heavy with power that it looked more like a rope. She could almost feel Hale through it.

Thor moved closer to it, sniffing the air, giving Oliver one last look. The dark vine at Thor's ankle pulsed and writhed harder. Oliver nodded, and Thor put his nose on the blue rope. The light flowed around him, moving snake-fast as it struck at the black thorny vine. The darkness split apart, and the tie flaked away like ash. Oliver fell to his knees, breath coming hard. Blood spotted his ankle where the vine had been.

'I'm okay,' Oliver said, reaching out as his wolf came closer. 'I'll see you on the other side?'

Staci smiled and leaned in to steal a quick kiss that turned into something deeper than they had time for. 'I won't leave you.'

The moment Oliver touched the light, she felt his pain come back. All of it all at once. She felt his broken bones and pain deep in his gut. The bullet wounds and the bruises. Each wound flared brightly, and then they were erased as the change took him.

Bones broke and twisted out of shape. Muscles ripped and stretched. Every breath burned like liquid fire. Her limbs felt like she'd been frozen and shattered. It went on and on. Never ending. She held onto Oliver through it all, offering her strength, everything she had. She wouldn't lose him.

Then it was done, and Staci fell into the darkness, welcoming the break.

THOR WOKE SLOWLY. HIS whole body ached. His wolf body. He searched for Oliver, but he slept. He needed much rest. More than Thor, so he left his human to sleep.

He tried to remember what had happened. He'd been in the dream place. Hale had helped them shift. It had hurt worse because of the wounds. Staci had been there. She had felt it all.

Thor growled, opening his eyes, searching. He had not meant for her to feel that pain. But she had helped. Given him strength and power. It had come with a cost.

Staci lay on the ground. Eyes closed, not moving.

Thor tried to get to his paws, trying to get to her. Clothes tangled him up, and hands held him down.

'Careful, she's okay, but I don't think she'd appreciate being clawed,' *Sam said. Her scent held no fear. She was a good alpha's mate, strong. Thor would tell Oliver he had been right when he woke.* ***'Will you let me help you?'***

Thor whined and nodded his head like he had seen Oliver do. Sam removed her hands and helped him out of the torn clothes so he could shake out his fur.

It was getting dark, and Sam had made her phone create a light to help them see. It made Staci all shadowy, but he could feel she was getting stronger through the mate link between them.

He carefully crept closer, going around to lie on Staci's other side. His mate was warm, smelling of storms and the coming lightning. Sam had brushed Staci's hair back from her face. He let her sleep like Oliver slept. They both needed much rest.

'I'm glad you're okay, Oliver,' *Sam said.*

He searched for others. Elliot smelled like cooked meat. Bad scent. Oliver would be sad he was hurt, but Thor did not care. Alpha and Lance held David down. He was half-shifted, stuck. Or slow. One arm twisted into a front leg, bald and deformed. The bottom jaw was longer than the top. His fingers were different lengths, claws on some.

David had liked control. Was funny that he did not have control now. Deserved this.

'Have you seen anything like this before?' *Hale asked, looking at Lance.*

'No. Backlash, maybe?' *Lance said, but he scented of uncertainty.*

Thor relaxed a little; David was not a threat like that. He turned back to Staci, tucking his nose against her neck. She was calm in sleep, not hurting, not afraid.

'Can you force him back?' *Lance said.*

Thor looked over, but they were talking about David still, not Thor. He relaxed again.

'Not without taking everything from him first,' *Hale said.*

'He doesn't deserve his title or position,' *Lance said.*

'Deserve or not, the rest of the prime alphas will attack us if I do it. They'd have no choice,' *Hale said.*

'Then let's leave him,' *Lance said.* **'He deserves worse.'**

What's happening? *Oliver asked, voice weak.*

David broken, *Thor said, sending Oliver the memories. Was easier than translating. Oliver liked to use many words when images were better.* **Is weak like he told us we were.**

'Oliver?' *Hale said. It was not the first time. Thor turned to him.* **'Can you try to force David to finish his shift?'**

Not my pack, *Thor said, though Hale couldn't hear him.*

'Even though the link is severed, you're a wolf and used to be part of his pack. Will you try?' *Hale asked, eyes still gold. But it was a request, not a demand.*

He also did not make Thor give Oliver back control. He would know it was Thor. Alpha always knows.

He trusts us, *Oliver said.* **Trusts you.**

Thor was a good wolf. Was worth trusting. Hale was a good alpha to think so. Would try to help David for their alpha, not for David.

Oliver's relief slipped over to Thor. He didn't like the deformity of David. It was a fear all Shifters had. Being stuck was worthy of fear.

Thor licked Staci's cheek as she slept. She tasted of tears, which made Oliver sad. But tears were fixed now. Oliver would see when she woke. She would be their mate. Maybe even pack.

Not without asking her first, *Oliver said.* **We've made enough mistakes without forcing Staci into something she didn't ask for.**

Thor ignored Oliver. Staci would want to be pack, Oliver would see.

Standing again hurt, but Thor ignored that too as he moved them closer. He wished for a human nose. David smelled bad, like old sweat and rotting blood.

Thor whined at Hale to let him know Thor was unhappy. Hale nodded. He understood. He could see and smell it, too.

David was worse close-up. None of the muscles moved under the skin now, and his breath was ragged and too fast. He was awake under that pain. Eyes unfocused but aware.

Thor sat beside him, considering the problem.

Can you help? *Oliver asked.*

Am smart wolf. Know many things, *Thor said. Was true. There was much knowledge as a wolf that his human half did not know and could not understand. Like the magic of pack. Old knowledge coming from the wolves that came before. Knowledge that would help in bad days if they came again.*

Helping David was easier than that. But it could kill him anyway. Not care if killed him, though, so would try.

Try not to kill him, *Oliver said, rolling his eyes. Oliver liked to do that many times. Thor did not understand why.*

Thor called to their magic. It was slow and still unfamiliar. Alpha. Or part of what made them alpha. But it was more than that. Thor used the part that wasn't alpha. He did not want David in his pack.

This magic would not have worked if the shift had not started. Or if Thor had been his human self. This magic had lots of rules. Lots of ways it could go wrong.

Thor stepped closer, letting his nose touch the stinking flesh. Magic crawled over David, pushing into muscle and bone. It took the memory of change with it. Sharing it with the body, reminding it what it was supposed to be doing.

The change started again. A bone snapped. Muscle tore. A howl ripped from David, short and sharp. Fur spurted out in clumps. The order was wrong as the body tried to catch up. The leg bone twisted into place, leaving muscle behind to catch up later.

Oliver winced as he remembered their own painful shift. But this pain was David's own fault, and Thor would not share Oliver's sympathy as it leaked over their bond.

Thor pulled back to sit on his haunches as the change finally finished. David was a dark brown wolf, so dark he looked black in the faded light. He was not awake. Had not been awake for most of it. Would have been better if he had. Could see what true pain was like. Maybe Thor should have stood on his wrist and let it not form.

Oliver didn't like the thought. Or that he'd agreed with Thor.

'I've only ever seen a Shifter's alpha be able to force a shift before,' *Lance said. He'd stepped back, giving space for the change.*

'Me too,' *Hale said, staring at David.* **But my wolf said it would work.'**

Have you always known how to do that? *Oliver asked.*

Am good wolf, *Thor said, avoiding answering. Was not human business to know about wolf magic. Oliver did not ask again.*

'You know we could just hand him over to the police and tell them that he shifted somewhere he shouldn't,' *Lance said, glancing at Thor.* **'After Oliver is safe.'**

'One semi-competent investigator later, and they're looking for two wolves, not one,' *Hale said.*

'You want to take him back to Sam's land, don't you?' *Lance said.*

Thor growled, then carefully moved his head from side to side like he'd felt Oliver do. It meant no. Not want David on their land.

'We can put him in a cage,' *Hale said, looking down at David.* **'I have one dismantled in storage.'**

Thor growled louder. He didn't like the cage either and liked that Hale had one even less.

It's better than David being free, *Oliver said, echoing the hatred of being locked up.* **And you know why a cage is sometimes necessary. Not everyone has our control when they're hurt.**

Killing would be better, *Thor said. But he did understand. Hated it. Hated that he understood even more.*

Thor stood and went back to Staci, leaving Hale to his decision.

'David should stay out for the rest of the night after a shift like that,' *Hale said.* **'We can set up the cage and get him locked up before then. After that, the prime alphas can deal with him.'**

'Elliot must have driven Oliver here, so we'll have two cars,' *Lance said.* **'Three, if we can find David's.'**

Thor tuned out the rest of the conversation as he lay down next to Staci again. He was careful not to touch her. She was still sleeping.

Do you have enough strength to shift us back? *Oliver said, nudging at the control.* **It's risky if anyone sees us like this.**

Thor was tired, but Oliver was right. It was risky; this wasn't their home. But Thor wanted to stay with Staci.

I'll take good care of Staci, *Oliver said.*

Not leave her? *Thor asked.*

Not unless she makes us, *Oliver said.*

Thor let the control slip over to Oliver as they changed. The pain was less this time but still more than usual. Too much energy had been used for it to be anything else.

OLIVER GROANED AS HE sat up. His stomach cramped painfully, and he felt hot and cold at the same time. He touched his chest, feeling the sharp spike of pain from where the bullet had penetrated. But there was nothing on his skin. No scar, no wound. Nothing.

He tried to stand and failed, his body warning him about how low on energy he was.

'Careful,' Hale said, putting one hand on Oliver's shoulder. Pack energy rolled over him, easing some of the pain. 'Sam will not be impressed if she healed you just so you can fall down dead because you overdid it.'

'I've survived worse.' Which was true about the shifting too often, not so much about the bullet wound. At least the reason there was no mark made sense if Sam had healed him.

Sam was kneeling next to Staci with only the light from her phone. Staci was pale in the poor light and still asleep. Some of the tightness in his chest eased.

'I think she's just exhausted from the storm and helping bring you back,' Sam said, answering Oliver's question before he could ask. 'She just needs some sleep.'

'Thank you,' Oliver said, throat tight. Staci had saved him. If not for her, he wouldn't have found his way back.

'You'd have been better staying as a wolf,' Hale said, handing him his combat trousers. The waist was torn, but there was enough material to tie it together and make himself semi-decent.

'Transporting one is going to be hard enough. I'd rather not get sent to jail after I've finally found my home,' Oliver said as he pulled the trousers on. They stuck to his wet skin, but he managed to get dressed without falling over.

Oliver didn't bother with his T-shirt, even though it was now cool. The material was more ripped than not. Any police with half a brain would be able to guess Oliver shifted, but as long as he was human, they couldn't prove it.

He looked around for the rest of the group. Lance was missing, as was David, which meant they were probably already in one of the cars. Elliot still lay alone at the edge of the clearing, skin pale with a wild pattern of pink marks. Part of Oliver knew he should check on his friend, but he couldn't make himself.

He moved to Staci's side and wiped the smear of mud off her face. He could feel her through their bond. She was exhausted but okay.

'You remember what happened?' Hale asked, kneeling next to Sam and touching her shoulder. She looked almost as tired as Staci as she put her hand over his.

'Yes,' Oliver said as he gently gathered Staci and lifted her into his arms.

'Good, then let's get to the hospital,' Hale said, glancing at Elliot. Oliver could see the reluctance, but Sam patted Hale's hand and stood.

'I don't need a hospital,' Oliver said.

'You almost died,' Sam said, lifting her chin. 'You need to get checked out.'

'How am I going to explain how I'm fully healed? Or why my own father shot me? Besides, I'm fine.' Oliver's stomach gave a savage twist as if to argue with him. 'Or I will be once I've eaten.'

Sam and Hale exchanged a look. They knew he was right. 'Staci and Elliot both need to get checked over,' Sam said.

'No hospital. Just need to sleep,' Staci said. Her voice was a whisper of its normal strength as she placed her hand against his chest. She didn't even open her eyes. 'Want to be with you.'

Oliver tightened his grip on Staci. Thor was still sleeping, but Oliver knew what his answer would have been to leaving Staci. 'I can take her home.'

'I don't like it, but Oliver's right. We can't explain most of what happened,' Hale said.

'What about him?' Sam's scowl grew deeper, and they all looked at Elliot.

'He's alive. Lance asked Zoe to meet us at the hospital. She's going to watch Elliot,' Hale said.

'Fine, but you're all coming to mine because at least if someone gets worse, I can help you,' Sam said, giving Hale a narrowed-eyed look like she expected him to argue.

Good alpha mate, Thor said sleepily.

She's definitely that, Oliver said. *Sleep, I'll take care of Staci.*

For once, Thor listened to him, and he drifted off, leaving Oliver alone in his head. Or nearly alone. He could feel Staci's pleasure at being in his arms and her exhaustion as she hovered at the edge of sleep.

He felt whole for the first time in a very long time. Even after how he'd been an idiot, Staci had come for him in his dream. Saved him.

After that, he was sure he could figure everything else out.

CHAPTER NINETEEN

Staci woke with a start. She lay on a soft bed, the smell of fresh linen and Oliver in her nose.

But that hadn't been where she'd fallen asleep. She struggled to separate the dream from reality. She'd been in the woods with Oliver. He'd been dying.

Staci opened her eyes. Oliver lay next to her, still and pale. A moment of panic hit her until she saw his chest move, breath coming slow and easy. He looked about as exhausted as she felt and could use the sleep. Instead, she took in the rest of the room.

It wasn't familiar. A large window on the far wall was open a fraction, letting in a light breeze. The pale curtains fluttered, and the morning light danced over the rest of the room. She'd been asleep all night? It didn't feel like it had been enough.

The floors were a dark hardwood, polished to a shine, and the walls a pale lilac. All the furniture looked as solid as the floor and just as well cared for.

She was wearing an unfamiliar T-shirt that smelled faintly of Oliver. He must have changed her while she'd been out, taken care of her. She smiled, pulling the T-shirt up to her nose.

She turned back to Oliver; he was awake, watching her with amber eyes. 'Hey.'

'Hey,' she said, flushing, feeling like he'd caught her doing something more than just pulling in his scent. She searched for something else to say that wouldn't sound stupid. 'Where are we?'

'We're at Sam's house. I was going to take you to the hospital, but you didn't want to go,' Oliver said. She remembered that faintly. Telling Oliver not to leave her. 'I would've taken you to yours, but I couldn't bear the idea of Florence kicking me out. So, I thought here would be better.'

A moment of panic flared. Florence would be worried sick. Staci sat up, holding the sheet close to her chest. 'Did you tell them where I was? My mum, Florence? They'll be—'

'I told Florence a version of the truth. Though I'm pretty certain I just convinced her we were having a dirty night away,' Oliver said, lip quirking as if he liked the idea that it might be true. She had to admit that she quite liked the idea of that herself. 'But she's fine. Both of them are.'

'Thank you,' Staci said, settling back down. The fear slipped away, and a measure of guilt replaced it. She needed to call Florence or go home since her phone was still at ranger headquarters. But she couldn't make herself move, not yet.

'Sam said we could stay here as long as you want.' Oliver sat up, the sheets curling up in his lap. There was no sign of his wound—not even a scar—it was like last night hadn't happened. He touched the spot on his chest.

'Are you okay?' Staci asked, wanting to place her hand over his, but she held back.

'It still feels bruised, but I'm fine. I promise,' Oliver said, brushing a strand of hair out of her face. 'Thanks to you.'

Staci wanted to lean into his hand, forget everything bad from the last day, and pick up where they left off in the storm shelter. But there were questions she needed answers to first.

'Were you going to tell me we were mates?' Staci asked, watching Oliver closely. He didn't look away, but she saw the pain that flickered through his face. 'I'll take that as a no.'

'At first, I didn't want to scare you off. Then my father came to town,' Oliver said, stopping to lean forward and cup her cheek. The connection between them flared to life. His regret was so intense she could feel it like it was her own emotion. How had she not realised before now that something was strange about feeling his emotions? 'I never wanted to hurt you. I wish I'd seen the truth sooner.'

'And now?'

'Now, I swear to you on my wolf that I will never leave you,' Oliver said, leaning forward to place his forehead against hers. 'I'm yours, always.'

Someone knocked on the door before Staci could say anything. It was soft, like they knew they were probably interrupting but didn't want to.

'Oliver?' Sam said, voice so quiet Staci almost didn't hear her. 'It's almost time. You've thirty minutes.'

His tension rocked up a notch. 'I'll be down in a minute,' he said.

There was no acknowledgement, but Staci assumed Sam had left. 'Time for what?'

'To meet with the prime alphas about my father,' Oliver said, his jaw muscle twitching like he wanted to say more. Or something else. 'They'll decide what happens next.'

'How's he going to defend shooting you?' Staci asked. Though she'd not seen his father pull the trigger, there was little doubt that it had been him.

Oliver looked away, pain and fear flashing through the link. 'My father shifted last night after Hale rescued me. He's not shifted back.'

Staci hesitated, wishing she knew more about how Shifter Magic worked. Not shifting back would mean he wouldn't have to explain his actions. 'He's hiding?'

'It doesn't seem like something my father would do.'

'What does Thor think?' Staci asked.

Oliver opened his mouth, but nothing came out. He turned to her, looking so lost that she reached out and took his hand. Emotions so complex and varied flared up in her mind and flickered so fast she couldn't name them. Except for one. How good it felt that she was touching him. How much he wanted her to keep doing it. She tightened her grip.

'My wolf calls him David now,' Oliver said, shaking his head like he was arguing with himself. Or his wolf. 'Thor doesn't know why David would hide. Someone who can't control themselves enough to shift is dangerous.'

'Will that affect what the prime alphas decide?' Staci asked.

Staci wanted to pull him to her in a hug so tight that she could peel away some of the pain in his voice, but he pulled away from her, moving to stand. He was clearly unconcerned with his nakedness. She'd a moment of déjà vu from the day before.

He pulled his jeans from a stack on the chest of drawers by the door. 'We don't know. This has never happened before. I've never seen or heard of a prime alpha losing control.'

'I want to come.'

'You should get some more sleep.'

'No.' She pulled back the sheets, trying to be as confident in the baggy T-shirt as he was naked. His gaze dipped down her body. Her flush followed his eyes, making her skin feel like it was on fire.

'No distracting me,' she said, bringing his eyes back to hers. 'I'm coming. Your father threatened my mate. I deserve to know how they're going to punish him.'

Oliver's eyes widened, and a slow smile spread over his lips at her words. 'Say that again.'

Out of everything she'd said, she knew exactly what he meant. 'My mate,' she said softly. Her skin tingled as she spoke, almost like the acknowledgement had its own power.

Oliver was across the room before the words had finished, mouth on hers, arms around her, pulling her flush against his body. His tongue slid inside her mouth, tasting every inch of her. She clawed at the jeans he'd just put on.

Another knock came, still soft. 'Twenty minutes,' Sam said, then Staci heard feet moving away this time as she didn't wait for a response. There was no way they'd burned through ten minutes kissing. Though her lips felt bruised.

Oliver cursed against her lips. Then, he relaxed his grip and pulled in a deep breath. 'Later.'

'Later,' Staci agreed. Despite what was to come, she felt light, though going down in Oliver's T-shirt might not inspire the image she'd been aiming for.

Oliver moved to a small pile of clothes on the dresser and brought them back to her. It was the clothes she'd left at headquarters yesterday.

'I had Lance pick them up for you,' Oliver said, handing her the pile with her phone on top. 'I thought you'd appreciate being connected to the rest of the world again.'

'Thank you,' Staci said, struggling to get the words out clearly as she took the pile. There were too many emotions, and she didn't know what to do with them.

She let him turn back to his own pile of clothes as she stripped and dressed in hers. She didn't know exactly where things would go from here, but this time, she wouldn't let anything get in their way. Not his father or her fear. Oliver was hers, and she'd make sure he knew she was claiming him.

The thought wavered for a moment at the word claimed. But it felt right.

Oliver opened the door for her once they were both decent, and she hooked her arm around his, letting the connection burst up. Oliver wouldn't be alone this time when he dealt with his father.

OLIVER DIDN'T LET STACI go until he walked into the kitchen, and even then, it was only long enough to get through the door before he took her hand again.

Not want to talk to alphas, Thor said. *Want to sleep next to mate. Am tired.*

I'm tired, too. We can sleep once all this is over, Oliver said. At least, he hoped they could. It all depended on how this meeting went. His father was in a cage in Sam's wood.

The prime alphas weren't going to like that at all.

'This is beautiful,' Staci said, taking in Sam's kitchen.

She wasn't wrong; it was impressive. The room itself was a large rectangle with old handmade solid wood cabinets covering the narrow back wall. A worktop and more cupboards ran under the window on the long wall until it reached an opaque glass door that led outside. A large old stone fireplace took up the other short wall, and pictures on the mantel showed Sam's family.

Someone had moved Sam's TV from the living room and set it up at the far end of the kitchen in front of the cabinets with a laptop, camera, and microphone. By the way that Sam was tucking away the wires, it had probably been her doing the technical part.

The screen was showing the camera's view. Five chairs sat around the solid wood table, with Sam's fireplace working to create an impressive backdrop. The set-up would make them look good.

'My grandfather made most of these cabinets,' Sam said, looking up at Staci. 'He built most of the house and the furniture in it.'

'You're lucky,' Staci said. 'My house is somewhat ... tired.'

'Your house is beautiful too,' Oliver said. Staci gave him a look. 'It's full of memories and your history.'

'You mean it's worn down?'

'I mean, it's a home, not a showroom like mine was,' Oliver said, and Staci flushed like he'd told her she was the one who was beautiful.

'As much as I hate to interrupt,' Hale said, 'we should get ready.'

Oliver nodded, tightening his grip on Staci's hand as he felt her nervous energy. Or maybe he was just feeling an echo of his own.

Not nervous, Thor said, shaking out his fur. *Bored of this hunt. Should have killed David.*

Oliver didn't bother to argue with his wolf as Hale sat in the centre, Sam beside him. Lance came in the back door, putting his phone in his pocket as he nodded at Oliver, then took the single seat to Sam's left. Oliver took the seat to Hale's right, and Staci sat on Oliver's other side.

Sam tapped on a keyboard Oliver hadn't noticed on the table, bringing up another screen. It started ringing a moment later. The Skype ringtone felt loud in the quiet room. Sam waited for Hale's nod before she accepted the call.

Five pictures appeared on the screen, names helpfully displayed under each box.

'This is pack business. Alpha Business,' Carwyn said before anyone else could. He was the Welsh prime alpha. He had white hair, a long beard, and was the oldest of the gathered men. That age had always made him think it entitled him to some extra respect. 'Anyone not directly involved in this matter should be excused.'

Not the greatest of starts. Oliver didn't move. That was a decision for Hale, not an old man in Wales.

'Everyone here is pack,' Hale said, giving Sam a smile before he turned to Oliver, then Lance. 'Or an alpha.'

'No one permitted you to have alphas in your pack,' Carwyn said, leaning forward.

'Carwyn,' Lachlan said, voice soft. He was a pale-skinned, grey-eyed bear of a man with dirty-blond hair. The few times Oliver had met him, he'd always had a calm, easy manner. 'We already discussed this matter. The decision was clear. If David chose to send his son—who was already an alpha—to Hale, we could hardly stop the inevitable.'

Hale twitched, the tiny movement telling Oliver he'd not known about this decision. Another secret his father had kept. Another lie. Staci reached out under the table, taking Oliver's hand. Their link flared up, making breathing easier. He clearly had a long way to go before he'd find his own balance. He squeezed her hand in thanks.

'One alpha,' Carwyn said, shaking his head. 'Not two.'

Lachlan smiled. 'Lance was already an alpha before he went to Hale's pack.'

Lance didn't react to his name being mentioned, but Carwyn half stood before he remembered he was in a call.

'This wasn't discussed—'

'Enough, this isn't the place or time for this conversation,' Alaric said, cutting in. He was square-jawed with hazel eyes, milky-white skin, and dark brown hair. 'We're here to talk about David.'

There was silence for a moment; the three men were clearly not happy with each other. But they did listen, which must have meant that Alaric had been voted in as the informal lead for this meeting.

'You said that David was … struggling,' Alaric said when no one else spoke, stumbling over the last word like he'd been going to say something else but had changed his mind.

'You should be asking him what he did to David,' Carwyn said. 'Everyone knows the two of them have been at odds ever since Hale became the Highland Rift Scar alpha.'

'You mean since Hale was fortunate enough to find living pack lands?' Noah said. He was a heavyset man, bald, in his fifties, with dark eyes. He was the alpha of the London Rift Pack, which covered the southeast of England. 'Yes, we're all aware of David's animosity.'

'David stole Oliver from my pack,' Hale said, somehow not letting the anger Oliver could feel seep into his voice. 'I took Oliver back. The backlash hit David mid-shift, and he got stuck.'

Too many voices talked at once for Oliver to make out who said what over the Skype link. Alaric once again shushed the group. Carwyn's face was red at another interruption.

'You didn't tell us he was stuck?' Alaric said.

'Oliver was able to push him through the end of the change into his wolf. But since he was violent and attacking my people before he started to shift, I thought it would be best to lock him in a cage for everyone's safety.' Hale paused, looking over the faces in the call. Then he added, 'At dawn, he woke but didn't turn back to human. It has now been a couple of hours, and nothing has changed.'

'I see,' Alaric said when no one else commented. 'Oliver was able to help him even though he was no longer pack?'

'Yes,' Hale said. But he didn't say how. That was a conversation that still needed to be had. Only the alpha of that Shifter was supposed to have that ability. Thor was being frustratingly vague on it.

'And your intentions for David?' Alaric asked, raising an eyebrow.

'He remains in a cage. But with him being a prime alpha, I didn't know what else to do with him. He's not my pack,' Hale said.

'It's interesting that this is how you have chosen to deal with the matter after he stole one of yours,' Lachlan said, voice carefully neutral. The suggestion that other options would be considered wasn't lost on anyone in the meeting.

'Lachlan!' Carwyn said, half standing again, slamming his hand on the table.

This time, Oliver couldn't help but look at Hale. There was nothing on his face that showed what he thought, and all that Oliver could smell was anger.

'I don't wish to be the prime alpha of Scotland,' Hale said, glancing at Oliver. 'But I won't allow David to harm my people.'

Carwyn didn't like that either. The growl rumbled over the speakers, making them crackle.

'George,' Alaric said, talking to the only member of the group who hadn't spoken. 'You're the closest alpha not on connecting land. Would you like to deal with this matter?'

George was the alpha of the Midlands Pack and the youngest in the group at just over forty. He had thick black curly hair, cut short to his scalp, deep ebony skin, and large brown eyes. He nodded, showing nothing of what he felt of the task. 'I will see if he can regain control and deal with the matter if not.'

'And if he's unfit. What happens to his pack then?' Hale said.

'Then we find a new prime alpha,' Alaric said, a smile playing on his lips. 'Whether or not they want the job.'

'That's not a decision you can make alone,' Carwyn said, a hint of a growl in his voice.

'Once George has evaluated David, we'll meet again and let everyone know what comes next,' Alaric said. 'Is there anything else that needs to be discussed?'

'There is another matter. David was working with a young weather warden, Elliot, and his mother to create a storm that would damage the town,' Lance said, leaning forward.

There was silence at the other end of the call, and Staci tightened her grip on Oliver's hand. He wished he'd had time to warn her they would be bringing this up here.

'You have proof?' Alaric asked.

Lance nodded. 'I have passed the details onto the appropriate authorities. They'll probably wish to investigate David's involvement. Along with a local councilwoman.'

'Very well,' Alaric said. Though it sounded more like a curse than the words had any right to. 'If that's all?' This time, there was silence. 'Then we're done.'

The call ended without any formality as they were kicked off.

'They're a bit bitchy,' Sam said, and Staci choked on a laugh. 'Are they always like that?'

Hale smiled faintly. 'Mostly.'

'Gawd, no wonder you don't want to deal with them,' Sam said, pushing her seat back. She dropped a kiss on Hale's mouth as she stood. 'I'm going to clean everything up, then make some food. You're all welcome to stay if you're hungry.'

Oliver's stomach growled in response to the suggestion, surging to the forefront, and Sam laughed again.

'Food it is, then,' Sam said.

'Does Lance really have proof that Joyce and Elliot created the storm deliberately?' Staci asked.

'Yes,' Lance said, answering before Oliver could. 'Evidence that they can't refute. They're going to go to jail for a very long time.'

'Thank you.'

'Anytime,' Lance said, giving them both a flash of his wolf's gold eyes. 'I told you we take care of our own.'

Like a pack was supposed to.

Oliver pulled Staci closer as their shared emotions threatened to overwhelm them.

They were home.

CHAPTER TWENTY

LANCE WATCHED AS JOYCE was brought into the police station. She held her head high, looking down at everyone around her. She wasn't in cuffs, which he'd been hoping for. But considering the sway she had, he'd probably been lucky the local cops had arrested her at all.

It had taken a few days for the authorities to review everything and get the warrant for Joyce's arrest. He kept expecting her to run during that time, but she'd not left town. Her arrogance had worked against her.

He and Zoe were sitting alone in the corner of the local police office while the Special Investigation Branch got all their ducks in a row. The burnt orange and off-white colour scheme made the place feel small and claustrophobic. Which it was.

There was one interview room, a cluster of desks in an open-plan office, a few meeting rooms, and a canteen down the hall. Downstairs, they had a few small holding cells, most strong enough to hold a Shifter. Not that they'd needed to use it for any wolves since Hale had been alpha.

'What do you think? She turns into a crying bag of shit the minute she's in the interrogation room?' Zoe asked. Going by the nervous energy of her wolf zipping across his skin, she was trying to distract herself. Being back in what must have felt like the centre of her old life couldn't have been easy. Especially not when the police had abandoned her after she'd been changed.

Zoe was still so new to being a Shifter that, in most other circumstances, he'd have made her stay away from something this personal. But she was strong and stubborn, and more to the point, without her help, he'd never have been able to pull off arresting Joyce.

Help distract her, Shade said. *Make feel better.*

But the distraction involved having a conversation. Lance had already let himself get too attached to the pack. Regardless of what Hale thought, there were better people for Zoe to rely on than him.

We help Oliver. Help Staci. Now we help Zoe, Shade said, a slight growl in his voice. He wasn't wrong. They'd helped Staci and Oliver. But neither of them was relying on him for support.

'She's too privileged to believe she's going to be punished for what she did,' Lance said at last.

Zoe let out a little snort. 'You might be right,' she said.

Letting the conversation die there would have been easy, but his wolf was right. A distraction would help.

'They'll charge her. She'll get a solicitor. They'll show her the evidence, which is overwhelming. She'll deny it. The Special Investigators will then petition to take the case to Edinburgh since it's a crime that involves magic abuse. She'll have no way to stop it. Then she may realise that she won't have her family's status to protect her anymore.' Lance paused to look at Zoe and added. 'Then she might cry.'

Zoe smiled. 'And Elliot?'

'If he wakes up, he'll definitely cry,' Lance said, shaking his head. Elliot was still in the hospital and hadn't woken since they'd dropped him off. Unlike Staci, getting hit by lightning had burned him pretty severely, and he was covered in Lichtenberg figures, pale pinkish tattoo-like marks. The Special Investigators had ensured the hospital was drugging him with small amounts of Rift venom just in case he woke. They didn't take any chances with magic. If he was innocent, they'd maybe apologise after it was all over. Maybe. 'Then he'll flip on anyone he has to to avoid jail.'

The Special Investigators came out of a meeting room at the far side of the room. Two women, both Elementals, in black suits and hair pulled up into a bun. Zoe stiffened a little at seeing them.

Lance let his wolf's power rise just a fraction, letting Zoe feel he was there. She relaxed a little. He might not be her alpha, but he was pack, and a little connection could help.

'Your wolf feels so calm,' Zoe said, glancing at him, then away. 'I can't imagine mine ever feeling that way.'

'It takes time,' Lance said, ignoring Shade as he preened under the compliment. 'I've had over ten years of practice. You're not even at a year.'

'Sometimes I think it won't matter how much time passes,' Zoe said, looking at her feet.

This was the most Zoe had ever opened up to anyone since she'd arrived last month. He wanted to tell her to talk to Hale, but she'd probably just close up again.

'What does your wolf want?' Lance asked.

'To hunt down those hurting the pack,' Zoe said, still not looking at them.

'So does mine,' Lance said, making her turn to him, judging if his words were genuine. She'd been a cop long enough to know the truth when she saw it. 'But we're still here, still human, letting the police deal with both troublemakers.'

'But what happens when I can't?' Zoe barely whispered the words. Her fear. Or part of it, anyway.

Humans were taught that Shifters were dangerous and that they should manage them with care. So, in the rare cases where they become Shifters themselves, that fear turned inwards.

'Me and Hale will hunt you down and put you out of your misery.' Lance spoke gently, making it a promise rather than a threat.

Tears gathered at the edge of her eyes, not quite falling. The scent of her relief wasn't exactly a surprise, but it made him sad. He hated that anyone felt that way about their wolf.

'Thank you,' Zoe said at last, taking a quick breath as she stared at the far wall.

'But I'd rather you didn't let it come to that,' Lance said. He put his hand on her arm this time until she looked at him. 'I'm here if you need to talk.'

Zoe's wolf rose around him a little stronger, and her eyes flashed to muddy amber. The energy was powerful, or at least it would be once it finished maturing. Right now, her wolf was little more than a pup.

'Your wolf is not your enemy, and not all the instincts are dangerous,' Lance said. He hesitated a moment before continuing, trying to ignore the stab of pain that came with every thought of his previous life. 'My wolf helped me track for the police. His instincts and understanding of the world are vastly different from mine.'

Shade missed those days, Lance realised with a start. Missed hunting in the city and showing off his skills. Shade tried to hide the thought, but it was too late.

Am happy here too, Shade said, showing him images of them hunting in the Rift. Lance filed the thought away for later to talk to his wolf, focusing on Zoe here now.

'Learn what your wolf sees, listen to her, understand her. It doesn't always have to be a fight,' Lance said.

Zoe didn't look convinced. It would take a lot more than one conversation to help her. But it was a start.

The Special Investigators came out of the room, scowling. Joyce had that effect on people.

'Solicitor,' Zoe said, letting the conversation shift away. 'You called it.'

Lance nodded as the Investigators came their way. This was the first step of many, but the pair had been arrested. From here, it was up to the courts, who hated magic-related crimes.

There was little chance of either Elliot or Joyce escaping justice. Lance would take that as a win.

A WEEK AFTER THE storm, Florence insisted Staci bring Oliver around for dinner. They'd mostly been sneaking moments together when they could, but it hadn't been easy with their work schedules and her mum. Once again, most of it was Elliot's fault. Those storm fragments had ruined the weather all around Huntly, and it needed a lot of managing to get it back to normal.

'Thank you for coming,' Staci said, leaning over to kiss his lips lightly as he stopped in front of her house.

Oliver put his hand on the back of her neck, and the light kiss turned into something else fast. He trailed kisses down her jaw, sending tiny streams of fire down to her core. She wrapped one arm around his neck to steady herself.

A door slammed somewhere nearby; Staci jumped and pulled away. Her neighbours might not appreciate the show. She was breathing hard, and that had just been a damned kiss.

'We should go inside,' Staci said, though most of her wanted to sneak back to Oliver's apartment.

Oliver nodded, looking at her with those glorious amber eyes. 'We can finish this later,' he said.

Staci's heart skipped a beat at the promise and reminder. He was staying. She wanted to lean over and kiss him again but didn't trust herself. They got out, holding hands like teenagers, as they headed to her house.

'Is it okay?' Florence asked, her voice coming from the kitchen as Staci opened her front door.

'Thank you, this is lovely,' a man's voice said. She knew that voice, but she couldn't quite remember where from. She hesitated a moment before continuing into the kitchen.

Florence was stirring a large pot on the stove. A man in his early sixties with a crooked nose, slate-grey eyes, white wispy hair, and a thick white beard sat at her kitchen table. The sun had tanned his skin a dirty, leathery brown since she'd last seen him. Jake. The town's old weather warden.

Her mum wasn't in the room, but Staci could hear the faint sound of the TV from the living room.

'You're late,' Florence said, giving Staci a knowing smile. 'I hope you're hungry. I've made your favourite stew.'

'It smells heavenly,' Oliver said, and she felt his hunger through their linked hands.

'Sit, sit. Talk to Jake while I finish preparing it. It will need some time to simmer.'

'Oliver,' he said as he offered Jake his hand. They shook before Oliver took a seat next to Staci.

'Nice to meet you. You're a ranger, right?' Jake asked, smiling when Oliver nodded.

'Yes,' Oliver said. 'For eight months now.'

'The rangers always took good care of me if I needed to go into the Rift Scar,' Jake said. He sounded wistful, which wasn't normally the reaction people had to going there.

'What brings you to town?' Staci asked, glancing at Florence. She looked pleased with herself. Something was happening.

'Retirement is boring,' he said. 'There's no challenge in it, and the local weather wardens get prissy when I try to help, even if it's free.'

Staci couldn't help but smile at the tone. This was from the man who had lectured her in depth about not interfering with his storms when she'd come back to town for a visit while she'd still been learning.

'I'm too old for most places to want to hire me. Too many fitter people to deal with their problems, they don't need an old man. Besides, I don't want something full time,' he said, glancing back at Florence. She flushed, then moved back to the stew, fussing over it.

Florence and Jake? Oliver nudged Staci, making her realise she was expected to say something.

'There was a position here. Whether the council will hire someone after everything that happened is another matter.'

'Yes, I heard. Lance told me about most of it,' Jake said. 'Nasty business. Never heard of anything like it. I'm really sorry you had to go through that.'

'Lance?' Staci asked, glancing at Oliver. She could feel his excitement through their link. Lance had asked Jake to help with Elliot? How had he even known who to call?

'Yes. He called me after the storm and asked me to tell the council whether what Elliot claimed was possible,' Jake said, scratching at his beard. 'I told them it wasn't. If Elliot ever recovers enough to stand trial, I'll be more than happy to provide the evidence to prove it, too.'

Staci didn't know what to say to that. It was her fault he'd been hit by the lightning. He'd been transported to a specialist unit down south, but so far, he seemed to be alive but unresponsive.

'After everything had settled down, I called Charles,' Jake said. Calling the mayor by name always felt strange to her. 'He told me what had happened to Elliot and that there's a position here.'

Staci nodded. That wasn't a surprise. He'd been the weather warden for a long time. The council would jump at the chance to bring him back. They'd probably want him full time. Her heart did a little flutter. He'd said that wasn't what he wanted, but ...

'But before I accepted, I wanted to talk to you about it first,' Jake said, glancing at Florence again. 'I know things haven't been easy with Elliot, but I'm not him.'

'I'm surprised the council didn't offer you a full-time position,' Staci said. Oliver took her hand under the table, offering reassurance.

'They didn't. Charles was very clear that you'd be the senior weather warden,' Jake said, smiling. 'I don't think I've ever seen him quite so riled up.'

Staci wasn't sure she believed him, but she also couldn't see why he'd lie. 'You're okay with that?'

Jake laughed. 'I can't promise it will always be easy, but I'll do my very best.'

The answer was about as honest as you could get. Staci looked at Florence, and she nodded. To be fair, this was probably the best offer Staci was likely to get.

'I don't have any issues with it,' Staci said, glancing at Oliver. More help meant more time with her mother and Oliver.

'Good. I'll tell Charles. He may call to check with you,' Jake said. He and Florence exchanged another glance, something unspoken passing between them. 'Charles also mentioned you wanted to know about your father.'

Chills ran down Staci's spine. She'd not been brave enough to ask Florence herself. Oliver ran his thumb over

Staci's wrist as he sensed the change in her emotions. That link between them was a little like a couple's cheat code. Blessing and a curse.

'Joyce said ...' Staci couldn't finish, she didn't know how.

Florence and Jake exchanged another glance. 'I'll tell you what happened if you want to know. I think your mother would if she could. You're not a child anymore,' Jake said.

Staci leaned a little closer into Oliver. She wanted to know, but at the same time, she was afraid. 'Yes,' she said, the word nearly catching in her throat.

'Your father was never trained because his dad died when he was still a kid, and there wasn't a school to send people to back then,' Jake said, shaking his head. 'Family was supposed to teach the kids, but your grandmother was human and didn't know how to find another Storm Elemental.

'Anyway, jump ahead a few years, and the town realised how much your grandfather had been doing to manage the weather, so they bring me in.' Jake winced. 'I'd been a weather warden a while by then. I knew within a week of coming to town why the weather was so bad.'

'My father,' Staci said, shivering.

Jake nodded. 'He was playing with it, letting small storms form with no thought of the consequences. It was easy for him. I tried to work with him and guide him, but he saw me as an interloper. Someone who had been brought in to replace him.'

Staci hesitated, not sure how to ask the first question that came to mind. It had felt good to be inside the storm, so much so that she could see how that could become addictive.

'Could he ...' Staci trailed off.

'Catch the lightning like you did? Be part of the storm?' Jake said gently, making her look up. He knew. Had probably always known. That's why he'd been so keen to train her. 'There are ways to mitigate the draw of the storm, like working as part of a team. But those who run the schools have always believed it was too dangerous to train people how to use Storm Magic like that. I told them what you had done, and their solution was just to focus on training you not to do it.'

Staci had more questions than she could count, but that wasn't why Jake was here now. Those could come later. 'Tell me the rest of the story,' Staci said.

'Things calmed down a bit when he met your mother, but as you got older, he meddled again,' Jake said. He paused like he wasn't sure if he wanted to continue. Florence sat down next to him, putting her hand on his.

'I should have done more, pushed him to go apprentice. Something. But I thought I could handle his interference.'

'No one knew how bad it was,' Florence said, tightening her grip on his hand. 'Frederick was good at making people happy. Making them think they were the only person in the world who existed when he spoke to you.'

'What happened?' Staci asked when both trailed off.

'There was a storm,' Jake said. 'A wild one. Mostly, I'd been able to dismantle the weather as he made it. But your father liked this one. He kept fighting me. Building it up.'

Staci remembered how hard it had been to manipulate Elliot's storm. How the storm had been almost aware and, with Elliot fighting her, she didn't know if she'd have been able to stop it if he'd not burned out first.

'We argued, and your mother gave us a good tongue lashing,' Jake said, a faint smile rising on his lips before it disappeared. 'I should have done something then, but I thought I could talk to him.'

So far, there seemed to have been little he could have done. But Staci didn't interrupt, afraid he'd stop talking.

'The storm was wild and out of control, and its core was above your house. I came as fast as I could. Your father was in the garden, soaked to the skin,' Jake said, hands twitching as he looked down, then back to Staci. 'He had you in his arms.'

Oliver's arm slid around her waist like he could protect her from this memory. 'I don't remember that,' she whispered.

'You were only four,' Florence said, a quiver in her voice. 'I came out of my house when I heard a noise. I've never been so terrified in my life. Your mother was screaming at him to put you down. But he wanted to show you lightning.'

Staci swallowed hard, feeling sick. That would have killed her or crippled her like Elliot.

'He wasn't doing it to hurt you; he was so pleased with his damned storm he wanted you to see it. Feel it like he did. He was so lost in the thing's power he couldn't even remember that it would hurt you,' Jake said, pulling at his beard. 'I got you away from him before the lightning hit him.'

Staci remembered Jake's face when he'd come to help her. His concern. Now, she was starting to see why. He had to have been worried that she'd follow in her father's footsteps. That's why Joyce had been afraid. She knew something of this, though maybe not the full story.

'What happened after that?' Staci asked when, once again, they paused.

Florence brushed imaginary crumbs off the table. 'Your mother kicked him out,' she said. 'Swore she'd never let him near you again.'

Jake patted Florence's hand this time. 'When your father returned to himself, he realised he'd gone too far. He chose to leave.'

Her mother had never said either of those, only that he'd left and wasn't ever coming home. But the pain in her voice when she'd said it had always stopped Staci from asking questions.

'What happened to him?' Staci asked. Though, what she really wanted to know was why he'd never tried to reach out once he was better.

'He told me and your mother that he was going to come with me and get training at the new magic college,' Jake said slowly. 'But I never saw him again after that morning. He'd burned his magic out, so I'd let him go say goodbye.'

'You couldn't have known,' Florence said. 'Even Melanie didn't know.'

'But If I'd just followed him,' Jake said, shaking his head. 'He wouldn't have had a chance to go.'

'He'd have just found another way, and you know it,' Florence said.

Jake didn't look like he believed her but slowly turned back to Staci. 'Your father disappeared. We found a letter after, saying he never wanted to risk hurting you or Melanie again.'

Staci's eyes burned as she tried not to let her tears fall. Was this supposed to make her feel better or worse? He'd tried to protect her, but he'd given up, too. What if the same thing happened to her?

'I'll never let that happen to you,' Oliver said, tugging on their bond like he'd sensed the direction of her thoughts. Or maybe she'd spoken out loud. Either way, it was a reminder that even if she got lost, he'd be there for her.

If Jake and Florence found Oliver's words odd, neither said it. She'd have argued if he'd said this to her a week ago. But now? He'd been inside her dream. He'd felt what she'd felt.

'Did you find him?' Oliver asked.

'No,' Jake said.

After everything they'd described about how much her father had been obsessed with the storm, she doubted he'd have been able to stop. If he was still alive, then someone would have found him.

He was dead.

She didn't know how she felt about that. Nor did she know if she felt better for knowing the truth.

'Is that stew I smell?' Staci's mum said in the doorway. 'It smells amazing.'

Florence wiped away a stray tear and rushed to Staci's mum's side, offering an arm. 'It is. And I made your favourite,' she said.

The moment gave Staci a chance to wipe her own tears. She wasn't sure what to do with the information. Had her mum known? Did it matter now?

'Staci, who's your lovely gentleman?' her mum said as Florence helped her to the chair away from the stove.

'This is Oliver,' Staci said, glancing at him as she took a slow breath, trying to push back the sadness. He showed no concern over the re-introduction.

'Are you staying for dinner, Oliver?' Staci's mum said, smiling at him. It wasn't easy to tell where her mum's memory was, but being remembered was always welcome.

'I'm staying, yes,' Oliver said, dropping a kiss on Staci's temple. 'Always.'

Staci smiled at him. She was starting to believe that promise.

EATING DINNER WITH STACI'S family and friends was a lot like he'd imagined growing up in a pack should have been. The conversation was stilted for a start as they struggled to shake off the sombre mood following Staci's family history. But before long, Jake was telling stories of Staci's first storm as his apprentice. Her mother talked about Staci's first day of school. Florence regaled them with Staci's pirate phase.

Oliver laughed so hard that the stew was cold by the time he finally finished his bowl. The scents of the room mingled until nothing was distinct except that it smelled like a real home. Staci was warm where she leaned against him. Their bond sent him happy contentment with the occasional burst of embarrassment as the stories made her cringe.

He almost ignored his phone when it rang, for a very different reason than before. He didn't want this moment to end. But there was still a lot going on to risk it. He excused himself from the table when he saw Hale as the caller ID.

'Everything okay?' Oliver asked, not bothering with a greeting. Hale never called just to chat.

'The prime alphas sent someone to tell us what happened with your father,' Hale said. His voice was oddly formal, which probably meant the person was there with him. 'Can you come to Sam's?'

Oliver bit down on a growl. They'd gone to Sam's house to find Hale? He wouldn't like that.

'I'll be there in forty minutes,' Oliver said, saying good-bye before he hung up and pocketed his phone.

'What's wrong?' Staci asked, coming up behind him to wrap an arm around his stomach and put a cheek against his back.

'I have to go see Hale,' Oliver said. 'Someone is here about my father.'

'I'm coming with you,' Staci said. She moved around so he could see her face, and the stubborn set of her jaw that he was starting to recognise meant she wouldn't budge.

'Thank you,' Oliver said, leaning down for a kiss. He might not like what his father had done, but he still didn't know how he felt about where this was going. A week of silence hadn't been a good sign for his father's fate.

They said their goodbyes to the others, leaving them to their old memories and joy. The drive took less than forty minutes because, at this time of night, not a single cop would be out this far from town watching for people speeding.

Benjamin wasn't the person Oliver was expecting to see when he entered Sam's kitchen. With his blond hair, stormy-grey eyes, and three-piece suit, the man looked too formal for the room or the cartoon coffee cup on the table in front of him. He was the reason Oliver had ended up at the Highland Rift Scar.

Vane, Benjamin's son, was one of the two wolves that Oliver had accidentally pulled into his pack. Benjamin had suggested sending Oliver away as punishment, and his father had jumped at the chance. The next day, Benjamin had given Oliver a lift to the train station, making it clear that he didn't think sending Oliver away was a punishment. It was a gift. It was only in the last week that he'd started to believe that was true.

'Oliver,' Benjamin said, looking him up and down, lingering on Oliver's eyes, but he said nothing about the colour, 'you look well.'

'Thank you,' Oliver said, tightening his grip on Staci's hand.

The back door opened, making them all turn as Vane stepped inside. He'd not changed much in the last eight months, except that he'd chopped his blond hair to nearly his skin. He was slim for a wolf, with baby-blue eyes and dimples that drew in every woman who saw them.

Pack, Thor said.

But Vane wasn't his pack any more.

Still pack, Thor said grumpily.

Vane saw him and stopped so suddenly that Lance, who'd been following behind him, nearly walked into his back.

'I'd like to petition to join the pack,' Vane said without even bothering with a hello.

'Hale—'

'No,' Vale said, interrupting Oliver. 'Your pack. I want to re-join your pack.'

Oliver stared at Vane. He'd only been part of Oliver's pack for an hour. Why the hell would he want to re-join?

We good alpha, Thor said like that was enough.

'I have agreed to my son's request, providing you and your alpha are agreeable,' Benjamin said to Oliver before turning back to Vane and adding, 'but a hello first might have been politer.'

Vane flushed but didn't backtrack on his request. Oliver looked at Hale, who nodded, which wasn't a surprise. They needed new pack members, especially ones who wanted to be here. But Oliver hesitated. Vane had a much safer and normal life back home.

'Why would you want to come live here? You would need to work in the Rift Scar. It's dangerous,' Oliver said. 'You could be an alpha back home, have your own pack.'

'I'm not strong enough to be an alpha,' Vane said, glancing at his father, then back at Oliver.

'Funny, I seem to recall you'd been doing just fine,' Oliver said. Vane had lost against Oliver, but he'd not been a slouch. 'Besides, you've plenty of time.'

'Not when my father is now the prime alpha,' Vane said.

Everyone looked at Benjamin. He didn't look like he had any more power than before. Didn't feel any different at all. But clearly, Benjamin liked to make people overlook him. A lot like Hale.

But if Benjamin was prime, that meant …

'My father?' Oliver asked, though he already knew the answer.

'He unfortunately fell ill quite suddenly,' Benjamin said, sounding like he was telling the truth. I suppose it could be considered the truth. 'It's rare in Shifters, but it's a very fast deterioration when it comes. He passed the pack to me before he died.'

'How did you keep him from hurting the rest of the pack?' Hale asked.

'Distance and that everyone in his pack, except his wife, were alphas. We were able to resist the call,' Benjamin said, letting out a sigh. 'He thought it strengthened him, but really it let us protect the others from him.'

'But not Oliver,' Staci said, her voice sharp. She'd moved up beside Oliver, not touching, but just there. He stayed silent, not arguing with her because she wasn't wrong. 'You didn't protect him.'

Benjamin gave her a quick once-over, but he turned back to Oliver when he answered. 'No one believed David would hurt his son, his own blood. His mother said David was gentle with Oliver. We shouldn't have believed her, but it's easier to believe that lie.' Benjamin shook his head. 'Then I saw his reaction when you stole Vane from me. The rage. The depth of his hatred.'

Good alpha, Thor said, but it was hesitant. If he'd been a good alpha, why had it taken him so long to help? *Not stronger than David.*

That was true. None of them were stronger. But together, they could have been. But they'd have suffered the same consequences that Hale had been trying to avoid. The prime alpha had to also want change, or there would be consequences.

'Why didn't you tell the other prime alphas about what was happening?' Hale said, moving forward so he could see Benjamin's face.

'They knew. They did nothing. It was David's land and business; if we wanted him out, we should find someone strong enough to challenge him.' Benjamin paused. 'I think some hoped you would do it, Hale. Though they'd have killed you for it, anyway.'

'Now you're one of them,' Hale said.

'I had suggested Oliver. It's his right as David's son,' Benjamin said. Vane made a noise like that was news to him. 'It was violently protested too by some. Age being the main objection that had any weight.'

'I don't want to be prime alpha,' Oliver said, shaking his head. 'I've met most of them. So far, I've not been impressed.'

'What happens now?' Hale asked, eyes on Benjamin. It wasn't exactly a challenge, but there was tension there.

Benjamin smiled. 'As prime alpha, my first intention is to leave this pack as it has always been. Independent.'

He was acknowledging he wasn't stronger than Hale; it was subtle, phrased like a favour, but it was there nonetheless.

'The prime alphas have agreed to your previous *request*. Those who are here may choose to stay or go as they please. You may, of course, also bring in other Shifters, providing they're working in the Rift Scar.' Benjamin paused at that one, judging Hale's reaction to the limitation.

It was an unusual one that no other pack had. Not even the London pack, which surrounded a Rift Scar. But it was better than any of them had expected to get at this point.

'Additionally, the prime alphas are *requesting*,' Benjamin said, emphasising the last word. Oliver doubted that was the word they'd used. 'That if you learn how the pack lands now feel alive, that you inform them.'

'If I learn the how of it, I'll consider the request,' Hale said. Nothing of his scent or power indicated that he'd lied.

'Now, back to my son,' Benjamin said, turning back to Oliver. 'Will you accept him into your pack?'

Vane had been quiet up until this point, staying out of the way. 'I spoke to the London Rift training centre, and they've got a programme starting next week with spaces.'

Oliver wanted to say no. Protecting Staci, Amelia, and Mitchel was too important to risk bringing more Shifters into his pack. But Vane hadn't come here to join the Rift Scar fight. He could have joined any Rift Scar. Hell, he could have joined Hale's pack for that.

'Why?' Oliver asked again.

'I'm not strong enough to be an alpha. I don't want to spend the next twenty years fighting off people who think they can beat me to gain status,' Vane said, which had a note of truth. It had been happening to Oliver since he'd first become a Shifter. Not to mention, it had been the reason Vane had challenged Oliver in the first place. 'But I can fight in the Rift Scar. I'm good enough for that.'

He was choosing to take the risk of the Rift Scar so he could join Oliver's pack? There had to be more than just challenges. He could join any rural pack and avoid that drama without having to sign up to work in the Rift Scar.

'That's not a good enough reason,' Oliver said, pressing for the truth.

Vane looked at his father like he wasn't sure if he wanted to speak, but after a moment, he straightened and turned back to Oliver. 'When you pulled me into your pack, I felt you; I felt the strength of your loyalty for your friends, how you'd do anything to protect those in your pack,' Vane said, a faint flush climbing over his neck.

'I realised I wasn't like that. I wanted to be stronger in a fight because it made me feel good, not to protect a future pack.' Vane winced like admitting that truth had cost him. 'I want to be part of a pack where they protect each other. I want to learn how to be that kind of alpha. That's why I want to join your pack.'

Oliver glanced at Benjamin. He didn't give much away, but it was obvious that this had surprised him too. Vane's admission can't have been an easy one for him.

Accept, Thor said, but didn't press to force Oliver to talk. The pack wasn't just Thor's alone. This was a decision they both made. *Need us. We keep him safe. Help teach.*

Oliver wavered for another moment. But in the end, he realised he couldn't turn Vane away, even if his first reason had been genuine.

'Yes,' Oliver said, turning to Vane. 'You can join my pack.'

Vane's smile damned near split his face. Oliver hoped Vane wouldn't regret it once he experienced Rift Scar reality. But if he did, Oliver would find him somewhere else safe instead.

'Good, then I'll pass the bonds now. Then when Vane finishes training, he can come straight home,' Benjamin said. Using the word home wasn't lost on any of them. 'And while we drive back to Glasgow, he can figure out how he's going to explain this to his mother.'

Vane paled a little but didn't change his mind. Taking Vane willingly from Benjamin was actually harder than stealing him had been, but Oliver wisely didn't say that.

They left not long after that. His little pack had grown, and once again, the new member was going out of range. But Amelia and Mitchel would be back soon, at least for a little while.

Am good alpha, Thor said. *We keep all safe.*

Yes, Oliver said. Because he was sure of one thing: he'd never let anyone hurt his pack like his father had hurt him.

CHAPTER TWENTY-ONE

It had been nearly two weeks since the storm. Now Jake was helping with the weather, Staci had found more time to spend with Oliver. But it still didn't feel like enough. She wanted more of him, time and connection, especially when his job was so dangerous, and her stomach dropped every time he went into the Rift Scar.

Thanks to Sam, she'd found a way to get it. If Oliver agreed.

'What if Oliver says no?' Staci asked as she rubbed her hands on her jeans. It did little to help as the clammy sweat returned moments later. Her stomach flipped around like it wanted to set up its own circus act.

'It's going to be okay. He's going to love it,' Amelia said. The tall blond woman was sitting at one end of Sam's kitchen table, eating her weight in bacon. Amelia had arrived back in town two days ago, and Staci had finally met her properly. 'Have something to eat.'

Staci shook her head. She was too nervous to eat.

'Oliver's not going to be the problem,' Sam said. She'd just got up to take the newest batch of bacon out of the grill. The smell should have been amazing, but it only added to the twisting in Staci's stomach.

'I won't do it if it's going to cause you problems,' Staci said, but that was the coward's way out. It wasn't that she didn't want to do this. She was worried that Oliver didn't want her to.

'I'll deal with Hale,' Sam said, smiling as she slid a few slices of bacon into a roll and nudged it towards Staci. 'But if you don't want to do this, you can back out at any point. I'm not even sure it will work.'

'It's not that I don't want to do it,' Staci said, fingering the roll, but she didn't pick it up. 'I just don't want to pressure him into thinking he has to.'

'You're his mate. Having you in his pack is all he wants,' Amelia said. She stopped eating and leaned forward. 'Trust me, I know. I can see it in his eyes when he watches me and Mitchel.'

Mitchel was Amelia's mate, just like Hale was Sam's, and Oliver was Staci's. But they were more than just mates. They were pack. Because Sam had been able to bring them in with her Earth Elemental Magic. It was a secret she had shared, even though if it got out, it could cost her life here.

Then Sam had said she might be able to make Staci part of Oliver's pack. But this wasn't just her choice.

'You're sure Oliver wants this?' Staci asked again. Oliver hadn't even mentioned it, though she understood why he hadn't. The secret wasn't his to share.

'Yes,' Sam and Amelia said together.

Sam sat and piled hot bacon inside her own soft white roll. 'If you want to wait, we don't have to do this today,' Sam said. She was patient, giving Staci room to think.

Staci didn't need room; she knew what she wanted. 'No, I want to do this.'

'Good, because they're almost here,' Sam said.

Staci concentrated. She could feel Oliver, feel him getting closer now as she looked for it. Sam seemed to always know where Hale was and how he was feeling—if he let her. But Staci had to search for her link, and all she could feel was a direction until she touched Oliver. The difference between being pack and mated and just being mated.

Staci made herself eat the bacon roll. It was amazing; the bacon was cooked just right, still juicy and the fat soft. They ate silently until Hale and Oliver came in through the back door.

Seeing him sent a thrill through her. No matter how many times she saw him, it never went away. He was hers. He made her feel safe and loved.

Both men looked around the room suspiciously. She managed not to shy away from Hale's eyes, though they remained human. Oliver had never changed back from his stunning amber since the fight with his father.

'What's going on?' Hale asked.

'I want to petition to join the pack,' Staci said, rushing the words out, watching Oliver as she remembered how he'd reacted when Vane had asked. 'I want to join Oliver's pack.'

Oliver went still. She wanted to get up and touch him, see what he felt, but he deserved privacy for this. The longer they were mated, the more she could understand his emotions, though not always the source. But sometimes, it could cause an echo. His joy would become hers, and vice versa.

'You want to be part of my pack?' Oliver said, coming to kneel in front of her. He didn't touch her.

'Yes,' Staci said, forcing herself to keep her hands on her knee. 'If you want me.'

Oliver looked at her for a moment. 'Yes,' he said, a smile nearly breaking his face. 'Yes, I want you there more than anything in this world.'

Without giving her a chance to speak, Oliver leaned forward, capturing her in a kiss. His joy spilt into her through the bond. Warm and bright, making her feel like she was wrapped in a soft blanket. She struggled to remember why she'd been worried.

Hale was speaking to Sam, but the words were lost as Oliver stole all of her attention.

Slowly, Oliver pulled back and knelt on the floor, not letting go of her hands. He looked at Sam. 'Can you do that?'

'I want to try,' Sam said, squeezing Hale's hand where he'd moved to stand next to her. 'Every time we've done it, someone has been hurt. It might not be possible. But I want to try.'

Oliver turned to Hale, body tense and worried.

'This might not be something you can change your mind about,' Hale said, watching Staci. 'We don't know enough about how the bonds work. About how the mate link works.'

'I want to be with Oliver. Being part of the pack makes the link stronger. It would let me feel he's safe at a distance rather than just where he is,' Staci said. 'And I want to give him the same, so he knows I'm fine when I work.'

Hale turned to Oliver, giving him a long, searching look. 'If you're both sure, I won't stand in your way,' Hale said, gently tucking Sam's hair behind her ear. 'I wouldn't have let anyone stand in my way if the positions were reversed.'

Staci let out a breath she hadn't meant to hold, then squealed as Oliver picked her up from the chair. He kissed her so hard she barely remembered to wrap her legs around his waist.

'Get a room,' someone said, voice too distant for her to care.

'My mate,' Oliver whispered against her lips.

'Mine,' Staci said.

She had everything she hadn't even known she wanted.

OLIVER STOPPED AT THE doorway to watch Hale. He'd turned Sam's garage into a gym, attaching the reinforced punching bag to a heavy support frame. He was punching a bag with careful strikes.

'What did Mitchel say?' Hale asked, pulling back from the punching bag.

Mitchel was a scientist who'd dedicated his life to finding a way to shrink the Rift Scar. He'd been studying the Scar's border ever since Oliver had brought Staci into his pack two weeks ago.

Oliver still couldn't believe she was in his pack. Just thinking about her brought a sense of her to his mind. She was outside, waiting for him.

'It's shrunk about half a mile,' Oliver said. 'He thinks it's stopped moving now.'

'Was he able to detect anything?' Hale asked, grabbing a bottle of water from a small bench nearby.

'No,' Oliver said, grimacing.

Mitchel had been very excited when Staci and Oliver had told him what they were going to do. A chance to see the change as it happened had made him sure he'd be able to detect something. But they'd all been wrong. Amelia was the only thing keeping Mitchel from being despondent at this point.

The faint scent of Hale's relief and then frustration peppered the room. Good results would have meant eventually letting everyone know about Sam, something that would hurt her. No results meant they couldn't fix the Rift Scar.

Would do same, Thor said. *Protect mate. Protect all the mates.*

Oliver couldn't argue with that.

'How's Mitchel?' Hale asked. That he asked at all meant a lot. Hale didn't know Mitchel well, but he was pack, even though he was a Frost Elemental.

'Coping. He's going to give it another week just in case, then head back south to continue his training to control his Frost Magic,' Oliver said, wishing he could punch the bag himself for a bit.

Thor didn't like it when Mitchel left. However, this time, Amelia was going to stay behind. She wasn't happy that Oliver had almost abandoned her to go to his father.

Told you was bad idea, Thor said. He'd said that a lot.

Hale nodded, rolling his neck. It cracked loudly. 'Was he able to narrow down how he thinks it's happening?'

'Too many options to be sure,' Oliver said. 'Currently, he thinks it's something to do with the fact our magic came from the Rift Scar, but it changed it when it infected us. But he has no idea why the Earth Magic is healing the land or why bringing in other Elementals is making it spread further.'

'At half a mile to a mile per mate, even if every member of the pack had one, we'd never be able to remove it,' Hale said with a sigh.

'Mitchel will keep studying it, keep looking for answers,' Oliver said. But they both knew it had been a hundred years already since the Rifts were first created, and no one had found a way to heal the land in all that time. The chances of them stumbling into it now were unlikely.

'Thank you,' Hale said, moving back to the punching bag.

'How many today?' Oliver asked, getting to the real point of him coming.

'One staying, two leaving,' Hale said, voice and scent showing nothing of his feelings.

That took them down to under twenty Shifters once everyone left. They needed replacements first, so it wouldn't happen straight away. Oliver ignored Thor's growl. His anger wouldn't help Hale.

'I'll call if Mitchel finds any changes,' Oliver said, turning to leave Hale to his stress relief.

The small hope everyone had found when the Scar first shrunk was disappearing quickly. Most of the prime alphas were calling their people home. IRS&D were ignoring that the Rift Scar shrinking had even happened.

Staci was sitting on the veranda steps as he stepped outside. Her face turned towards the sun. She turned to him as he started towards her.

He let go of the worry and stress. Everything else would be figured out eventually, but for now, he and Staci had a date.

'I love you,' Oliver said, kissing Staci as she stood.

Staci smiled, leaning into him. She tasted like strawberries that they'd bought for their picnic. 'I love you, too. Now let's go, I'm starving. And your wolf needs a work-out.'

Oliver picked up the basket at her feet, revelling in Staci's calm lack of concern at the idea of his wolf running around the woods. A few weeks ago, he couldn't have ever imagined the peace of being with her, of her acceptance.

The pack lands only enhanced the feeling. He was home, safe and loved. Looking at Staci, he could see she felt the same.

THE LIFE AND CHAOS OF A RETIRED OLD GOD

Humour, Magic and Old Gods who should know better: A Collection of Ernie Smith Short Stories

Being retired was supposed to be easy. No drama, no family, no problems. Considering Ernie is a god, he should've known better.

In this collection of short stories, Ernie struggles to live a quiet life as Death loses his scythe, a genie wants a holiday, and Ernie's family keeps dropping in.

Then there's Ragnarok. Because who doesn't need an end-of-the-world event to keep things calm and quiet?

But it doesn't stop there. This collection contains a brand new bonus short story where Ernie is asked to mediate a feud between Dragons. With tensions running high, maybe the poker game wasn't the best idea.

Also included in this collection is a series of flash fiction originally published on my blog. Follow Ernie as he deals with Cupid shooting the wrong person, Wererabbits for April Fools, Santa stuck in the chimney, and what happens to snowmen when the weather changes.

The Life and Chaos of a Retired Old God is a collection of humorous short stories where Ernie learns that quiet is the last thing he's going to get.

https://jemmaweir.com/books/the-life-and-chaos-of-a-retired-old-god/

WISHING FOR TRUTHS

Contemporary Fantasy Short Story

Vanessa considers her mother's drinking and crazy schemes her biggest problem. Until she meets the Genie.

When Vanessa finds a bottle on her doorstep, the last thing she expects is a wish-granting Genie. What could go wrong with a wish for her two friends and herself? Everything.

On top of that, her mothers' newest scheme is starting to unravel, and the only help Vanessa can think of is the Genie. But he's refusing to come out of his bottle. Now Vanessa must use nothing but the truth to help her friends before her mother ruins everything.

This is a story about wishes gone wrong and a Genie who isn't telling the whole truth, served with a dash of Romance.

Buy this Short Story now and join Vanessa as she learns what it means to 'be careful what you wish for.'

https://jemmaweir.com/books/standalone/wishing-for-truths/

Want to Read more from me?

Want to keep up to date on new releases and get some free stories? Join my newsletter by clicking on the link below.

https://www.jemmaweir.com/newsletter

Or you can follow my blog or Social media below:
https://www.jemmaweir.com
https://www.facebook.com/JemmaWeirAuthor
https://www.instagram.com/jemmaweir

www.ingramcontent.com/pod-product-compliance
Lightning Source LLC
Chambersburg PA
CBHW050957180726
48291CB00006B/1871